Cadenza

Rockliffe Book 6

STELLA RILEY

Cover by Ana Grigoriu-Voicu, books-design.com

CONTENTS

Page

PROLOGUE

VIENNA, March 1778

The performance finished in a flourish of technical brilliance as the soloist brought the lengthy cadenza of Bach's fifth Brandenburg Concerto to its conclusion. For a handful of seconds as the last notes died away there was utter silence … and then the room erupted into a storm of enthusiastic applause. The young man rose from the harpsichord to look at his audience with a faintly bemused expression. After a moment, he remembered to bow and did so awkwardly, one hand on his heart and a lock of brown hair dropping over his brow. And finally he summoned a shy smile which caused three young ladies in the front row to heave soulful sighs and make frantic use of their fans.

When, some minutes later, he was allowed to leave the platform he found Herr Krassnig purring with satisfaction.

'A triumph, my boy. By tomorrow, your name will be known to everyone who matters and Vienna will be yours for the taking. Now … go and accept the accolades. Be charming.'

If anything, Julian Langham looked even more bemused.

'Charming?' he echoed. 'How do I do that?'

Herr Krassnig sighed. 'Then try 'modest' instead. But do *not* promise any private performances. If you wish to make a living, you will leave future engagements to me.'

By the following afternoon, his head still ringing with praise and applause, Julian continued to feel as if he was floating in a bubble that might burst at any moment. He dealt with it by locking his door and hiding in his work.

The primary theme of the *scherzo* in his head swelled to a *crescendo*. Alternately playing a few bars and committing them to paper, he was oblivious to everything … until Frau Bessler in the rooms upstairs began banging on the floor, causing things to vibrate. Julian stopped what he was doing and reluctantly opened his ears to reality.

Somebody was hammering on the door to the street.

Sighing, he went to open it and then, staring blankly at the thin, bespectacled fellow on his doorstep, said, 'Who are you?'

'English, if you please,' snapped the little man. 'I do not speak German.'

Blinking, Julian switched to his native tongue and asked the question again.

'I am Benjamin Fellowes of Bartle, Bartle & Fellowes. You will have been expecting me.'

'I wasn't – and can't imagine why you'd think so. What do you want? I'm busy.'

Mr Fellowes surveyed him from head to foot, taking in uncombed hair and a severely frayed dressing-robe, flung over shirt and breeches. Repressing irritation, he said, 'Perhaps you would be good enough to invite me in?'

'What for? I don't know who you are so I've nothing to say to you. Go away.'

Julian moved to close the door. Mr Fellowes put his foot in it.

'My lord, do you *never* read your correspondence?'

Recollection stirred vaguely in a corner of Julian's mind. He said, 'You're here about *that*? Why? I wrote back explaining that you had the wrong man.'

'And we have written three times *since* then stating most emphatically that we do *not*.'

'Oh Christ,' he muttered, stepping back. 'I don't recall any other letters. But if it will put an end to this nonsense, come in and say your piece. I haven't got all day.'

Mr Fellowes – who had survived an unpleasant channel crossing, endless hours in a poorly-sprung carriage and a great deal of indigestible food – cast him a look of dislike.

'I would have been happy to have resolved this matter from my office in London. So if my presence here is an inconvenience, you have only yourself to blame.'

'If you say so.' Shutting the parlour door behind them, Julian folded his arms and stared at his visitor. 'Your letter said I'd inherited some title or other – and I replied that you must have me mixed up with somebody else. That was clear enough, wasn't it?'

The lawyer held on to his severely strained patience.

'You are Julian Langham – only son of Francis Langham and his wife, Maria, now deceased. Grandson of Hector Langham and --'

'Spare me the last dozen generations. So far as it goes, you have it right. What of it?'

'Your grandfather was a nephew of the second Earl of Chalfont. The fourth earl died over a year ago, leaving no legitimate male children, brothers or nephews. It has taken months to trace both the male and female lines for the last three generations in search of an heir and thus prevent the title dying out. There is only one possible candidate, sir. You.'

There was a long, long silence. Then Julian said flatly, 'No.'

'I can assure you that there is no mistake, my lord. The papers will prove --'

'I don't *care* what they prove. And the title can die out with my very good will.'

Mr Fellowes looked shocked. 'But you are the fifth Earl of Chalfont and --'

'No. I'm not. I'm Julian Langham, musician. I don't want a bloody earldom I never heard of and you're wasting your time.' He wrenched the door open. 'Good day, sir.'

Having got this far, Mr Fellowes was not about to give up. He said severely, 'There is more than a title at stake here, my lord. There is also responsibility for the land and the folk whose livelihoods depend on it. Allow me to explain ...'

The annoying voice faded as the final phrase of the *scherzo* drifted tantalisingly back. If he didn't capture it soon, it might escape again. His eyes strayed to the half-written page on the harpsichord and his fingers to the quill lying on top of them.

'My lord!' snapped the lawyer. 'Will you *please* give me your attention? This cannot be left unresolved. An earldom is no small matter.'

'It is to me,' retorted Julian, frustrated by losing the elusive phrase yet again. 'I didn't ask for it. I don't want it. And my life is here.'

A disparaging glance about the cluttered, shabby room made Mr Fellowes wonder why Langham still hadn't asked the blatantly obvious question that would have been any normal man's response to the first letter. But since this omission was actually to his own and his partners' advantage, he said merely, 'You don't understand, sir. If you --'

'No. It's *you* who doesn't understand. I've spent seven years scraping a living giving music lessons and accompanying mediocre singers. And that coat,' he pointed across the room, 'is the first new one I've had in the last three. All of this was for the future I've wanted since I first touched a harpsichord at the age of eight.' He stopped, breathing rather fast. 'Yesterday, I gave my first paid recital. Yesterday, I *finally* brought an audience to its feet. Today, Vienna knows my name and I have a promise of three further engagements. *Today*, Mr Fellowes, is my *beginning*. And your earldom has no place in it.'

Finally accepting that he was not dealing with a rational being who would relieve Bartle, Bartle & Fellowes of the whole Chalfont mess by grabbing the offered title with both hands, Mr Fellowes said deviously, 'Would not Vienna be more intrigued to learn that its rising star is an English nobleman?'

Julian, who would never have thought of that, frowned, struck by uncertainty and a measure of confusion. 'I don't see what difference that makes. And if taking the title means living in England --'

'Permanently? It need not. Sign the papers, visit your estate and settle any outstanding matters there ... I imagine it would take no more than a few weeks.' Mr Fellowes paused, then added persuasively, 'My partners and I will be happy to defray your travel expenses, my lord - so I beg you to at least consider it.'

Julian hesitated and then said slowly, 'I could consult Herr Krassnig, I suppose.'

The lawyer had no idea who Krassnig was and didn't care. Doubtless the man would be delighted to learn that his protégé was an earl.

'A capital idea. Do that without delay.' He grasped Julian's unresisting hand and shook it. 'But I have taken enough of your time and should leave you to your work. There is no need to show me out. I will call tomorrow to learn your decision. Good day, my lord.'

Somewhat dazed and with a vague feeling of disquiet, Julian watched him go. Then, shrugging slightly and telling himself he'd mention the matter to Herr Krassnig later, he banished it from his mind and went eagerly back to his *scherzo*.

ENGLAND

Summer, 1778

CHAPTER ONE

'Mama,' remarked Arabella Brandon to her cousin and best friend, 'says it is time I stopped moping.'

Continuing to peruse the last custard tart, Elizabeth said, '*Were* you moping? I hadn't noticed.'

'That's because I wasn't.' *I was shocked and confused, then furious. And later, ashamed and frightened*, thought Arabella. *But not heart-broken. Never that.* 'I'm just tired of being everybody's favourite topic of conversation.'

Her family meant well, of course. But she didn't need reminding of that day six months ago when the future she'd expected to have had been snatched away. Of sitting like a stone amidst an outbreak of complete pandemonium; of her eldest brother with his hands around Andrew Forrester's throat, while the two younger ones shouted a mixture of abuse and questions; and finally her mother's voice demanding calm. Every word was engraved on her memory in perfect detail.

'Enough, all of you! Adam, Leo – be quiet! And Max ... let Andrew go, please. This is not his fault – nor is it helpful. We shall all take a seat and discuss the situation reasonably.'

Adam and Leo had sat down and the shouting had stopped. Reasonable discussion, however, had been out of the question.

'Discuss it?' snapped Max, giving his oldest friend's throat one last squeeze before shoving him away. 'What is there to discuss? After keeping Belle waiting for three bloody years, David has jilted *her – and without even being man enough to tell her so himself!'*

'You think I'm happy *about it?' croaked Andrew. 'But until his letter arrived this morning, we had no idea! And with him in Massachusetts, I can't exactly get my hands on him, can I?'*

'It wouldn't make much difference if you could,' growled Max. 'But if ever I lay eyes on him again --'

'Sit down*!' said Lady Brandon. And when, with reluctance, they had done so, 'Good. Now, Andrew. What precisely did David's letter say?'*

'Not nearly enough,' he replied, casting a wary glance at the three Brandon men. 'He was wounded in a skirmish, sent to

recover at the home of a Boston family and nursed by the daughter of the house – whom he appears to have married.' For the first time, he looked at Arabella. *'Belle ... I can't tell you how sorry I am. The very least David owed you was to write and tell you himself. I can't believe that he hasn't done so.'*

'I can,' muttered Adam. 'He was always leaving somebody else to clean up his mess.'

For the first time since the news had exploded like a faulty petard, Arabella drew an unsteady breath and forced herself to speak. *'It's very stupid of me ... but I don't seem able to – to believe that David would do this. Are you quite sure it isn't a mistake?'*

His jaw tightening, Andrew said, *'I wish to God it was. But given the time the letter has taken to reach us, he must have been married for at least two months.'*

And that was when Arabella had risen from her seat, made her excuses and left them. She'd locked herself in her bedchamber and forced herself to face the fact that, after a betrothal of almost three years during which she had refused a London season and waited patiently for him to return from the colonies and marry her, David had abandoned her without a qualm. And worse even than that ... he had done it knowing perfectly well that she couldn't marry anybody else.

Pushing the memory aside, she looked at her cousin and said thoughtfully, 'The truth is that I probably fell out of love with David long before – before it happened.'

'Then perhaps – bad as his behaviour was – it's a blessing in disguise.'

A *blessing*? Arabella had to bite back hollow laughter. It wasn't a blessing. It was a disaster. A disaster that was as much her fault as it was David's. She had known right from the first that she should never have given in to his pleas and persuasions ... but, having done so, she'd comforted herself with the knowledge that it wouldn't matter because one day they'd be married. Except that now, that wasn't going to happen. And she couldn't tell anyone – not even Lizzie – how big a problem that was.

She said dryly, 'I wouldn't exactly call it that. But I'm tired of hearing Adam and Leo talking about what they'd like to do to David. And I'm *particularly* tired of being an object of sympathy – which mostly isn't sympathy at all but just a way of crowing over me.' She paused, plucking at a fold of her skirt. 'I finally let Mama bully me into attending the York assembly last week and had to put up with Sarah Fanshawe pressing my hand and telling me how *deeply* she feels for me. I thought I was going to be sick.'

'Understandable,' agreed Elizabeth, finally tearing her eyes from the tart. 'She did her best to get David herself. Now, jealousy will have turned into gratitude for a lucky escape.' She paused for a moment and then said, 'But Belle … you can't let girls like Sarah influence your life.'

'I'm not.'

'Aren't you? Then why are you hiding?'

'I'm *not* hiding. I just … I don't feel much like going into society.' Arabella pushed the plate containing the lone tart in the other girl's direction. 'Eat it. You might as well. I know half the reason you come here is for the cakes.'

Elizabeth laughed. 'It's *one* of my reasons, certainly. There's nothing like this at home.' She reached for the tart but before biting into it, said, 'You're changing the subject. Why?'

Arabella took her time about answering, conscious as she often was of the differences between her life and that of her cousin. Their mothers were sisters; but while Arabella's mama had married the district's biggest and most affluent landowner, Elizabeth's had fallen in love with a gentle and wholly unworldly cleric. And where Arabella had three brothers and a very handsome marriage portion, Elizabeth was the eldest of three sisters none of whom could expect more than five hundred pounds apiece. Inside this room, the gulf between the two girls didn't exist. Outside it, because Arabella had every material advantage and Elizabeth little but her undeniable beauty, the contrast was huge.

At length, she said reluctantly, 'Mama says it's time I put the past behind me and began again. She's also decided that since

I'm no longer betrothed, I ought to have a London season. And guess whose help she's hoping to enlist.'

Elizabeth narrowly avoided choking on her tart.

'She's written to the duke?'

'Yes. Or to be more precise, to the duchess.'

'Heavens!'

'Exactly. At the moment I'm clinging to the possibility that nothing will come of it. The relationship isn't exactly close, is it? Our mothers only ever met his Grace once, years ago; and every mention of him in the society pages makes him sound positively formidable. As for the duchess, none of us know *her* at all. She may not even be aware of the connection. And if that's so, I can't see why she would agree to sponsor a girl she never heard of before.'

'But if she *does*,' offered Elizabeth, carefully keeping any note of wistfulness from her voice, 'only think how exciting it could be. Balls, parties, the opera; Vauxhall and Ranelagh ... driving in Hyde Park. As a relative of the Duke of Rockliffe, you'd be invited everywhere. You'd probably enjoy it.'

Arabella's eyes grew thoughtful.

'I might enjoy it if you and I could go together.'

Elizabeth concentrated on dusting sugar from her fingers.

'You know that can't happen. The expense would be enormous and --'

'Mama would help. She's offered before and would again.'

'I know – and it's kind of her. But Papa is adamant about not accepting what he regards as charity.'

'Then we could share,' persisted Arabella. 'I have more gowns than I need and we are of almost exactly the same size. Also, if the duchess invites me, I don't see why she wouldn't invite you, too, since you're no less related to the duke than I am. In fact, why don't we find Mama now and --'

'Belle, no. It's lovely of you to think of it – but it won't do. You know it won't. And not just because of the money. Papa will say a visit to London would only leave me neither fish nor fowl – which it probably would.' Elizabeth took a long breath and then said, 'I wasn't going to mention it just yet ... but I've started looking for a position.'

'*What?*'

'Don't sound so shocked. It had to happen at some point. I'm twenty-three years old and --'

'That's not exactly ancient, is it?'

'It's nearly two years older than you,' retorted Elizabeth. 'But the point is that, given my circumstances, I'm very unlikely to marry, so finding a suitable position will help the whole family – particularly Flora and Tilly.'

'What sort of position?'

'As a governess, perhaps ... or a companion to some elderly lady.'

Arabella looked horrified. 'Lizzie ... you *can't*. Does Aunt Maria know?'

'Yes, I can – and of course Mama knows. To be honest, I'd prefer some measure of independence to dwindling into an old maid in the place I've lived all my life.'

'Will being an old maid somewhere else be any better?' demanded Arabella mutinously. Then, seeing her cousin's expression, 'I'm sorry. That was horrid and I didn't mean it as it sounded. But this isn't right – it just isn't. I'd always hoped that one day perhaps you and Adam might ... well, you know.'

Elizabeth's colour rose a little. There had been a time not so long ago when she had hoped the same thing but nothing had come of it. She said, 'Adam is my first cousin – just as you are. No one would have been happy about a match between us. Look, Belle ... can we please stop this? Nothing is decided yet – not me taking a position or you going to London – so there's no point worrying about it.'

'Perhaps not,' agreed Arabella, with all the appearance of giving way but thinking, *And until things are certain, there's still a chance of changing them. We'll see.*

* * *

Unaware that her cousin was about to embark upon a renewed campaign to enlist her mother's help in overcoming the Reverend Marsden's scruples about accepting financial assistance,

Elizabeth went home to contemplate an advertisement she had cut from the *Morning Chronicle* a week ago and already knew by heart.

Mature lady required to oversee the running of a gentleman's establishment and also regulate the care of young children. Flexible terms upon application.

Elizabeth wasn't sure what 'flexible terms' meant. What she *was* sure of was that there was something unusual about someone seeking a combined housekeeper-governess, since both roles were full-time occupations. Despite this – or perhaps because of it – the advertisement intrigued her. At first, she told herself she was merely curious. Then she told herself that the best way of learning how to apply for a position would be to actually *do* it. And finally, she assured herself that, since twenty-three could hardly be considered 'mature', there was no possibility of her application being successful. Really, she thought, it couldn't do any harm just to send an enquiry. She was unlikely to even get a reply. So no one need ever know anything about it, need they?

Making sure that Mama was busy in the garden, Flora copying out Papa's sermon and Tilly, out on the regular round of sick-visiting, Elizabeth sat down to compose a mature-sounding letter, describing her various capabilities in an only *slightly* exaggerated way which absolutely did *not* count as lying.

* * *

Finally yielding to Arabella's persistence, Lady Brandon had a long conversation with her sister and an even longer, but wholly unproductive one, with her courteous and completely intractable brother-in-law.

'It is not merely a question of money, Louisa – though I believe in doing the best I can for my family whilst living within my means,' said Josiah gently. 'But I am also conscious of what will ultimately be best for Elizabeth. Such entertainments as she would find in London cannot help but leave her dissatisfied with life when she returns home – as, inevitably, she must.'

'*Is* it inevitable?' asked her ladyship bluntly. 'She might attract a husband.'

'In the highest level of society with a dowry most would call negligible? Even you must admit the unlikelihood of that.'

'Not necessarily. Lizzie is a beautiful, sweet-natured girl so it is by no means inconceivable that a gentleman might want her just for herself. Also, she would be presented to society as a relative of the Duke of Rockliffe. I imagine some men might find that connection more valuable than money.'

'I suppose that may be true,' replied the reverend, 'although such an attitude does not recommend itself to me. Neither can I approve of the moral laxity of the *haute monde* – or want my daughter exposed to it.'

Louisa sat up very straight.

'Whose morality are you questioning, Josiah? Rockliffe's – or that of his duchess?'

'Neither. It is not for me to judge them.'

'Quite.' Putting aside her annoyance, she said, 'If Lizzie should be invited along with Belle, Maria is quite happy for her to go. You are aware of this?'

'Of course. And in most respects relating to the rearing of our daughters, Maria's word is law. But not,' he concluded, 'in this one.'

'I see.' Louisa rose and shook out her skirts. 'In that case, there is no more to be said.'

* * *

Ten days later, letters arrived at both Brandon Lacey and the Knaresborough vicarage.

Elizabeth managed to extract hers from amidst the rest of the post and tuck it away for perusal later, in private.

Lady Brandon, meanwhile, read the Duchess of Rockliffe's friendly and forthright missive, then went in search of her daughter. She found her, clad in an old gown and a broad straw hat and carrying a basket containing bread, cold meat and ale.

'Max hopes they'll finish pulling the flax today so none of them will remember to eat,' explained Arabella. 'I've asked Hawkes to send supplies down for the workers but thought I'd take this to the boys myself and see how they're getting on.'

Her mother nodded. The bond between Arabella and her older brothers was uncommonly strong. They had helped her climb trees and caught her when she fell out of them; they'd taught her to ride nearly as well as they could themselves and how to fire a pistol and what to do if a fellow didn't keep his hands to himself. Max, in particular, had tried to be the father they had all lost when Arabella was twelve and he himself just shy of twenty. It had made Louisa's decision never to consider replacing the love of her life easier on all of them.

'Then I won't keep you,' she said, smiling. 'I merely wanted to tell you that the duchess has answered my letter.'

Arabella set the basket down with a little thump. 'And?'

'And she will be delighted to present you to society, suggests that you travel to London within the next month and very much looks forward to welcoming you. You can read her letter for yourself later – she writes with genuine warmth and kindness which I'll confess is a relief.' Louisa eyed her daughter shrewdly. 'Why don't you look thrilled?'

'I should, shouldn't I?' Arabella sighed. 'But I'm not sure I want to go.'

'Why not?'

Because if I receive an eligible offer of marriage, I'll be expected to accept it, she thought despairingly. *But unless it comes from a gentleman who doesn't regard virginity as a prime requirement, I can't – and that's not a question I can very well ask him.*

She said, 'There are girls who know about David jilting me and who will be making their curtsy this season. I can't ... I just can't bear the thought of having to go through it all again.'

'That is understandable – though as a guest of the Duke and Duchess of Rockliffe, I doubt that kind of gossip need concern you. But we can discuss that later – as well as the fact that, without being asked, the duchess has included Elizabeth in her invitation.'

Arabella's expression brightened. 'Really?'

'Yes. But don't expect anything to come of it. Although I'll speak to him again, I doubt your Uncle Josiah will budge. Now – take the boys their meal. And talk to Max.'

By the time Arabella arrived on the scene, two footmen were already handing out parcels of food and drink to the tenants and estate workers, while her brothers – coatless, hatless and as filthy as everyone else – were wandering around, speaking to this one or that before raiding the contents of their sister's basket and settling down to their own meal. Leo found a place under a tree, with the inevitable sketch-pad; Adam and the blacksmith indulged in a heated discussion which, knowing Adam, probably had something to do with weapons; and Max dropped on the grass beside Arabella, saying, 'Not that I don't appreciate it, but what brings you down here? You've never liked seeing the flax fields stripped.'

'Silly, isn't it? But it's so beautiful when it's in full flower and still pretty when it goes to seed.' She shrugged. 'Do you ever wonder what Great-Great-Grandfather Gabriel would think if he could see Brandon Lacey now?'

'Every year, Belle.' Max reached for a stone-ware bottle and half-drained it. 'At lambing, at first-clip and at shearing; when we plant the flax and when we pull it. Everything we do here is based on what Gabriel started. The only things that have changed are the size of our holdings and more modern equipment. I like to think he'd approve.' He reached for another slice of pie and looked sideways at her. 'Now. Why are you *really* here?'

'Isn't bringing you food enough?'

He shrugged, took a bite of pie and waited.

Arabella sighed. Of all her brothers, Max had always known her best.

'Mama has heard from the duchess.' Briefly, she told him what she knew of the duchess's letter, concluding with, 'But even though Lizzie has been invited as well, Mama says Uncle Josiah *still* won't permit her to go.'

'Uncle Josiah means well but is completely mutton-headed at times,' responded Max without heat. 'This is the best chance Lizzie will ever get and it's short-sighted of him not to recognise it.'

'If she doesn't come to London, she'll be taking a position as a governess or some such. She's already talking about it. So she *needs* this, Max. She needs it more than I do.'

'No. You both need it equally. Lizzie, because she deserves more out of life than she's likely to get. And you because you've let David's defection turn you into a hermit.'

'I have not.'

'You have ... and in certain senses, I can understand why and sympathise.' He fell silent for a time, as if deciding whether or not to say what was in his mind. Finally, however, he said, 'Although I was furious for your sake when Andrew brought us the news, I always thought it unlikely that the attachment between you and David would weather such a long separation. Clearly, his didn't ... and I don't think yours did either. But you're not the girl you were before any of this happened; the girl who liked stupid jokes and rode like the wind and ran barefoot on the grass.' He paused and shrugged again. 'I don't know why that is – and I'm not asking. But selfishly, I'd like my sister back.'

Tears stung Arabella's eyes and she turned away to hide them.

Max reached out and folded her hand in his. 'Go to London and enjoy yourself – unless you *want* to spend the rest of your life never seeing anything beyond Yorkshire?'

'Oh.' She had never looked at it in that way. 'No. I don't.'

'Good. So come riding with me tomorrow and show me that my intrepid little sister – the girl who always gave as good as she got and laughed while she was doing it – hasn't disappeared for good.'

* * *

Elizabeth brooded over the letter like a sparrow with a hen's egg. Because it was so unexpected, she hadn't given any consideration to the possibility that her application for the mysterious position might be accepted. That it *had* been was therefore both baffling and awkward. And then there was the strangeness of the reply itself.

It had been written, not by her prospective employer, but by a doctor claiming to be that gentleman's friend and neighbour.

I have undertaken this task on his lordship's behalf, it said, *because in this matter, like so many of the others currently facing him, he has no experience. His situation is this. He has recently inherited a title, along with all the responsibilities that go with it. Shouldering these burdens has required personal sacrifice on his part; but though he is doing his best, he is struggling. My wife and I have concluded that if his lordship's household and the children within it were regulated by a woman of sense and firm disposition, he would have one less cross to bear. I have no hesitation in describing him as an honourable man, Mistress Marsden, and you may count on the support of my wife and myself, at need. It is my hope that you will not only accept the challenge but be in a position to shoulder it soon. If you have doubts, a trial period would be acceptable. I look forward to hearing from you,*

P. Featherstone, Physician

Beckingham, Nr. Newark, Nottinghamshire

There was a second sheet, promising reimbursement of her travelling expenses and outlining a modest stipend for the first three months – to be paid whether or not she remained for the entire period and re-negotiated at the end of it. It all sounded eminently fair and very respectable. Unfortunately, because Elizabeth hadn't been able to supply any references, it also sounded a bit too good to be true.

The question, she decided, was whether or not she wanted to accept the offer. If she didn't, she had merely to write back saying that she was no longer available. But if she *did* ... she could do nothing further until she had spoken to Mama. And that meant showing her Dr Featherstone's letter.

Mama read it ... then read it again. Finally, she looked up and said, 'How did you manage this, Lizzie? What did you say that brought you the offer of this position, despite being unable to supply a character?'

'I didn't lie,' said Elizabeth quickly. 'I said that my circumstances dictated the necessity of seeking suitable employment – the inference being that I hadn't done so before. Then I just described the things I do here. Household matters, helping out at the charity school ... that sort of thing.' She hesitated, before adding uncomfortably, 'I *may* have given the impression of – of being a little older than I actually am. But mostly, I think it's come about because this newly-titled gentleman is somewhat desperate.'

'Well, there I agree with you. One would think such an inheritance a good thing … but from what the doctor says, the poor man is quite distracted. Of course, since he is clearly a widower, the children must be a worry to him. It is a pity we are not told how many there are and of what ages. It is also remiss of this doctor not to include their father's name and precise direction. Rather odd, in fact.'

Elizabeth had thought the same thing but discovered that she didn't want to dwell on possible stumbling-blocks. She said, 'I didn't expect to be offered the post, Mama. But now I have been, I'd like to consider whether or not to accept – with your and Papa's permission, of course. However, before any definite decision can be made, I must write again insisting on more information – not just about the children but about the gentleman who would be my employer. Does that sound sensible?'

Maria Marsden looked thoughtfully at her eldest daughter.

'You are always sensible, Lizzie … and I will speak to your father, if that is what you want. But let us be clear. As I have said before, there is no need for you to take up paid employment unless you really wish to. I do not want one of my girls sacrificing themselves for the others.' She paused, sighing. 'It is unfortunate that your papa is so blinkered in the matter of London. Having shared Arabella's education, you possess all the same accomplishments and are as fit to enter polite society as she. Both I and your Aunt Louisa have done our best, of course – but there is no shifting him once his mind is made up.'

'No,' agreed Elizabeth, somewhat hollowly. 'I know. But I want … I don't think I can simply continue as I am for the rest of my life. So if you and Papa are agreeable, I believe I might like to go to Nottinghamshire for a trial period. Then, if I am unhappy there or not suited to the work, the situation will be easily remedied, will it not?'

* * *

By the time Arabella and Elizabeth met on the following afternoon, replies had been despatched to both the Duchess of Rockliffe and Dr Featherstone.

'Mama sent Uncle Josiah a note telling him that the duchess invited you as well as me,' said Arabella the instant they were alone. 'Did he tell you?'

Elizabeth sat very still and looked at her hands. 'Mama did.'

Arabella muttered a word she'd learned from her brothers and promised never to repeat. Then she said, 'He isn't being fair. If you ask me, he isn't even being very Christian.'

'Stop it, Belle.' Elizabeth's voice was weary. 'I knew he wouldn't change his mind. And it doesn't matter anyway. I've been offered a post as a – a sort of housekeeper-cum-governess in Nottinghamshire – and, subject to more information and Papa's agreement, I intend to accept it.'

Arabella stared at her incredulously and said flatly, 'A housekeeper.'

'Yes.'

'In Nottinghamshire.'

'Yes.'

'Do you even know where that *is*? No.' This as Elizabeth would have spoken. 'Don't tell me. I don't *care* where it is. Don't do this, Lizzie. Please don't!'

'And do what instead? Stay here helping Mama with the house and Papa with the parish? Because with or without the duchess's invitation, I am not going to London. So can we please, *please* stop talking about it? It doesn't do any good. In fact, it makes everything worse.'

For a second, Arabella froze. Then, absorbing the bleakness in her cousin's blue eyes and feeling thoroughly guilty, she whispered, 'Sorry. I'm sorry, Lizzie. It was stupid of me not to realise how much you wanted ...' She stopped. 'You always behave as if everything is all right. But it's not, is it?'

'No,' agreed Elizabeth with a careful lack of expression. 'It's not.'

There was a long silence while, frowning, Arabella pleated and re-pleated a fold of her taffeta skirt. Then she looked up, her expression rather odd, and said, 'If you *were* to go to Nottinghamshire ... when might you be leaving?'

'It isn't settled yet so I can't say. But soon, I hope. Why?'

Arabella opened her mouth, closed it again and eventually said carefully, 'Because I've just had what might be a brilliant idea. Or then again, not. So I think I'll keep it to myself until I know one way or another.'

CHAPTER TWO

The new Earl of Chalfont looked up from the letter Dr Featherstone had handed to him and said vaguely, 'I daresay this female will be as good as any other.'

'We can but hope so – since hers was the only application,' retorted Paul. 'As you can see, she's making her acceptance of the position conditional on receiving more information. Once she has it, she could be here inside the month. Will you hold out that long?'

They were sitting in a corner of the Dog and Duck where, when he remembered to eat at all, Julian generally took his main meal of the day. Even after six months in the neighbourhood, he was still the object of curious stares because nobody could equate the title with his shabby, unkempt appearance.

He shrugged in answer to his friend's question.

'Things can't get any worse than they already are.'

'It will be easier when the harvesting is over.'

'Will it? Why?'

'One thing less to deal with?' Paul studied him without appearing to do so, noting the signs of sleeplessness and the utter bleakness in the dark green eyes. 'Has there been any word at all from the lawyers?'

'No. I've stopped expecting it. They got me here so they could make Chalfont's problems mine instead of theirs.' His mouth twisted wryly. 'If I hadn't been such a naïve idiot, I might have known better than fall for it. But I was and I did ... and now I'm stuck with it. I'm drowning under debts I didn't create and boundary disputes and ... children.'

'Yes. How is it going with them?'

'The same as always. They're supposed to be attending the parsonage school but no one knows where they are half of the time – though they usually turn up for meals.'

'It's to be expected. They had been running wild for the best part of a year before you took them in. I'm sure the villagers are duly grateful.'

'Not that I've noticed,' muttered Julian, pushing aside his half-full plate. 'The women still won't take work in the house in case I've inherited the fourth earl's habit of siring bastards. But the complaints have stopped – so that's something, I suppose.'

The complaints aren't why you took the little pests to live in your house though, are they? thought Paul. *You did it because they had nowhere else to go.*

He had first met Julian Langham six weeks after his arrival in the district and mere days since – to everybody's astonishment – he had given a home of sorts to the three illegitimate offspring of his predecessor.

That meeting lived in Paul's mind. It had been raining. Soaked to the skin and as white as his shirt, Lord Chalfont had arrived at his door carrying an unconscious boy, wrapped up in his own coat. He'd said, 'Please ... he fell and I don't know what to do.'

'Fell?' Having taken the child inside and laid him on the table in his surgery, Paul had begun checking for broken bones. 'Where?'

'In the hall. He was sliding down the bannister and – and he fell.' Julian had swallowed hard, looking as if he wanted to vomit. 'About eight feet, on to the flagstones.'

'Well, he doesn't appear to have broken anything so it's likely he's just ... ah.' The child had groaned, eyelids fluttering. 'He's starting to come round. Which one is he?' And when his lordship hadn't immediately replied, 'What is his name?'

'I don't know. I haven't ...' He stopped, looking helpless. 'They d-dart about, you see.'

What Paul had seen was that the new earl's teeth were chattering with cold and shock ... and that he looked on the verge of both physical and mental collapse. He'd concluded that, whoever this man was, he wasn't what anyone had been expecting; and in the months since then, he'd had no reason to change this opinion.

'They baffle me,' said Julian suddenly.

The abrupt words brought Paul's mind back to the present. He said, 'Who?'

'The children. They rarely speak to me but sometimes I see them watching. It's … unnerving.' He stared into what was left of his ale as if expecting it to provide answers. Then, glancing up, 'You haven't told her, have you? Mistress … whatever her name is. You haven't told her about the children. Not properly.'

'No, I haven't – and I won't be completely forthcoming when I reply to this.' Paul pocketed the letter and grinned suddenly. 'I'd feel guilty about that if I didn't suspect there are things she hasn't told *us* … such as why, lacking a character from a previous employer, she didn't ask the local clergyman or doctor to supply one.'

'Perhaps she didn't think of it.'

'Julian, most people aren't as vague as you. Of course she thought of it.'

'If she understands children, I don't care. I don't know the first thing about them.'

'Not even having been one yourself?' objected Paul, managing not to laugh. 'And being around other boys your age?'

'No. We lived in a fairly remote spot and I was an only child, so Mother wouldn't hear of me going away to school. I had a tutor and, for a time, also a music teacher until I went to Cambridge.' A faint smile tugged Julian's mouth. 'You look appalled. But it wasn't that bad. As long as I had music, I didn't need anything else.' The smile slid away, as he contemplated the ruin of his hands. Long-fingered and elegantly-boned, they were littered with scratches, the marks of old blisters and the beginnings of calluses. 'In truth, if I had that now I'd be coping better with the rest of this mess.'

Surprised that he hadn't understood this before, it was several moments before Paul spoke. But finally he said, 'Aren't you finding any time at *all* to play?'

'Play what? The harpsichord is still not in working order.'

'But you've been repairing it since you first got here!'

'With insufficient time and none of the proper materials,' muttered Julian. 'Strings were broken, the jackrail was split and half the jacks were damaged. Nearly all the dampers had rotted and mice had been nesting on the soundboard, for God's sake. I told you all that.'

The doctor stared at him in exasperation

'Julian ... I can name every bone in your hand and tell you more about your liver than you'd really want to know – but the internal workings of musical instruments are as big a mystery to me as they are to most other people. However ... I gather what you're saying is that you haven't played a note since you left Vienna. Is that right?'

'Yes.'

'And it's killing you.'

Julian hunched one shoulder and said nothing.

Paul stood. 'Get up and come with me.'

'What? Why?'

'If you'd made any attempt to get to know your neighbours instead of going about with your head down and your hands in your pockets, you'd be aware that your struggles to mend matters at Chalfont without raising rents haven't gone unnoticed. There are people who would help if you asked them. But you don't ask. You hide.'

'I don't --'

'Reverend Hassall would have been happy for you to play the church organ. Did you think of that?' Paul's determination to sound bracing rather than sympathetic came out more gruffly than he had intended. 'But I forgot. You don't attend church, do you?'

'I went once.' Julian shifted uneasily. 'I'd intended to speak to the vicar. But the regular organist has rheumatism in his hands and --'

'He does. Is less than perfect playing too painful for you to listen to?'

'No. What hurt was knowing what that must mean to him. And that hearing me play wouldn't have made him feel any better.'

The air hissed between Paul's teeth. He said, 'Ah. My apologies.'

24

'It doesn't matter.' He rose. 'I should go back. Ridley thinks the weather may break before we've got the last of the --'

'You can spare another hour. It's time you discovered that the heap of firewood you are trying to mend isn't the only harpsichord within reach.'

Panic swept over Julian's face and he froze.

'No. I can't. It's been six months. I can't play in front of anybody. I --'

'You may not be offered the chance. But if you are, whether or not you do so is up to you. Now ... stop arguing and come with me. Like you, I've work to do this afternoon.'

Between the Dog and Duck and the pretty villa on the edge of the village, progress was halted several times by persons wishing to pass the time of day with the doctor and be introduced to the new earl. An unpleasant mixture of shyness and embarrassment rolling about his chest, Julian flushed and fidgeted as he tried to make the correct responses. Paul began by wanting to laugh. Then he started to notice that Julian's obvious awkwardness was doing him no disservice – on the contrary, in fact. People seemed to find it endearing.

The door of the villa was opened by a neat maid who cast a doubtful glance at Julian, then beamed at the doctor.

'Are the ladies at home, Millie?' he asked. 'And if they are, do they have a few minutes to spare for me?'

'They've always got time for you, sir – you know that. One moment and I'll --'

'Dr Featherstone!' said a resonant contralto from the far end of the hall. 'This is a pleasant surprise. Bea? Oh – there you are.' This as another lady emerged from an open doorway. 'We have visitors and can therefore quite legitimately put off the household accounts until tomorrow.'

'Excellent,' said the second lady. 'Millie – tea in the drawing-room, if you please.'

'That's exceedingly kind, Miss Beatrice but we won't stay,' said Paul, smiling. 'I merely hoped you would allow me to present Lord Chalfont to you. Julian – Mistress Caldercott and her sister, Miss Abigail Caldercott.'

Finding himself impaled on two pairs of bright hazel eyes, in the faces of two ladies of middling years, Julian mumbled something and managed a reasonably creditable bow. The ladies curtsied and Miss Abigail said, 'We've been wondering when we would finally meet you, my lord. Now come in, sit down and tell us what we may do for you.'

He cast a glance of agonised appeal at the doctor, reluctantly trailed the Misses Caldercott into the drawing-room ... and then stopped dead, his gaze transfixed by the pretty, rosewood instrument by the windows. Paul said something but he didn't hear what it was or which of the sisters replied. All he knew was that there was a gaping hole inside him and across the room was the dual-keyboard miracle that could fill it.

Miss Abigail captured some small part of his attention by laying her hand on his sleeve. She said, 'Dr Featherstone says you play. Is that right?'

He nodded. 'I ... yes.'

She looked up into his face and was shocked by what she saw there. Avid hunger mixed oddly with something that looked like terror. Drawing him a couple of steps closer to the harpsichord, she said, 'Then, if you wish to try our instrument, please feel free to do so while the doctor takes tea. You will not disturb us in the least – will he, Bea?'

'Not at all, dear.'

'There. You see?' She lifted the lid, put the strut in place and heard his indrawn breath. 'Just sit down here and take your time.' Then, turning away and as if ignoring him, 'Ah ... and here is the tea. Thank you, Millie. Bea – will you pour or shall I?'

Julian stood like a stone for several minutes, then stroked the edge of the casing with reverent fingers. But finally the lure of the keyboard became irresistible and he sat down before it. He lifted a hand, realised that it was shaking and restored it to his lap. He took several deep breaths. Finally, before he could change his mind, he reached out and played a swift chromatic scale, followed by a series of equally rapid arpeggios. Behind him, silence fell. Unaware of it and frowning a little, he concentrated on a single note ... first alone and then in both major and minor triads. The frown deepened; he pulled a small tuning-hammer from his pocket and rose to look inside the instrument. Head bent, he said as if to himself, 'The F above middle C is flat.'

'Is it?' Miss Beatrice was surprised. 'Are you sure, my lord? It sounds perfectly all right to me and without a tuning-fork --'

'It's flat and I don't need a fork,' he mumbled. One hand delicately adjusted the tuning-pin, the other repeatedly tested the offending key until it grew fractionally sharp. Harpsichords, as he knew only too well, had a habit of tricking you. For a couple of minutes more, he continued playing the same key, over and over until the string settled to the place he wanted it and stayed there. Only then did he sit down and run through the same checks as before and until he was satisfied.

Unfortunately, the comfort of a mundane task he'd performed hundreds of times evaporated in the face of the knowledge that now he must either play something or get up and walk away. He couldn't walk away any more than he could stop breathing. He wanted to play; the need was so acute his chest ached with it. But his brain was saying, *What if I can't? What if my hands don't remember? What if it's all gone?*

Dread paralysed him. For twenty years, he had practised for five hours a day – often more. He had no idea how even a week without playing a note could impair his ability – let alone six months. He'd told Paul he couldn't play in front of anyone; but that wasn't the problem. What was stopping him now was the mind-numbing possibility that he wouldn't be able to play at *all*.

Sweat crawled between his shoulder-blades. He thought, *I have to face this. I have to get past it. If I don't ... if I can't ...*

He shut his eyes, lifted his hands and plunged, without pausing to think, into Bach's *Fantasia in C minor*. And the world which had been off-key for so long ... so very long ... was suddenly in tune again.

The opening cascade of notes, the militant chords and the complex base line rang out crisp and sure. It was a virtuoso piece. He could have chosen a score of easier ones but, subconsciously, he had chosen this because, among its many challenges, the

Fantasia demanded the one thing which, just at present, he didn't have. Confidence.

All his doubts and fears fled. Everything vanished except the music. And when he finally brought the piece to its darkly dramatic finale, it was on an outpouring of pure triumph.

Four-and-a-quarter minutes. He knew to a fraction how long it took to play this piece. A little over four minutes … yet here he was, shaking in every muscle, heart pounding and breathing as if he had run a mile. He hauled in a ragged breath, pressed the heels of his hands to his eyes and let gratitude and relief overwhelm him.

Oh God. Thank you. Not gone. Out of practice, yes … but not gone.

The acute silence after the last note died away lasted only a handful of seconds. Then four people burst into applause. Having forgotten anyone was there, Julian started and turned. Not just the doctor and the middle-aged sisters but also the little maidservant in the doorway; all of them on their feet, wildly clapping.

Stalking across the floor to grip his shoulder, Paul said baldly, 'I'm sorry. I had no idea. Nothing you've said prepared me for …' He stopped, shaking his head. 'I expected you to play well. But what I just heard was worthy of the concert platform.'

'Not really,' came the embarrassed and typically literal reply. 'The trills weren't as smooth as they ought to have been and I missed a couple of *appoggiaturas*. I'm a bit rusty.'

'Rusty?' It was Miss Abigail who spoke. 'Really? Young man … if you think practise can better *that* performance, you had better come here regularly and make it so.'

Julian stood up, his face lighting into a rare and spectacularly sweet smile.

'May I? Truly? It wouldn't be an intrusion?'

'Dear boy,' said Miss Beatrice, reaching out to fold one of his hands in hers, 'it would be our very great pleasure.'

* * *

For the first time, Julian walked the mile back to Chalfont Hall without his heart plummeting further at every step. Where life had been a black hole, there was now a glimmer of light. After he had been absent from Vienna for almost two months, Herr Krassnig had written making it plain that either he returned immediately to fulfil the engagements awaiting him or his career in that city was finished. Julian would have sold his soul to go back. In truth, he'd have sold it never to have left. But return hadn't been possible and still wasn't; and now, though he might never give another concert, at least music was no longer completely denied him ... so he need not starve.

Having lured him to Chalfont, Bartle, Bartle & Fellowes had promptly terminated their services. It had not taken Julian long to understand why. Aside from the debts racked up by the fourth earl, there was a boundary dispute with one of the estate's neighbours. Mr Bascombe claimed that a stream which had once fed both estates had been diverted in Chalfont's favour. Maps which ought to have proved or disproved this accusation were unaccountably missing and legal action was looming ever closer. Seeing this, knowing of the debts and realising that there was scant chance of being paid, Bartle, Bartle & Fellowes had washed their hands of the Chalfont earldom.

For the rest, tenants' cottages had been allowed to fall into even greater disrepair than the main house, some fields had remained uncultivated for more than three years and the entire estate was teetering on the edge of bankruptcy. Inevitably, the land was entailed and nothing in the house – neither paintings nor furniture – was in remotely marketable condition. So with the need for money being critical, Julian had sold the contents of the stables; a fine black gelding, a pair of chestnuts and a smart carriage.

This had helped but didn't solve the problem. Julian had been on the point of turning his back on the whole sorry mess and taking sufficient money to get him back to Vienna when he'd found out about the children. Three of them; two boys and a girl, ranging in age from six to twelve – and all the result of the previous earl's indiscriminate couplings with tavern-wenches and village girls. And though Julian could have walked away from the title and the estate in a heartbeat, he found he couldn't turn his back on the children.

No-one seemed to know where their mothers were and they had been fostered by a village woman until, no longer being paid for their keep, she'd turned them out of doors. Since then, they had apparently been sleeping in one of Chalfont's empty barns and foraging for food as best they could – mostly, if the villagers were to be believed, by stealing it. When Julian had first come across them, gaunt, filthy and ragged, the two boys had faced him with mistrustful, challenging stares while their small sister peeped out from behind them. Then all three had fled.

It had taken days to find them again and when he'd done so and tried telling them they could live in the house, they hadn't believed him. He eventually persuaded them by having Mistress Phelps leave the kitchen door open and food waiting just inside it. Now they inhabited the suite of rooms that had once been the nursery and schoolroom and ignored Julian more or less completely. This, since children were an alien species, suited him perfectly well … but left him aware that he probably ought to be doing more if only he'd known how. And that was why he had listened when Paul and Janet Featherstone had said he must employ a female to do what he could not.

He supposed he ought to tell the children about that. He thought the little girl might like having a lady looking after them. But all the boys would see was that their days of doing pretty much as they pleased were numbered.

* * *

From the upper floor windows, three young faces watched him walking towards the house. Tom, the eldest of them, said, 'Why is he coming from the village not the farm?'

Rob merely shrugged. Six-year-old Ellie said, 'He looks different. Happy.'

'Happy?' Rob nudged her teasingly. 'How do you work that out?'

'Don't know. He just does.' She stood on tiptoe on the stool that enabled her to see over the high windowsill. 'I think he's whistling.'

'Whistling?' scoffed Tom. '*Him?* Nah.'

Rob lifted the catch and opened the window a few inches. They all listened.

'See?' said Ellie, smugly. 'He *is* whistling. Told you.'

Tom grunted. 'He usually looks like he's lost a shilling and found sixpence.'

'I think he's lonely,' offered Ellie. 'We've got each other. He's got nobody.'

His lordship having disappeared inside the house, the three of them abandoned the look-out post and wandered back to sit on the hearth-rug.

'He's friends with the doctor,' said Rob. 'But *something's* cheered him up, so p'raps this'd be a good time to talk to him.'

'About what?' asked Tom. 'And he don't *want* to talk to us. Makes that clear enough.'

Rob shook his head. 'Maybe he thinks *we* don't want to talk to *him*.'

'And we don't.'

'You mean *you* don't. I wouldn't mind.'

'Nor me,' said Ellie. 'It's better here. There's something to eat every day and proper beds and nobody chasing us off and --'

'All right – so it's better. But why is he doing it? Why is he letting us live here when he don't have to? He's not kin ... he ain't got money. He could chuck us out just like that!'

'He wouldn't,' said Ellie uncertainly.

'But he *could*,' snapped Tom. 'And then where would we be? Back where we was before – that's where! And that's why we can't trust him or rely on always living here. There's no saying how long it'll last.'

'Maybe there would be if we got to know him a bit,' Rob suggested. 'It's right what you said, Tom. He didn't have to take us in – but he did, didn't he? And the only thing he said we gotta do is go to lessons at the parsonage which ain't so bad.'

'And he don't shout at us,' said Ellie. 'Not ever.'

'What's wrong with the pair of you?' demanded Tom angrily. 'So he's put a roof over our heads and he don't shout. So what? It don't mean it'll always be that way. And what does he do at night in that room downstairs? It's the only locked door in the whole house. He don't even lock his bedchamber … I know 'cos I went through it. But that room is locked whether he's in it or not. Why? What's he up to in there? He could be doing *anything*.'

'Cutting up dead animals or boiling down children to make glue.' A voice from behind the partly-open door caused the three of them to nearly jump out of their skins and stare, half-petrified, as the earl strolled in and looked down on them.

Tom turned scarlet and said nothing. Ellie looked as if she was about to burst into tears. And Rob stood up, saying shakily, 'G-Glue?'

Julian nodded. He felt awkward and stupid but he knew better than to walk away from what he'd overheard. 'Lucky I don't need any, isn't it?'

Deciding that he didn't *look* angry, Rob said hopefully, 'You was joking, right?'

'Right,' agreed Julian. 'But if what I'm doing in the library is bothering you, I had better put your minds at rest. Come along.'

'I don't want to,' quavered Ellie. 'Not if there's dead animals.'

'There aren't. Not one.' Julian held out his hand to her. 'Come and see.'

'You promise?'

'I promise. No dead animals and no glue-pots. Nothing at all scary.'

'All right.' Ellie scrambled up, put her small hand in his and said shyly, 'I don't care what you was doing. It was Tom, mostly.'

'Shut up,' hissed Tom, getting to his feet. 'No tale-telling. We stick together.'

'And so you should,' agreed Julian mildly, leading them from the room and down the stairs. 'I don't blame you for wondering, Tom. I don't even mind you going through my things – though I'd rather you didn't.' Having reduced all three children to silence, he continued to the library door and inserted the key in the lock. 'What's in here, however, is a different matter and means a great deal to me … though I think you'll find it disappointing.'

And he opened the door. The children stared. Sofas, chairs and tables had all been pushed against the walls, leaving just one item standing in solitary splendour in the centre of the room amidst a litter of strange tools, pieces of wood and lengths of wire.

'What is it?' breathed Ellie, still clinging to his hand.

It occurred to Julian that it had been idiotic to expect them to recognise something they could never have seen before. He said, 'It's a musical instrument – a bit like the organ in the church. It's called a harpsichord.'

There was a long silence and then Rob said, 'Can you play it?'

'Yes – though not at present because it's broken. I'm trying to mend it ... and the room is kept locked because I don't want anyone else to touch it.'

Half under his breath and half not, Tom uttered the worst curse he knew and walked out. Ellie's fingers tightened on Julian's hand and Rob said, 'He don't mean it, sir. He --'

'I know. It's all right.' Julian summoned a smile. 'Now ... any other questions?'

'Yes.' It was Ellie who spoke. 'When it's all mended, will you show us how it works?'

CHAPTER THREE

The response to Elizabeth's letter arrived four days after she had sent it and answered all the questions she had asked. Since she had no reason to be suspicious, she didn't notice the careful wording. She merely gained her parents' agreement that it all sounded very suitable, wrote a brief reply and then sent a note to her cousin. Two hours later, having been given no chance to say more than that she would be taking up the position in three weeks' time, she found herself listening to Arabella's notion of a brilliant idea.

'Stop!' said Elizabeth, pressing her hands against her face. 'Just stop for a moment. Are you seriously suggesting that we change places and impersonate each other?'

'Just the changing places part. I don't think impersonation need come into it.'

'How can it not? Heavens, Belle – are you *completely* mad? It is the most ridiculous idea I ever heard. It will never work.'

'Yes it will. And it isn't nearly as difficult as it sounds. Think about it.'

'I don't *need* to think about it. It's you who needs to do that. How you can possibly suppose we'd get away with it? We'd be found out. You know we would.'

'Eventually,' grinned Arabella. 'We'd be found out *eventually*. But by then, you would have had a few weeks in London and I'd have had some time away from everybody who knows about David and the rest of it – and a bit of an adventure as well. It's perfect.'

Elizabeth shut her eyes for a moment and then, opening them again, said, 'Don't think for one moment that I'm agreeing to this. But if you want to explain exactly how this marvellous scheme of yours is supposed to work, I'll listen.'

'Well, obviously I haven't got all the details worked out yet --'

'Obviously.'

'-- but we've got three weeks in which to plan it properly. Basically, however, it's quite simple. We begin our journeys together; me, to London and you, to – to wherever it is. Don't interrupt – we can find a map later. At the last stopping point before we go our separate ways, we change places. You travel on to London and I go to the place *you* were going that I can't remember the name of,' said Arabella triumphantly. 'Easy!'

'Easy,' echoed Elizabeth in hollow accents. 'And what happens when we get there – or haven't you considered that yet?'

'Nothing happens. That's the beauty of it. Neither the duke and duchess nor your gentleman-employer have ever seen either of us so they won't know the difference, will they?'

'I suppose not. But --'

'They'd have no reason to suspect we're not who we say we are. And since we're almost exactly the same size, clothes won't be a problem --'

'I suppose your maid won't be a problem either,' cut in Elizabeth dryly. 'Or did you imagine that Aunt Louisa would permit you to travel without her?'

'Annie will do as I say ... and if the worst comes to the worst, I'll bribe her.'

'Brilliant. And when she makes a mistake? When she calls me Miss Lizzie in front of one of the duke's servants or, worse still, the duchess? What then?'

'We'll have to rehearse her so she doesn't.' Flushed with enthusiasm and excitement, Arabella looked her cousin in the eye and said, 'We can do this. I *know* we can. And it isn't as though we'd be doing anything so very terrible. Uncle Josiah wouldn't have agreed to you accepting this position if he wasn't convinced of its respectability so I'll be perfectly safe. As for London ... the duchess invited both of us, so you're as entitled to go as me.'

It occurred to Elizabeth that it had been a long time since she'd seen her cousin so full of bubbling animation; not, in fact, since before David had set sail for the colonies. But though it seemed a pity to dampen her spirits, Arabella really must be made to think. So she said, 'None of this alters the fact that what you're suggesting means deceiving both of our families – not to mention the duke and duchess and goodness knows how many others along the way. *You* may be comfortable with that but I'm not.'

'Well, perhaps I'm not *entirely* comfortable with it ... but there's no actual harm in it. If Uncle wasn't so stubborn, there'd be no need for any of this because we'd be going to London together. I wouldn't mind that so much. But as things are, I'd really rather not go at all just at present and I'm *certainly* not ready to go husband-hunting – which is what the duchess will expect. She's probably already lining up potential suitors.'

'How would my being there change that?'

Arabella gave a laughing shrug. 'By dividing her attention. You're prettier than me – no, don't argue. My mouth is too wide, my chin is too pointed and my nose is what polite people call retroussé. As for my hair ... the less said, the better. The duchess would see all that right away. Then she'd notice that you are the graceful, ladylike, impeccably mannered one and I'm the hoyden ... so she'd concentrate her efforts on you instead of me.'

'And there I was thinking it was my company you wanted,' sighed Elizabeth. 'Thank you so much.'

'Don't be silly. Of course it would be that, too. But it's not going to happen, is it? And since only one of us can go, I think it ought to be you rather than me.'

'I see.' There was a very long, thoughtful pause; and then, 'Why are you so desperate to avoid London, Belle? Is there something you're not saying?'

'No! And I'm *not* desperate. I just don't want to do it yet.' Aware of a need to hide her expression before something in it gave her away, Arabella rose and walked to the window, saying, 'I'm not ready, Lizzie. Next year, perhaps – but not now.'

'If we do what you suggest, the duchess won't be inviting you next year.'

'Then I'll cross that bridge when I come to it.' Hauling in a deep breath, Arabella turned back to face her cousin. 'Can you stop raising objections long enough to admit that you're tempted? That, unlike me, you'd *love* a taste of society and all that goes with it.'

'Of course I'm tempted. Aside from you, I can't think of any girl who wouldn't be. But none of this is as straightforward as you're making it sound.'

'I know that. But --'

'I'm not sure you do. For example, let us consider what you'll be doing while I'm going to balls and parties and driving in the park. You may *think* you want to get away from everyone but you can't possibly want to spend weeks acting the part of a housekeeper and managing somebody's children. Could you even *do* it?'

'Of course. How difficult can it be? I know about household management – not as much as you do perhaps, but enough. And a housekeeper doesn't dust and sweep and cook herself, does she? She oversees the other servants. As for children ... ha!' She gave a snap of her fingers. 'I have three brothers, remember.'

'All of them older than you.'

'That's immaterial,' retorted Arabella breezily. 'Leo and Adam aren't so much older than me that I can't remember all the things they got up to when they were home for the holidays from Eton. Young children ought to be easy compared to them. How many did you say there were?'

There was a long, resigned silence. Finally, Elizabeth said, 'I didn't – because you didn't give me the chance. But there are two boys and a girl, aged twelve, nine and six respectively.'

'Well, that doesn't sound too bad. What about their father?'

'Oh – you'll *like* that bit. Their father is an earl. Lord Chalfont of Chalfont Hall, if you please.' And with a swift, mischievous smile, 'He *might* be young and gorgeous ... but from the little we know so far, I wouldn't care to rely on it. He's probably some middle-aged distant relation who never expected to inherit and is therefore now over-doing his attempts to live up to the title.'

'Who are you telling, Lizzie? Me or yourself?' retorted Arabella. And then, 'You're thinking about it, aren't you? Despite everything you've said, you are actually considering falling in with my utterly splendid plan.'

* * *

Julian learned that Mistress Marsden had accepted the position within his household over supper with Paul and Janet Featherstone. He liked Janet. He'd never had a sister but somehow she felt like one. Consequently, she was one of only three women with whom he was comfortable – the other two being the Misses Caldercott. Younger ladies, with their lingering, speculative glances, scared him to death.

Taking Mistress Marsden's letter from Julian, Paul said, 'I'll write back arranging to collect her from the Woolpack in Newark – unless you'd rather go yourself?'

'No! That is ... not really.' He thought for a minute and then said, 'Now it's definite, I suppose I should tell the children.'

'That should be interesting. How do you think they will take it?'

'Tom will probably swear and walk off. Rob and Ellie ... I don't know.' Setting down his knife, he gave a brief account of his visit to the nursery floor and its aftermath, adding, 'I haven't laid eyes on Tom since then. But Rob sometimes comes to the fields and waves to me from the fence. And Ellie ... Ellie waits for me on the drive and walks back chattering about her lessons.' He stopped and took a gulp of wine. 'She holds my hand.'

There was a brief silence as Paul and his wife exchanged glances.

'Well, that's a start,' said Janet, putting a bowl of potatoes at his elbow. 'At least you know their names now. But, aside from explaining matters to the children, there are a few other things you should do prior to the advent of Mistress Marsden.'

'Such as what?' He looked at the potatoes as if mystified by their presence and then transferred a couple of them to his plate.

'Such as having a bedchamber and sitting-room made ready for her, perhaps?'

'Oh. Yes. I hadn't thought of that.'

'Why are we not surprised?' murmured Paul, with sardonic amusement. 'You *did* realise that the lady would be living in the house?'

'Yes, of course.'

'There is no 'of course' with you, Julian,' remarked Janet calmly. 'If your mind is on something else – as it all too frequently is – you don't remember what was said to you ten minutes ago. However, let us concentrate on making Mistress Marsden welcome, shall we?'

He nodded and smiled, the picture of tractability. 'How?'

Janet eyed him resignedly. Not for the first time, she wondered how he managed to be completely beguiling and, at the same time, so utterly exasperating that she wanted to shake him. He was ridiculously good-looking, of course. Slightly curling, glossy mahogany hair which, even untidy and over-long as it was, probably had girls wanting to run their fingers through it; eyes of dark, forest green set below straight brows and above well-defined cheek-bones; and most dangerous of all, that shy, sweet smile, guaranteed to pierce even the stoniest of hearts. Even his physique – though still a trifle thin – had begun, during these recent months of manual labour, to gather a little extra muscle. Janet could quite imagine foolish girls sighing over him. Julian, of course, would either fail to notice them or run a mile.

Now, she said patiently, 'A bedchamber and sitting-room? I will help, if you wish.'

'Thank you.' Julian laid down his knife again, half the food on his plate still untouched. 'I'd be very grateful. But I know you are busy and wouldn't want --'

'Have you any idea where to begin?'

'No.' Another hint of a smile. 'None at all, actually.'

'That's what I thought. So finish your dinner and pay attention.' She waited until he began eating, then said, 'You have Mr and Mistress Phelps living in – he for the heavy work and outside jobs, she as your cook. In addition, their niece comes in for a few hours a week to clean – though, from what I've seen, Ginny Brent's idea of cleaning doesn't encompass anything above or below eye-level. So before Mistress Marsden arrives and takes one look, then gets back on the next Mail Coach, her task needs to be made less daunting – which means hiring more maids.'

'The village girls won't come,' said Julian, not raising his eyes from his food.

'That was before they knew anything about you. It's different now. Mistress Hobbs near the bakery is struggling to make ends meet since she was widowed and she has two daughters, both seeking positions. If you can pay them, they'll come – and what's more, they'll live in. But until we get that settled, I'll bring my own girls and we'll make a start. Your floors haven't been scrubbed or waxed in living memory and the main rooms need a thorough scouring --'

Julian's knife clattered on the plate. 'Not the library. My harpsichord --'

'Fine.' Janet's patience was further strained by the fact that her husband was clearly struggling with a desire to laugh. '*Not* the library. But the parlour, the dining-room, the great hall ... and a bedchamber for Mistress Marsden – all of which I'll oversee myself. Are we agreed?'

'Yes, ma'am,' said Julian meekly. 'Thank you.'

'Don't be too grateful,' offered Paul, re-filling all three wine glasses. 'She's been itching to get her hands on your mausoleum for weeks.'

'I never called it a mausoleum,' objected Janet, colouring a little.

'It's what you meant,' he grinned. 'So, Julian ... you're still working on the harpsichord? Even though you go to the Misses Caldercotts' for an hour or so every other day?'

'It's not enough,' came the blunt reply. 'But I don't want to wear out my welcome.'

'There's no danger of that, I suspect.'

'Indeed not,' agreed his wife. 'Both ladies take great pleasure in what they call their 'private recitals'. And Miss Beatrice is awestruck by your ability to tune their instrument purely by ear.'

'Yes.' Paul lounged back in his chair. 'I was wondering about that myself.'

Julian's shrug suggested that the matter was of minor importance. He said, 'It's a facility I have; an ability to identify any note without a point of reference and hear the true centre of it. Some people call it perfect pitch.' He paused and then, smiling crookedly, added, 'It's not as rare as you might think. Mozart has it as well. And truthfully, it's more of a curse than a blessing most of the time.'

'Why?'

'Violins,' came the dark reply, accompanied by a faint shudder. 'And singers.'

* * *

'We can't go on like this,' announced Arabella flatly. 'We've been going back and forth over the same ground for four days. It's time to make a decision. If we don't, the entire question will be redundant because there won't be sufficient time to plan the thing. So … what is it to be?'

Elizabeth shut her eyes and tried to think. Her good sense and upbringing were saying one thing, while everything inside her shouted another. Finally, drawing a long unsteady breath, she said, 'All right. I'll do it.'

Arabella gave a wide, delighted grin.

'At last! You won't regret it, Lizzie – I promise you won't.'

'Since I already doubt my sanity, I hope you're right. So … where do we start?'

'With the main problems we'll have to overcome.' Arabella reached into her pocket and flourished a folded sheet of paper. 'Fortunately, I have a list.'

'A list. Yes. Of course you do. I might have guessed.'

'There's nothing wrong with being prepared.' Arabella sat down, giving her striped polonaise a cursory twitch. 'The first three points are the most difficult and, though finding a solution may take time, I thought we should at least be aware of them. First off, there's Annie. As you said, we'll need to get her full cooperation. Secondly, there is the possibility that Mama will want one of my brothers to escort us south. And thirdly, there's the matter of writing and receiving letters – and I really think there's only one way around that.' She looked up, dark grey Brandon eyes bright and determined. 'You write to my family and I'll write to yours.'

'*What?* That won't work for a minute.'

'It will. I can't remember the last time Mama or any of my brothers saw my handwriting. When was the last time Aunt Maria saw yours?'

'I …. don't recall.'

'That's because there's no occasion for it. Neither of us has ever been from home, have we? And our handwriting isn't *that* dissimilar.'

'It isn't only the handwriting,' protested Elizabeth. 'You'd still sound like you.'

'Well, how else is it to be managed? How can either of us write letters pretending to be the other one without knowing what to write *about*? And we'll be receiving letters as well, remember – in addition to which, you'll be staying in a ducal household, so Mama will expect letters from London to bear Rockliffe's seal. Don't you see? Writing letters on each other's behalf is the only way we can make this work.'

Elizabeth massaged her temples. 'I'm beginning to wish I'd never agreed to it.'

'You'll get over it,' grinned Arabella. 'Now ... I'll deal with Annie. And *if* Mama raises the subject, I'll set about persuading her that Max is too busy to undertake a return-trip to London, Adam will soon be off to visit his friend's wretched fencing academy in Paris and Leo ... well. Let's be honest. Leo attracts trouble like a magnet. We'll be *much* safer travelling under the protection of a couple of outriders. That should do it, don't you think?'

'Probably,' agreed Elizabeth, reaching to take a macaroon from the tray. 'But there are greater problems than the ones you've listed. What about the girls we know who are likely to be in London at the same time? The ones you were so eager to avoid ... and who will know at a glance that I'm not you.'

Arabella's smile was seraphic. 'There were only three. Angela Kingsley, Dorothea Henderson and Sarah Fanshawe. But as it turns out, none of them will be making their curtsy this season.' A gurgle of decidedly wicked laughter weaving through her voice, she said, 'Measles.'

'Measles?'

'Yes. Dorothea's brother told Max that it's gone through Miss Atherton's Academy like a plague. They've all come out in spots ... and none of their mothers are letting them *near* London until the marks fade. Fate, Lizzie, is on our side.'

'So it would seem – though you might show a glimmer of sympathy.'

'For *Sarah Fanshawe*?' demanded Arabella, by no means deaf to the quiver in her cousin's voice. 'I'm not such a hypocrite – and I didn't think you were, either. But the most important thing is that you needn't worry about being recognised. One problem less.'

'And when the masquerade is over? What do we do then? We can't exactly just switch back to being ourselves, can we? Somehow, we're going to have to manage things so that we return home together – and that isn't going to be easy.'

Arabella took the last apricot tart and bit into it.

'The timing of that part will mostly depend on the length of your visit. The duchess hasn't said how long it will be, so we can't plan for it. But when you know, you can write to me. I'll resign the housekeeper post and we'll meet at the same coaching inn where we parted company.'

'And if the duke sends me home in one of his own carriages – as he's almost certain to do? What then?'

'When you're safely away from London, you'll tell the coachman you wish to collect a friend *en route*. We can resume our own identities somewhere between there and here and no one will be any the wiser.'

This all sounded rather too easy. 'You don't think the coachman might start to wonder when he sees that we've exchanged clothes?'

'I doubt coachmen and grooms ever notice what one is wearing,' returned Arabella with what her cousin privately considered was naïve optimism. 'However ... speaking of clothes, now would be a good time to make sure my gowns fit well enough. Come on.'

Elizabeth rose, saying, 'What are you going to tell Annie?'

'The truth. She's sure to have a great deal to say but if we throw ourselves on her mercy and make her believe she's part of the secret, she may come round more quickly.'

On being told what was in the wind, Annie did indeed have a great deal to say – most of it concerned with the fact that Miss Belle ought to be past the age of indulging in wild pranks and a final, doom-laden prophecy that it was all going to end in tears.

But when none of this had any noticeable effect and she had laced Elizabeth into a pink flowered polonaise, very similar to the one Arabella was wearing, professionalism took over and she said, 'That looks very well on you, Miss Lizzie and nobody'd know it wasn't made for you. Just needs a bit of adjustment with pinning the over-dress to allow for you being a bit fuller in the bosom than Miss Belle.'

'You just had to point that out, didn't you?' muttered Arabella whilst slanting a laughing glance in Elizabeth's direction. And then, 'Well. We make quite a pair, don't we?'

The cousins stood side by side before the mirror, one in green-striped satin and the other in rose pink tiffany. They were the same height, of very similar build and both fair ... but there the likenesses ended. Where Arabella's eyes were dark grey, Elizabeth's were the blue of forget-me-nots; and while Arabella had inherited the silver-gilt hair which recurred in the family every generation or so, Elizabeth's curls were the same true gold possessed by their mothers.

Annie sniffed. 'It's a shame you can't both go to London. I'll give you that much. But I'm not happy about letting you go off on your own, Miss Belle – and not just 'cos her ladyship and Mr Max will have my head if anything happens to you, neither. So you'd better sew it all up tight if you want me to keep quiet about what the pair of you are up to.'

'We will – I promise.' Arabella dropped a kiss on her maid's cheek. 'We'll plan every detail. And what can possibly happen to me? Lord Chalfont is an earl!'

'I don't see as that makes it any better,' replied Annie darkly. 'From what I can make out, when it comes to gentlemen, the higher the title the worse they behave.'

* * *

Having cornered the children in the nursery-suite between supper-time and bed, Julian closed the door behind him and leaned against it in what he hoped was a casual pose but which would also shore up Tom's escape route. He said, 'There's something we need to discuss ... so perhaps you could all sit down?'

Rob and Ellie settled on the battered sofa; Rob looking a little wary and Ellie expectant.

Tom remained standing, his expression a mixture of anxiety and belligerence. He said, 'If'n you're going to put us out, just bleeding say it. No need to *discuss* it, is there?'

'If I *was* going to do that, I should think there would be *every* need,' replied Julian evenly. 'But since I'm not, I suggest you sit down and listen.'

Ellie reached up and tugged at her brother's hand.

'Sit down, Tom. It's all right. Sir Julian don't lie to us.'

Julian found himself repressing a grin. *Sir Julian, indeed. Where had that come from?* But he continued to watch Tom until the boy hurled himself ungraciously into the nearest chair and then said, 'I won't turn you out, Tom. You have my word.'

'And that's supposed to mean summat is it?'

'Stop it, Tom!' hissed Rob. 'Just stop!'

'Yes.' Tiring of twelve-year-old bravado, Julian detached himself from the door and stepped aside. 'But if my word isn't good enough for you, you're free to leave at any time.'

There was a long, unpleasant silence during which colour ebbed from Tom's face, Ellie looked ready to burst into tears and Julian held his breath. Then Rob said rapidly, 'Just shut up, Tom. Ellie's right. Sir's never lied to us. So button it and listen, will you?'

Tom shrugged and picked at his cuff, saying nothing. Taking this for temporary capitulation, Julian said, 'Thank you. I came up to tell you that, since I don't know anything about looking after children, we'll be getting help.'

'What sort of help?' asked Ellie.

'A lady. Her name is ...' He stopped, scouring his brain. *What was her name? Marshall? No. Marsden. That was it.* 'Her name is Mistress Marsden and, as well as being a sort of housekeeper, she will know how to care for the three of you better than I do.'

'I don't need no sodding female looking after me,' growled Tom.

And, 'You look after us well enough,' offered Rob.

'Better than *anybody*,' said Ellie stoutly.

'Kind – but untrue. Tom ... the lady is coming whether you need her or not. And since you will have to moderate your language once she arrives, you may as well begin now.'

'What's that supposed to mean?'

'It means,' said Julian firmly, 'that you will stop swearing.'

'Or what? You'll hit me?'

'Oh, something *much* worse than that. I'll tell Mr Phelps that you'll clear away that heap of muck behind the stables. He'll be happy to be spared the task himself ... and since your mouth is a midden, the rest of you might as well smell like one.'

Hours later, crouched over the harpsichord as he attempted to re-fit the jackrail, Julian was still wondering where the words had come from and whether to congratulate himself for handling Tom tolerably well or worry that the boy might decamp in the night. It was a relief, therefore to find Tom at breakfast with the other children on the following morning ... silent and mulish but still physically present.

It was a long, gruelling day. The sky was heavy with the promise of a storm and every pair of hands was needed to get the last of the harvest, such as it was, into the barns before the heavens opened. By the time it was done, thunder was rumbling in the distance and Julian felt as if his back was breaking. But there at the end of the lane, little Ellie sat patiently waiting for him.

Although she took his hand just as she always did, she neither skipped along at his side nor chattered about her day. Instead, she walked in silence for a time before finally saying, 'Is this lady who's coming nice?'

It ought to be the easiest thing in the world to simply say yes ... but he couldn't do it. Not only because he actually *was* incurably truthful; but because, for some reason, Ellie *believed* that he was. So he said, 'I haven't met her so I don't know for certain. I hope so. Dr Featherstone found her for us and she sounds quite nice in her letters.'

Ellie digested this for a moment or two. Then, with a tiny tremor in her voice, she said, 'What if she isn't? Mistress Clack who we used to l-live with wasn't very nice. And Mistress Hassall read us a story about a wicked stepmother. What if this lady is like them?'

Something unpleasant coiled in Julian's gut. He stopped walking, sat down on the stone wall and lifted the child up beside him.

'The wicked stepmother was just a story, Ellie. It wasn't true. And Mistress Marsden isn't going to be your stepmother anyway. She'll be a sort of a cross between Mistress Hassall and Mistress Phelps. But I'll make you a secret promise.'

Ellie's eyes grew round. 'Just between you and me?'

He nodded. 'If the lady isn't nice ... if she hurts or frightens you ... you will tell me and I'll send her away. How's that?'

'You promise?'

'I promise.'

Just for an instant, she beamed at him as if he'd given her the earth. Then, snuggling against his side so that, without him knowing how, his arm ended up around her, she said, 'I'm glad you came, Sir Julian. Everything is better now. You won't go away, will you?'

Julian stared sightlessly at the hedge on the other side of the lane and resolutely pushed back the familiar desolation. 'No,' he said. 'I won't go away.'

CHAPTER FOUR

At Brandon Lacey, the day of departure dawned on a sky heavy with the promise of rain. Arabella told herself it was merely the gloomy weather that was robbing the occasion of what ought to have been a glorious sense of freedom and adventure and wondered if Elizabeth felt the same.

To prevent their mother being inconvenienced, Max had hired a comfortable travelling carriage, together with a driver, a very muscular groom and two outriders. Luggage was strapped to the roof and a fully-laden picnic basket stowed under one of the seats in case of emergency. Both families gathered in the courtyard to bid the girls farewell and everyone hugged everyone else.

Max waited until last. Then, gathering Arabella close, he said, 'Enjoy it, love. Make the most of every minute. But if you're not happy ... if, for any reason, things don't go well and you want to come home, write to me. To *me*, Belle. I won't ask questions. I'll just come and get you. Is that clear?'

Arabella's vision wasn't. Now, as so often during these last days, she ached to confide in her favourite brother ... but she knew she couldn't. Max might know her inside out and trust her judgement but if he knew what she was planning to do now, he would end it in a heartbeat. Pressing her brow against his shoulder, she said unsteadily, 'Yes. Thank you.'

'Don't be an idiot.' He hugged her closer still and dropped a kiss on her hair. 'Just take yourself off to London and bring all the young bucks to their knees.'

Elizabeth's leave-taking was much more restrained. Her sisters looked uncomfortable; her father delivered a fond sermon full of useless advice; and her mother held her tight and whispered, 'If it turns out to be a mistake, don't be afraid to admit it and come home. You'll do that, won't you?'

'Yes, Mama.' Elizabeth's lips felt numb. 'I'll do that.'

After that, and seemingly in no time at all, they were off in a flurry of waving and last-minute good wishes. Once out on the open road, Arabella and Elizabeth exchanged long, silent glances and clutched the other's hand. Watching from the backward-facing seat, Annie said, 'Coachman says it's a fair way to Newark, so there's time to change your minds and do what everyone *thinks* you're doing.'

'Do you want to change your mind, Lizzie?' asked Arabella.

Elizabeth drew a careful breath. 'No. Do you?'

'No.'

'Well. That's that, then. Boot and saddle, as Max would say.'

At first, the novelty of setting out into the unknown made time pass quickly. But after the first change of horses, the scenery outside the carriage window lost its appeal and the cousins decided to kill the hours by going over and over every detail of their plan until both they and Annie could recite it to music. By the time they stopped for the night at the Golden Lion in Ferrybridge, Annie was no longer stumbling over calling Elizabeth Miss Belle and all three of them were stiff, tired and not looking forward to an early start and a longer day of travel.

'If thou wants to make it t'Newark before dark, we'll be leaving by seven in't morning at latest,' announced the coachman. 'His lordship said as you've rooms waiting at the Woolpack and it's my job to see you get to 'em – so no arguments.'

Elizabeth sighed, Arabella groaned and Annie muttered beneath her breath. But all three were ready to board the carriage at the appointed time on the following morning though none of them were happy about it.

The second day's travel seemed endless. Annie managed to doze for a large part of it. With a sort of tension building with every mile, Arabella and Elizabeth talked very little, each busy with her own thoughts.

The carriage rattled into the centre of Newark shortly before six in the evening and drew up in the busy yard of the Woolpack. Inside, however, the innkeeper's wife welcomed them with a cheerful smile and led the way to spacious and comfortable rooms, promising them dinner within the hour. When she had gone, Elizabeth said, 'I thought I was hungry. Now I'm not so sure.'

'I know. I feel the same.' Arabella looked at their trunks, sitting innocently side by side. Both had been meticulously packed in readiness for the morrow, so that only the uppermost garments needed to be exchanged and thus enabling Elizabeth and herself to travel onwards with the other's luggage. 'Stage-fright, do you think?'

'Last chance to change your minds, more like,' offered Annie flatly. 'You both better be absolutely sure what you're doing. If something goes wrong for either of you, there's going to be no putting it right.'

'Thank you for those words of comfort, Annie,' said Arabella sweetly. 'They've made us feel *so* much better.'

And suddenly, she and Elizabeth were laughing.

* * *

Morning came, bringing rain.

'Quite lucky, really,' observed Arabella, sounding more cheerful than she felt. 'You'll be able to put up the hood of my cloak so the entourage won't get a good look at you.'

'And what about you?' Elizabeth stood still while Annie finished fastening her into Arabella's exceedingly smart claret-coloured travelling dress.

'I'll stay out of sight until you've gone, then wait in the coffee-room for Dr Featherstone.' She smoothed the unfamiliar dark blue cuff and discovered that her fingers weren't quite steady. 'The next Mail Coach isn't due in until eleven, and he promised to be here by ten … so I'll be gone before the inn gets busy.'

'You shouldn't be alone in a public inn, Miss Belle,' muttered Annie. 'If this comes to light, Mr Max will have a fit.'

'So you've said. Frequently.' She pointed at Elizabeth and, despite the snakes writhing inside her ribcage, managed a valiant grin. 'And *that's* Miss Belle. I'm Mistress Marsden … efficient housekeeper and Generalissima of the schoolroom.'

It was perhaps fortunate that a tap on the door heralded a maidservant telling them that the coach was loaded and ready to depart. Elizabeth and Arabella looked at each other, swallowed hard and indulged in one final hug.

'Take care, Belle,' whispered Lizzie. 'It all sounded fine but if it's not --'

'It *will* be fine,' replied Arabella firmly. 'Don't worry about me. Just make sure you enjoy yourself. And write. I want to know all about the balls and parties and what the duke and duchess are like. Now go – before we're both in floods of tears. You too, Annie.' She pressed a guinea into the maid's hand. 'Buy yourself something pretty in London and look after 'Miss Belle'. We're both depending on you. *Go!*'

With the most painful moment behind her, Arabella stood at the bedchamber window and watched Elizabeth and Annie climb into the carriage. Then the coachman set it in motion and it rattled out of the yard ... and out of sight; her last link with her usual life, gone. Well, she had wanted escape and adventure, hadn't she? And this moment was the beginning of it. So she stiffened her spine, pulled the bell for the maid and, when the girl appeared, asked for someone to take her trunk downstairs. Then she descended to the coffee-room and settled at a table by the window to wait.

It was the first time in her entire life that Arabella had been completely alone in a public place and for a few minutes she felt unpleasantly conspicuous. However, it gradually dawned on her that no one was taking any particular notice ... not nearly as much, she realised, as they would have done had she been wearing her own elegant clothes instead of Elizabeth's more well-worn and conservative ones. She supposed she looked like what she was pretending to be; a genteel female on her way to a new position. That was encouraging because, if that was what the handful of people coming in and out of the coffee-room saw, there was no reason why Dr Featherstone would not see the same. On the other hand, thought Arabella and trying not to smile, it wouldn't hurt if the good doctor was either elderly or a bit short-sighted.

Outside, the rain was getting heavier and beginning to beat against the window. A curricle pulled into the yard and a fair-haired gentleman of roughly Max's age dropped down, tossed his reins to a nearby ostler and vanished inside the inn. Arabella sighed, tried not to fidget and wondered what the time was.

Silently damning the weather, Paul Featherstone narrowly avoided colliding with the innkeeper's wife. Stepping back with a smile and an apology, he said, 'Good day to you, Maggie. Are you still baking the best mutton pies in Nottinghamshire?'

'Aye – and in Lincolnshire, too,' she retorted, laughing. 'If you've business in town and want to come back around noon, I'll prove it to you.'

'Though there's nothing I'd like better, I can't. The rain is bidding fair to become a deluge so I'll be staying no longer than it takes Davey to water my horses. And the only business I have today is to collect a young woman who lodged here last night. One Mistress Marsden?'

'Young woman?' The landlady stared at him. 'Young *lady*, more like. You'll find her in the coffee-room, sir – and glad to be removed from it, I'll be bound.'

A faint frown lit Paul's eyes but he said lightly, 'Then I'd best go and tell her that deliverance is at hand, hadn't I? Thank you, Maggie.'

Having always suspected that Mistress Marsden's letters weren't telling him everything, Paul thought he had been prepared for the unexpected. A single glance was sufficient to tell him how wrong he had been ... and it stopped him mid-stride.

Good God, he thought. *Surely* that *can't be her? I doubt she's a day over twenty.*

Turning away from the window, Arabella met the fair-haired gentleman's expression of shocked disbelief, realised that this must be Dr Featherstone and felt suddenly panicky. *He knows I'm not Lizzie*, was her first guilty thought. Then, *No, that's stupid. He can't know – how could he?* And finally, the answer came to her. *Lizzie said she'd given the impression of being older. How* much *older, for heaven's sake? Forty?*

Wiping every vestige of expression from his face, Paul walked to her side and, with a slight bow, said, 'Mistress Marsden, I presume?'

She nodded and got to her feet. 'Yes. And you must be Dr Featherstone.'

'I am indeed. Please sit down again, ma'am. My horses need a brief rest and perhaps you would care for some coffee or a cup of chocolate to warm you before we set off? As you can see, the weather is deteriorating.'

'It certainly is,' agreed Arabella resuming her seat, hoping she sounded suitably blasé and as if sitting in taverns with strange gentlemen was an everyday occurrence. 'Thank you. Chocolate would be very welcome.'

He nodded to her and walked away to place the order, whilst trying to decide what he ought to do. She was far too young and Maggie Rowell was right about her being a lady. Not that that precluded a need to earn her own living, of course – but her age certainly did. Julian needed a woman of sense and character, not a schoolroom miss. Paul drew a long breath. *All right*, he decided. *I've got half an hour in which to find out what she's made of and, if necessary, send her back where she came from.*

Returning to the table by the window, he sat down facing Arabella and said, 'Forgive my bluntness, Mistress Marsden – but I daresay you will recall that we advertised for a *mature* lady. Exactly how old are you?'

Arabella turned scarlet and narrowly avoided spluttering at him. Then, pulling herself together, she lifted her chin and lied. 'I am twenty-five, Dr Featherstone. How old are you?'

He managed not to laugh. 'My age is of no consequence, ma'am. Yours, unfortunately, *is*. What experience do you actually have of overseeing the running of a household – or of managing young children, come to that?'

'Did I not tell you those things in my letters?'

'Yes. But you also admitted that you had no previous employers – neither did you seek character references from persons who might have supplied them.'

Not being sure how to respond to this, she said cautiously, 'Such as whom?'

'Such as the local clergyman, perhaps?'

'That would be my father,' said Arabella triumphantly whilst simultaneously suppressing a faintly hysterical giggle at the thought of asking Uncle Josiah to recommend her as a housekeeper. 'I imagine you might have considered that somewhat biased.'

'The doctor, then – or the squire or any reputable person of your acquaintance?' said Paul impatiently. Then, 'When you meet Lord Chalfont ... or rather *if* you do ... you will appreciate my concerns.'

A maid arrived with a cup of chocolate and a half of home-brewed. As soon as she had set these down and stepped away, Arabella said sharply, 'What do you mean – *if*?'

'At present, I'm inclined to think that his lordship's best interests as well as your own will be better served by putting you on the York Mail which will be here,' he drew a watch from his waistcoat pocket, 'in roughly twenty-five minutes.'

Her breath leaked away and she felt suddenly cold. She had never considered the possibility that the doctor might take one look and find her unsuitable. It was a disaster that couldn't be allowed to happen – not with Elizabeth already on the road to London and no way to contact her.

Looking him in the eye and keeping her voice as steady as she could, she said, 'Since you have told me very little about him, I can't speak for Lord Chalfont. But I think *I* am better placed to decide what is in my best interests than you are, sir. I am fully capable of running a moderate-sized household and – and I've helped in the village school so I'm quite accustomed to dealing with children.' She stopped and, still holding his gaze, 'I realise that you were expecting someone a little older but --'

'Quite a *lot* older, ma'am,' retorted Paul.

'But you shouldn't judge by appearances. I'm more capable than I look – truly I am.'

'You're certainly tenacious,' he agreed with a hint of grim amusement.

'I need the position,' she shrugged. Then, hopefully, 'And as I recall it, a trial period was offered, was it not?'

There was no denying that. There was also no denying, thought Paul reluctantly, that the girl wasn't lacking either spirit or determination. Perhaps he *was* wrong to judge purely by appearances. Perhaps ... just perhaps ... she might not be so very unsuitable after all. The trouble was that the risk would be Julian's, not his.

He said slowly, 'A trial period it is, then. One month.'

That wouldn't do. Elizabeth would be in London longer than that.

'Two months,' said Arabella firmly. 'You can't expect me to prove myself in less than that – given that it appears there are challenges I was not previously made aware of. I am not a miracle-worker, Dr Featherstone.'

Paul realised that he was starting to like her. Despite the pulse he could see hammering in her throat, she was holding her ground and refusing to back down. He had to admire that. He also had to admit that anyone dealing with Julian required resilience and a strong vein of obstinacy. Mistress Marsden, it seemed, had both.

Smiling for the first time, he said, 'Very well, ma'am. You win. Two months it is.'

Relief washed over Arabella. She said earnestly, 'Thank you. I shall make sure that neither you nor his lordship regrets it.'

'I'll hold you to that.' Paul got to his feet. 'We should be on our way before the road turns to mud. Is that your trunk in the hallway?' And when she nodded, 'Good. Drink your chocolate and I'll get it loaded. All being well, we'll be at Chalfont in time for tea.'

Arabella watched him go, her heart beating unpleasantly fast. It had been an alarmingly close call ... and she still had the earl to face. She could only pray that he would be less inclined to quibble.

* * *

It was an unpleasant journey. The rain continued unabated and, from time to time, lashed in on them under the hood of the curricle. Arabella hugged her cloak around her, felt her hair begin to droop in the damp and was glad the doctor was concentrating on his horses rather than forcing her to make conversation.

When they finally arrived, she had only the briefest glimpse of Chalfont Hall before the doctor helped her from the curricle and swept her inside out of the rain. Putting back her hood,

Arabella had a confused impression of dark, oak panelling and then a red-haired lady wearing a faint frown was stepping towards her, saying briskly, 'What a horrid journey you must have had. Let me take your cloak – it's quite soaked.'

'Y-Yes,' agreed Arabella weakly. And attempting to sound cheerful, as she surrendered the sodden garment, 'But at least we are here now.'

'Indeed you are.' Behind the girl's back, Janet raised her eyebrows at Paul, who answered with an unhelpful shrug leaving her with no option but to plough resolutely on. 'I am Mistress Featherstone, by the way. I hope my husband has been looking after you?'

'He – he's been most kind.'

Swallowing a grin at her tepid tone, Paul said, 'Janet – where's Julian?'

'I've no idea. He was here a minute ago but --'

'I'm here.' Emerging with ill-concealed reluctance from the shadows of the staircase, his face pale and empty of expression, Julian bowed and said woodenly, 'Welcome to Chalfont, Mistress Marsden.'

All the air in Arabella's lungs seemed to leak away. *This* was the earl? This breath-takingly handsome man who looked about the same age as her brother, Adam? It wasn't possible. She shot a look of confused enquiry in Dr Featherstone's direction.

He nodded his confirmation. 'Lord Chalfont, ma'am.'

She managed a curtsy. 'My lord.'

There was a sudden deathly silence during which his lordship looked anywhere but at Arabella. Stepping into the void, Janet said, 'Let me show you to your rooms. Paul ... have Phelps bring up Mistress Marsden's luggage and send one of the maids with tea.'

Paul started to offer to fetch the trunk himself but Julian cut across him saying abruptly, 'No – let Phelps do it. I – I'd like a word with you. Now.'

Having a fair idea of what was coming, Paul sighed and followed Julian into the clean but still dilapidated parlour, murmuring 'Yes, I know and I agree. She's not at all what we expected. She claims to be twenty-five – though I don't believe that for a minute. And that flawless curtsy coupled with the cut-glass accent bereft of any hint of Yorkshire is --'

'What does any of that matter?' Julian burst out. 'I can't – I *can't* have her here. You have to take her away.'

This was a much more extreme reaction than Paul had anticipated. 'Why?'

'*Why?* You've seen her. Why do you *think?*'

'I don't know. That's why I'm asking.'

'She – she's much too young and far too pretty!' With a massive effort, he managed to stop himself blurting out, *Girls like her scare the hell out of me. They tie my tongue in knots and make me feel like an idiot.* 'She's got to go.'

Far too pretty? thought Paul, baffled. *That's interesting – because aside from unusual hair and nice eyes, she's nothing out of the ordinary.*

In the brief glance which was all he'd allowed himself, nothing Julian had seen was ordinary; not the heart-shaped face nor the halo of silvery-fair hair ... and certainly not those lovely dark grey eyes. She was beautiful and thus, to him, terrifying – as a consequence of which he was desperately scraping his mind for acceptable reasons to get rid of her.

'She'll never manage the children. Tom will run rings around her. And God knows what people will make of her being here alone with me barring a couple of servants! They'll say she's my m-mistress or some such rubbish. I can't have her here, Paul. I just *can't!*'

'Stop panicking for a moment, will you? I was half-inclined to send her home but she's determined and not easy to dissuade, so I eventually agreed to a two month trial period. If, by the end of it, you --'

'Two *months*? No. I won't have her living in the same house, seeing her every day, having to *talk* to her and – and --'

'And what?' Paul grinned at him. 'What's the matter? Afraid you won't be able to keep your hands off her?'

'*No!*' snapped Julian, appalled. 'No, of course not. I wouldn't – I would never --'

'I know that. If I didn't, I'd have put her on the York Mail. Take a deep breath and calm down, will you? It's eight weeks, Julian – not a lifetime. And she might decide to leave before then. But in the meantime, just give her a chance. She may surprise us.'

* * *

After Mistress Featherstone left, Arabella lingered over her unpacking as long as she dared. The bedchamber and adjoining sitting-room she had been given were comfortable, if shabby, and the view from the windows over rain-soaked fields, less than inspiring. However, none of that was what was bothering her. Dr Featherstone, she decided darkly, ought to have told her about the earl … who was nothing like the middle-aged widower she'd expected. Adam was twenty-eight. Unless the earl was a good deal older than he looked, possession of a twelve-year-old son made him an exceptionally precocious youth – a concept she found she preferred not to contemplate. And why had he behaved so oddly? Arabella knew she hadn't been looking her best but she didn't think she looked awful enough to account for his expression of utter alarm. It was all very bewildering. And she hadn't laid eyes on the children yet.

Having tidied her hair as best she could and changed into the least creased of Elizabeth's gowns, the inevitable could be delayed no longer. She left her room and went downstairs. The hall was deserted and she had no idea which of the doors led where, so she strode to the nearest one, put her hand on the latch … and nearly jumped out of her skin when a young voice nearby said clearly, 'You can't go in there.'

Arabella wheeled round to find herself under the scrutiny of three pairs of eyes. It was uncanny. A second ago, they hadn't been there. But now there was a scowling, dark-haired boy, his arm looped around the newel at the foot of the stairs; a younger, tow-headed boy, sitting four steps up; and a small girl with big brown eyes, staring at her from three feet away.

Ellie's words also reached the dining-room where Julian was pacing back and forth in an attempt to convince himself that he could survive the next hour or so. While Paul had been driving to Newark, Janet had insisted that – for this evening at least – dinner should be served correctly and that Julian must sit down at the table with Mistress Marsden to make her feel welcome. He must also, she had said, make an effort with his appearance. So here he was, hair neatly tied and wearing his only decent coat, condemned to an evening of pure torture.

He had never met a pretty young woman who wasn't terrifying. They *looked* at him. And it wasn't *just* looking. They either wore an expression which suggested they knew something he didn't … or, worse still, they gazed at him expectantly, as if waiting for him to say something in particular. And because he didn't know what that particular something was, his brain had a tendency to freeze completely.

On the other side of the dining-room door, one such female was encountering the children for the first time. Julian knew he ought to help with this. Instead, despising his cowardice, he stayed where he was and listened.

In the hall, Arabella swallowed, summoned a smile and focussed on the easiest target.

'Can't I? I didn't know that. Thank you for telling me.'

Ellie nodded. 'It's locked, anyway. Nobody's allowed in because of the harpy cord.'

'The harpy cord? I don't quite --'

'Harpsichord,' said Tom. 'The heap of rubbish nobody's allowed to touch.'

'It is *not* rubbish!' Ellie swung round on him. 'Just you wait till it's mended.'

'Hell will freeze first,' came the derisive reply. Then, turning a hard stare on Arabella, 'Just so you know … that's Rob and that's Ellie. I'm Tom. And I don't need no nursemaid.'

Being very familiar with male pride, Arabella knew the correct response to this.

'You didn't need to tell me that, Tom. It's perfectly obvious that you can look after yourself.' She smiled at Rob and Ellie. 'I hope you two aren't going to say that *you* don't need me either because that will mean I've come an awful long way for nothing.'

Rob grinned back. 'We'll let you know. Mistress Marsden … right?'

'Quite right – but a bit of a mouthful, don't you think? How about Miss B-Lizzie?'

'Miss Blizzy?' asked Rob cheekily.

'Lizzie,' said Arabella, furious with herself for the slip. 'It's short for ...'

The words withered on her tongue as the earl stepped into the hall wearing an expression that defied interpretation and very obviously avoiding her eyes. She thought, *He doesn't like me. We've barely exchanged a word and already he doesn't like me. Why?*

Ellie, meanwhile, skipped across to take his hand, saying, 'Can we show Miss Lizzie our rooms and take her to meet Missus Phelps and --'

'Tomorrow,' said Julian, managing something vaguely resembling a smile. 'You can do that tomorrow. For now, go and see what Mistress Phelps has for your supper.'

They clattered away towards the kitchen, leaving Julian feeling exposed and awkward.

Indicating the room he'd just left, he said, 'Ma'am?'

'Thank you, my lord.'

The dining-parlour was cavernous, dismal and contained a large table, with places set at either end. *Well*, thought Arabella, *that speaks volumes. And he's left the door open. Is that to safeguard my reputation or because he's afraid I'll throw myself at him? With looks like that, I daresay he's used to girls drooling over him. And there's no denying those eyes of his are extraordinarily --* She checked the thought before it could go any further. *But he won't find me drooling. I'm accustomed to handsome men. There are three of them at home. And David was pretty, too ... so I don't judge by looks any more.*

She sat, straight-backed, on an over-stuffed horsehair sofa, watched him pull the bell to let the servants know they could serve dinner and decided to leave conversation up to him. Just when she was coming to the conclusion that he wasn't going to open his mouth, he said stiffly, 'Did you have a pleasant journey?'

'Very pleasant, thank you. I travelled as far as Newark with my cousin.'

'Ah. That was ... fortunate.'

'Wasn't it? She is on her way to visit relatives in London, so we were able to begin our respective journeys together.' She waited and, when he said nothing, added, 'Of course, thanks to the rain, the ride from Newark to here was less enjoyable. But it was very kind of Dr Featherstone to collect me.'

For the space of a heartbeat, the long-lashed green eyes flicked to her face before going back to studying the carpet. He said, 'I don't keep a carriage.'

That possibility hadn't previously occurred to Arabella. What titled gentleman *didn't* keep a carriage? On the other hand, she suspected that if Lord Chalfont had come to Newark himself, she might currently be on her way back to Yorkshire. Annoyance began tugging at the edges of her mind. Forcing herself to ignore it, she said pleasantly, 'I understand you have only recently inherited your title, my lord.'

'Six months ago,' said Julian, managing not to add, *Six months and a bloody lifetime*. 'The estate has been ... neglected.'

A maid came in and set a tureen of soup on the table. Casting a brief yet oddly indulgent glance at the earl, she said, 'Milord, ma'am ... if you'd like to be seated, I'll serve.'

Remembering just in time that he was supposed to pull out a chair for his guest, Julian did so before walking the length of the table to take his own place. The maid ladled soup into bowls and offered each of them the basket of rolls, saying cheerfully, 'Fresh-baked this afternoon, sir.'

'Yes. Thank you ... er ... Rose?'

'Violet, sir,' corrected the girl. And on her way from the room, sounding as if she wanted to pat him on the shoulder, 'Now, you just have that while it's hot. I'll bring the beef when you're ready.'

Silence fell again. They ate – or at least, Arabella did. The earl, so far as she could see, spent the time stirring his soup and reducing the bread to crumbs. He still didn't look at her. Finally, laying down her spoon and letting irritation get the upper hand, she said, 'I'm not a basilisk, you know.'

Julian's eyes flew to hers and the spoon slipped from his grasp, sending soup splashing on to his fingers. 'I beg your pardon?'

'I said I'm not a basilisk – or a Gorgon or Medusa – or any of those things in mythology one can't look in the eye without dire consequences.' She offered him a cool smile. 'I just thought I'd mention it.'

Colour crept across his cheekbones and, picking up his napkin, he concentrated on wiping soup from his hand. 'Forgive me. I didn't mean to be rude.'

Light finally dawned. Eyes widening in fascination, Arabella thought, *He's shy. Painfully, miserably shy. Oh dear.* She said quietly, 'Of course not. It's a bit difficult isn't it – sitting down to dine with a complete stranger?'

'Yes.' Janet had told him he must get to know Mistress Marsden. He just wished she'd also told him how he was supposed to do it. 'Yes, it is.'

'I daresay you have a lot of questions.' She smiled encouragingly. 'Under the circumstances, it would be amazing if you didn't – so ask them, by all means.'

God, he thought dismally. *There are probably a dozen things I ought to ask but I've no idea what they are.* Staring into the soup, he muttered, 'I haven't thought about it.'

'Oh. Well perhaps we might try it the other way around. Since I'm here to oversee your household and your children, I shall need to understand your exact requirements.'

Not having any requirements, exact or otherwise, Julian temporised.

'I'll trust your judgement.'

Arabella didn't find that helpful but could hardly say so. Fortunately, Violet replacing the soup with beef and an array of vegetables temporarily suspended the need for conversation. However, as soon as they were alone again, she persevered.

'Perhaps you could tell me a bit about the children?'

'Such as what?'

'Well … how long is it since your wife died?'

'*Wife?*' For the first time she had his whole attention. 'What wife? I've never been married. What on earth made you think --?'

'The fact that you have three children,' cut in Arabella acidly, before she saw both the alternative explanation and the pit yawning at her feet. 'Oh. I see. They – they're --'

'Not mine,' blurted Julian. 'Illegitimate, yes ... but not mine.'

For a second, she didn't take it in. Then she managed to say weakly, 'N-Not?'

'No.' Julian had assumed that Paul would have spared him this task on the drive back. Clearly, he hadn't. 'I inherited them from the fourth earl along with everything else.'

Arabella tried to take this in. 'And – and their mother?'

'Mothers. Plural.'

'Oh. That is ...' She stopped, frowning. 'But how is it that *you* are responsible for them?'

He shrugged, looking uncomfortable. 'Someone had to be.'

'You're saying no provision had been made for them?'

'Not after their father died – and precious little before it. The only thing the fourth earl was generous with was his seed. Of course, if he'd --' Glimpsing her expression, Julian stopped abruptly and said, 'I probably should have left out that bit about the fourth earl's --'

'Yes,' she said, before he could repeat it. 'You p-probably should have done.'

He eyed her uncertainly.

'I'm sorry. It's just ... I'm not very good at conversation.'

Arabella stared at him, torn between laughter and the suspicion that this was probably a massive understatement. Taking a second to wonder how Elizabeth would have coped with a man who said the first thing that came into his head, no matter how inappropriate, she said, 'I think I'm more relieved than shocked.'

'Relieved?'

The laughter she had been suppressing escaped in a series of deliciously infectious gurgles that the earl's confused expression only made worse. Finally, still struggling to breathe, she said, 'Don't worry. I'm not having hysterics.'

'That's a relief.' Her skin was flushed and her eyes brilliant, but it was the warm, musical ripple of her laughter that caught in his chest and held him captivated. 'Then what is so funny?'

'The fact that what you've just told me is better than what I believed earlier.'

'Which was?'

'That you – that you'd fathered a child around the time you first started shaving,' replied Arabella, promptly relapsing into a fresh fit of giggles. 'I must admit that I found that a b-bit worrying.'

'More worrying than being employed to look after the late earl's by-blows?'

All signs of amusement fled.

'Yes. And if that remark was designed to test my attitudes, consider yourself answered. They are *children* … and the circumstances of their birth are no more their fault than they are yours. But you already know that, don't you? Otherwise they wouldn't be here.'

He nodded and muttered something that sounded like another apology.

'You have nothing to apologise for, my lord – nothing at all.' She frowned a little. 'How on earth were they managing before you came here?'

'God knows.'

'I see. Then I hope the fourth earl is roasting somewhere very hot.'

'Yes,' agreed Julian. 'So do I. Because if he'd married one of the boys' mothers, I needn't be here.'

CHAPTER FIVE

With the exception of an odd look from the coachman, Elizabeth's journey from Newark to Stamford proved uneventful. She and Annie awoke the following morning to intermittent drizzle which, for an hour or so, they seemed to out-distance. But by the time they reached Huntingdon it had caught up with them and was steadily becoming heavier. The coachman, hopeful of reaching St Neots before dark, sent for food to be brought to the carriage and stayed only long enough for a change of horses.

'How much further is it?' asked Annie, trying to relieve the cramp in her shoulders.

'Two more overnight stops – if we're lucky and the weather doesn't get any worse,' replied Elizabeth, smiling sympathetically. 'Not much fun, is it?'

'Not *any* fun,' grumbled Annie. 'The only bit of me that doesn't ache is my bum – and that's because I can't feel it no more.'

Rather than quibble with the maid's choice of words, Elizabeth said, 'I wonder how Belle is getting on? And what the earl is like?'

'So long as he's gentleman enough to keep his hands to himself, it doesn't much matter what he's like. As to the rest ... right now, Miss Belle's more comfortable than you and me.'

Conversation lapsed and they stared gloomily out on the sodden countryside. By mid-afternoon, Huntingdon was behind them but progress through the wet grew increasingly slow.

Beginning to feel alarmed, Elizabeth said, 'Perhaps we should have stopped in Huntingdon, rather than pressing on. I'm sure one of the inns could have --'

Her words were cut off as the coach rounded a sharp bend, sending both herself and Annie sliding to the other side of their seats. Then, before either of them could right themselves, the carriage continued careering sideways – fast and amidst a good deal of shouting from the box – until it lurched to a violent, tooth-rattling stop and landed half on its side to the ominous sound of splintering wood and shrill complaints from the horses.

Entangled with each other on the floor, Elizabeth and Annie tried to scramble up but froze when the coach began to slide again and the driver yelled, 'Don't move a muscle or we'll be at the bottom of the bloody bank!'

Elizabeth looked up at the other window and discovered she could see nothing but sky. She didn't dare raise herself up to peer through the one directly above her head.

'This,' she remarked, through slightly chattering teeth, 'isn't g-good.'

'You can say that again.' Annie's face was unnaturally white. 'I think my ankle's broke.'

'Sit tight and don't fret, ladies,' called Jessop, the more senior of the two outriders. 'Once the coachman and groom are down and we've got the horses unhitched, we'll have you out in no time.'

Elizabeth devoutly hoped so. She reached for the maid's hand, saying optimistically, 'It's probably just a sprain, Annie. That hurts more than one might think.'

Annie said nothing but her fingers tightened on Elizabeth's like a vice.

Although it seemed endless, the wait while voices outside conferred was probably no more than five minutes. Then the far door opened and Jessop peered down on them. He said, 'We're going to open the door you're jammed up against. If we try and lift you through this'n, there's a good chance we'll dislodge the carriage further. So I want you to move slow and gentle-like, one at a time and find something to hang on to. Can you do that?'

'We'll try,' said Elizabeth. 'But Annie's ankle is hurt.'

'I'll manage.' Annie's voice was faint but determined.

'Good girl. Clem and me are coming round to your side. Shout out when you're ready.'

Inch by inch, Elizabeth managed to get to her knees and let down the window nearest to her so that she could put her arm through and cling on to the outside of the carriage. She said, 'Now you, Annie. Wedge yourself into the corner and try to reach the strap.'

Annie's first move, made clumsy by pain, caused the carriage to shudder. Faces appeared at the window, someone shouted, *'Whoa!'* and Elizabeth stopped breathing. Mercifully, however, they remained where they were and Annie finally managed to grab the strap.

Afterwards, Elizabeth never remembered quite how the outriders managed to extract them from a drunkenly-leaning carriage, poised on a steep bank above the river. Realisation that the only thing stopping them from sliding down into the water was a single boulder, wedged where the front nearside wheel had once been had made the bottom of her stomach fall away. A second realisation was no better. They were on a deserted stretch of road, possibly miles from the next inn; the coach, according to the almost distraught coachman, had suffered worse damage than that mangled wheel and needed extensive repairs; and, as if all that wasn't bad enough, the rain had become torrential.

Clem set off to locate the next village, while Jessop helped the coachman and groom with the tasks of calming the frightened horses, removing the luggage from the roof and preventing the carriage sliding further down the bank by propping it up with stones purloined from a nearby wall. Elizabeth and Annie sat on their trunks, side by side in the deluge, feeling like orphans of the storm.

After a while, Annie said, 'I thought we were taking the Great North Road all the way?'

'We are. This is it.'

'Then why are we the only ones on it?'

'This awful weather, I expect. How does your ankle feel?'

'Sore. Must've just wrenched it like you said.'

'Well, at least that's *one* piece of good news,' said Elizabeth, trying to sound cheerful despite the fact that, having soaked through her hood, water was trickling down her neck. 'Hopefully, Clem will be back soon with help.'

'If he finds any,' said Job's Comforter. 'Looks like the back of beyond to me.'

More time passed. More rain fell. The men decided the carriage was as secure as they could make it and Jessop set off in Clem's wake. The groom walked the horses up and down to combat the chilling effect of the rain. Clem didn't come back and the sky darkened. And then, just when Elizabeth was beginning to think they were all doomed to spend the night here, she heard the rumble of carriage-wheels travelling in the same direction they'd been taking themselves. Shouting to the groom to keep the horses back, the coachman readied himself to flag down the oncoming vehicle. Four matched greys drawing a smart, if exceedingly muddy, chaise rounded the bend that had been their own undoing ... then slowed to a stop.

'Oh thank God,' whispered Elizabeth, hauling herself to her feet. 'Thank God.'

The coachmen exchanged a few terse sentences and the new arrival jumped down to speak to the carriage's occupant. Elizabeth was just wondering at the seeming delay when her own coachman waved her over, calling, 'It's all right, Mistress Brandon. This gentleman will take you and your maid as far as the next inn. When Clem gets back here with a cart, we'll send your luggage after you. Now ... let's get the two of you out of the wet.'

'But what about you and --?'

'Don't you worry about us, Miss. Just hop inside so the gentleman can get on his way.'

Seeing little choice and longing to get out of the rain, Elizabeth climbed into the carriage and, half-blinded by her hood, stretched out a hand to help Annie. It wasn't until they were both seated and the carriage jerked forward that she looked at their rescuers. Two men ... a gentleman and his valet, by the look of them. The valet smiled faintly and acknowledged her with a polite nod but did not speak. The elegant dark-haired gentleman said nothing either. He merely raised his eyes from the book in his hand, subjected her to a chilly regard and moved his glossy boots away from her dripping hem.

Elizabeth felt herself flush. She didn't need the disparaging look in those tawny-gold hawk's eyes to tell her that she and Annie were hopelessly bedraggled. But she pinned a smile to her lips and said, 'Thank you for helping us, sir. It is most kind of you and we are extremely grateful.' Then, when he merely inclined his head a fraction, she persevered with, 'Allow me to introduce myself. I am Mistress B-Brandon of --'

'Of Brandon Lacey in Yorkshire,' he said, his voice soft and somewhere beyond bored. 'Yes. So your coachman said. As to my help ... on such a day, I could scarcely refuse.'

But on another day you would have? thought Elizabeth. But keeping the smile firmly in place, she said, 'And may I know to whom I am indebted?'

'Sherbourne,' he said unexpansively. And turned back to his book.

Elizabeth and Annie exchanged glances, then looked at the valet. One corner of his mouth curled and he rolled his eyes in the direction of his employer. Despite her current misery, Annie was forced to stifle a giggle.

'I saw that, Frayne,' said Sherbourne without raising his eyes from the page. 'We need not discuss it. But you may wish to consider the question of exactly how valuable I find your undoubted ability with boot-blacking.'

Mr Frayne's grin widened. He cleared his throat but said nothing.

Elizabeth's sodden petticoats were clinging to her legs and her feet felt like ice. Unlocking her jaws and ignoring the fact that their rescuer clearly didn't want to talk, she said, 'Do you know how far it may be to the next inn, Mr Sherbourne?'

He sighed, looked up and said, 'Lord.'

'I beg your pardon?'

'*Lord* Sherbourne ... as in the earl of. But in answer to your question – no. I am lamentably unfamiliar with this stretch of road.'

Effectively silenced, Elizabeth went back to staring through the window. After a time, Annie whispered, 'What are we going to do if they can't mend the coach?'

'Hire another one, I suppose. But there's no use worrying about that now. The most important thing is to find shelter as soon as possible and – ah!' Elizabeth broke off. 'There's Clem, on his way back with a cart. That's a relief. At least we can count on dry clothes.'

Annie opened her mouth to reply but closed it again when Elizabeth shot her a warning look and shook her head. If his lordship wanted silence, silence he should have.

In a long, covert perusal, Elizabeth took in the earl's black hair, narrow dark brows and chiselled bones. He was good-looking in a severe sort of way; it was a pity that he was also cold, forbidding and a hairsbreadth from rude.

The chaise trundled cautiously on through the rain. Annie started to shiver. Elizabeth passed the time hoping that the staggering amount of money Arabella hadn't let her refuse at Newark would cover the expense of hiring another coach. It had been meant to cover additional necessities in London. But first they had to get there.

Dusk was approaching when, from the forward-facing seat beside his master, the valet rubbed a hand over the misty window and said, 'Lights, my lord.'

Lord Sherbourne slid a gilt-edged card into his book and closed it. 'An inn?'

'I believe so.'

'Excellent.'

Elizabeth tilted her head, trying to see what he had been reading only to find the characters on the cover unfamiliar.

Greek? she wondered. *He's passing the time reading Greek?* And then, *Now why should that make his behaviour seem marginally less unacceptable?*

The chaise came to a halt. The groom leapt down, opened the door and said apologetically, 'Mr Cox says we'll not get any further today, my lord.'

'I believe I had guessed as much. You had best see about rooms, Frayne.' Letting the valet precede him, Lord Sherbourne descended without haste and turned to offer Elizabeth his hand. 'Ma'am?'

She hesitated for a fraction of a second before placing her fingers in his. They were firm and, unlike his demeanour, warm.

Releasing them as soon as she could, Elizabeth pulled up her hood and walked swiftly inside the small, half-timbered inn.

Stepping away from his lordship's valet, the landlord greeted them enthusiastically.

'Welcome to the Oak, my lord. Bedchambers, we can do and as good a dinner as you'll get this side of Biggleswade. But as I was just explaining to your gentleman, private parlours we don't have – though you'll maybe find the coffee-room private enough tonight, with no other guests and the weather as it is.'

A faint frown touched Sherbourne's brow but he said, 'For myself, that will do admirably. But perhaps the lady might prefer --?'

'No,' said Elizabeth quickly. 'A bedchamber and a hot bath is what I require most – aside from the arrival of my luggage, of course. And I have no objection to dining in the coffee-room.'

The inn-keeper nodded, summoned a maidservant and issued the necessary orders. His lordship, however, looked thoughtfully at Elizabeth and, with only the merest suggestion of reluctance, drawled softly, 'Then, since we are to share the coffee-room, perhaps you will do me the honour of dining with me, ma'am?'

'Oh.' Taken by surprise, not sure what she wanted to say but aware that there probably wasn't much alternative, Elizabeth felt herself flush. 'I – that is most kind of you, my lord but – but I am loth to inconvenience you.'

His smile, though fleeting, was not without irony.

'No inconvenience, ma'am – otherwise I would not suggest it.'

* * *

Later, soaking gratefully in hot water while Annie stood at the window looking out for Clem with their trunks, Elizabeth said, 'If this village is as small as I think it is, I'm not sure where we're going to get another carriage.'

'If it carries on raining like this, we won't need one,' replied Annie grimly. And then, 'I don't think you ought to be dining alone with that man, Miss Lizzie. Let me tell them to serve your dinner up here.'

71

'No.' Elizabeth laughed. 'He's not exactly the susceptible sort, is he? And some practise talking to fashionable gentlemen would be useful – assuming his lordship doesn't sit down to dine with a book in his hand. Meanwhile, you can take your dinner with his valet. He probably won't gossip ... but one never knows.'

In a bedchamber on the other side of the corridor and having unpacked a suit of black brocade, the valet said neutrally, 'Did you believe what the young lady's coachman told you, my lord? About her travelling to London as the Duke of Rockliffe's guest, I mean?'

Sherbourne shrugged. 'I see no reason not to do so.'

Frayne continued finishing brushing the coat and turned his attention to laying out the cream embroidered vest to be worn beneath it. 'She is a beauty.'

'Yes.' A pause; and then, 'Was there some particular point to that observation?'

'No, my lord.'

'Good.' He stood up and prowled to the window. 'Speak to Cox. Find out our chances of getting more than a mile or two from this place tomorrow.'

'You don't think it likely?'

'I suspect not. And given the reasons for my early departure from Whitcombe Park, it is a damned nuisance. However ... I live in hope.'

'Mistress Brandon will have even greater difficulties.'

'Mistress Brandon is not my responsibility,' said the earl coldly. 'And I will thank you for not attempting to make her so.'

* * *

Downstairs in the coffee-room, Ralph Harcourt, Earl of Sherbourne, sat in a corner and brooded over a bottle of canary. With the most extreme reluctance, he had been on the brink of offering for Anna Whitcombe when the letter demanding his presence elsewhere had arrived. The reprieve was a relief. Although every bit as lovely as the young woman upstairs, Mistress Whitcombe was also one of the most tedious females he had ever met. Not that this was the reason for his unwillingness to commit himself. *That* stemmed from the feeling that marrying an heiress was tantamount to selling himself ... merely in a more socially acceptable manner than that employed by his youngest brother. Ralph didn't mind selling his title; he didn't even mind that well-dowered Anna had been hanging out for the highest rank she could buy for the last two seasons and was only considering him because there were no marquises or dukes currently available. What stuck in his throat was the knowledge that the title came with his person attached to it. Unfortunately, whether or not he did so for money, marriage was a necessity. The earldom, as he knew only too well, required an heir; because the prospect of his brother Cedric stepping into his shoes didn't bear thinking about.

Mistress Brandon hesitated in the doorway, elegant in midnight blue taffeta and blonde lace. Ralph hadn't needed his valet to point out that she was beautiful. Even cold, wet and still shaken from the accident, that fact had been evident. Now, of course, she looked stunning; the perfect English beauty ... all rose-petal skin, shining gold curls and wide forget-me-not eyes. A visual delight and possibly even a temptation if one had the remotest interest in well-bred innocents – which, with a week of Anna Whitcombe's company fresh in his mind, Ralph did not.

Rising, he bowed politely and asked if she would care for a glass of wine.

Elizabeth hesitated, then decided on caution. 'Perhaps later ... with dinner.'

In truth, the confidence she'd felt upstairs had evaporated the second she'd walked into the room and come face to face with an epitome of self-assurance and worldly sophistication. He was also better-looking than she had thought; tall, well-made and with an in-built grace, all wrapped up in something that made her senses prickle.

Ralph saw the sudden, almost imperceptible wariness and had no difficulty interpreting it. It was so ludicrous that he nearly laughed. She was no more at risk with him than she would be with an octogenarian priest. But they never realised that, did they? Thanks, presumably to their mothers, they always thought one of two things. Either that they themselves were completely irresistible … or all men were wholly governed by their reproductive organs.

He smiled at her and watched the blue eyes widen. Then she answered his smile with a demure one of her own, before sitting down and saying prosaically, 'I don't suppose that you know exactly where we are, my lord?'

'We are in the village of Offord Cluny, some five miles south of Huntingdon,' he replied, remaining on his feet but retrieving his half-full glass of wine. 'More than that, I am afraid I cannot tell you.'

'It's a small place, then?'

'Exceedingly small. You are wondering, I imagine, where – should it be necessary – you will find a replacement conveyance.'

She nodded. 'My – my brother arranged the entire journey. And now I have two outriders but no carriage for them to … to …'

'Outride?' suggested his lordship helpfully.

Elizabeth nodded. 'Exactly.'

'Are either of them reasonably intelligent?'

'Yes. Max wouldn't have employed them if they weren't.'

'In that case, I suggest you hand over the task of carriage-hunting to them.'

She regarded him gratefully. 'I hadn't thought of that. Thank you.'

'My pleasure.' He glanced towards the door, as a pair of maids appeared, carrying covered dishes. 'Ah. It would seem that dinner is about to be served. Perhaps I can tempt you to that glass of wine now? Drinking alone is a very bad habit … and I have no wish to add to the many I already possess.'

His last words and, more importantly, something about the not entirely bland tone in which they were uttered brought the blood to Elizabeth's cheeks and made her glad to be spared the need to reply. She took her seat at the table, accepted a steaming slice of beef pie and let the silence linger.

Mentally smiling, Sherbourne passed her a dish of buttered potatoes and then, as if he didn't already know the answer, said, 'May I ask your destination?'

'London.' Elizabeth paused and then decided there could be no harm in speaking openly. 'I am to spend a few weeks with the Duke and Duchess of Rockliffe. My mother is a distant connection of his Grace and the duchess has kindly offered to present me to society.'

Odd, he thought, obliquely scrutinising her. *What is she … twenty one or two? Surely she should have made her curtsy years ago.* He said, 'Your first visit to London?'

'Yes.' The obvious question sprang into her mind. 'Do you … are you perhaps acquainted with the duke?'

'We have met. I cannot claim close acquaintance.'

'I can't claim any at all. What is he like?'

'He is … singular. What you might call a law unto himself.' Ralph considered revealing Rockliffe's best-known trait, but decided against it. She would doubtless discover that for herself quickly enough. And if Rockliffe ever found out that she had spent an evening alone with the Earl of Sherbourne in a remote country inn, she'd discover something else entirely. 'He is also, as one might expect, extremely influential.'

Elizabeth eyed him meditatively over the rim of her wine-glass. Then, setting it down, she said, 'That isn't very helpful. Perhaps you didn't mean it to be.'

A gleam of something she couldn't identify entered eyes that were suddenly more gold than hazel. 'You malign me.'

'No. I don't think so. After all,' she added, without first stopping to think, 'you've already admitted to possessing a quantity of bad habits.'

He was surprised into laughter. '*Touché*, Mistress Brandon.'

Both his laughter and the reminder of who she was supposed to be discomposed her for a moment and she murmured, 'Perhaps – though I shouldn't have said it.'

'Why not? Or do you never do things you ought not?'

'No.' Elizabeth saw the trap and stepped away from it. 'I don't.'

'What a pity.' He lounged back in his chair and trapped her eyes with his. 'You do not know what you are missing.'

Both posture and tone suggested that he would be happy to teach her. An odd sensation flickered somewhere deep inside her and she swallowed hard, thinking, *Is he teasing or flirting ... or is he, God forbid, actually a* rake? *Whichever it is, I need to stop this conversation right now.*

'And therefore I am *not* missing it,' she said firmly. And before he could answer, 'But we were talking about the Duke of Rockliffe.'

'*You* were,' he agreed amicably. 'I was attempting not to. However --' He stopped as his valet materialised in the doorway. 'Well, Frayne? Is the inn on fire?'

'Thankfully not, my lord. But the news isn't good.'

Ralph's eyes narrowed. 'Go on.'

'The rain still hasn't let up and the river's been rising for several hours. A few miles from here, the St Neots road crosses a bridge. The word in the tap-room is that heavy debris has been washed downstream and smashed into one of stanchions. The bridge being old and already crumbling, the local squire sent men to find out if it's safe to use. They said it isn't – so he's ordered them to block it so carriages can't pass until it's been repaired.'

Elizabeth watched Lord Sherbourne's mouth set in a hard line and though his voice remained soft as ever, she heard steel in it as he said, 'I cannot be delayed here that long. There must be an alternative route.'

'Not without turning back towards Huntingdon, apparently – and the general view is even that may be impossible with the road as it is.' Frayne spread his hands helplessly. 'I'm sorry, my lord. But it looks as if we're stuck here.'

Ralph drew a harsh breath and nodded. 'Very well. Thank you, Frayne.'

The valet withdrew and the frowning hazel eyes returned to Elizabeth.

She said carefully, 'This is ... unfortunate.'

'Unfortunate?' The smile he gave her was sharp as a blade. 'What a perfectly delightful euphemism. It makes it all sound *so* much better, doesn't it?'

CHAPTER SIX

Arabella started to recognise the hitherto unforeseen snags of her new situation on the following morning when she tried to deal with her hair. Having never previously done much more than plait it, she swiftly discovered that getting the unruly mass to behave needed more hands than she had. In the end, after struggling fruitlessly for nearly half an hour, she bundled it into a knot at her nape, anchored it with every hairpin she possessed ... and hoped for the best.

Downstairs, there was no sign of either the earl or the children but she eventually found a maid dusting the parlour. The girl smiled at her, dipped a curtsy and said, 'Good morning, ma'am. If you was wanting breakfast, you'll find it in the kitchen.'

'Thank you. Would you point me in the right direction ... er ...? I'm sorry. I don't know your name.'

'I'm Rose, ma'am. It was my sister, Violet, who served you and his lordship dinner last night. If you'll just come with me, I'll introduce you to Cook – Mistress Phelps, that is.'

'I don't mean to interrupt your work, Rose --'

'That's all right, ma'am. Mistress Featherstone – that'd be the doctor's lady – said we was to make you feel welcome and help you settle in.' The maid gave a conspiratorial grin. 'No use expecting his lordship to do it.'

Somewhat taken aback both by this frank remark and the tone of amused affection in which it was uttered, Arabella followed Rose from the room saying, 'Have you and your sister worked for Lord Chalfont for a long time?'

'Oh no, ma'am. Violet and me have only been here a fortnight. Afore that, none of the young women in the village would take work at Chalfont – the old lord being what he was. But now his young lordship has been here a while, everybody can see he's a very different kind of gentleman. And Mistress Featherstone told him straight that, with you coming, he'd have to get extra help in – which turned out lovely for Vi and me.' She breezed into the warmth of the kitchen. 'Martha, here's Mistress

Marsden. She'll be wanting a cup of tea and whatever else you've got, I'll be bound.'

Still reeling slightly from the torrent of information she had been given *en route* from the parlour, Arabella smiled weakly and said, 'I'm pleased to meet you, Mistress Phelps – and I'm sorry to be putting you to extra trouble by being so late down.'

Martha Phelps, a plump comfortable-looking woman in her late fifties, dried her hands on a cloth and smiled. 'It's no trouble – so don't you go apologising, ma'am. Bound to take you time to get into the way of things. You just sit there and I'll put the kettle on. Rose, cut some bread, will you? And Violet – lay a place for Mistress Marsden.'

Violet gave the new arrival a brief but openly evaluating glance. She said, 'Bet none of this is quite what you were expecting, is it?'

'Why do you say that? ' Arabella sat at the table and looked around at the spotlessly clean but sparsely equipped kitchen. 'Actually, I'm not sure *what* I was expecting.'

'More staff, a less shabby house and somebody more like a titled gentleman than his lordship,' came the brisk reply. 'If you'll forgive me saying so, ma'am, you sound like a lady – and you've the manners of one, too.'

'Thank you.' Deciding to establish her credentials as fast and briefly as possible, Arabella said pleasantly, 'My father is a vicar and my mother has high standards. But our family is not affluent and I have two younger sisters at home.' She shrugged. 'One of us needed to take suitable employment and, as the eldest, that one was me. But I won't pretend that I've run a large household before because I haven't. I know I have a lot to learn … and I'm hoping I may count on all of you to help me.'

Mistress Phelps set a cup of extremely strong tea at her elbow and went back to toasting bread. She said, 'That's honest, at all events. You can stop looking down your nose, Vi – since it's clear Mistress Marsden isn't looking down hers.'

'I wouldn't dream of it,' agreed Arabella, sipping her tea. 'Where are the children?'

'At the vicarage,' replied Rose, setting butter and honey within reach. 'Mistress Hassall, the vicar's lady, gives lessons for three hours every week-day morning. They'll be back here a bit after noon; Martha feeds 'em, then turns 'em loose till tea-time.'

'They don't have any sort of routine?'

'Not so far. His lordship wouldn't know where to start and we've all got enough to do in the house.'

Arabella nodded and drew a long breath. 'How long have they been here?'

'Nigh on as long as his lordship.' Mistress Phelps put a plate of only slightly-burned toast in front of Arabella. 'Before that, they was running wild about the village, stealing food and sleeping in one of the barns – Ma Clack having tossed 'em out after the old earl died and the money stopped coming.'

Arabella looked up from buttering the toast. 'And their mothers?'

'Both the boys' mothers were women the old earl picked up in Newark – tavern wenches, most like. They left their mistakes on his doorstep and disappeared off back where they came from. Little Ellie's mama was different. She was a village lass who came here as a maid. No more'n seventeen, she was and pretty as a picture,' said the cook grimly. 'She died when the baby came.'

'And that was when girls wouldn't work here no more,' added Rose.

'I ... see. And you say all three children ended up homeless?'

'That's right.' Violet sat down on the other side of the table. 'Nobody'd take in all three and young Tom wouldn't let 'em be split up. At first, a few folks tried to help ... but having blankets pinched off the line and loaves left to cool vanishing from window-ledges soon got on everybody's nerves. So they was left to their own devices until his young lordship found out about them.'

'He needn't have done anything,' said Mistress Phelps. 'They wasn't his responsibility. But he took 'em in and they've been here ever since. They live on the old nursery floor and eat down here with us.'

'Not with Lord Chalfont?' asked Arabella, trying to establish a clear picture.

Mistress Phelps laughed. 'Bless you, no, ma'am. His lordship's the gentlest, sweetest gentleman in all creation – but his head's in the clouds most of the time.'

'He tries, though,' offered Rose. 'Ridley – he's the land-agent – says his lordship don't know one end of a plough from the other but he rolls up his sleeves and works alongside the men when extra hands are needed.'

'Which is most of the time,' added Violet. 'And he hasn't put the rents up – which everybody thought he would, knowing he'd inherited nothing but debts.'

'When he treads mud into the house, he always apologises,' said Rose.

'And remember that terrible suet pudding?' Mistress Phelps shuddered. 'It was awful but he actually *ate* some of it … then he smiled and thanked me.'

Arabella was beginning to understand why these three women regarded the earl with such protective indulgence. It was also clear that whatever his lordship had been doing before inheriting the title had done nothing to prepare him for occupying it. Pushing her half-eaten toast aside, she said, 'Where was his lordship before he came here?'

'Foreign parts,' said Mistress Phelps darkly. 'Don't know where – just not in England.'

'And what was he doing there?'

'He's never said.'

The three women exchanged glances. Then, in hushed tones, Rose said, 'There's the harpsichord. He spends hours there most nights working on it. But the room's always locked so none of us have ever seen what he's doing.'

Although this endorsed what the children had said the previous evening, Arabella thought repairing a harpsichord a very unlikely pastime for a gentlemen and wondered if it was merely a smokescreen for something else. The trouble was, her imagination wouldn't stretch to what he might *really* be doing. Rising, she said, 'Thank you for breakfast, Mistress Phelps – and to all of you for helping me understand a little about how the household works. I take it that there are no other servants?'

'There's my husband, ma'am,' said Mistress Phelps. 'He does the outside work and anything heavy. He's cleared out the room across the passage so you can use it as an office. You'll find the household ledgers in there – and pen and paper, if you're needing them.'

'I *would* like to write a letter to my mother, telling her that I've arrived safely. But later, would one of you have time to show me around the house?'

'I'll do it.'

Arabella blinked. Of the three of them, Violet was the last one she had expected to volunteer. But she said, 'Thank you. That would be kind. Shall we say in half an hour?'

* * *

The freshly-painted office was small but it contained the basic essentials. Arabella sat down at the somewhat scarred desk and, drawing a long, bracing breath, prepared to write a very careful letter to Aunt Maria; a letter which, without exactly lying, gave the impression that Lord Chalfont was a good deal older than he actually was and made no mention of the fact that the children were the illegitimate offspring of the previous earl.

It wasn't easy but she eventually accomplished it to her satisfaction and set it aside, intending to ask someone – probably Mr Phelps – to take it to the village for posting. Then she went in search of Violet and said, 'I'd like to see the nursery rooms but it might be best to let the children show me those. So perhaps you and I can tour the bedchambers and reception parlours? It seems quite a large house.'

Violet nodded and reeled off numbers. Then she said, 'Pardon me for remarking on it, Mistress Marsden, but it don't look to me as if you're used to doing your own hair.'

Surprised into laughter, Arabella said ruefully, 'That obvious, is it?'

The girl grinned back. 'I doubt it'll last the morning.'

'So do I – and it took ages. That's why I was so late. But at home I had my – my sisters to help. The youngest has a talent for it.'

'So have I,' replied Violet composedly. 'And I'll dress it for you, if you like.'

This was even more surprising.

'You have no idea how tempting that offer is – but I'm not here as a guest and I'm sure you already have enough to do. It would be wrong of me to cause extra work.'

'I wouldn't mind.' She paused. 'I'd like to train as a ladies' maid and practising with you would be a good way to start. I reckon you know how a proper ladies' maid goes on – what she does and so forth.'

'Yes,' agreed Arabella slowly. 'My cousin has one. Her family is much better-placed than mine ... but she and I spend a lot of time together. Her maid is very good at her job – though a bit too bossy at times.'

'So you could help me learn – in return for me doing your hair?'

'Yes. If you're sure it won't cause trouble with your sister or with Mistress Phelps.'

'It won't.' Violet held out her hand. 'Do we have a deal, then?'

Still somewhat bemused, Arabella accepted the hand and shrugged. 'It would seem so.'

* * *

After a tour of scrupulously clean bedchambers furnished with balding rugs and moth-eaten hangings, some of them also bearing signs of mildew and damp, Arabella had a fairly clear idea of the previous earl's neglect and the financial straits of the current one. However, she refrained from remarking on it and instead, praised Rose and Violet for their diligence. Then she informed Mistress Phelps that, as of the following day, she wanted the children to take their noon-day meals with her in the dining-room.

Rose and Violet burst out laughing.

'Oh dear,' said the cook. 'Are you sure, ma'am? They're little savages at table.'

Arabella hid her inner qualms behind an air of determination.

'Then it's time that was remedied. But the dining-table is enormous. Last evening, his lordship and I were virtually shouting at each other down the length of it. Do you think Mr Phelps might be able to remove some of the leaves – if Lord Chalfont won't mind?'

'Lord Chalfont won't notice,' grinned Violet. 'When we said his head was usually off somewhere else, we weren't joking.'

'In that case, do it. I will begin familiarising myself with the household accounts and, when the children have eaten, perhaps someone could let me know? I want them to show me their own rooms. Oh – and one other thing.' She stopped on her way to the door. 'I asked the children to call me Miss Lizzie so perhaps you might all do the same? Ma'am makes me feel like my grandmother.'

Arabella soon discovered that accounts ledgers were not her greatest strength but she persevered until boisterous young voices alerted her to the return of her charges. Mentally girding herself for a struggle, she closed the books and straightened her spine. This, she told herself, was a matter of starting as one meant to go on; kind but firm.

It was Ellie who came to fetch her.

'Are you coming to see our own special rooms, Miss?'

'Right away. I've been looking forward to it all morning.'

Behind their small sister, Tom regarded her with suspicion and Rob with curiosity.

Tom muttered, 'I'll bet you've seen 'em already.'

'No. Since they're *your* rooms, that wouldn't have been polite,' she replied pleasantly. 'Shall we go?'

The nursery suite proved light and spacious; two bedrooms, leading off a large area that had once been used for both lessons and play. There were a couple of battered desks, an ancient sofa and several balding rugs but everything was clean and looked comfortable. Shelves held a couple of dozen books, most of which appeared to be on the verge of falling apart and there were a few toys here and there … board games and a doll with no hair, most noticeable amongst them. Arabella wondered how much chance there was of better curtains and cheerier covers for the children's beds – and then had an idea.

Families kept things. *Hers* certainly did. The attics at Brandon Lacey were stuffed with long-gone-by items that no one had ever bothered to throw away. Pieces of furniture, old pictures, trunks full of out-dated clothes. She remembered her brothers squabbling over Great-Great-Grandfather Gabriel's buff coat and back-and-breast from when he'd fought under Oliver Cromwell. If this house was the same, there was no saying *what* she might find upstairs. And even if there was nothing useful, the children would enjoy the hunt.

She said, 'This is nice … though I think we could make it even nicer. I'll speak to his lordship about it. In the meantime, I suppose you need some new books, don't you?'

'Why?' asked Rob. 'We do our reading in lesson times – not here.'

Arabella sat down on the lumpy sofa and looked at them.

'Are you telling me that none of you have ever read *any* of those books?'

'Why would we?' scoffed Tom. 'There's better things to do.'

'That is a matter of opinion,' remarked Arabella. 'But what *do* you do with your afternoons?'

'We go outside, mostly.'

'To play, you mean? Or do you sometimes help his lordship on the farm?'

Tom gave an unpleasantly sarcastic laugh.

Rob said uncertainly, 'He's never asked us to help.'

'And if he did?'

'I … wouldn't mind.'

'Nor me.' Ellie sat down beside Arabella. 'Sir Julian's nice. He's kind to us.'

'For as long as it suits him,' added Tom under his breath.

The difference in their attitudes to the earl wasn't hard to understand, thought Arabella. Tom, as the eldest and having probably known very little kindness in his life, was naturally wary of trusting it now; Rob, she suspected, was torn between wanting adult male companionship and loyalty to his brother; and little Ellie plainly regarded 'Sir Julian' with a great deal of affection, if not actual love. Rob could easily be won over, she thought. But Tom was a very different matter and was going to require some deft handling – preferably by the earl himself. For now, however, she decided to release the children to their usual pursuits while she planned her strategy. Changes and the establishing of a routine could wait until tomorrow. She did, however, see the wisdom in warning them of *one* imminent change – which was sufficient to send Tom off muttering scornfully.

Informed by Rose that his lordship took his dinner on a tray in the parlour, Arabella said she would be quite happy to take hers in the kitchen.

'That's not fitting, Miss,' said the cook flatly. 'You shouldn't be eating with us.'

'Well, I'm not going to sit in the dining-room on my own – never mind putting someone to the trouble of serving and clearing,' retorted Arabella. 'The kitchen will do perfectly well until we can persuade Lord Chalfont to change his ways. After that ... well, we'll see. Though I shouldn't be dining with him either, should I? And he's so shy that I doubt he'll want me to.'

'Probably not used to talking with young ladies,' suggested Mistress Phelps.

'A fellow with looks like his?' Violet laughed. 'Go on with you! He probably has girls falling over each other to catch his eye.'

'If you ask me,' said Rose slowly, 'I think he's miserable. He don't say anything about it but I reckon he never wanted to come here at all – let alone stay.'

Later, standing at one of the windows that overlooked the drive, Arabella watched Ellie waiting patiently for the earl to return to the house and then walk back holding his hand and talking non-stop while he, head bent, appeared to listen intently to every word.

While she found it curiously touching, it also reminded her of something he'd said about the fourth earl on the previous evening.

If he'd married one of the boys' mothers, I needn't be here.

* * *

'Miss Lizzie says that, after lessons tomorrow, we're going to have our dinner with her in the dining-room,' said Ellie at length and sounding suitably impressed.

'Does she?' asked Julian neutrally. 'Why?'

'To learn table-manners.' She looked up at him, plainly confused. 'What are they?'

'Using your knife and fork properly and not spilling food everywhere,' he told her. And with an internal grimace, added, 'And making polite conversation.'

'Oh.' Ellie considered this and then, deciding it didn't sound too bad, said, 'She seems nice. And she's pretty.'

'Yes.' *Too pretty*, thought Julian, edgily. *And when she laughs … God.* 'I'm glad you think you'll like her – but it's early days, yet. What do Tom and Rob think?'

'Rob's all right. Miss asked if'n we helped you on the farm and Rob said he'd like to.'

'And Tom?'

She shrugged and her face clouded over.

'Tom says eating in the dining-room and reading books except in lessons is stupid.'

'Ah.'

Ellie stopped walking and stared into his face.

'Why is Tom always angry with you?'

Julian drew a long breath.

'It's not so much that he's angry as that he's not ready to trust me yet.'

'He *is* angry though. Nearly all the time.'

I know, thought Julian. *He's angry about the world in general and a part of him is constantly screaming that life isn't fair. I wonder what he'd say if I told him that I know exactly how that feels?* But he squeezed the child's hand and said, 'He'll get over it eventually. And in the meantime we should be patient with him because, deep down, he doesn't want to be angry at all. He just can't help it.'

* * *

Unable to decide, on the strength of a single meeting, what to make of Mistress Marsden, Julian took the safest option and avoided both the lady and the possible dangers of the dining parlour. Purloining bread, cold meat and a small tankard of ale from his own kitchen, he reached the library undetected and locked the door behind him. Then he sat on the floor to eat his meal and evaluate how much progress he might expect to make with the harpsichord before exhaustion overcame him.

He was surprised – even startled – when Mistress Marsden began creeping into the fringes of his mind. Normally when he was in this room he thought of nothing outside it, the harpsichord claiming his entire attention. Yet once or twice he caught himself wondering if she really *was* unlike the young women whose bold stares and peculiar air of expectancy left him feeling self-conscious and anxious. Last night she hadn't seemed frightening. She'd treated him much the same as Janet Featherstone and the Caldercott ladies did ... which would have been reassuring if she hadn't been young and pretty and possessed of a warm, melodic laugh; a laugh which made his insides uncurl and yearn to hear it again in order to recapture the elusive phrase it had brought to mind. A rondo in a bright key, he decided. G major, perhaps?

He stopped eating, suddenly made acutely uneasy by ideas and feelings he didn't understand. True, Mistress Marsden didn't seem to be like those other girls ... but different didn't necessarily mean safe. And if she was already putting these peculiar and unwelcome notions in his head, she might be dangerous in other ways entirely. Setting aside Mistress Phelps' over-cooked beef, Julian pushed to his feet and turned his attention to the only thing that would, when in working order, make his life more bearable.

Once upon a time, the harpsichord had been a thing of beauty, its case ornamented with inlaid mother-of-pearl and ormolu. Now it was covered in deep scratches, burns from carelessly placed cheroots and the other assorted evidence of years of ill-usage. Julian minded this quite a lot in the sense that he didn't understand how anyone – even his lecherous sot of a predecessor – could subject a musical instrument to such treatment. But the external damage was as nothing when compared to what had been done to the inside.

He didn't think he would ever forget his first sight of it. The harpsichord had been left open, the lid hanging forlornly on one hinge; mice had been in it, their droppings everywhere; strings had been snapped or perhaps chewed through. And worst of all, a bottle lay on its side, having disgorged the best part of a pint of claret over the soundboard, the jacks and the dampers. The instrument was so badly wrecked that it had looked beyond saving. And it had made him physically sick.

He had been labouring over it for months, always at night when his work outside on the estate was done. Although he had arrived at a point where there was light at the end of the tunnel, there was still much to be done before it would be playable. Tonight's job was that of continuing to replace the rotting dampers.

Julian pulled off his cravat, rolled up his sleeves and set to work.

CHAPTER SEVEN

The rain stopped overnight and morning dawned on weak sunshine but the landscape about the Oak remained woefully sodden. Having obtained her permission the previous evening, Lord Sherbourne instructed his valet to send one of Mistress Brandon's outriders off to check the state of the road. The report the man brought back did nothing to improve his lordship's mood.

'So,' he said grimly to Frayne. 'We are stranded here for today at least.'

'It would seem so, my lord.' The valet was perfectly aware of both the need for haste and the reason for it. He was also aware that the earl's temper was unlikely to survive the enforced delay intact. He said, 'The best we can hope is that conditions improve by tomorrow. I'm told that if we go back towards Huntingdon and branch off south, the lane will bring us back on to the North Road just below the damaged bridge. Meanwhile, if your lordship would care for breakfast, it is being served in the coffee-room. I believe Mistress Brandon and her maid are already downstairs.'

'Oh good,' breathed Ralph. 'Another hour of polite conversation. How delightful.'

While Annie devoured kippers with every sign of enthusiasm, Elizabeth pushed egg around her plate and said, 'We're going to be travelling at least two days longer than we expected – more, if the roads don't dry out or we can't find a carriage. I'll have to write to Aunt Louisa or she'll start to worry.'

'Mind what you say about his lordship, then. It won't help matters if she thinks Miss Belle's stuck here with a rake.'

'Keep your voice down,' hissed Elizabeth. 'And we don't *know* he's a rake.'

'I'd lay money on it.' Annie shrugged and waved a piece of kipper on the end of her fork. 'But even if he's not, her ladyship won't like the sound of him – mark my words.'

'Good morning,' said a soft voice from behind them. 'Or, then again, is it?'

Annie narrowly avoided choking; Elizabeth's fingers clenched on her coffee-cup.

'N-Not particularly,' she said, turning and managing a smile. 'Jessop says there is little chance of travelling so much as a mile today.'

'So I have heard.' Sherbourne strolled to the sideboard and helped himself from the covered dishes there. 'Will the delay cause the duchess concern?'

'Not immediately, since it wasn't possible to predict the precise day I would arrive. But if the delay is protracted ... yes, I imagine so.'

'Then let us hope that it is not.' He took a seat at another table and addressed himself to his breakfast – a clear indication that he wasn't feeling sociable.

Elizabeth gave Annie a meaningful look and said quietly, 'If my cloak has dried out, please see what can be done with it. And ask the innkeeper for writing materials.'

'Very good, Miss Belle.' Annie rose, dropped a curtsy and went out.

Elizabeth poured a second cup of coffee and tried not to look at the earl. From the corner of her eye, she could see that he had produced the book he'd been reading the previous day and was once more apparently engrossed in it. A rake who read Greek seemed an unlikely combination ... unless she was wrong on one or both counts.

A maidservant came in bringing paper, pen and ink and proceeded to clear away the breakfast things. 'Will there be anything else, ma'am?'

'No,' began Elizabeth. And then, 'Yes. If I leave letters here, will they be collected and sent on?'

'Yes'm. The coach usually comes through every Thursday and Saturday – though it mightn't, this week.'

Nodding her thanks, Elizabeth drew the paper in front of her and began by scribbling a frantic note to Arabella. Then, silently praying that her cousin had been right about their handwriting not arousing suspicion, she embarked on the more difficult letter to her aunt.

Dear Mama, she wrote. *Please do not be alarmed but heavy rain is currently making the roads impassable and thus delaying our journey …*

Ralph finished his breakfast and crossed the room in search of fresh coffee. He hadn't intended to engage Mistress Brandon in conversation, yet he heard himself saying, 'I gather there *is* someone who will worry?'

'My mother,' replied Elizabeth, looking up, 'and also the cousin who travelled with me as far as Newark. What of you, my lord? I had the impression that you were anxious to complete your journey.'

'I am. But it appears Nemesis has other plans.' He returned to his seat and picked up the book, his mouth curling slightly. 'Perhaps I threw down an unwitting gauntlet.'

'I'm sorry. I don't follow.'

'The *Iliad*,' he replied, gesturing with it. 'It is some years since I read it and I had forgotten just how much of it is about Fate. Lots of wrath and revenge as well, of course – but I hope we may escape those.'

'Do you believe in Fate?' asked Elizabeth, curiously.

'I accept its existence. Don't you?'

'I don't know.' She thought for a moment. 'I find it hard to believe that all our lives are part of some grand plan and that everything happens for a reason. In fact, I *don't* believe it. You and I are here because it rained.'

'Are you sure? How do you know that the rain was not the work of cosmic forces?'

'*Cosmic forces*?' she echoed. 'Doing what, exactly?'

'Throwing you and I together in this particular place and time.' The hazel eyes regarded her with not unfriendly mockery. 'Or is that too fanciful for you?'

'Much too fanciful – and for you, too, I should think. Why on earth would Fate – or anything else for that matter – want to do that?'

'I don't know. The Greek gods are both whimsical and inscrutable. Did Paris know why the gods chose *him* to award the golden apple? Of course he did not.'

Elizabeth gave him a long, level look.

'You don't believe any of that, do you?'

'Not a word,' he replied coolly. 'Man was given free will and his course through life is not pre-ordained. He is responsible for both his triumphs and his sins.' A sharp-edged, slightly crooked smile dawned. 'But it would be comforting, would it not, to sometimes believe otherwise?' And he turned calmly back to his book.

She continued to stare at him for a moment, not sure what any of that had been about but entirely positive that she shouldn't be finding him quite so intriguing a puzzle. Then she addressed and sealed her letters and walked out.

Upstairs, Annie had managed to restore the cloak to some semblance of respectability and was giving it a final brushing. Without looking up, she said, 'What was his high-and-mighty lordship talking to you about?'

'Fate,' she said. And thought, *Or so it seemed on the surface.* 'And mythology.'

'*Mythology?*' scoffed Annie. 'Heathen claptrap is all that is. Monsters and folks running about half-naked.'

Elizabeth gave a gurgle of laughter. 'That's one way of looking at it.'

'It's not decent, Miss Lizzie. I knew from the start he wasn't to be trusted. So for the Lord's sake, have some sense tonight and take your dinner up here with me.'

'I'll think about it,' murmured Elizabeth, knowing already that she wouldn't. She was perfectly well aware that Lord Sherbourne wasn't a gentleman Papa would approve of – or even Mama, come to that. But since their acquaintance was destined to be short-lived, there could be little harm in taking the opportunity to play with fire.

By mid-afternoon, Ralph's temper was balancing on a knife-edge. The letter from his youngest brother which had provoked this journey might turn out to be just another instance of Bertram's chronic idiocy. Equally, however, it might not. And if the latter proved to be the case, every hour Ralph was delayed in this benighted place, bereft of further communications, might result in the kind of trouble he was bent on avoiding. There had been numerous times in his life when the notion of Cedric locked up out of harm's way had possessed a lot of appeal. But not this way. *This*, if Bertram had it right, couldn't be anything but bad news.

If he had hoped that the mildly risqué style of his conversation last night and the peculiar nature of his discourse this morning might have given Mistress Brandon a distaste for his company, he was disappointed. Wearing the same gown as the previous evening, she joined him in the coffee-room and immediately said, 'My lord, Jessop believes it may be possible to get as far as St Neots tomorrow and, all being well, hire a conveyance there. Since I understand that you must go in that direction yourself, I wondered if … if you would be kind enough to allow my maid and I to travel that far with you? I am very sorry to ask but I don't see any alternative.'

In truth, she had *no* alternative. He had known that all day and been waiting for her to realise it. He also knew that he could not refuse. So he inclined his head and said smoothly, 'Of course, ma'am. It will be my pleasure.'

'You are very good. Thank you.'

'Not at all.' He waited until she was seated before resuming his own chair. Then, deciding he might as well find out more about her than her eventual destination, he said, 'You are from Yorkshire, I believe. A large county with which I am unfamiliar, I am afraid.'

Good, thought Elizabeth. And then, realising that since, sooner or later, she would have to start being Arabella, it might as well be now, said, 'My home is in the North Riding, near Knaresborough. There have been Brandons there for generations.'

'And your family?' he asked lightly.

'Well, Mama, of course … and I have three brothers, all of them older than me.' She paused, letting her expression darken a little. 'Papa died ten years ago so Max – my eldest brother – inherited the barony before he was twenty.'

Ah. Not Miss Nobody from nowhere then, but the sister of a baron, thought Ralph. And with some amusement, *Did she toss that information at me in a clumsy attempt to put me in my place and keep me there?* But he said merely, 'I inherited my grandfather's title only a year ago. However ... am I correct in guessing that your brother prefers to spend his time on the family estates rather than in London?'

'Max has visited London from time to time – as have Adam and Leo – but never for extended periods.' Elizabeth offered him a tentative smile. 'Perhaps their pursuits while there differ from your own, my lord.'

His amusement deepened. 'That may be so – though I am not at all sure what leads you to suppose it. Is it my own pursuits you consider dubious ... or those of your brothers?'

Realising she had dug an unwitting pit for herself, Elizabeth flushed.

'I – neither one. That wasn't what I meant at all.'

'I am delighted to hear it.' He rose, offering his hand. 'Dinner ... and most fortuitously timed, would you not say?'

Not surprisingly, Elizabeth did not know *what* to say and therefore, wisely, said nothing. The look in those knowing eyes did not improve matters. Lord Sherbourne, as she had known from the first, wasn't *safe*; unfortunately, something about him was more compelling than she wanted to admit even to herself. So she decided that, since playing with fire clearly needed skills she did not possess ... and that allowing herself to form an attraction to any man at all was pointless, the sooner she and his disturbing lordship parted company, the better.

* * *

His lordship facilitated this by demanding an early start – which had them leaving the Oak at a little before nine in the morning. Annie wedged herself into a corner, looking sulky; Lord Sherbourne buried his nose in the *Iliad*; and, trying to ignore both of them, Elizabeth stared out of the window, earnestly praying that the rest of her journey would prove less fraught than the last two days had done.

Their progress – circuitous to avoid the damaged bridge – was less than brisk but Lord Sherbourne's chaise finally pulled in to the busy yard of the White Horse shortly after noon. Helping Elizabeth down, Ralph said, 'If you and your maid go inside and order food, I will find out what carriages may be for hire.'

Elizabeth nodded and did as he suggested. Half an hour later, he joined her wearing an expression that made her heart sink.

Coming quickly to her feet, she said, 'What is it? What's wrong?'

'This inn possesses only one travelling carriage and it has already been commandeered by a gentleman in similar straits to your own. The George, further along the street, keeps only a couple of gigs suitable for short, local journeys and though I have sent Frayne to another inn on the edge of town, I do not hold out much hope – it being a smaller establishment than either of the others. I am told that the Mail is due through here tomorrow … but that will not do at all.' Ralph paused, his mouth growing tighter by the second. 'I am sorry.'

Despite her increasing consternation, Elizabeth thought she could guess the cause of that grim expression. His honour as a gentleman – which had probably been drilled into him since he was three years old – would force him to take her at least as far as the next main town. And he clearly hated the idea.

As steadily as she could, she said, 'Thank you for trying, my lord. You have been extraordinarily kind. But you must not feel that you have any further responsibility to --'

'Spare me the brave protestations, ma'am,' he cut in coldly. 'Despite the danger to your reputation of continuing to travel in my company, you must know as well as I that I cannot in all conscience abandon you here.'

'Yes, you can. You can simply return to your carriage, unload my luggage and --'

'If you think that, at this point, obstinacy is remotely helpful, you are singularly naive.' Then as Frayne appeared in the doorway, 'Anything?'

'No, my lord. Nothing.'

'Very well. Tell Cox to make ready to depart.'

Frayne vanished and Elizabeth said flatly, 'Go, by all means. But I'm not coming.'

'And do what instead?' he demanded. Then, when she hesitated, 'Ma'am, since I intend to make Stevenage by dark, I do not have time to debate the matter. I would therefore appreciate it if you would just *stop talking.*'

Elizabeth's jaw dropped. 'I beg your pardon, my lord, but --'

And that was as far as she got before his hand closed on her elbow with a grip that brooked no refusal and hinted at temper barely held in check. Marching her smartly out into the yard and ignoring her attempts at protest, he bundled her back into the carriage and then, turning on Annie, said implacably, 'You, too. In.'

'No!' she said, trying to stand firm. 'I'm not letting you abduct Miss Li-Belle like this. I --'

With one hand, he propelled her head-first into the carriage.

'If I was abducting her, *you* would not be here,' he snapped, climbing in behind her and slamming the door. 'As it is, I am doing only what needs to be done and would prefer to simply get on with it.' He rapped on the roof of the carriage and it jerked forwards. 'Mistress Brandon ... your outriders, as you will see if you look through the window, are continuing to accompany us. They are now doing so at my expense rather than your own – no, please allow me to finish – in the event of further catastrophe or the need to travel after dark. The point is not negotiable and therefore not open for discussion. In fact, you will have my undying gratitude if you will kindly refrain from discussing anything at all for at least the next half hour.' And so saying, he dragged the *Iliad* from his pocket and dived into it.

* * *

By the time they reached Stevenage, the mood inside the carriage had improved very little. No one had spoken a word that was not strictly necessary and, of the four of them, Frayne was the only one who did not appear either angry or uncomfortable. Indeed, catching an errant gleam, Elizabeth suspected that the valet was finding the entire situation hugely entertaining.

She would have been surprised had she known that Lord Sherbourne had spent a substantial part of the journey feeling thoroughly annoyed with himself and trying to determine precisely why he was so eager to wave goodbye to his passengers. True ... Mistress Brandon's skirts took up a great deal of room, forcing him against the side of the carriage and meaning that he couldn't stretch out his legs without kicking either Frayne or the damned maid. But that really wasn't sufficient reason for either his loss of control at St Neots or the grumbling resentment he still felt when they pulled into the White Lion in Stevenage.

Sweeping inside, he ordered rooms, dinner and stabling. Then, leaving Elizabeth to her own devices, he promptly vanished. Scowling at his retreating back, Annie muttered, 'If I had a few toadstools, I'd know what to do with them.'

Elizabeth shook her head. 'No, you wouldn't. He may be rude and insufferably overbearing but he *has* done us a favour. And at least you don't have to dine with him – speaking of which, I'll need a fresh gown. Let's see which one is least crushed.'

Although it boasted no private parlours, the White Lion provided guests with a large, comfortable dining-room. Becomingly gowned in leaf green taffeta and hoping the earl had stopped sulking, Elizabeth walked in to discover that he wasn't there at all. Instead, a pair of fashionably-dressed matrons perched on the window-seat, from which they had a clear view of the comings and goings in the yard below.

'There is definitely a crest on that carriage,' said one of them. 'Whose, do you think?'

'Too much mud to tell,' yawned the younger lady. And then, seeing Elizabeth hovering in the doorway, 'Ah. A fresh face, thank goodness! Please do come in, ma'am. After two days trapped in the chaise together, my cousin and I are fast running out of conversation.' She rose, smiling. 'Allow us to introduce ourselves. I am Philippa Sutherland and this is Lady Davenport. How do you do?'

Elizabeth curtsied, smiled shyly back and said, 'Arabella Brandon, ma'am – and delighted to make your acquaintance.'

Invited to sit with them and promptly informed that they were on their way into Cambridgeshire to support Lady Davenport's youngest sister through her first confinement, Elizabeth did not see any harm in revealing her own destination. And though some latent instinct warned her to omit any reference to Lord Sherbourne, a seemingly amiable if rather direct question left her unable to be similarly reticent about the Duke of Rockliffe ... at which point the ladies became very friendly indeed.

'Ah!' said Lady Davenport, as if a mystery had been solved. 'Did I not say, Philippa, that a chaise bearing a crest had arrived? It must have been yours, Mistress Brandon.'

'Mine?' echoed Elizabeth, caught unawares. 'No. That is – it belongs to – to another traveller who --'

From just beyond the door, Sherbourne heard her losing herself in a tangle of potentially dangerous admissions. Moving quickly to put a stop to them, he walked in saying, 'I believe the carriage under discussion is mine.' And only then realised he had made a catastrophic mistake.

There was an abrupt silence, during which Lady Davenport's smile became something very different and Lady Sutherland turned perfectly white, her eyes locked with those of the earl. Just for an instant, Ralph felt himself struggling to breathe. Then Lady Davenport said frigidly, 'Lord Sherbourne ... a surprise indeed.'

'Yes. I'm sure it is.' Quite how, he did not know, but somehow he got the words out and even managed a bow. 'How do you do, Philippa? I trust Lord Sutherland and the rest of your family enjoy their customary good health?'

'It has certainly improved recently,' she said stingingly. 'Remind me, my lord ... how many months *is* it since you were last in town?'

With an unpleasant jolt, Elizabeth recognised that this was less an undercurrent than a thirty-gun salvo. She opened her mouth on some innocuous remark but was forestalled by his lordship, who said, 'Several. I am flattered that you noticed.' And before her ladyship could respond, he shot a pointed glance in

Elizabeth's direction and, bowing as if to a complete stranger, said, 'Ma'am.'

Are we not to know each other? wondered Elizabeth, baffled. But, responding to his cue, she curtsied and murmured, 'Sir.'

'I think, Charlotte,' said Philippa clearly, 'that I would prefer to dine in our rooms after all, would not you?'

'Absolutely. Not a doubt of it. And Mistress Brandon ... perhaps you will join us? After all, we can't leave you to dine unchaperoned with a – a --'

'An unmarried gentleman?' suggested Ralph, willing the Brandon chit to accept before things got any worse. 'Were those the words you were looking for?'

'Not precisely,' she snapped. 'Not at all, in fact.'

'Beg pardon, Miss Belle,' said Annie, bustling in without warning, 'but his lordship's man brought the other bag up and I found the shawl we were looking for. Here it is.'

If the atmosphere had been unpleasant before it was now positively toxic; so much so that even Annie noticed it and added awkwardly, 'Sorry for interrupting.'

Stepping away from Elizabeth as if fearing contamination, Philippa Sutherland said, 'There is no need to apologise. You have cleared up our misconceptions beautifully. Come, Charlotte.' And the pair of them swept from the room in a cloud of disgust.

Ralph briefly shut his eyes and tried to shake off the feeling of dizzying unreality. Then, having told Annie to get out, he impaled Elizabeth on an acute stare and said, 'How much did you tell them?'

'I – not very much. Does it matter?'

'Matter? Oh no. Charlotte Davenport is one of the biggest gossips in London, of course ... but no. The fact that she has just seen us together and drawn her own conclusions does not matter in the least. *What did you tell them?*' And when she hesitated, 'For God's sake, madam! At least assure me that you did *not* mention Rockliffe?'

'I can't,' whispered Elizabeth, as comprehension slowly dawned.

'*Hell.*' He swung away towards the fireplace and, glancing over his shoulder at her, said coldly, 'You *do* realise what they are thinking, do you not?'

She shook her head, though she had an unpleasant premonition that she did.

'No? Then allow me to enlighten you. They believe that we are lovers.'

'L-Lovers?' She could feel herself turning scarlet. 'No! Surely they can't --'

'They can. And they will make certain that their suspicions reach the duke's ears. Not,' he added bitterly, 'that they will have to try very hard to do that.'

'What do you mean?' She was starting to feel slightly sick. And when he merely shrugged and said nothing, 'It may not be as bad as you think. They aren't travelling to London. They're going to --'

'They could be going to the Outer Hebrides,' he snapped, wheeling to face her. 'My lovely simpleton ... you really have no idea, do you? They will write letters to their friends. And their friends will write letters to *their* friends ... with the result that, in a week or less, London will be awash with the news that a young, unmarried connection of the Duke of Rockliffe is Ralph Sherbourne's latest mistress. And his Grace's likely reaction to that is something I would rather not contemplate.'

'I'll explain,' said Elizabeth desperately. 'When I explain that you've merely helped me out of a difficult situation and – and that whatever he has heard is merely the result of ill-natured women jumping to conclusions ...' She stopped, frowning. 'Why *are* they ill-natured? Why would they immediately think the worst?'

Sherbourne dropped into a chair, crossed one long leg over the other and contemplated her with an acid-edged smile. He said, 'That took a while, did it not? But I knew we would get there eventually – even though two days' exposure to my immense charm has naturally made it inconceivable to you that there could be people who might dislike me.'

'Not at all,' she retorted. 'But why *them*?'

For a moment or two, he wondered what she would say if he told her what Philippa had once meant to him and the hopes he'd thought they shared ... before her brother's death had changed everything; everything, that was, except the way he still felt about her. If he'd explained that for two months, he'd sliced his heart open writing to her every day and begging, not for forgiveness, but simply not to be condemned unheard. Until the day all his letters had been returned unopened ... along with the announcement of her wedding to Phineas Sutherland.

But Arabella Brandon did not need to know any of that – and neither would it help. So he drawled, 'They have their reasons. It doesn't matter. What *does* matter is preserving your reputation. As a general rule, I would say that Rockliffe's influence is sufficient to put an end to any scandalous suspicions. But if, in this particular instance, he feels that only action will serve ... well. Let us hope it does not come to that.'

'Why? What will he do?' asked Elizabeth. And then, eyes widening with horror, 'He – he won't challenge you to a *duel*, will he?'

Ralph gave a wholly unamused laugh. 'No. For numerous reasons, that is the very *last* thing he will do. Nor does he need to when he can actually do something more helpful and much, *much* more final.' He paused, eyeing her sardonically. 'He can insist that we marry.'

CHAPTER EIGHT

Arabella had not expected her first meal with the children to be a resounding success and it wasn't. All of them bolted their food; none of them knew how to use a knife; and her first attempt at civilised conversation resulted in an immediate and very necessary lecture on not speaking with one's mouth full. By the time it was over, she had a monumental headache and therefore decided that the battle to make them sit still and read could wait until the following day. There was a need for more books anyway – few of those in the schoolroom being in readable condition; but it wasn't going to be possible to find others while the key to the library door remained in the earl's pocket.

By the time Arabella hadn't clapped eyes on his lordship for forty-eight hours, she came to the conclusion that he was avoiding her – which in some respects wasn't a bad thing but, in others, was a downright nuisance. So when she virtually collided with him in the hall after dinner, she stopped him in his tracks by saying brightly, 'Good evening, my lord. May I have a word, please?'

Although seemingly not the alarming species of female he had expected, Julian was still acutely wary of Mistress Marsden. 'I – yes. I suppose so.'

This was hardly encouraging but she persevered.

'I wondered if it would be alright to raid the attics.'

'The attics?'

'Yes. The children's rooms could be made more cheerful and it occurred to me that, among the bits and pieces that were discarded years ago, might be things that could be useful. Old toys, perhaps. And curtains.'

'Curtains?' Julian was starting to feel as imbecilic as he doubtless sounded.

'Yes,' agreed Arabella. 'Do I have your permission to look?'

Since it didn't require money, he didn't know why she was asking. Preparing to make his escape, he said, 'By all means.'

'Thank you. And there's something else, if you wouldn't mind.'

Reluctantly, Julian halted and turned back. 'What?'

'Are there books in the library?'

'Books?' He frowned, as if a library containing books was an alien concept. 'I think so.'

'Good. I would like to look through them, please.'

His expression grew instantly mistrustful. 'Why?'

'The children need to practise their reading,' she said patiently. 'Unfortunately, the books in the schoolroom are dropping apart so I am hoping the library holds something suitable and in better condition. May I have the key?'

He was shaking his head before she had finished speaking. 'No. I'm sorry ... but no.'

'Why not?'

'I work in there. I don't ... I just prefer no one else goes in.'

Since this was exactly what both children and servants had warned her to expect, Arabella was ready for it.

'Even,' she suggested reasonably, 'if you go with me and I promise not to touch anything *but* the books?'

For a seemingly endless moment, he stared mutely at the threadbare carpet, his shoulders tense and his hands clenched in his pockets. But finally, hauling in a long breath, he said, 'Very well. Come with me.'

Following him across the hall, Arabella experienced a small quiver of trepidation. She'd been *told* what lay behind that locked door but wasn't sure she believed it. As far as she was concerned, it could be anything. For all she knew, he might be holding satanic rituals or painting lewd pictures on the walls. So when he turned the key, opened the door and gestured for her to precede him, she had to force herself not to hesitate.

Since half of the windows were shuttered, it took her eyes a moment to adjust to the gloom. But when they did ... she saw that there was indeed a harpsichord. It stood forlornly in the centre of the room and somehow commanded her attention, blinding her to the bookshelves filling two of the walls.

Behind her, Julian closed the door and pointed. 'You wanted books. There they are.'

'Yes.' She ventured a few steps nearer the instrument, close enough to see that, though attached, all the strings were lying loose. 'Ellie thinks you are mending this.'

'I *am* mending it,' he said tautly. 'Please don't touch anything.'

Still faintly incredulous, Arabella said, 'Do you know *how*?'

He stared at her as if she was deranged, words tumbling through his head. If someone handed him the right parts and materials, he could build a harpsichord from scratch. It might not be pretty; but it would play perfectly – which was the only thing that mattered.

Eventually, he snapped, 'Of course I bloody know!' And then, flushing, 'I beg your pardon. I shouldn't ... I didn't mean ... it's just that yes, I know *exactly* what I'm doing. Only a complete idiot would blunder about inside an instrument like this if they didn't.'

'No. Of course,' she said hastily. 'I'm sorry. It was a stupid question.' She looked back at what she was beginning to suspect was a labour of love. 'Is this what you did before you came here? Repaired harpsichords?'

'No.' He drew an odd impatient breath. 'Do you want to look for books or not?'

'Yes.' But she didn't do it. Instead, putting her hands behind her back so as not to alarm him, she circled the instrument, absorbing what it told her until light dawned, blinding in its intensity. She said softly, 'You play, don't you?'

He didn't answer but she could feel the tension in him from eight feet away so she kept her eyes on the once-exquisite casing of inlaid fruitwood, now marred with deep scratches and marks from carelessly-placed glasses. 'It must kill you to see it in this condition.'

Forcing himself to speak, he muttered, 'The outside isn't important.'

'Perhaps not – but it's a pity.' Arabella looked at the pristine dual-keyboard, gripping her hands together to stop one of them reaching out. 'You've cleaned the keys.'

Julian choked back an acrid laugh. He had done more than that. He'd dismantled both keyboards. For nearly a month, the ivory and ebony keys had lain on an old sheet like extracted teeth, as he meticulously cleaned, restored and checked the underside of each one for any sign of worm. Putting them back where they belonged had taken a week. If he told her that, she'd probably think him mad.

Instead, she looked at him with respect and said, 'How long have you been doing this?'

He opened his mouth to tell her to take what books she wanted and go.

'Since I first realised I was trapped here,' he said. And promptly squeezed his eyes shut for a second, appalled that he'd said the words out loud. 'I'm sorry. That was unnecessarily dramatic. Would you mind leaving the books until another day? I have ... things to do.'

Arabella nodded. She was beginning to realise that she had been tapping on a nerve and it was about to snap. Turning to go, she said, 'Thank you for showing me, my lord. The work you are doing here is truly remarkable.'

She was four steps down the hallway when she heard him say, 'Julian. Lord Chalfont is ... somebody else. I'd prefer you called me Julian.'

Then the door closed between them and the key turned in the lock.

* * *

Julian was used to the routine at the Misses Caldercott's villa. He wasn't allowed to touch the harpsichord until he drank a cup of tea and ate a slice of whatever tart Cook had baked the previous day. He had the time this took down to a minimum, scalding his mouth with the tea and disposing of the tart in four bites. Miss Abigail then reproved him for ruining his digestion and Miss Beatrice patted his hand and called him a foolish boy. Then and only then did they let him alone to play.

He had vaguely noticed some days ago that the angle at which the harpsichord stood had been altered slightly, putting his back to the window. This morning, the sun streamed in behind him and a pleasant breeze played on the nape of his neck. He loosened his fingers with a series of rapid scales and arpeggios, followed by the playful *Courante* from one of Bach's Suites. Then, with barely a pause, he embarked on the *scherzo* he had composed shortly before leaving Vienna. It was the first time he had risked playing anything of his own ... but the ladies need not know who had written it and he wanted to know if it still satisfied him. It did; in fact, it made him smile, so he played it again, more quickly this time. Then, before Miss Beatrice – it was always she who asked – could demand enlightenment, he did something else he hadn't tried before and launched into the *Allegro* from Mozart's newest concerto. This would be something else the ladies were unlikely ever to have heard ... and Mozart's genius would render his own efforts easily forgettable.

Though a challenge, playing any part of a concerto without the orchestra wasn't impossible; it merely required rather more concentration than usual. It had taken Julian months to get hold of the music and nearly a fortnight to completely master all three movements. But he considered the piece one of Mozart's best ... lively and complex but holding a melody that stuck in one's mind afterwards. Perfect, in fact.

When the last notes died away, he sat motionless letting the echo of them clear from his head. He was still doing it when a man's voice said loudly, 'Why's he stopped?' And was swiftly followed by a chorus of annoyed shushing. Julian turned sharply towards the open window, half-stumbling to his feet when he saw upwards of a dozen villagers gathered among the rosebushes in the Misses Caldercott's front garden.

'Oh dear,' sighed Miss Abigail from behind him. 'I *told* Millie to keep them quiet.'

For a handful of seconds, heart thudding inside his chest, Julian remained rooted to the spot as if he didn't know which way to turn. His audience didn't wait for him to decide. It burst into ragged but wholly enthusiastic applause, over which somebody shouted, 'Play another, m'lord!' ... the call quickly being taken up by others.

From the back of the little crowd and into a brief, expectant lull, Paul Featherstone trapped Julian's gaze and said, 'No point in crawling back into your shell now, Julian. So take a bow and give them an encore, why don't you? God knows, entertainment is a rare commodity hereabouts.'

Julian looked out on the hopeful faces in the garden. For an instant, they became the audience he'd performed before in Vienna; three hundred ladies and gentlemen, powdered, perfumed and clad in bright silks and satins. Something faintly hysterical stirred inside him, producing a brief genuinely amused laugh. Then he did one thing they expected of him ... followed by another they didn't. He swept a flourishing bow and, in the resurgence of applause that greeted it, sat down again and took them by surprise with a medley of well-known tunes. *Barbara Allen* slid seamlessly into *Robin Adair*; *The Vicar of Bray* became a foray into *The Beggar's Opera* with *How Happy Could I Be With Either*; and *Rule Britannia*, played as a theme with variations, served as a finale. Wide grins broke out, feet tapped, a few brave souls even sang along. And when it was over in yet more applause, Julian realised that the laughter and genuine pleasure of these ordinary folk meant just as much as a standing ovation in a concert-hall.

When they finally started to melt away, he looked at the Caldercott ladies and said, with an attempt at severity, 'Did you arrange that?'

'No. It's been going on for a while – though previously, they stayed out of sight,' said Miss Beatrice, her cheeks pink with excitement. 'This morning was different. Myself, I rather suspect Dr Featherstone.'

'Who – me?' grinned Paul, stalking in to clap Julian on the shoulder. 'Well done. You'll never hear the last of it, of course – but that was a nice thing you did. Give your next recital on Sunday after church and you'll have the whole village there. Play a reel and they'll be dancing in the street.'

'On a *Sunday*?' murmured Miss Abigail sardonically. 'God forbid!'

Paul laughed and shook his head. Then, briskly, 'I have to go, Julian. But first tell me how it's going with Mistress Marsden.'

Three people waited while Julian dragged his mind back from wherever it had been.

'Well enough, I suppose.' He thought for a moment. 'Ellie likes her.'

'Excellent. And what of you? Do *you* like her?'

Yes, he thought; but with ingrained caution, said merely, 'She is ... different.'

'Different?' echoed Paul, amused. 'In what way?'

'Well, she doesn't seem to mind when I say the wrong thing ... or look at me as if she's either waiting for me to be charming and witty or – or evaluating my stud potential. And Ellie says she can climb trees.'

Miss Beatrice smothered a laugh. Miss Abigail said unsteadily, 'Yes. That is *certainly* different. You must bring her to tea one day. I'm sure Bea and I will enjoy meeting her.'

* * *

While Julian was giving an unintentional performance, Janet Featherstone had been paying a surprise call on Arabella. In her usual down-to-earth fashion, she said, 'How are you coping?'

'Quite well, I think. As yet, I'm concentrating on getting to know the children and trying to establish a routine for them. I'd like to add a few lessons but I'm not sure what they learn at the vicarage.'

'Reading, writing and basic arithmetic. They sing hymns, recite prayers and occasionally she reads them a Bible story. Nothing at all to fuel their imaginations or create enthusiasm.' Janet examined the lemon tart on her plate. 'I see Martha Phelps' pastry-making skills are no better than the rest of her cooking but I don't suppose Julian complains.' She paused, glancing sideways at Arabella. 'Speaking of Julian ... how are you getting on with him?'

'Until yesterday, I'd hardly seen him. At first, I put his manner down to shyness ... but it's more than that, isn't it? He's almost reclusive.'

'Yes. You know about the harpsichord, I suppose? That music is the love of his life?' And when Arabella nodded, 'My guess is that he's spent so much time communicating with a keyboard, he's forgotten how to communicate with people. If, that is, he ever knew.'

'Have you heard him play?'

'No – but Paul has. Apparently, he's exceptional – which isn't to be wondered at after seven years studying in Vienna.'

'Seven *years?*' gasped Arabella.

'Yes. And he'll talk about Vienna with moderate comfort; the music, his studies, other musicians he met. But try asking about the last few weeks before those weasely lawyers tricked him into coming here and he slams an invisible door in your face.'

'What do you mean – they tricked him?'

'They lied,' said Janet flatly; and proceeded to explain. 'He never meant to stay ... but after he found out about the children, he didn't know how to leave. Those first few months, it was like watching someone die by degrees. He's been better since Abigail and Beatrice Caldercott offered him the use of their instrument and he'll be better still when he's finished repairing the one here. But if what Paul and I suspect is true, there will always be a part of him missing.'

'And what *do* you suspect?'

'That his ambition was to be a concert performer ... and that he'd been on the brink of achieving it when the lawyers found him.' Janet shrugged and rose, pulling on her gloves. 'We may be wrong ... but if we aren't, he's wasted here.'

'If you aren't,' said Arabella slowly, 'it isn't any wonder he's miserable. Because he is, isn't he? I suspect that is why he closes himself off.'

'And bottling it up compounds the problem.' She looked Arabella in the eye. 'I've half a mind to ask what you're doing here, Mistress Marsden – since everything about you is telling me you've never worked for a living and probably don't need to do so now. But I won't. I'll merely leave you with a challenge. Persuade Julian to talk.'

Arabella stood up and hoped the fact that her nerves had gone into spasm didn't show. She said, 'You think I can succeed where you and your husband have not?'

'I think it's worth a try. It's harder for him to run away here. So all you need is some perseverance ... and the right lever.'

* * *

Luncheon in the dining-room with the children was only marginally less fraught than it had been the day before … but, after it, Arabella insisted they remain seated, produced the books she had found in the schoolroom and, when Tom scowled, said firmly, 'Half an hour, and then we'll have some fun. Tom and Rob, you'll have to share for now but that means you can help each other. Start with *Jason and the Golden Fleece.* And Ellie … you can sit with me and we'll read *Figgy The Magic Dog* together.'

Once Tom and Rob realised that Jason was a hero on an epic quest, they settled down better than Arabella had expected and Ellie enjoyed *Figgy* so much that she insisted they read it twice. The half-hour passed quickly and, at the end of it, Arabella said, 'Now … who's in the mood for a treasure-hunt?'

'Me!' said Rob and Ellie in unison. To which Rob added, 'Where, Miss? Outside?'

'No. We're going to search the attics for ancient, long-lost riches. Or in my case, new curtains for your bedchambers.' Tom swore under his breath and Arabella fixed him with a withering stare. 'You can join in or not, Tom. It's entirely up to you. But what you will *not* do is use language like that in my hearing. Do we understand one another?'

He nodded and mumbled, 'Sorry. I forgot.'

'Good. Then let's march. *En avant, mes braves*!'

Within half an hour, everyone was filthy but having too good a time to care. Even Tom, who had begun with an expression of ostentatious boredom, grew somewhat more animated when Ellie heaved an antiquated musket from a trunk and asked Miss Lizzie if it could be made to work.

Suspecting that it couldn't but alarmed in case it could, Arabella sat down to give it a thorough examination. By the time she was satisfied that the thing contained neither powder nor shot and was frozen at perpetual half-cock, Ellie had lost interest – having discovered a pair of doleful-looking puppets – and Rob was busy assembling a troop of toy soldiers. Tom, however, who had been looking over her shoulder with close attention and a glimmer of respect, said, 'How did you know how to do that?'

'My brother said that if I wanted to learn to fire a pistol, I must first learn how to look after it,' she replied. 'This musket is old but, in essence, not so very different from a modern firearm.' She handed it to him. 'It's never going to work again. But with some gun-oil and a bit of effort, you may be able to get most of the parts moving. And taking something apart is the best way to learn how it works.'

Tom accepted the gun with a grunt that Arabella decided to interpret as 'thank you'.

When the clock in the hall chimed four and Ellie immediately said she was going to meet Sir Julian, Arabella decided that they had done enough for one day. Gathering up the various lengths of velvet and brocade she had unearthed herself, she said, 'Take the things that you want, then wash your hands and get rid of the cobwebs.'

'Can we *really* keep the toys?' asked Ellie doubtfully.

'Of course. These and any others you find.'

'You mean we can do this again?' asked Rob, bright-faced under the dirt. 'There are some skittles but I couldn't find them all.'

'Try again tomorrow.' She hesitated and then, aware that no one at Chalfont either knew or cared about the proper protocol, said, 'Ellie ... will you do something for me? Will you tell his lordship that I'll expect him in the dining-room at six o'clock?'

'With clean hands,' replied Ellie promptly. It had been the day's first lesson.

Arabella swallowed a laugh, hoped his lordship had a sense of humour and said solemnly, 'Yes. With clean hands.'

* * *

Julian didn't know how he felt about dining with Mistress Marsden again.

Somewhere at the back of his mind was the idea that it might be pleasant not to eat alone. Also, he liked watching her as she talked ... and especially liked hearing her laugh. But the prospect of having to make conversation tied his stomach in knots.

He made himself as presentable as possible and, having gone downstairs early, found her putting the finishing touches to a small vase of wild roses. Tossing a teasing grin over her shoulder, she said, 'Did Ellie tell you to wash your hands?'

'Yes.' He held them out. 'Do you want to check?'

'No. But you can tell her that I did. She'll like that.'

'She likes *you*,' said Julian baldly. And managed not to add, *She thinks you're pretty.*

'I hope so.' Having asked Violet not to begin serving immediately, Arabella took a seat beside the empty hearth and waited to see if his lordship would follow suit. If he thought she only wished to discuss the children, he might relax a bit. 'Rob is a happy, good-natured little boy ... but Tom is still very wary. I'm not sure how to mend that, other than by --'

'Giving him a musket?' interposed Julian mildly.

'Oh.' Her colour rose a little. 'Ellie told you about raiding the attics?'

He nodded. 'In detail.   However ... about the musket?'

'It's old and will never fire again. But Tom seemed interested – the first time he's been interested in *anything* – so I gave it to him to take apart.' Arabella hesitated. 'I know I should have asked your permission --'

'Why? With Tom, anything is worth a try. He thinks that, sooner or later, I'll toss them out. Nothing so far has convinced him that if I was going to do that, I wouldn't have brought them here in the first place.'

'Have you told him that in so many words?'

'I thought I had.' Perching on the arm of a chair, he met her gaze with a diffident one of his own and said, 'I should try again, shouldn't I?'

'It certainly wouldn't hurt.' She smiled cheerfully at him and changed the subject. 'Mistress Featherstone called on me this morning to ask how I was getting on ... and probably also to make sure I wasn't making your life a misery. I gather that she and her husband are good friends of yours.'

'They've both been very kind,' agreed Julian. And then, making an effort, 'As it happens, I saw Paul in the village. He asked after you as well.'

'I can imagine.' Sudden and involuntary laughter danced in her eyes and quivered in her voice. 'I suppose he told you he nearly sent me packing at Newark?'

He nodded, wanting only to look and silently begging her to laugh aloud.

'Not that I can blame him,' Arabella went on truthfully. 'I realise I'm not what you asked for ... or much like a real housekeeper.'

'I don't know what a real housekeeper is supposed to be like.'

'I've gathered that.' This time she did laugh. 'And am suitably grateful.'

Julian drank her in, realising that he was staring but seeming unable to stop. He said abruptly, 'The Caldercott ladies told me to invite you for tea.'

Accepting the change of subject without a blink and pretending she'd never heard the name before, Arabella said, 'The Caldercott ladies?'

'Miss Abigail and Miss Beatrice. They live on the edge of the village.' He hesitated, then added, 'They've been allowing me to play their harpsichord.'

'Oh. That is good of them. But I imagine they enjoy listening to you.'

He flushed a little, considered telling her what had happened that morning and then, deciding it would probably come out wrong, said instead, 'Yes. I ... think so.'

'Mistress Featherstone mentioned that you studied music in Vienna.'

Fortunately, Violet entered bearing portions of trout which gave Julian the opportunity to merely nod while they took their seats. Arabella tried a bite of dried-up fish, watched his lordship prodding his piece with his fork and, deciding a casual approach might be best, said, 'It's not good, is it? Mistress Phelps seems to cook everything to death. But I suppose she came with the house?'

'Yes.' He ate some of the trout and said, 'It's not so bad. I recall a suet pudding that was truly terrible.'

She giggled. For an instant before he looked away again, that vulnerable green gaze rested on her face as if she'd done something remarkable. Feeling her colour rise but determined not to lose this more relaxed mood, Arabella said, 'She felt bad about that. She didn't expect you to eat it and was impressed that you did.'

'I suppose I was hungry,' he muttered.

'No. You were just too kind to hurt her feelings. However, I was going to ask about Vienna. This is the first time I've left Yorkshire – so Vienna sounds positively exotic.'

'Exotic? No. At least, I didn't find it so. But beautiful; bitterly cold in winter; and bursting with music and musicians.'

'Which is why you were there.' *And probably why you wish you still were*, thought Arabella. Abandoning the trout, she said, 'Did you meet anyone famous?'

'That depends on your definition. Have you heard of Wanhal or Pleyel?'

She shook her head. 'Should I have done?'

'They're well known in Europe, though perhaps less so here. But --' He stopped as Violet replaced the trout with mashed potatoes and something smothered in sauce. Peering cautiously at what lurked beneath, he said dubiously, 'Lamb chops, I think.'

Arabella poked at her own portion. 'And the sauce?'

He tasted it. 'Possibly something to do with tomatoes?'

She watched him hack through the meat, work at chewing it and eventually swallow.

'Better than the suet pudding?'

'Marginally.' And then, just as she put a forkful of potato in her mouth, 'I know Wolfgang Mozart.'

She managed not to choke and eventually croaked, '*Mozart? Really?*'

Julian nodded, his eyes on his plate. 'He'd just resigned from his post in Salzburg and was spending a couple of weeks in Vienna before seeking a new position. There was a private party and he performed his newest concerto – the E flat major. Someone I knew introduced us and told him --' He stopped abruptly.

After waiting a second or two, Arabella prompted, 'Yes? They told him what?'

Herr Krassnig had told Mozart that if he heard his compositions played by Herr Langham he'd be a lot less satisfied with his own renditions. But that was *definitely* something that couldn't be repeated without sounding conceited.

'It doesn't matter. But the result was that the two of us got together over a pianoforte, taking it in turns to play this and that whilst arguing over phrasing and dynamics.' Keeping his eyes on his plate and sawing heroically at a chop, he added, 'It was a long evening with a good deal of wine. It ended with us both passed out on the floor.'

'You and Mozart got *drunk* together?' she demanded, delighted shock illuminating her face. 'Truly?'

'Yes.' He looked across at her, then away again, mumbling, 'I suppose I ought not to have mentioned that bit.'

'Why not?' Arabella abandoned her food and, leaning her elbows on the table, cupped her chin in her palms. 'Was it fun?'

'The parts I can remember were.' Her laughter caused his insides to lurch. 'The knives grinding in my skull next day weren't.'

'No. I imagine not. What is he like?'

'Mozart?' Julian thought for a moment, wondering how best to describe genius. 'He's young, loud and exuberant. Maybe a little brash.'

'Younger than you?'

'Six years younger. And destined to be the greatest composer of his generation.'

'You said you were playing the pianoforte that night,' she said consideringly. 'I've been meaning to ask you about that. Why do you play the harpsichord instead?'

'I prefer the sound,' he shrugged. 'It's more delicate and intimate than that of the pianoforte. And virtually all of the music I enjoy playing – Bach, Scarlatti and Rameau, for example – was written for the harpsichord, so is best performed on one.'

Arabella hesitated and then, because his lordship seemed to have forgotten his shyness and was opening up to her more than she'd expected, she said tentatively, 'When the harpsichord here is fully repaired ... will I hear you play?'

He gave a small, wry laugh. 'Undoubtedly. More than you want to, I imagine.'

CHAPTER NINE

The Earl of Sherbourne's coach drew up outside Wynstanton House in St James Square at a little before five in the afternoon. The last day of the journey had been accomplished in something approaching frosty silence caused by Elizabeth's appalled reaction to the notion that she and the earl might be expected to marry.

She had said, 'No. Absolutely not! It's the most ridiculous – not to say impossible – thing I ever heard. I can't – and I *won't*.'

And Ralph, unaware that her attitude had nothing to do with him personally and *everything* to do with the fact that she wasn't who he thought she was, had been more offended than he cared to admit. In truth, he suspected that it would be a cold day in hell before Rockliffe either suggested or even permitted a marriage between them – regardless of what gossip Philippa stirred up. In a sense, that was a pity because Ralph had to marry *someone* … and he recognised that he could do much worse than beautiful, well-connected Arabella Brandon. Her reaction, therefore, struck him as vaguely insulting.

However, when the chaise came to a halt and both Frayne and Annie had stepped down to see to the unloading of the luggage, he unlocked his jaws to say, 'If the duke is at home, it will be best that I speak with him immediately.'

'No. It will be best if I explain the circumstances and tell him that, regardless of anything he may hear, you have behaved impeccably. If he accepts my word – and I don't see why he shouldn't – you may be spared the need to speak with him at all.'

Ralph found that he couldn't be bothered to explain how unlikely this was. He merely said, 'As you wish. But I would appreciate it if you refrained from giving the impression that I am reluctant to face him.'

'Of course I won't!'

'Excellent. Then I will bid you *au revoir* – since, society being what it is, we are bound to meet again. Frayne … see Mistress Brandon to the door and help Cox with her luggage.'

Rendered speechless by his cool dismissal, Elizabeth was on the pavement before she remembered her manners. Equally cool, she said, 'Goodbye, my lord. And please accept my deepest gratitude for your help.'

Then she swept up the steps to the door as it swung open to reveal an imposing black-clad butler she might have taken for the duke himself had she not known better.

'Mistress Brandon? Please come in, ma'am. Their Graces have been expecting you for some days and will be most relieved at your safe arrival. Henry, William ... pray attend to the trunks and convey them to the Jasmine Suite. Mary ... show Mistress Brandon's maid upstairs.' He cast an all-encompassing glance at Frayne's retreating back and the muddied crest on the earl's carriage but forbore to remark on it. 'Please follow me, ma'am. Her Grace will wish to welcome you and show you to your rooms herself.'

'Thank you,' said Elizabeth, responding to Annie's anguished glance with what she hoped was an encouraging nod when all the time she was aware of the massive hall, the wide marble staircase and paintings that would have graced a palace.

Oh dear lord, she thought, *What have I done?*

For this, Elizabeth realised with sudden, sickening clarity, was where it all truly began. Although her journey had been beset with obstacles, her part in the Grand Masquerade had been easy compared with what lay ahead. *Now* she had to start being Arabella in earnest. She had to remember that her aunt was her mother, her father was her uncle, her cousins were her siblings and her sisters were her cousins. It hadn't sounded so very complicated before. Perhaps it still wasn't. But one thing was clear. She had better begin thinking of both families in terms of their pretended relationship rather than in mental translation; because it needed only one tiny, stupid slip and the game would be over.

The butler halted outside a pair of double doors, tapped and then opened them.

'Mistress Brandon has arrived, your Grace,' he announced.

'What?' asked a disembodied voice. Then, 'Thank goodness!'

'Indeed, your Grace. I have taken the liberty of bringing her up directly.'

Pink-cheeked and with a lock of hair falling over one eye, the duchess's head appeared from behind a sofa. 'Arabella! At last – no, Vanessa! Don't --' This as something hit the polished floor with an ominous crack, followed by a baby's giggle. 'It is *not* funny. Mama is not laughing.' Simultaneously disentangling herself from her skirts and picking up her small daughter, Adeline struggled to her feet and said, 'Forgive me for just a moment, Arabella. She's terrifyingly quick – and this room is full of delightful temptations.'

Vanessa grabbed a handful of her mother's necklace and said, 'War!'

'War, darling? Surely not.' Sailing across the room, she handed the child to the butler, saying, 'Take her ladyship to Lily, Symonds and send tea, please.'

'Certainly, your Grace,' said Symonds.

Both his bow and his exit were somewhat spoiled when her small ladyship hit him on the nose shouting, 'Gah!'... and totally ruined when he jiggled her on his arm and walked away saying, 'Gah to you, too, little madam. Gah, indeed.'

Catching the surprise in her newly-arrived guest's eyes, Adeline said, 'Symonds is quite wonderful – the nearest thing Vanessa will ever have to a grandfather.' Then, taking Elizabeth's hands and drawing her into a warm, scented hug, 'Welcome, my dear. Tracy said he'd heard dire reports of the state of the roads further north but, even so, I was starting to worry. *Was* it the weather?'

'Yes, your Grace.' Elizabeth allowed herself to be drawn down on a sofa beside the duchess. 'A two-day deluge ... amongst other things.'

'Well, I want to hear all about it – but so will Tracy.' Adeline smiled at her. 'He is from home just at present but will dine with us this evening ... so rather than make you tell it all twice, shall we save the tale until then?'

Elizabeth smiled and nodded, half relieved by the temporary respite and half not.

A footman arrived with the tea-tray, bowed and left.

'Your mama's letters didn't tell us how very pretty you are,' remarked Adeline, reaching for the tea-pot. 'But that's to her credit. Most mothers rhapsodise over their daughters' looks whether there's any basis for it or not.' She paused. 'It is a great pity that your uncle wouldn't permit your cousin to join you for this visit.'

'He felt that it would not ultimately be to Lizzie's benefit.'

'And how did Elizabeth feel? Or you, come to that.'

At this precise moment, Elizabeth felt she was walking over very thin ice. She said, 'We were both disappointed. We've shared everything for as long as I can remember, you see.'

'Very clearly. And it renders your uncle's attitude even more regrettable than I'd previously thought,' came the blunt reply. She smiled suddenly, 'But *you* are here. And we intend you to enjoy yourself.'

'Thank you, your Grace. I'm sure I will.'

'Good. Perhaps we can begin by dispensing with my title. Cousin Adeline will do, don't you think? Not strictly accurate – but as close as we can get. For the rest, in a few weeks' time when you have some acquaintances and become accustomed to society, we shall hold a ball. But next week, I am giving a small supper-party to introduce you to our closest friends. How does that sound?'

'It sounds very kind, your – I mean, Cousin Adeline – if a little alarming.'

'It need not. Among them are a number of young married ladies you will like very much – indeed, I think we will pay calls on some of them in advance of my party. Now ... finish your tea and I will show you to your rooms while there is still time for you to rest before dinner.'

The Jasmine Suite comprised bedchamber, sitting and dressing rooms, all of them furnished in shades of dusky rose and palest green. In the middle of it and assisted by a second and very smartly-clad maid, Annie was busy unpacking. The duchess said, 'Ah – Jeanne. No doubt you've given Miss Arabella's maid all manner of useful information.'

'I've tried, my lady,' agreed Jeanne, with a small curtsy. 'I've also rung for a bath, Miss Arabella – it should be here directly.'

Jeanne left. And, glancing around the room as if to assure herself that everything was as it should be, Adeline said, 'I'll leave you to settle in – oh, there is a letter awaiting you which I'm sure you will want to read. If you need anything further, don't hesitate to ring.'

'A letter?' asked Elizabeth, as soon as the duchess had gone. 'Where is it?'

'Looks like it's from Miss Belle,' said Annie, handing it to her. 'I'll wager she hasn't got rooms as lovely as these. I've never seen the like!'

Elizabeth skimmed the few lines Arabella had written the morning after her arrival at Chalfont. *The estate is run-down and impoverished; the earl is young, outrageously good-looking and shy; and the children belonged to his predecessor. Nothing here is what we thought but I think I'll like it. I'll write again when I know more.*

'Is that it?' sniffed Annie, when Elizabeth had read it aloud. 'Not very helpful, is it?'

'No. But she'd barely arrived – just as we have.'

'That's as may be, Miss Lizzie. But --'

'Stop. Don't make that mistake again. From now on, I'm Miss Belle – even in private.' And do *not* tell her Grace's maid about Lord Sherbourne. It's bad enough that I've got to explain him to the duke and duchess.'

'You haven't met the duke yet, then?'

'No. I'm to have that honour this evening at dinner. So decide what I ought to wear and get the creases out of it, please. I'll need every ounce of confidence I can muster.'

* * *

A couple of hours later, his Grace of Rockliffe strolled into the house and found his wife curled up in her boudoir with a book. Her hair was loose and she was wearing a cream lace chamber-robe, prettily threaded through with pale blue ribbon. Rockliffe took a moment to enjoy the picture she made and then crossed to tip her face up for a kiss before sitting beside her. He said, 'How many priceless family heirlooms did Vanessa break today?'

'Only the small Chinese vase.'

'Only?' He winced, thinking of its age and rarity. 'Ah well ... I suppose one must be grateful for small mercies.'

'Yes. I don't think either of us will miss the ugly Chelsea shepherdess or the fretwork bon-bon dish.' She slid beneath his arm and leaned against his shoulder. 'Symonds told you that Arabella has arrived?'

'He did. He also told me something else ... but I am attempting not to jump to hasty conclusions. What is she like?'

'Well-mannered and extremely pretty. If, as we understand, she also has a substantial dowry, there won't be any shortage of potential suitors.'

'Unless my memory fails me, we did not promise Louisa a son-in-law.'

'No, we didn't. But after the debacle with that other young man, it would be a miracle if she wasn't hoping for it.' Adeline frowned slightly. 'Arabella didn't mention him. Perhaps I didn't give her the opportunity ... or perhaps it's too soon.'

'Or perhaps,' said Rockliffe, tugging lightly at a ribbon here and there, 'she prefers not to talk about it at all. If so, I sympathise. On occasion, I also find myself in favour of not talking ... such as now, for example.'

* * *

Having been directed by a helpful footman, Elizabeth entered the blue salon to find it occupied only by a tall and very handsome dark-haired gentleman, exquisitely clad in pearl grey brocade. For an instant, she thought that this couldn't possibly be the duke ... and immediately realised that it could not be anyone else. Hovering uncertainly two steps into the room, she managed a deep curtsy but failed to make her tongue work.

Amusement lurking in his eyes, Rockliffe strolled over to take her hand and bow over it. He said, 'Welcome to Wynstanton House, Arabella. I rejoice to find you safe and well. No doubt writing materials were hard to come by?'

Elizabeth's heart sank and she swallowed.

'I – I'm sorry, your Grace. I should perhaps have written ... but because of the damage to the bridge, the people at the inn thought the Mail coach might not arrive, so it seemed I would get here before any note did.'

'I see. And did you also apply this logic to your family?'

'No. I left a letter to be sent when the coach *did* come.'

'Good.' He smiled suddenly. 'There is no need to look so worried. Since I find delivering homilies fatiguing, I do not make a habit of it. Please ... sit. Adeline's tardiness is entirely my fault but she will be with us shortly.'

Elizabeth perched on the edge of a chair. With the exception of that devastating smile, everything else about him was formidable enough to make her dread the evening ahead. What she and Arabella had done was quite bad enough without the additional complications posed by the Earl of Sherbourne.

The duke poured two glasses of wine and handed her one of them.

'I hope,' he said, 'that your mother and aunt are in good health?'

'Yes, your Grace. They are both very well – as are m-my brothers and cousins.' In the hope of avoiding questions similar to the ones asked by the duchess, she said, 'The duchess – oh. She says I am to call her Cousin Adeline but ...'

'Then by all means, do so,' said Rockliffe smoothly. 'You were saying?'

'We talked about m-my cousin and though I conveyed Lizzie's gratitude for your kind invitation and her regrets at being unable to accept it, I ought perhaps to have explained that her situation has changed.'

'In what respect?'

'She has taken up a position in the Earl of Chalfont's household.'

'Chalfont?' The dark eyes grew thoughtful. 'Interesting. I take it that the current earl has inherited the title quite recently?'

'I believe so. He advertised for a lady to oversee his house and children ... and he lives near Newark, so Lizzie travelled with me until we parted company there last Friday.'

'And the Reverend Marsden considered this arrangement more suitable than a sojourn in my house?' murmured Rockliffe. 'No – you need not answer that.'

'Answer what?' asked Adeline, arriving just in time to hear this. And to Elizabeth, 'Has he been intimidating you?'

'*He*,' drawled the duke, turning away to pour wine for her, 'has been doing no such thing. And I am standing right here, you know.'

'No one could possibly overlook that fact.' She accepted the glass he offered her and added, 'But you *can* be intimidating … and when you are, people tremble.'

'Really? I must remember to look out for that. It certainly doesn't happen at home.'

Adeline laughed and turned to Elizabeth, taking in her silver-grey taffeta.

'That is a very pretty gown … but, if you'll forgive me saying so, not your best colour. If you feel sufficiently restored tomorrow, I believe I will take you to Phanie's.'

It was towards the end of dinner when fruit and sweetmeats had appeared on the table and the servants withdrew for the last time, that Rockliffe finally approached the subject that had been ruining Elizabeth's appetite throughout. Idly fingering a fruit-knife, he said, 'And so, Arabella … tell us about your journey.'

Controlling both face and voice to the best of her ability, she said, 'As I told Cousin Adeline earlier, the rain began as we left Newark and continued, getting heavier all the time. We had just got past Huntingdon, when the accident happened.'

'Accident?' asked Adeline quickly. 'Were you hurt?'

'Fortunately not.' Elizabeth proceeded to describe the position and condition of the carriage – along with the difficulty of getting to the nearest inn and out of the rain. In an attempt to delay the inevitable she also included a good deal of superfluous detail which Rockliffe eventually interrupted.

'May we assume you were rescued from this sorry plight?'

'Yes. A chaise and four came along and – and took us to the nearest inn. During the evening, we heard that the nearby bridge had been damaged and been closed to traffic.'

'I was wondering where the bridge came into it,' murmured the duke. And in response to his wife's enquiring look, 'It was mentioned earlier. But I interrupt. Do go on, Arabella.'

'Well, the rain finally stopped overnight but the road was a quagmire so we were stuck there for another day. During it, I learned that repairs to my own carriage were going to take considerable time, which meant I would need to hire another. Lord Sherbourne said I would have to go to St Neots to do that --'

'Sherbourne?' interposed Rockliffe flatly.

'Yes. Did I not say?'

'No. You did not.'

'Oh. Well, it was he who rescued Annie and me from the roadside.' Somehow, Elizabeth managed to summon a smile. 'Since he would be travelling through St Neots himself, he offered to take me there and help find a replacement vehicle.' Seeing the duke and duchess exchange seemingly expressionless glances, she added quickly, 'He was very helpful. I don't know how Annie and I would have managed otherwise.'

'And did his lordship succeed in hiring a carriage in St Neots?' enquired Rockliffe.

'He tried. Unfortunately, it wasn't possible. But he – he refused to abandon me so we continued as far as Stevenage yesterday and finally arrived in London this afternoon.'

'Let me see if I have this correctly,' said Rockliffe. 'Your carriage suffered an accident on Sunday and, today being Wednesday, you have been in the Earl of Sherbourne's company for four days. Is that right?'

Elizabeth nodded uneasily. She sensed that, quite aside from the fact of her having travelled unchaperoned with a gentleman, Sherbourne's name had not been well-received. She said rapidly, 'My maid was with me – and nothing at all improper occurred. His lordship was a perfect gentleman the entire time. I realise it wasn't ideal --'

'Not *ideal*?' echoed Adeline. 'That is one way of putting it.'

'Quite,' agreed the duke and, with a glance at his wife, 'Which brings me to the other thing Symonds mentioned. Arabella ... the earl delivered you to this house in his own carriage. He did not, however, leave his card or even see you to the door. Did it not occur to him that I might conceivably wish to have a few words with him?'

'It did and he wanted to,' admitted Elizabeth, beginning to regret her obstinacy. 'I told him not to. I said that I could explain everything to you myself.'

'And he accepted that?'

'I ... didn't give him a lot of choice.'

Rockliffe sighed. 'Arabella ... please think very carefully. With the exception of innkeepers and the like, were you seen in his lordship's company by any other travellers?'

Her heart sank a little further. 'Yes. Two ladies at the inn in Stevenage. But they were travelling away from London --'

'Who were they?'

'Lady Davenport and Lady Sutherland.'

This produced another – and this time, catastrophic – silence.

'Ah. That renders one question unnecessary.' His Grace's voice remained as smooth as ever but the set of his mouth told a different story. He said, 'Adeline ... I take it I need not explain why the presence of Philippa Sutherland was singularly unfortunate?'

'No. It's clear enough,' she replied acidly. Then, to Elizabeth, 'Did you give them your name – or tell them you were coming here?'

'Yes. It – it was before Lord Sherbourne came into the room and I didn't know – didn't realise that I shouldn't.' She gripped her hands hard in her lap. 'His lordship asked me the same questions and was as – as put out by my answers as you are.'

'Put out? I'll wager it was a bit more than that,' said Adeline. 'Tracy, if this gets out – and it will – Arabella's reputation will be in shreds before anyone even sees her.'

'Quite.' The dark Wynstanton eyes rested broodingly on Elizabeth. 'The usual way a gentleman repairs damage to a lady's good name is by marriage. But in the unlikely event that Ralph Sherbourne *were* to offer and even if you were willing, there is not the slightest chance that I could counsel your family to consent to it.'

She stared back in surprise. 'Why not? Oh – please don't misunderstand. I've no desire to wed Lord Sherbourne. But he seemed to think you might insist upon it.'

'Did he indeed? A further example of why his lordship and I need to have a little talk,' returned Rockliffe. 'As to why ... let us merely say that I do not care for the gentleman's reputation. A fact of which I am quite sure he is already aware.'

* * *

A short distance away in Curzon Street, the Earl of Sherbourne eyed his youngest brother with acute disfavour. He said softly, 'I am at a loss, Bertram. The garbled communication I received from you at Whitcombe Park informed me that Cedric was in ... how did you put it? Yes. A spot of bother. Nothing, you said, that I would not be able to mend with a mere snap of my fingers. Am I remembering this accurately?'

Bertram shifted uneasily. 'Yes.'

'Furthermore, instead of writing to me immediately from Gardington, you wasted three days travelling to London to do so.'

'Well, I couldn't remember where you'd gone so I had to come here to ask old Hetherly. And it took a bit longer because I racked up at the Pheasant on the way and there was a pair of bruisers due to fight the next day so --'

'Stop.' Ralph had always known Bertram was an imbecile – yet at times the degree of it still had the power to astound him. 'Knowing the situation ... knowing that my presence was urgently needed ... it did not occur to you that a certain amount of haste was required?'

'I thought a few days wouldn't make any difference. Not really. And I thought there was a good chance Ceddie would talk his way out of it before you got there.'

'You *thought*, Bertram? That must have been a novel experience. And since we are none of us any longer in the nursery, I would appreciate it if – in my hearing, at least – you could call Cedric *Cedric*.' Ralph drew a long, restraining breath. 'Why is it that as soon as I turn my back, one or other of you wastes no time in creating an unholy mess?'

'It's not *that* bad. And you can fix it easy enough. Go down to Gardington – come the earl over this Belcher fellow – and the thing's as good as done. Ain't it?'

'No. It is not. *This Belcher fellow*, as you put it, is in fact Mr Belcher of Finchley Farm. He is a respectable man, a pillar of the local community and his acres flank mine.' He paused, trapping his brother in a look of icy fury. 'And you think that Cedric's seduction of the man's daughter is *a spot of bother* that may be *easily fixed*?'

'Well, maybe it's a *bit* worse than I thought,' Bertram conceded, 'but you'll be able to buy Belcher off, won't you? Reading between the lines, I reckon that's all he wants.'

Ralph had scant faith in his brother's ability to see what was in front of his nose, let alone read between the lines. 'If this was about money, Mr Belcher would not have taken the somewhat drastic step of confining Cedric to Gardington. How has he managed that, by the way? My own experience of Cedric's ability to slip through one's grasp is that it would be easier said than done.'

'They've got him locked up in the old gamekeeper's cottage with the girl's brothers making sure he don't get away,' came the blithe reply. 'Didn't I mention that?'

* * *

Belcher's daughter, for God's sake, thought Ralph grimly a little later, when he'd shut himself in the library away from Bertram's particular brand of inanity. *Doesn't Cedric possess even half a brain?*

Not that it mattered. He couldn't go racing off to Dorset or anywhere else until he'd faced Rockliffe. Arabella Brandon might think that unnecessary but Ralph knew better – and if he left town now, the duke would add cowardice to whatever else he was currently thinking.

Pinching the bridge of his nose between finger and thumb, Ralph felt the familiar frustration wash over him. He was mortally sick of cleaning up after his brothers – both of whom were equally stupid. He would happily wash his hands of the pair of them had it not been that every idiocy they committed rebounded on him.

His own reputation wasn't spotless, of course – though, since shortly before inheriting the earldom, he had been making efforts to repair it. And the truth was that he had never been as black as he was painted. Yes, he had lovers; but he restricted himself to ladies who knew the game and were free to play it; and he'd never forced a woman in his life. Indeed, from the moment he'd first laid eyes on Philippa Wilkes to the day whatever hopes he'd still been clinging to came crashing down around him, he'd remained celibate as a monk.

But his sexual activities were not the real problem. The sin that still, seven years on, hung around his neck was the thrice-damned duel which had resulted in the death of Edgar Wilkes. Ralph realised that it had been a mistake to leave the country. If he had stayed, he might have shouted out the truth of what had happened until at least *some* gentlemen began to believe him. But he hadn't. He had left the task of clearing his name to his second, Richard Lazenby. And though Richard had done his best, Ralph's absence had damned him.

It didn't matter that he had spent the last nine months at Gardington, learning to become a responsible landowner or that his last liaison had been nearly a year ago. As for what had happened last night … unexpectedly coming face to face with Philippa after so long had left him off-balance. And Fate had plainly been enjoying a joke at his expense when, of all the women in the world, it had sent her to catch Arabella Brandon in his company … unchaperoned at a public inn. No one was going to believe that he had merely been conveying the girl, unsullied as the day she was born, to Wynstanton House. And finally, to cap it all, he was going to have to go to Dorset and use whatever means it took to placate Jeremy Belcher and prevent a new scandal resounding throughout the county.

Really, he thought, *it was enough to make one wonder if God and Nemesis shared the same lamentable sense of humour.*

CHAPTER TEN

Arabella's days began to fall into a pattern. She spent the half hour before breakfast giving Violet instruction on the duties of a ladies' maid while the girl dressed her hair – almost, Arabella was surprised to find, as well as Annie did. She conferred with Mistress Phelps on what was to be served for dinner and attempted, so far without noticeable success, to persuade the cook that vegetables did *not* need to be boiled into a pulp or meat roasted until it was a shrivelled travesty of its former self. She enlisted Rose's help to transform the materials she had brought down from the attic into bed covers and she devised a new and different afternoon lesson for the children.

The note Elizabeth had written from the Oak at Offord Cluny finally arrived and, after telling of the carriage accident but insisting that neither she nor Annie had been hurt, its disjointed and very un-Lizzie-like nature sent Arabella into fits of semi-shocked laughter.

He's an earl, Belle. Very good-looking and sophisticated – but I'm convinced he's a rakehell. Not that he's actually done *anything. But there's something about the tone of his voice and the look in his eyes and he says things I don't know how to answer. I'll have to dine with him again tonight and the mere thought is giving me butterflies. I hope* your *earl isn't like this one.*

No, thought Arabella, smiling a little as she folded the letter and put it away. *Aside from the good-looking part, my earl isn't at all* like that. *Actually, he's not like anybody. He's shy and kind … and rather lovely.*

Arabella hoped that, like her morning routine, dining with his lordship would also become a habit – but she suspected that forcing the issue might ruin the progress she had made thus far. Consequently, when she entered the dining-parlour at the usual time and found him already there, she felt a burst of unexpected pleasure.

Julian said, 'I'm told that, after he'd shot an arrow in Harold's eye, Norman built a big castle by the sea and a bloody tower in London.'

'Ellie said?' laughed Arabella. 'Well, she's right in most respects.'

'Getting it right is less important than enthusiasm. And you gave her that.'

She coloured a little. 'Thank you. That was the idea.'

Violet came in with soup and bread. When she had left them to eat, Arabella asked Julian about the farm ... what animals were kept, what crops planted and how many tenant families depended on the estate. Having reeled off the relevant numbers, he said, 'Ridley, the steward, is an old man and, as you are aware, there is no money for improvements.'

'Sometimes money isn't what is needed so much as a new way of looking at things,' she replied. 'What I *don't* understand is what on earth the fourth earl did with his time.'

'Aside from bedding every female within reach, you mean?' And when she made a small choking sound, 'Sorry. But it isn't as if you didn't already know. As to the rest, he drank. According to Phelps, he fell down the stairs and broke his neck whilst drunk.'

An idea occurred to Arabella but she decided not to mention it just yet and instead said, 'How is the harpsichord progressing?'

The joy in his smile stopped her breath for a moment.

'It's ready for tuning.'

She beamed back at him. 'Is that very difficult?'

'No. Just time-consuming.'

She thought for a moment and then said slowly, 'It's probably an idiotic question ... but how can you tune the harpsichord when there are no notes there to begin with?'

'You start with just one. Everything else follows from that.' Julian swallowed some soup, gathered his nerve and said, 'I'll show you, if you like.'

The offer took her by surprise and it required effort not to pounce on it.

'Yes, please. I'd like that very much.'

'You could look for the books you want at the same time.' He glanced up again. 'Ellie likes the story about the dog. Perhaps we can find a similar one.'

We? Was that the beginning of acceptance or even a tentative friendship? Arabella smiled at him and said gently, 'Yes. Perhaps we can.'

The rest of the meal being no better than usual, they did not linger over it and half an hour later they were standing beside the harpsichord while, at Arabella's request, Julian identified the various parts. More confident than she had ever seen him, he said, 'The player depresses the key but the jacks do most of the work. Look. As the key goes down, the jack rises and the quill plucks the string. When the key is released, the jack descends and the damper – that bit of felt there – silences the note. Here, the jacks were in such a bad state that they all had to come out ... and most of the dampers had rotted and needed replacing.'

'It looks like new,' remarked Arabella.

'A lot of it is,' he replied, pulling the tuning-hammer from his pocket. 'That's why it has taken so long. As for tuning ... you see this pin here?' And when she nodded. 'Play the A above middle C.' He glanced around. 'Sorry. Do you know --?'

'Yes.' She depressed the key, saw the jack move but heard nothing. 'What now?'

'Wait while I tighten the string to a point where it becomes viable.'

He fitted the tuning-hammer to the wrestpin and began gently turning it. Arabella opened her mouth on a question, then closed it again. As if he knew what she had been about to ask, he slanted another smile at her and said, 'Yes. I *am* tuning the right one. The strings have been lying slack for a while so, in addition to their natural cunning, they've grown lazy.' He paused, eyes locked on what his hand was doing. Then, 'All right. Play the A again now.' She did and the key rewarded her with a low-pitched and decidedly unmusical groan. Arabella laughed, half-intrigued, half-delighted. Julian forced himself to keep his mind on what he was doing. 'Good. Now we begin. I'm going to tune the string and you're going to continue playing the note at a steady tempo until I tell you to stop.'

Gradually, the pitch of the note rose until it was ringing out cleanly.

'Close,' he muttered, now barely touching the pin, 'but still flat. It needs to be over-tuned until it's slightly sharp.'

'Why?' she asked. 'And how do you know that note *is* A?'

'I just do. As for why ... as soon as I stop tormenting it, the string will relax. It's a little trick harpsichords have.' He straightened and turned to look at her. 'Now I have the A, I'm going to tune the F a third below it, then the C a third above. As I said, it's not difficult – it just takes time.'

'It looks difficult to me,' observed Arabella. 'And it must take a lot of patience.'

'Yes.' He hesitated. 'I'm going to continue with this. If ... if you want to look through the books, please do so.'

'Are you sure? Won't I be disturbing you?'

'No. Once I start concentrating, I'll probably forget you're there,' he said. And wondered if, tonight, that might not be true.

It took Arabella quite some time to find half a dozen books that might possibly be suitable and all the time she was hunting the shelves she was aware of the constant repetition of sound as Julian moved on from triads to fifths. She noticed that, at some point, he had discarded both coat and cravat and was working in his shirt-sleeves; and when, despite the fading light, he persevered with his task, she went quietly about the room, lighting candles. She thought he muttered his thanks but couldn't be sure. Smiling to herself, she sat down in a corner to look through the books she had chosen ... only to discover that her gaze was constantly drawn to the man by the harpsichord.

Arabella had believed herself immune to masculine beauty. Growing up with three outstandingly good-looking older brothers tended to do that to one. Now, however, she found herself noticing a cameo-pure profile ... a firm, well-shaped mouth ... forest-deep eyes fringed with sable lashes; and more than any of those, his hands. Elegantly-boned yet strong; patient, confident and clever. Something about those hands produced an odd frisson of heat which, in turn, was responsible for her gathering her books and slipping softly from the library, silent as a ghost.

Julian knew when she left. Having sensed her presence through every minute of the last hour, he immediately felt the lack of it. The endless routine of his fingers halted and he drew a long breath to clear his chest of feelings he didn't understand. Then, straightening to ease the ache in his shoulders, he went back to work.

* * *

On the next two nights, Arabella fell asleep to the distant sound of steadily repeated notes as Julian continued tuning the harpsichord. She would have liked to go down and join him but knew that – even if he welcomed her company – it would be wiser not to do so. After leaving him that first night, she had lain awake pondering and then feeling again the reaction she'd experienced whilst simply watching his hands. If it had not been completely new to her, she might have put it down to physical desire ... but she knew that couldn't be right. If it *had* been, she would surely have experienced something similar during those two so-deeply-regretted occasions with David; but she hadn't.

She wrote another letter to Aunt Maria filled with the doings of the children, Mistress Phelps culinary mistakes and virtually no mention of the earl. Then, having completed it to the best of her ability, she went up to the nursery to ask the children if they would take it to the village for posting on their way to the vicarage next morning. Even before setting foot through the door, she realised that something was – if not actually wrong – at least unusual. Instead of being at the end of the lane waiting for Julian to come home, Ellie was with her brothers and saying mulishly, 'I won't. He followed me and I'm keeping him.'

'He *followed* you because you were feeding him bits of the bun Marjorie at the bakery gave you,' said Tom, irritably. 'And you can't keep him. He ain't yours to keep. Anyway, Sir won't let you.'

'He will *so*! He will if I *ask* him.'

Pushing open the door, Arabella saw immediately what the problem was.

'Oh dear,' she said mildly. 'Don't tell me. Figgy?'

'Yes.' Ellie clutched the dirty brown-and-white bundle of fur even closer and said, 'And Sir Julian *will* let me keep him. He *will*!'

Shoving the letter in her pocket, Arabella sat down and put her arm about the child.

'He *may* do, if the dog doesn't belong to someone else – but we will have to ask him. Rob ... go down and find out if his lordship is --' Then, hearing feet taking the stairs two at a time, 'Never mind.' And quickly, as Julian erupted through the doorway looking anxious, 'It's all right. She's fine. It is merely that she has ... brought us a visitor.'

'Figgy's not a visitor,' mumbled Ellie stubbornly. 'He's staying.'

'Figgy,' repeated Julian. Letting out a breath, he looked at Arabella, 'Ah.'

'Quite. He followed Ellie home ... though not, Tom says, without some encouragement. And as I was just about to explain, before we can consider Figgy's future, we need to know whether or not he already has a home elsewhere.'

'I told her and told her,' said Tom. 'But she wouldn't listen.'

'I'm sure you did your best, Tom.' Julian hesitated and then dropped on his haunches in front of Ellie, watching the bedraggled, filthy creature lick her chin. 'I understand you wanting to keep him. But if he is some other child's pet, that wouldn't be fair, would it?'

'No. But he isn't.'

'We don't know that for certain --'

'Yes we do. He was *hungry*.'

'Perhaps. But that doesn't prove anything, Ellie. And you wouldn't want me to be accused of stealing him, would you?'

Cunning, thought Arabella, hiding a smile as, for the first time, Ellie looked uncertain.

'You didn't steal him. You wasn't even there.'

'No. But it is what people might think.' Keeping his face perfectly solemn whilst pressing home his advantage, Julian said, 'I could go to prison.'

'No!'

'Yes. And that's why we have to find out where he came from.'

'All right.' Ellie's mouth trembled and she heaved an immense sigh. 'But when you're sure he doesn't have a home, *then* can I keep him?'

Arabella shook her head at Julian and mouthed, *No promises.*

'We'll see.' He stood up. 'Tom ... perhaps you'll help me sort this out? I have to go into the village anyway, so if you can find something to serve as a leash, we'll take Figgy with us and see if anyone claims him.'

'And if they don't, you'll bring him back?' demanded Ellie, tears sparkling on her lashes as she reluctantly allowed her brother to take her pet. 'Please. You will, won't you?'

'One thing at a time,' said Julian. 'First, let Tom and me see what we can find out.'

Trying to hide his pleasure in being asked to help, Tom produced a length of fraying cord that had once held back the curtains and, making a loop at one end, dropped it over the dog's head. 'Come on, Figs. Time for a walk.'

Ellie burrowed miserably into Arabella's side and, seeing the indecision in Julian's face, Arabella pulled the letter from her pocket and said cheerfully, 'Off you go – and please take this to be posted. And when you're back, we'll have a picnic tea in the garden with Mistress Phelps' freshly-made gingerbread.'

As they left, she was fairly sure she heard a voice mutter, 'Gingerbread? God help us.'

* * *

Mistress Marsden had advised him to speak plainly to Tom and, since walking to the village took roughly twenty minutes, Julian realised that this was probably as good a time as any to do so. His difficulty was in knowing quite where to start and he was still trying to work this out when Tom said, 'Ugly little bugger, ain't he? Oh - sorry. I didn't mean --'

'It's all right.' Julian flashed the boy a grin. 'Just between you and me – yes. He is.' And then, before the moment was lost, 'Look. I think it's time we got something straight. I know you've always had to look after Rob and Ellie and I don't blame you for still feeling responsible. But I'd like you to trust my word on just one thing, if you can.'

136

'What?'

'Chalfont is your home – and always will be as long as I have any say in the matter.'

There was a long silence. Then, gruffly, 'I reckon I knew that.'

'You did? Oh. Well ... good.'

'In the beginning, I reckoned you'd be like everybody else and get fed up with us. And I didn't think you'd stay – not with the way things are.'

Julian drew a long breath and said, 'I won't lie to you, Tom. At first, I didn't mean to stay – not because of anything here but because I wanted the life I had before I came. Accepting that I couldn't have it, was ... hard. Some days, it still is. But when I took you and the others in, I didn't do it thinking I could walk away any time I chose. I knew I was making a permanent commitment.'

'A commitment?' asked Tom. 'What's that?'

'A sort of promise. The kind you can't break.' He paused, wondering how much to say; and then, knowing Tom was no fool, forced himself to continue. 'I think you know how matters stand at Chalfont and that I'm not the best man to mend them. The land hasn't been farmed properly for some years and your – your father left --'

'Don't call him that!' Tom burst out. 'He weren't no father to any of us. He – he just had his fun with our mothers till they weren't no more use to him. As for us, we could've starved in a ditch for all he cared.' He swallowed convulsively. 'Oh he dumped us on Ma Clack, all right – but that was just to get us out of the way. And *she* didn't want us, neither. All she ever cared about was the money. I don't remember Rob coming. But I was six when they brought Ellie ... and I remember how the old witch went on and on about him not paying her enough to take in all his by-blows.' He stopped, breathing hard. 'So don't call him our father. He was a bigger bastard than any of us!'

If there was a right answer to this, Julian didn't know what it was so he said quietly, 'I'm sorry. And for what it's worth, I don't disagree with anything you've said.'

'You never met him, did you?'

'No. I'd never even heard of him until the lawyers found me
– and the degree of relationship between us is so remote as to be
laughable. But the lawyers just wanted to pass the estate's
problems and debts on to somebody else ... and, as it turned out,
that somebody was me.' He smiled wryly. 'I never wanted to be
an earl. I still don't.'

They walked along in silence while Tom chewed this over.
Finally, he said, 'Where was you before?'

'In Vienna.'

'Where's that?'

'In Austria. If you're interested, I'll find a map and show you.'

More deep thought and then, 'Can I ask you something?'

'Of course.'

'Why does that harpsichord matter so much? I mean, why do
you spend hours every night trying to fix it?'

The unexpectedness of this caused something inside Julian's
chest to twist. He thought, *God. How do I explain that to a child
... to anyone, really ... in a way that makes sense?*

'If Rob and Ellie were suddenly taken away and you didn't
know if you would ever see them again, how would you feel?'

The boy opened his mouth to speak, then abruptly closed it
again. After a long moment, he said, 'I don't know. I think ... I
think it'd be as if some of *me* was missing.'

'Yes,' agreed Julian simply. 'That's how I feel when I can't
play.'

Once in the centre of the village, he said, 'Where were you
when Figgy appeared?'

'Near the bakery. Are we *really* going to call him that?'

'Unless you find his home or can persuade Ellie otherwise, I
fear so. Ask in the shops and anyone you meet – whatever you
can think of. I'll take Miss Lizzie's letter to the inn and see if there
are any for me, then I'll catch up with you.' He grinned suddenly.
'Good luck.'

The only letter awaiting collection at the Dog and Duck was a
further communication about the diverted stream. Groaning
inwardly, Julian shoved it in his pocket and set off to find Tom.
This, due to the number of people who stopped him to ask when

he would give another concert from the Misses Caldercott's parlour, took longer than expected. But he eventually rounded a corner and spotted Tom at the end of the road, facing five other boys. For a split second, Julian thought nothing of it. Then a number of things struck him. One of the boys was holding a hefty piece of wood; Tom's cheek was bleeding; he was clutching Figgy to his chest; and the ground around him was littered with stones. Even as Julian started to run, one of the five threw another and snarled, 'Hand over the runt, bastard – and maybe we won't give you a pasting. He ain't yours anyway.'

'He ain't yours neither.' Tom was too busy ducking and trying to edge away to notice Julian's approach. 'If nobody owns him, my sister's keeping him.'

'Who says?' jeered one of the others, letting another stone fly. 'That molly lord up at the hall? Think we're scared of him?'

Julian scooped up a stone from somebody's flower-bed and slowed his pace despite the anger beating in his chest. Tom had seen him. Good. He signalled to the boy to wait.

His voice low and furious, Tom said, 'He ain't no molly.'

'Course he is. He plays music, don't he? Like a *girl*.'

Tom dodged another missile. 'Say that to his face, would you?'

'Any time,' boasted the ringleader, starting to close in.

'How about now?' asked Julian. And, as all five wheeled to face him, 'Go on. I'm listening.' He waited, tossing the stone casually from one hand to the other. And when none of them spoke, 'What? Nothing to say? Now why am I not surprised?'

The bullies exchanged uneasy glances and started shuffling away. One of them mumbled, 'Didn't mean nothing, mister.'

'My lord,' said Julian. 'You didn't mean anything, *my lord*. And please have the guts to stand and face me. Tom ... do you know their names?'

'Yes, m'lord,' he agreed, entering into the spirit of the thing. 'All of 'em.'

'Excellent. And have they troubled you – or Rob or Ellie – before?'

This time, Tom stared at his feet and scuffed one boot on the cobbles.

'I'll take that as a yes.' Julian let his gaze stray over the miscreants. 'Odds of five to one and wanting the dog in order to give it a kicking say a lot about you. Your fathers must be so proud. But the fun is over. *This* time I shall merely speak to your parents and to the Reverend Hassall. However … if anything like this occurs again, you may count on my doing something much, much worse. Do I make myself clear?'

They shuffled some more and nodded.

'*Do I make myself clear?*' he repeated, in a tone Tom had never heard before.

'Yes.'

'Yes *what?*'

'Yes, m'lord.'

'Good. Now get out of my sight.' And when they fled, he tossed the stone away, saying, 'Come on, Tom. Let's go. And you'd better bring bloody Figgy.'

It was a while before either of them spoke but eventually Tom said, 'Would you have thrown that stone?'

'No. But it didn't hurt them to wonder.' Julian glanced at him. 'I hope I've frightened them sufficiently. But if I haven't … if anything of the sort happens again, you will tell me.'

'You frightened 'em all right,' agreed Tom, his voice oddly thick.

'You will *tell* me, Tom. I mean it. I can't protect you properly if I don't know what's going on. And being your guardian is about more than putting a roof over your head. So if anyone bullies you … if anyone so much as looks *sideways* at you … you will tell me.'

With a small choking sound, Tom swung away hauling Figgy with him and sat on the stone wall, dragging his sleeve across his eyes. Julian shoved his hands in his pockets, wondering what he'd said to provoke this reaction but knowing better than to remark upon it. After a moment, he strolled over to sit beside the boy and simply waited.

'Sorry,' said Tom, at length. And then, 'Guardian? Is – is that what you are?'

'In an unofficial sort of way ... if that's all right with you?'

'Yes. I reckon so.'

'Good.' He sought for a way to lighten the moment and eventually said, 'Did you know that when Miss Lizzie first came she thought I was your real father.'

Tom's jaw dropped. 'She never!'

'She did. It gave her a very odd idea of me.' And when the boy looked at him, 'I'm twenty-eight, Tom – and you are twelve. Work it out.'

'Oh. Right.' A grin dawned and then evaporated. 'What did she say when you told her who Rob and Ellie and me *really* are?'

'She was relieved. Better that, she said, than working for the kind of loose-screw who went about siring children at the age of sixteen,' said Julian, amusement warming his voice. 'And for God's sake, don't tell her I told you. I'm fairly sure I shouldn't have done.'

Tom sat a little straighter. 'Miss Lizzie's all right, isn't she?'

'Very much all right – which is fortunate since, like a lot of other things, we appear to be stuck with her.' He felt the boy shift enquiringly. 'Well, I'm stuck with Chalfont and you're stuck with me ... and we're both stuck with bloody Figgy.'

He was finally rewarded with a chuckle. 'That's the second time you've called him that.'

'I know. Consider it a special occasion. And don't quote me. Miss Lizzie won't like that either.' Julian paused again and then said, 'Shall we walk on?'

'Yes.' Tom stood up. 'Let's go home.'

* * *

As promised, Arabella – enthusiastically assisted by Rob and Ellie – had organised a picnic on the hayfield that might once have been a lawn. Leaving the children to their own devices, she poured Julian a cup of tea and said, 'Gingerbread?'

'No thank you. I prefer to keep all my teeth.'

She grinned and sat down at his side on the blanket.

'What happened today?' And when he didn't immediately answer, 'Tom has a cut cheek, a bruise forming on his jaw and I've never heard him laugh before. What happened?'

Julian shrugged. 'A small incident in the village. And we ... talked.'

'Ah. I see. Male solidarity?'

'Something like that.' He glanced at her. 'What would you know about it?'

'I have brothers.' She trapped his gaze. 'Tell me.'

'I made it clear that this is his home and answered his questions as honestly as I could.'

'And the cut cheek?'

'A skirmish with some village bullies. He surprised me there. He wouldn't give Figgy to them. And he defended me when they called me a m--' Julian checked his unruly tongue just in time. If she didn't know what a molly was, he preferred not to be asked to explain it. 'They called me something rude and said I play music like a girl.'

Arabella's mouth quivered. 'And what did Tom say to that?'

'He could see me behind them so he asked whether they'd say it to my face.'

'And did they?'

His eyes rested on her with mild impatience. 'What do *you* think?'

'They didn't. So well done – and well done to Tom, too. I'm proud of you both.' She scrambled to her feet as if embarrassed and called to the children. 'Who's for a game?'

'Me,' said Rob and Ellie instantly. 'And Figgy,' Ellie added.

Tom groaned but volunteered to fetch the ball and the hoop.

Julian remained cross-legged on the grass, looking suspicious. 'What game?'

'Nothing very complicated. Just a lot of running about, trying to get the ball and score points by throwing it through the hoop Tom's hanging in that tree.'

He shook his head. 'I'll watch.'

She laughed down at him and stretched out her hand. 'Coward.'

As it always did, her laughter coiled through his chest and lingered there. He took her hand and let her pull him to his feet, saying, 'I'll make an idiot of myself.'

'*You* will?' grinned Arabella. 'Try doing it in petticoats!'

The game began sedately enough but swiftly descended into a chaotic scramble with a great deal of shoving, yelling and barking. When Rob and Ellie complained that it wasn't fair Sir Julian being taller than the rest of them, he held the ball out of their reach and volunteered to quit the field.

'Don't you dare!' said Arabella breathlessly. 'I'm winning.'

He raised one brow and tossed the ball through the hoop. 'You *were*.'

Tom swooped on the ball and successfully winnowed a path between his siblings only to be brought down by Figgy. Ellie cheered; Rob dived for the ball at the same moment as Arabella; and the resulting collision sent her slamming into Julian's chest.

His arms went round her automatically and for perhaps three seconds, they remained perfectly still, startled green eyes locked with grey ones in which laughter was fading into confused awareness. Equally muddled, Julian slowly – and very reluctantly - released her and stepped back with a brief, muffled apology.

'It is I who should apologise,' she said awkwardly. 'I trod on your foot.'

'Did you? I didn't notice.'

Oblivious to undercurrents, Ellie tugged Arabella's hand.

'Aren't you playing, Miss Lizzie?'

'What? Oh. Yes.' She swallowed hard. 'Yes. Of course I am. Now ... who's winning?'

CHAPTER ELEVEN

At breakfast on the morning following his arrival in London, Lord Sherbourne's letters included a polite note from the Duke of Rockliffe, bidding him to call in St James Square at eleven o'clock that morning. It could not, Ralph noticed, be described as an invitation ... a fact which told him that the interview would be no less unpleasant than he had anticipated. A trip to Dorset, he reflected grimly, as he pushed his plate aside in favour of more coffee, was likely to have proved preferable.

Rockliffe received him in the library and offered him a seat.

The earl said, 'Thank you – but I will stand. This need not take long.'

'I beg to differ,' returned Rockliffe. 'And since there are numerous other matters on which we may disagree, I see no need to add to them unnecessarily. Please sit down.'

Reluctant and already feeling at a disadvantage, Ralph did so.

'I assume Mistress Brandon has given you the salient facts about her journey?'

'She has. She has also assured both the duchess and me that your conduct towards her was above reproach.'

'If that is a question, I am not sure what answer you require,' snapped Ralph coldly. 'You have Mistress Brandon's word. That should be enough. If it is not, I fail to see how mine will satisfy you.'

'I would like to hear it, nonetheless.'

'You think I ruin innocents? Acquit me. I have never done so.' He drew a breath and tried to leash his temper. 'You need not have ordered me here this morning. I had every intention of calling upon you at the first opportunity. But for Mistress Brandon's obstinacy yesterday, I would have left my card with a message telling you so. As it is, ask your questions and let us have this over with.'

'As you wish. How badly damaged was the carriage?'

'The front near-side wheel was crushed and the coachman suspected a broken axle. From what I saw, the boulder the carriage had crashed into was the only thing stopping it from sliding down into the river.'

Rockliffe was frowning slightly. 'A lucky escape, then.'

'Yes. When I arrived, Mistress Brandon and her maid had been sitting in the rain for nearly an hour. I presume you would not have wished me to leave them there?'

'You presume correctly. Had help been sent for?'

'Yes. One of the outriders had --'

'Outriders?'

'She didn't mention those? There were two of them. They accompanied us throughout and I paid them off yesterday.' Ralph held the duke's gaze with an implacable one of his own. 'In the unlikely event that Mistress Brandon has been less than clear, allow me to reiterate. At both our enforced two-night stay in Offord Cluny and again at Stevenage, she and her maid shared a bedchamber. On all three evenings, there being no other choice, we dined together in a public room. Had it been possible to hire a carriage for her at St Neots, she would have completed her journey as she had begun it. Since it was not – and leaving her stranded without transport was out of the question – I had no choice but to take her with me. But from the time I first met her to the moment I set her down at your door, she was in no sense compromised.'

'Until Stevenage,' observed Rockliffe mildly.

'Indeed. I did not know of the presence of Lady Sutherland and her cousin – nor they of mine. By the time I arrived on the scene, the damage had largely been done. They knew who Mistress Brandon was and where she was going. My appearance was all it took for them to leap to the wrong conclusions.' Ralph paused and then said tersely, 'You know, of course, who Philippa Sutherland is – or was – in relation to myself?'

'Yes. Rumour has it that Philippa Wilkes, as she was then, might have married you had you not shot and killed her brother. Is it true?'

'Yes.'

'Making it the crux of the matter regarding her attitude towards you.'

'It would seem so.'

'In which case we can rely on Lady Sutherland shouting what she knows ... or rather what she *thinks* she knows ... to the world.'

'I am as aware of that as you could possibly wish.' Ralph knew what had to be said next and had come prepared to say it. 'If Mistress Brandon's reputation is damaged through Philippa's rantings ... be assured that I am willing to give her my name.'

The silence that followed this was profound. Finally, Rockliffe said, 'My congratulations, Sherbourne. You have surprised me.'

'Yes. I thought I would.' The words contained a hint of bitterness. 'You believe I have no honour worth mentioning, do you not?'

'I thought,' corrected his Grace gently, 'that you would baulk at repairing a situation which, in essence, was not of your making. However, let us hope that such a sacrifice will not become necessary. I believe I still wield some influence.'

'Undoubtedly. You intend to brazen it out?'

'In part. I also intend to lie.' A faint smile dawned. 'Lady Sutherland was mistaken in thinking my young cousin unchaperoned but for her maid. An elderly aunt also made the journey with her but, on that particular evening, was overcome with a megrim.' Rockliffe paused, shrugging slightly. 'It is unlikely that anyone will question my word. And it is a lie which, if asked, you will corroborate.'

'I see,' remarked Ralph sardonically, 'that you have it all worked out.'

'I hope so.'

'How fortunate.' He rose, conscious of an odd tight feeling in his chest. 'Otherwise you might have been forced to acquire me as a relative.'

The duke also stood. 'I am rarely *forced* to do anything. But you are right in thinking that I do not consider you a suitable husband for Arabella ... though perhaps less so than if you had not offered. However, I would prefer that she finds a gentleman who *wants* rather than is merely *willing* to marry her. Doubtless you see the distinction. I will also admit that, in certain respects, your own reputation would be a matter of concern.'

'Of course. We are once more back to the matter of the duel, are we not? God forbid that you should have a murderer in the family.'

'One would certainly rather not,' agreed Rockliffe urbanely. And then, 'At the time, I recall your second ... Mr Lazenby, was it? ... telling a different and somewhat peculiar story.'

'So peculiar, in fact, that no one believed it.'

'Should they have done?'

'What do you expect me to say?' demanded Ralph aridly. 'That Richard was lying? And what is the point in my saying anything? Edgar Wilkes will still be dead. So I thank you for asking – but I believe I will decline.'

* * *

At Phanie's exclusive establishment, the Duchess of Rockliffe said, 'The cornflower embroidered taffeta and the rose-sprigged cream silk, Arabella – and please do not argue. I promised your mother that you would have gowns in the latest mode ... and one cannot do better than Phanie.'

Feeling awkward and embarrassed, Elizabeth managed a smile but said, 'It is very generous of you, Cousin Adeline. But if – if there is to be any talk --'

'There will not be any talk because Tracy will not permit it,' said Adeline, calmly. 'Now ... I think we might pay a call on Lady Amberley. You will meet her again on Friday, of course, but Rosalind has a way of silencing gossip and there is no harm in sewing a few seeds in advance. Ah – I ought to warn you that she is blind. It isn't at all obvious. But I recall wishing someone had told me rather than assuming I knew.'

When they arrived in Hanover Square, the butler informed them that the marchioness was taking tea with Lady Cavendish.

'Excellent,' murmured Adeline. 'Dolly will be helpful, too.'

Unsure what this might mean, Elizabeth followed the duchess and found herself facing two ladies; the older, extremely modish and the younger an exquisite brunette.

'This is a pleasant surprise,' said the dark-haired lady when Barrow had announced her unexpected guests. And with a tiny laugh, 'Actually, Dolly and I were just talking about you.'

Elizabeth's heart lurched. Surely Lady Sutherland could not have set tongues wagging already? But Adeline merely smiled and said, 'Well, if you were wondering whether Arabella had arrived at last – here she is. Lady Amberley and Lady Cavendish, my dear. Two very good friends of mine.'

Elizabeth curtsied and then, rather shyly, took the marchioness's outstretched hands.

'Welcome,' said Rosalind, drawing the girl down to sit beside her. 'Did you have the most horrendous journey?'

'It wasn't without adventure,' agreed Elizabeth dryly.

'I'm not sure whether it was an adventure or a *mis*adventure,' remarked Adeline. 'But, in a nutshell, after Arabella's carriage came to grief, she and her maid were rescued from the roadside by none other than Ralph Sherbourne.'

'Goodness!' exclaimed Dolly Cavendish. 'I'm surprised he didn't simply drive on by.'

'He was quite kind,' offered Elizabeth. 'Although it was clear he didn't welcome our company. But the roads were dreadful and my coach was badly damaged so … '

Seeing Elizabeth hesitate, Adeline said briskly, 'So Sherbourne brought her to London himself. They were together for four days. However, since Arabella's maid was with her the entire time and his lordship behaved like a gentleman, it wouldn't have mattered had they not been seen in each other's company.'

'By whom?' asked Rosalind.

'Philippa Sutherland.'

There was a tiny incredulous silence. Then Rosalind said uncertainly, 'Wasn't her brother the man Sherbourne killed in a duel some years ago?'

'Edgar Wilkes. Yes.'

Elizabeth's breath leaked away. She thought weakly, *Oh. That explains a lot.*

'There was more between Kilburn – as Sherbourne was then – and Philippa Wilkes than the duel,' said Dolly. 'Oh, that's all anyone remembers now. But before it – *until* it – the whole of society was enjoying watching Kilburn walking around heart-on-his-sleeve, stars-in-his-eyes besotted.' She shrugged. 'It isn't hard to understand that Philippa couldn't or wouldn't marry her brother's killer. Kilburn, of course, went to lick his wounds in France ... and came back the discreet rake he is now. It makes one wonder whether Philippa cut deeper than one would have imagined possible. Certainly Sherbourne shows no sign of risking his heart again, despite every pretty young widow in London competing for his reputedly talented attentions.'

'Dolly,' said Adeline aridly, 'will you please stop shocking Arabella.'

'I'm not shocked,' lied Elizabeth weakly. 'But I'd like to ask something, if I may?'

'As long as it isn't about what her ladyship thinks Sherbourne's talents are.'

'It isn't. I wondered why you all seem to dislike him.'

'Not me,' declared Rosalind immediately. 'I've never met the man.'

'No more have I,' admitted Adeline reluctantly. 'I've merely seen him from time to time – though not often, since few hostesses invite him.'

'I've met him,' said Dolly, smiling at Elizabeth. 'But after days in his company and no pre-conceived ideas, what did *you* make of him?'

'He's clever ... yet also somehow confusing.' *And alarmingly attractive.* She hid that thought with a slight shrug. 'The perfect manners make it impossible to really *know* him but also prohibit dislike. And if he hadn't helped Annie and me, we would probably still be stuck in St Neots.'

* * *

Five busy days after arriving in St James Square, Elizabeth prepared to meet some of the duke and duchess's closest friends. She tried to be comforted by the assurance that the gathering was both small and informal; she also tried to rid herself of the idiotic wish that Lord Sherbourne was to be present. She might not be sure what he was really saying half of the time but at least his face was familiar. And since learning that, contrary to expectations, his lordship had signified his willingness to wed her should the need arise, Elizabeth's feelings towards him had gathered an element of something she could not quite identify.

'Chin up, Miss,' said Annie bracingly as she put the finishing touches to Elizabeth's hair. 'You look a treat. That polonaise could've been made for you.'

'It *was*,' muttered Elizabeth. 'How many times must I remind you to be *careful*?'

'I *am* careful when anybody's about.' Annie tweaked a curl into place. 'There. Perfect, if I do say it who shouldn't. Now ... off you go, Miss *Belle*. And enjoy yourself.'

She joined the duke and duchess in the drawing-room just as sounds from below betokened the first arrivals.

'Cassie and Sebastian,' said Adeline. 'I particularly asked them to be early.'

Within an hour, four of the five couples had arrived – as had the duke's friend Mr Fox, thus giving Elizabeth her first glimpse of the fashions favoured by the Macaroni club. As for the other gentlemen – my lords Amberley and Sarre, Mr Audley and Lord Harry Caversham – all were elegant, good-looking and possessed of easy charm. All bowed over Elizabeth's hand ... after which, she found herself surrounded by their ladies.

It took less than five minutes for Elizabeth to understand why Cousin Adeline had wanted Cassandra Audley to arrive first. The two of them were the same age and similar in nature, so Elizabeth liked Cassie immediately. She also liked Caroline, Lady Sarre. And though the seeming ebullience of Rockliffe's sister, Lady Elinor Caversham, took a little more getting used to, her forthright friendly acceptance was hard to resist.

Last to arrive – and greeted with much good-natured banter – was the duke's brother, Lord Nicholas Wynstanton and his beautiful red-haired wife. With an elegant shrug, Madeleine informed the company that she was reforming Nicholas's time-keeping by degrees, since rapid adjustments represented too great a shock to his system.

Towards the end of supper, Rockliffe proposed a toast of welcome to Arabella and then, having briefly described her journey said, 'Sherbourne is convinced that Philippa Sutherland will try to make mischief – and I agree. Therefore, should anything be said in your hearing, I would be obliged if you would look suitably mystified and remark that surely her ladyship must be mistaken. Mistress Brandon's elderly aunt was travelling with her as chaperone, was she not?' He paused and, with a sardonic smile, added, 'She wasn't, of course. So please do not allow yourselves to be drawn into supplying details.'

'Goodness,' remarked Nell Caversham a little later when the gentlemen had gravitated to the card table, leaving the ladies to gossip amongst themselves, 'You had Ralph Sherbourne all to yourself for four whole days?'

'Not entirely,' said Elizabeth. 'My maid and his lordship's valet shared the carriage with us. And he spent most of the time reading.'

'*Reading*?' echoed Nell, as if she'd been told Sherbourne had passed the journey painting his toenails pink. 'How disappointing! When Cassie and I made our come-outs, there were at least half a dozen girls who were desperate to catch his eye but he never showed the least interest – which naturally made him all the more attractive. And there's no denying that he *is* attractive.'

'Looks,' remarked Cassie, 'are beside the point. The only time I met him, he behaved atrociously.' She looked at Madeleine. 'He's been out of town since last November. Now he's back and presumably aware that he has a four-month-old nephew. Do you think he will try to mend matters between himself and Genevieve?'

'And demean himself by associating with a lowly gaming-house proprietor?' asked Madeleine acidly. 'I doubt it. Neither can I imagine either Genevieve or Aristide welcoming any such overtures.'

Adeline smiled at Elizabeth and said, 'Genevieve is Sherbourne's half-sister and she is married to Madeleine's brother who owns a very successful gentleman's club. I don't suppose the earl mentioned any of that to you?'

'No. Neither of us talked about anything of a personal nature.'

'Do you know what *I* think, Adeline?' said Nell suddenly. 'I think you should have invited him this evening.'

'Sherbourne?' laughed Cassie. 'I'd like to have seen his face if she had!'

'No.' It was Caroline who spoke. 'Nell has a point. The best way to make Philippa Sutherland's gossip appear ridiculous is to demonstrate gratitude and a degree of friendship towards Sherbourne for rescuing Arabella from an awkward situation.'

Elizabeth said hesitantly, 'I seem to be putting everyone to a great deal of trouble.'

'Nonsense,' retorted Nell. She looked at Adeline. 'It's the Cavendish ball next week. Dolly won't have invited Sherbourne since he's only now returned to London. But I imagine she *would*, if someone asked her to. What do you think?'

There was a brief silence. Then Adeline said, 'Yes. I'll call on her tomorrow. Well done, Nell – it's a good idea. I wish I'd thought of it.'

* * *

Lord Sherbourne, meanwhile, was in Dorset and riding to Finchley Farm. He was not looking forward to the coming interview. He was fairly sure he knew how it would end. The only thing he could look forward to was seeing Cedric's face when he knew it too.

He was received by a very grim-faced Mr Belcher and, having apologised for being unable to arrive sooner, added, 'You also have my sincere apologies for this whole unfortunate affair. However, while someone retrieves my brother, perhaps you and I can discuss what is to be done.'

'My sons are fetching him now,' replied Mr Belcher. 'As to what's to be done ... there's only one thing I know that will repair the damage.'

'Ah. Marriage.' Exactly what he had expected. 'Is that what your daughter wants?'

'It's what he promised her before he took her maidenhead. Let's be clear about this, my lord. My Jenny is no light-skirt and she'd not been with a man before your damned brother came along with his fancy manners and promises.'

'I'm sure. But candour compels me to admit that Cedric is weak, stupid and irresponsible. Does Miss Belcher want that sort of husband? Do *you*?'

'Trying to talk me out of it, are you? Well, it's no more than I expected.'

'You mistake me, Mr Belcher. I am merely pointing out what you would be getting,' sighed the earl. 'Forgive me for asking ... but is your daughter with child?'

'She might be. It's too soon to tell.' The farmer turned his head. 'Sounds like Mr Harcourt's about to join us. He was damned lucky my boys didn't knock seven bells out of him. It was only Jenny shouting that he was going to marry her that stopped 'em. But none of us trusted him not to disappear – which is why we've had him under lock and key.'

'I had been trying something of the sort myself,' murmured Sherbourne.

The door opened and Cedric appeared, flanked by two of Mr Belcher's brawny sons. He looked grubby, dishevelled ... and frantic. His first glimpse of his brother produced a look of wary relief and he said unsteadily, 'Ralph – thank God. They've been keeping me a prisoner. *Me*! In a bloody *hovel*! You've got to make them let me go.'

'I don't have to do anything, Cedric. As usual, you find yourself in a mess of your own making. Sit down.'

'But they've got it all wrong! She – she chased after me and – and, no matter what she says, I wasn't the first. There'd been others. Why won't anybody *believe* me?'

'Shut your filthy mouth or I'll shut it for you,' growled one of Jenny's brothers.

Cedric quailed and directed a pleading stare at his brother. 'Ralph – *please*!'

'*Sit down*.' Although his voice was no louder, there was disgust and menace in the earl's tone. Then, when Cedric had been shoved into a chair, he said coldly, 'You have just been given some good advice. Heed it.' He turned to Mr Belcher senior. 'I suggest that your sons leave this matter between the three of us for the time being … but to perhaps find out if Miss Belcher wishes to join us?'

'Aye. That'd be best.' With a jerk of his chin, Belcher told his sons to leave and, when they had done so, he glared down on Cedric, saying, 'You're a bloody disgrace, young man. And if you try blackening my Jenny's name again, I'll let Aaron and Ned give you a lesson you won't forget in a hurry.'

'Do not,' added Sherbourne, 'expect me to protect you. I have done that for the last time. Henceforth, you reap what you sow.'

Mr Belcher shot him a look of mingled surprise and approval. Then the door opened again … and Jenny stepped hesitantly into the room.

She was a pretty child … child being the operative word since Ralph didn't believe she was a day over seventeen … and possessed of blue eyes, glossy brown curls and a body just blossoming into womanhood. Flags of colour flew in her cheeks and her eyes darted around the room before fixing themselves on Cedric with an expression which, in Ralph's opinion, his brother didn't deserve. He stepped forward, bowed and with an encouraging smile, said, 'Please sit down, Miss Belcher. There is no need to be embarrassed – or to fear that I blame you for any of this.'

'Oh.' She perched on the edge of a chair. 'You d-don't?'

'No. Your father says that my brother promised you marriage. Is that true?'

She nodded vigorously. 'Yes, my lord. If he hadn't, I'd never have – have --'

'I didn't,' blurted out Cedric. 'On my honour, Ralph – I --'

'If you had even a shred of honour,' came the cutting reply, 'we would not be having this conversation. Now be silent. I will tell you when you may speak.' He turned back to the girl. 'He offered marriage. And you believed him?'

'I – yes.' She bit her lip and her eyes filled with tears. 'I shouldn't have, should I?'

'No. The only thing about Cedric on which one may always rely, is his ability to lie. However ... knowing this, is it remotely possible that you *wish* to marry him?'

'Y-Yes, my lord. I believe I l-love him.'

'God help you, then,' breathed Sherbourne. And to her father, 'The final word has to be yours, Mr Belcher. The only other thing I can offer is financial compensation ... if you feel that worth discussing.'

'I don't. If it turns out Jenny is expecting, money isn't going to mend matters, is it?'

'No. It is not.'

Cedric looked disbelievingly at his brother. He said, 'Ralph? You – you're not going to make me marry her, are you? You *can't*. I don't *want* to be married!'

'Then it is a pity you did not think of that sooner,' said Sherbourne, icily dismissive. 'Very well, Mr Belcher. Have the banns called and send me word when the ceremony is to take place. In the meantime, I suggest that you continue to keep my brother contained – though *not*, perhaps, in the gamekeeper's cottage? I will have his clothes sent from Gardington. And at some point, we should consider where he and your daughter are to live once they are married. It will not, I regret to say, be in my house.'

Cedric erupted from his chair and grabbed his brother's arm.

'Ralph – what the hell are you doing? Trying to frighten me? You can't *mean* this – you *can't*! You've got to get me out of it!'

Shaking himself free and stepping back, Sherbourne said, 'No. I am done with you, Cedric. In future, you can go to the devil your own way.'

CHAPTER TWELVE

Arabella stared at the letter, her vision blurred. She had known it would be from Aunt Maria. Of course she had. What she *hadn't* expected was for it to release a flood of homesickness. Suddenly, more than anything she wanted a letter from her own mother or from Max; and because she knew she wouldn't get either for as long as she stayed at Chalfont, stupid tears welled up. Blinking them back, she told herself not to be an idiot. In two months, three at the most, she would be home again, the adventure behind her ... and everything would be just as it was before.

Except that it wouldn't, would it? The knowledge came unbidden and not entirely understood. *After this ... after Julian and the children and everything here ... how can things at home ever be just as they were*?

Arabella dried her eyes, blew her nose and straightened her spine. Then she asked herself the obvious question. If Max arrived at the door right now to take her home ... would she want to go? And the answer, without even having to think about it, was that she wouldn't. Not yet. Not until she knew Julian better; not before the harpsichord was fully restored; and not until she had heard him play it.

For now, however, it was time to embark on her mission for the day. In truth, there were two missions – though the second might well depend on the success of the first. So as Violet was finishing her hair, she told her what she wanted to do.

The girl's jaw dropped. 'Go down the cellars? Me? No. I'm sorry, Miss Lizzie – but no.'

'We'll take a couple of lanterns and --'

'No, I tell you! It'll be black as pitch and there'll be rats.'

'Then we'll take a shovel to hit them with. Come on, Violet. Ladies' maids have to be intrepid. It isn't all hair-tongs and goffering irons, you know. Please? I promise it won't take more than ten minutes.'

'Oh bloody hell. Alright. Ten minutes, then. But if we get bit by rats --'

'We won't,' agreed Arabella, refusing to contemplate this possibility. 'Let's go.'

'What do you want in here, anyway?' asked Violet, as they opened the cellar door and peered down into the depths. 'Smells as if something died down there.'

Arabella decided not to think about that either. Holding her lantern in one hand and her skirts clear of the filth in the other, she trod carefully down the stairs. She said, 'The late earl was a drunkard. If he kept wine, this is where it will be.'

'But he's been dead nigh on eighteen months. Anything that's left will have gone off.'

'Perhaps – perhaps not.' She reached the foot of the steps, lifted the lantern high to send the light as far as possible ... and saw the racks. They weren't by any means full but equally, they were not empty. Arabella said, 'Come here and hold my lantern.'

A scurrying sound kept Violet glued on the second step from the bottom.

'*Violet!* The sooner I look at these bottles, the sooner we leave. Now *come here*!'

'Oh lord!' moaned the maid, edging her way across the floor. 'Do hurry up, Miss.'

Arabella shoved the lantern at her and started sliding out bottles. She might not drink wine herself very often, but Max and Adam had taught her what to look for on a label. By the time she had examined half a dozen she realised that, as she had hoped, the fourth earl had a decent palate and that, since it had been properly stored, the wine should be as good as it had ever been, if not better.

Grinning in triumph, she carefully put all but one of the bottles back and said, 'Thank you, Violet. I've found out what I wanted to know. Let's get out of here.'

* * *

Julian was on the barn roof, re-laying shingles under the direction of Mr Ridley. As usual, he was wearing neither coat nor cravat, his shirt-sleeves were rolled up and the usual stubborn lock of hair was curving about his cheek. To Arabella, experiencing a complex mix of sadness, affection and anger, he looked beautiful.

'You bain't doing that right,' observed Mr Ridley complacently. 'You bain't overlapping 'em proper.'

'I am doing exactly what you told me,' replied Julian through his teeth. 'And the reason I am doing it at *all* is because you can't be scrambling about on a roof at your age. So hold your tongue and check the gates haven't mysteriously opened themselves again.'

The old man gave a sour laugh and hauled himself to his feet.

'Ain't no mystery – and did it first thing.' He winked at Arabella and turned to go. 'Show some muscle, m'lord. There's a pretty lass here admiring you.'

Startled, Julian glanced round. 'Oh – Mistress Marsden. Wait. I'll come down.'

When he was safely on the ground, she said, 'You asked me to use your given name. I'll do it if you stop calling me Mistress Marsden.'

He looked away and then back, as if hiding a thought. 'What would you prefer?'

It came to her that what she'd *prefer* was the thing she couldn't have. The children called her Miss Lizzie and she didn't mind that. Having Julian use a name other than her own somehow brought home the extent of her deception. She wished she hadn't said anything. But it was too late to go back so she swallowed the odd lump in her throat and said, 'Elizabeth?'

Julian nodded. 'Elizabeth, then. Now … what brought you out here?'

She opened her mouth to tell him and instead, gesturing to the barn roof, said, 'You shouldn't be working as a labourer. Is there no one else who could do that?'

'Not today. And with the corn still in there and Ridley convinced we'll get rain overnight, it won't wait.'

The anger she'd felt earlier re-surfaced. A thousand pounds or even five hundred would make such a difference here. Day after day, the man in front of her struggled to hold everything together without help or hope. *If Max was here*, she suddenly thought … *if Max could see what I see, he would help. I know he would. But he's not here, nor can he be and nor can I ask him.*

She said baldly, 'There's a quantity of good wine in the cellar.'

'Wine?' he asked blankly. Then, 'What of it?'

'You can sell it. If it is as good as I think it is, it should fetch a fair price.' She paused, then added, 'I brought a bottle upstairs so that we can make sure it hasn't deteriorated.'

For a long moment, Julian simply stared at her. Then he smiled; an inviting, half-sweet and half-wistful smile. 'You want me to come inside and drink wine with you?'

Oh don't, she thought helplessly. *Don't smile at me like that.*

'Perhaps after you've finished the roof? I wouldn't want you to risk a broken neck.'

'No more would I.'

'Later, then. I don't know why I was in such a hurry to tell you.' She gave a tiny laugh which, even to her own ears, sounded self-conscious. 'Stupid of me.'

'No. It wasn't. Today … hasn't been going well. The possibility of making a little money is a much-needed bright spot. So thank you.'

Arabella nodded and walked away, her mind a seething mass of emotions.

Julian watched her until she vanished from his sight round a corner. Then he hauled in a long, unsteady breath and thought, *A bright spot? Yes. But it isn't the wine. It isn't even that she thought of it and went into the cellar to find out. The bright spot is her. Elizabeth. It's the easy affection she gives the children … and trying to help in other ways because she sees how bad the need is. It's listening to her laugh and being able to talk to her without feeling clumsy or stupid.* He shoved his hands through his hair, aware of a constriction in his chest. *But I can't – I mustn't – allow myself to rely on any of it because she may not stay. And if she doesn't … well, I won't think of that.*

* * *

They met, as usual, in the dining-parlour.

Arabella smiled brightly at him and said, 'Is the barn roof watertight?'

'I hope so.'

'Good.' She hesitated briefly. 'What was that you and Ridley were talking about this morning? Something to do with gates being opened?'

He shrugged. 'Mr Bascombe, whose lands lie alongside mine, has a grudge regarding a stream. He has been threatening legal action for some time now but never taken the final step. He just sends somebody to open gates so the few sheep we have get out.'

Arabella frowned. 'That is iniquitous. He should be stopped.'

'Yes. But it isn't that simple.' Julian drew one finger down the dusty bottle beside him on the dresser. 'Is this part of your hoard from the cellar?'

'Yes.' She allowed him to change the subject and put the Bascombe problem aside for consideration later. 'I've opened it and allowed it to stand but couldn't find a decanter. It's a 1772 burgundy from the Auxerre region.'

'And that is good?'

'It comes from a reputable vineyard,' Arabella temporised, unable to say that it was a label she had seen at home. 'As to taste, I'm no expert.'

'Unfortunately, neither am I.' Flinging an unexpected grin in her direction, Julian poured two small glasses, then turned and handed her one of them with a slight bow. 'Your very good health, ma'am.'

'And yours, my lord,' she retorted, before taking a cautious sip and promptly wrinkling her nose. 'Oh. It's very dry.'

Julian examined his glass against the light and then tasted it. It *was* dry … but also rich and smooth. Compared to the cheap wine he had always been accustomed to it was nectar. He took another very appreciative sip and said, 'How many bottles are there?'

'Of this specifically? I don't know. Altogether? Seven or eight dozen.' Arabella reached over and tipped the contents of her own glass into his. 'It must be worth something, mustn't it?'

'I imagine so. But to sell … it would have to go to Newark.' He thought for a moment. 'There's a monthly auction.'

'Perfect!' Arabella's face was suddenly vivid with excitement. 'If it was advertised and if there is more than one gentleman interested in buying ... what do you think?'

What Julian thought was that she looked warm and beautiful and he wanted something he wasn't allowed to want. He said, 'I think we can only hope.'

She sensed but didn't understand his withdrawal.

'You're right, of course. I'm getting carried away.'

I wouldn't mind carrying you away, said an unruly and startling voice in his head before he silenced it.

'And why not? I would never have thought of it and I'm grateful.'

'Don't be. It was just an idea. It might have been nothing.'

'No,' he said simply. 'It wouldn't. You didn't have to do anything ... but you did.'

A wave of increasingly familiar confused tenderness engulfed her. Before he could see it in her face, she turned away to pull the bell summoning Violet with their dinner. 'I had another idea as well. It concerns the local corn-mill.'

Julian's brows rose. 'It's for sale.'

'I know. I saw it in the newspaper. It has been for sale for months and, for some incomprehensible reason, no one has yet bought it.' Arabella continued fussing with the table-settings so she wouldn't have to look at him. 'I can't understand that. How are you and the tenants and everybody else managing?'

'This is the first year in the last four that Chalfont has grown corn – or much of anything else, for that matter. As to the mill, Mr Bascombe has one.'

'So everyone mills their corn there?'

He shook his head and, with rare acidity, said, 'Bascombe doesn't allow that. He forces them to sell their corn to him for less than market price, then mills it himself.'

'Does he, indeed?' Both Arabella's tone and the glint in her eyes boded ill for Mr Bascombe should he ever cross her path. 'So put a spoke in his wheel. Lease the corn mill.'

Julian blinked. 'Lease it?'

'Yes. Just for a trial period to begin with. It can't be that expensive and you could recoup some of the cost by charging your neighbours for the use of it. More importantly, it would get your own corn out of the barn and off to market ... and give other folk an alternative to Mr Bastard.'

'Bascombe,' he corrected on a tiny choke of laughter.

'Yes. Him.' Arabella turned back to finish re-arranging the table.

For what seemed a very long time, Julian stared at her slender back ... at the velvet skin of her neck and the cunningly-piled silver-gilt hair above it ... and discovered that he felt slightly dizzy. Finally, in a voice not quite his own, he managed to summon a few suitably innocuous words.

'How do you know these things? I'd never have thought of them.'

By the time she looked at him, he had his expression under some kind of control. Her brows rose and she laughed. Somewhere in the dim recesses of his mind was the knowledge that she had no idea what that did to him.

'It's only common sense,' she said prosaically. 'We can't have the corn going mouldy in the barn, can we? And I want you free to finish tuning the harpsichord so that I can finally hear you play.'

* * *

'I shudder to recall,' said Paul Featherstone, as he and Julian carried wine from the cellar to the farm's only cart, 'how close I came to dismissing Mistress Marsden before you'd even seen her. She's a mystery though, isn't she?'

'Is she? Why?'

'She's here because she needs to earn her living ... yet she knows a good bottle of wine when she sees it and has no trouble working out the cost versus benefit of leasing the mill? How many impoverished vicar's daughters are there, do you think, who could do that?'

'I don't know.' *And I don't care*, said that extremely active little voice in his head. 'It doesn't matter. She's good with the children.'

'Ellie likes her,' sighed Paul. 'I know. You told me.'

'It's not just Ellie. They all do – even Tom.'

Paul looked sideways at him. According to what Mistress Marsden had told Janet, it was Julian himself who had eventually won Tom over. But aware that probing did more harm than good, he said merely, 'Have you made a decision about leasing the corn-mill?'

'I'd like to. It makes sense. But we're barely making ends meet as it is. And the children need new shoes.' He let out an angry-sounding breath and added, 'In truth, they need new everything because nothing fits any more – but shoes are the priority.'

Resisting an impulse to curse, Dr Featherstone dug in his pocket, pulled out five guineas and slapped them in Julian's hand. 'Take it!' he snapped, when Julian tried to refuse. 'Don't be so bloody stubborn. Call it a loan, if you must. You can pay me back when the wine is sold. In the meantime, buy the shoes, rent the mill and treat yourself to a haircut. You look like a damned pirate.'

* * *

The wine was put in to the following week's auction and an offer was made to lease the corn-mill. Three days went by during which, just when Arabella had thought the tuning process was complete, Julian had begun the entire exercise again. Consequently, for the past three nights, she and the children had fallen asleep to the accustomed lullaby of endlessly repeated notes. Tonight, however, it was absent and Arabella drifted off vaguely supposing that Julian was either attending to a different task or had simply gone to bed like a normal person.

She dreamed she was in the York assembly-rooms with Mama. It was a concert and someone was playing Bach. For a time, she floated pleasantly with the music. Then she stirred, reluctantly coming half-awake. She turned over, searching for the dream that the music told her was still there. And in that second, she was suddenly fully alert and sitting up, her heart pounding. She hadn't been dreaming. Someone *was* playing Bach.

Arabella hurtled out of bed, grabbed her chamber-robe and flew out on to the landing. From the floor below, the music flowed on unabated; from above her, three tousled heads leaned over the bannister. She smiled, put her finger to her lips and beckoned them down. Quiet as mice, the four of them tiptoed down the stairs to the turn above the hall ... and there they halted, frozen into immobility.

For the first time, the library door stood open, its interior lit by three branches of candles. And in the centre of that circle of light was the harpsichord ... and Julian.

It was a moment like no other Arabella had experienced or could ever have imagined. The air in her lungs was replaced by painful sweetness and she wondered distantly if this was how magic felt. He looked so beautiful there ... so relaxed and confident and at home. And the sounds he was coaxing from that poor, abused instrument would have made angels weep. Her knees gave way and she sat down on the stairs, aware that the children were curling up about her. Tom looked amazed; Rob, fascinated; and Ellie's face simply glowed.

Bach became Mozart, then something hauntingly lovely that Arabella had never heard before ... then Bach again. He allowed no time between pieces. Indeed, Arabella wasn't sure he even knew they were there. He was in a world of his own ... *his* world; the place where he was most completely himself. Every now and then, he tilted his head over the keys, a frown or smile touching his face, as if something had surprised or particularly pleased him; sometimes he played whole passages, eyes closed, head thrown back and wearing an expression that was almost pain; yet the cataract of beauty cascaded flawlessly and unhesitatingly on.

There wasn't a single sheet of music in front of him. Every note he played was transmitted from his head to his hands with a quality of depth and feeling that, by turn, suggested joy or loss or triumph. Even when he played Bach, crisp and precise as it was, there was somehow an implicit mood or a feeling Arabella had never before suspected; and favourite, familiar pieces she had known for years were transformed into something fresh and new. There was so much more here than the manual dexterity required of any skilled performer. There was an indefinable quality that made one listen, not with one's intellect, but with one's heart. And the only word she knew that might describe it was genius.

It wasn't until Ellie yawned and sagged against her shoulder that Arabella realised how long they had been sitting there ... all three children, perfectly silent. Turning, she whispered, 'Take Ellie up, Tom – and go to bed yourselves. Leave the doors open if you want to ... but his lordship could play for hours yet.'

Tom nodded, lifted his sister and went quietly up the stairs. Rob hesitated a moment and said, 'How does he *do* that?'

'I don't know. Ask him tomorrow.'

He nodded and reluctantly followed the others. Arabella remained where she was for a time, aware that Julian was repeating something he had played earlier; the lovely bitter-sweet piece that bore no resemblance to any composer she knew. Then she rose and went quietly down to stand at the library door.

The piece came to an end and, for the first time, he did not immediately begin another. Instead, he said, 'How long have you been listening?'

'A while. Since you left the door open, I presumed that it was all right.'

He turned his head, his expression faintly baffled.

'I opened the door because it improves the acoustics.'

'Oh.'

'But I don't mind an audience. Did you enjoy it?'

'*Enjoy* it?' she echoed, incredulously. 'Julian, there aren't words. I have never heard anyone play like that – or even imagined that anyone *could*.'

He turned back to the keyboard, a small smile curling his lips. 'Thank you.'

Arabella detached herself from the door-jamb and crossed to stand over him with folded arms. 'Don't thank me, you idiotic man. Just tell me the truth. You're a concert performer, aren't you?'

'I ... would have been.'

'What does that mean?'

'The day before the lawyer found me, I'd just given my first recital.'

'In Vienna?'

He nodded and, lifting his hand, played a series of idle chords. 'I had three further engagements – one of them at the Belvedere. Instead, like the idiot you just called me, I came here expecting to go back … only to find I couldn't.'

For a moment, she was speechless. Janet had called his current life a waste. Janet, thought Arabella grimly, didn't know the half of it. She said abruptly, 'What was the piece you were playing just now?'

'Which one?'

'You'd played it earlier on as well. You played lots of pieces I couldn't name but could guess the composer – but not that one.' And when he said nothing, 'You know perfectly well which I mean. The one that made me want to laugh and cry at the same time.'

'Did it?' Pleasure flared in his eyes before his lashes hid it. 'That's nice.'

'Isn't it?' said Arabella sardonically. Then, 'Are you going to admit that you wrote it – or do I need to fetch the red-hot pincers?'

Julian kept his eyes on his hands. 'Did you really like it?'

'I loved it.' She fell silent, frowning a little. Then she said, 'This is ridiculous. You can't squander the rest of your life here. There must be something we can do.'

He shook his head, recognising the need to be cautious. He was on an emotional knife-edge born of the long-awaited freedom to play whatever he wanted for as long as he liked. And the music, more potent than any drug, was still inside him. He gave a derisive laugh.

'There isn't. Arranging a concert requires money and patronage. Nobody in England has ever heard of Julian Langham and the Earl of Chalfont is a bloody farmer. Do you think,' he finished with unusual asperity, 'that if there was the remotest chance of pursuing the career I've spent more than half my life working towards I wouldn't have found it by now?'

And before she could reply, he declared the conversation over by plunging into the Bach *Fantasia*. Arabella watched for a minute, half-inclined to stop him but choosing instead to sit on the floor at his side and let him play the piece through to the end. Then, before he could embark on something else, she said flatly, 'We *are* going to talk about this.'

'No. *We* are not.' He glanced sideways at her, then away again. He needed to play something else – anything else. It was the only way he could keep his mind off the fact that she was sitting there in her night-rail and wrapper with all that incredible hair tumbling down her back. 'I've already told you that there is no point – and *why* there isn't. Talking – *thinking* – doesn't help. I know that you mean well but some things can't be mended. Be satisfied with the wine and the corn-mill.'

'I can't. Music – this,' she touched the harpsichord, 'means everything to you.'

'Yes. What else is there?'

There was no satisfactory answer to that so she said slowly, 'Little – perhaps nothing, right now. But in time, that will change. You will meet someone and --'

'Are you talking about *marriage*?' he asked incredulously. 'That is about as likely as the concert platform. The title means nothing; the estate is a hairsbreadth from bankruptcy; and I have three illegitimate children. What woman would take that on?'

I would. The words rang inside her head without her having any idea where they had come from. *Stupid*, she told herself, *stupid, stupid, stupid – in every conceivable way*. She said carefully, 'If those are the only things she sees, she wouldn't deserve you anyway.'

The pit of his stomach seemed to drop away and he shut his eyes. Then, opening them, he said, 'I'm sorry. I think you should go.'

Arabella thought so too but she did not budge. Inside, she was a seething mass of frustration. Patronage and money, he'd said ... and she was fairly sure that the Duke of Rockliffe could provide both. Unfortunately, any approach she made would bring his Grace to Chalfont, thus ending her time here and Lizzie's stay in London.

But surely there was only one question which mattered. Which was more important? The masquerade ... or the life Julian deserved? And the answer was glaringly obvious.

Setting further thought aside for the moment, she got up from the floor and perched on the bench beside him, saying curiously, 'What is it called ... your own piece?'

'Nothing. I don't name them.' She was too close. He could feel the warmth of her against his side and smell the lavender-water she'd used to rinse her hair. He shifted to the far edge of the bench only to find that it wasn't far enough. 'It's just a sarabande.'

'Them?' She pounced on the word and turned her head to look at him. 'You don't name *them*? How many pieces have you written?'

'I've never counted. Three sonatas, a couple of toccata and fugues and a scherzo or two. I don't know.' He shrugged. 'I only keep the good ones. The others go on the fire.'

'*You burn them?*' Arabella stared at him in pure disbelief. 'Are you *completely* insane?'

'No.' He risked a sideways glance. 'I don't think so.'

'Who *says* those pieces are no good?'

'I do.'

'Exactly.' She stood up to loom over him. 'Do you suppose that *Mozart* burns music no one but him has ever heard because he decides it isn't good?'

'What has that to do with anything?' He rose and found himself facing her at inescapably close quarters. 'I'm not Mozart.'

'No, you're not. But perhaps you are as good. Perhaps you could be *better*.'

Julian's tension fractured and he laughed.

'Stop!' She grabbed his arms and shook him. 'Stop it! It isn't funny. You are burning *music*. *Your* music. How can you? It – it's downright *wicked*.'

The laughter dried in his throat. Not because, ludicrous though her faith in him was, it overwhelmed him but because the world had narrowed to the fact that the only thing separating her skin from his was the thin lawn of his shirt-sleeves. He couldn't think. He was drowning in grey eyes, full of passionate accusation and certainty ... all of it centred on him. It was too much. His hands moved of their own volition. One slid into her hair, while the other found her waist as he closed the space between them ... and then his mouth was on hers.

For the merest instant before the absolute rightness of it settled over her, surprise stopped Arabella's breath. Then there was nothing but him; nothing but the joy of his embrace and the gentle, questioning touch of his lips which she answered by putting an arm around his neck to draw him closer. A welcome, a promise, an invitation.

Her hair was cool silk in his fingers, the curve of her waist soft and warm, her mouth hot and sweet. Time ceased to exist and reality shifted. Desire blossomed, but though he acknowledged its presence, he felt as if he was hovering on the brink of something greater; something beyond the scope of his imagination ... like a concerto, as yet unwritten. It both lured and confused him. So he released her and stepped back to where the ground was safer until he could make sense of it.

The kiss had lasted mere seconds but when she looked at him, he saw his own startled awareness mirrored in her eyes. Clearing his throat, he struggled to find something to say and eventually settled for, 'Should I apologise?'

Arabella moistened her lips. 'Not on my account.'

'Then I won't insult you by lying. I know I shouldn't have done it and that it mustn't be repeated.' He stopped, as if puzzling something out. 'I could blame the music, I suppose. Sometimes ... afterwards, I'm not – I can't --' And stopped again, unable to explain how everything in him was very near the surface at such times

'Oh – I think the music had something to do with it,' she said softly. 'For both of us. Goodnight, Julian.'

And walked quickly away, leaving him alone.

* * *

She checked on the children and then climbed into bed knowing that she wouldn't be able to sleep. His kiss – every bit as beautiful as his music – had nearly been her undoing. Not in the physical sense, of course. Regardless of the fact that it had been lovelier and more pleasurable than David's kisses had ever been, and she'd have liked to stay in his arms forever, she had learned her lesson on that score. If he hadn't drawn back, she would have made herself do so. No. What she had wanted – and what she had very nearly *done* – was to end the deceit by telling him the truth; who she was, why she was there instead of her cousin ... everything. But that wasn't something to be blurted out on the spur of the moment with no thought to the consequences. Changing places had been her idea. She had talked Lizzie into it, so had no right to risk exposure without consulting Lizzie about that too.

But for reasons she wasn't yet ready to explore or even acknowledge, she wanted to be honest with Julian. After tonight, the pretence was no longer remotely acceptable; and ending it would not merely salve her conscience but might also bring advantages. Of course, in addition to Julian, she would have to confess to both her mother and Rockliffe. But that done – and assuming that the heavens didn't fall – she could approach the duke on Julian's behalf. She could cajole Max into making the Chalfont estate a loan. She could even allow herself a small, private and very unlikely fantasy that could solve every one of Julian's problems if neither Rockliffe nor Max would do so.

Her brain was reeling with too many ideas and the echoes of music.

First things first, thought Arabella. *Tomorrow morning, I'll write to Lizzie.*

* * *

Julian also lay awake. His blood was singing ... and it wasn't solely due to the music. Sexual gratification had never been a priority. He could go for months without missing or even thinking about it. His two brief liaisons had come about because the girls in question had pursued him – presumably because they considered him either attractive or some sort of challenge. During the short time each affair had lasted, they had seemed satisfied with his performances in bed but found them insufficient compensation for his behaviour outside it. Julian couldn't blame them for that. He supposed that one's lover forgetting one's existence half of the time might be a bit annoying. But Elizabeth was different. In the last few days, he'd caught himself thinking about her a great deal – more, in fact, than was either comfortable or wise. He looked forward to seeing her every evening and tried to think of things that might make her laugh. And tonight, when he had started to play, it hadn't been for himself alone.

The temptation to kiss her which had been lying in wait for some time had finally proved irresistible. Immediately, he had known that he wanted her; almost as immediately, he had been aware that there was – or could be – more to it than that. It wasn't a feeling he knew or could understand and it had been sufficiently alarming to stop him doing what he shouldn't have been doing anyway. She hadn't seemed to mind him kissing her but that didn't mean she would welcome him doing it again, possibly even more than once. He hoped she knew that he wouldn't have tried to take it any further. If she didn't … if she doubted his intentions, she might leave; and since he couldn't risk that happening, kissing her wasn't a mistake he could afford to make again.

He told himself he shouldn't feel like this – whatever *this* was. He should concentrate on practical matters such as how to find the money to pay for a new plough, the current one having outlived its useful life a decade or so ago. The trouble was that he seemed incapable of stemming the tide of stupid happiness that washed over him when she smiled or laughed … or merely entered the same room.

Was this what love felt like? He didn't know. He had never experienced it. But tonight – and entirely separate from the heightened emotion he always got from playing freely and at length – he'd had a dizzying sense of possibility. And had no idea what to make of it or how to find out if it had been purely in his imagination.

CHAPTER THIRTEEN

Having lingered at Gardington for several days to deal with matters brought to his attention by his steward, Lord Sherbourne returned to Curzon Street the night before the Cavendish ball and was astounded to find an invitation to it. He wasn't unacquainted with Lord and Lady Cavendish; no one in society was. But he couldn't think of a reason why he would receive an invitation from them when he had never done so before. Since, however, it would be stupid not to attend, he sent a footman round with an acceptance along with his apologies for not having responded sooner.

As soon as he walked into the ballroom, having exchanged greetings with his host and hostess, things that had puzzled him very quickly became clear.

Lord Nicholas Wynstanton dropped a heavy, if apparently amicable, hand on his shoulder and said, 'Sherbourne. We heard you might be joining us this evening. Come and take a glass of wine in the card-room.'

'That is extremely civil of you,' replied Ralph. 'Later perhaps?'

'Why not now?' asked Nicholas, smiling but not releasing his grip. 'Numerous other friends eager to drink with you, are there?'

'Probably not. But one prefers to have a choice in the matter.'

'Then let's make it look as if you have one.' Cheerfully manoeuvring towards the card room, Nicholas added softly, 'It wouldn't do to have folk think there's bad blood between us ... now would it?'

There being no answer to this, Ralph didn't attempt to make one.

Inside the card room and occupying a group of armchairs near the hearth were Amberley and Lord Harry Caversham. The obvious choices, Ralph supposed; Rockliffe's brother, his oldest friend and his brother-in-law. He found himself envying the duke's ability to keep things in the family. It was a comfort he himself had never possessed and was never likely to. Now he remained silent and waited to find out what these men wanted with him. Whatever it was, he doubted he would like it.

Harry Caversham held out his hand, saying pleasantly, 'Good evening, Sherbourne. You haven't been around much recently, I believe?'

'No. I have spent some months in Dorset.'

'Familiarising yourself with your estates?' asked Amberley, handing him a glass of wine. 'The early stages take time, do they not?'

'Indeed.' Ralph made no attempt to drink. Instead, letting a cool glance stray past the marquis and Lord Harry to land on Nicholas, he said, 'What may I do for you, gentlemen?'

'You can listen,' returned Nicholas flatly. 'The ladies believe a show of friendship will cast doubt on any gossip before it becomes a problem. We ... have our doubts.'

'Of course.' His smile was faintly acidic. 'Am I supposed to reassure you?'

'You can try.'

'Nicholas.' Amberley sighed faintly. 'We know you don't like Lord Sherbourne but --'

'No. I don't.' Dark eyes met and held the earl's tawny ones. 'Quite aside from everything else I and the rest of the world knows of you, my lord, Aristide Delacroix is not merely a friend of mine but also my brother-in-law – as he is yours. And your sister could have done much worse for herself. I hope I'm making myself quite clear?'

'Admirably so,' said Ralph. 'However, I don't imagine you brought me here purely to hear that. So perhaps we might come to the point?'

Harry laid a restraining hand on Nicholas's sleeve, saying, 'Leave it, Nick. You've said your piece ... but his lordship is quite right. We're under orders to make it look as though we're all getting on like a house on fire – and this isn't the way to do it.'

'I just wanted to make the position plain.'

'And you have done so.' Amberley raised his glass and low-voiced but firm, said, 'We are attracting attention. So smile, gentlemen and let us toast ... something.'

'Our accord?' suggested Harry, grinning. And before anyone could object, 'Here's to it!'

All of them drank; all of them smiled; all of them knew it for the charade it was.

Amberley, however, decided that it was time to address the situation. He said, 'We're all aware that you helped Mistress Brandon out of extreme difficulty and behaved impeccably towards her throughout. We're also aware that it was sheer bad luck you were seen together by Philippa Sutherland, of all people. Tonight is about telling the world not to believe everything it may hear. The suggestion is that you dance with Mistress Brandon – just once, in order not to raise speculation of an impending betrothal – and perhaps also Lady Elinor and the Countess of Sarre.' He paused and added, 'My wife, of course, dances with no one but myself.'

'And you can forget both my wife and Cassie Audley – neither of whom are predisposed in your favour,' advised Nicholas. 'So – do we have an understanding?'

'Oh yes,' Ralph replied, his tone rather more clipped than usual. 'You have made yourself abundantly clear, my lord. Do I have everyone's leave to go?'

'Don't be an ass, Sherbourne,' said Harry, by no means unkindly. 'We're trying to help, believe it or not. And when you've done your duty in the ballroom, perhaps you'd care to join me for a hand or two of piquet. Amberley is too good for me and Nick, no challenge at all … so I'd be happy to try my luck with you.'

* * *

Clad in the embroidered blue silk delivered only that afternoon from Phanie's, Elizabeth stood at the edge of ballroom with Adeline and Cassie and tried not to look like the country cousin she undoubtedly was. The room was vast, elegantly-appointed and ablaze with candles. There were banks of flowers and greenery, an orchestra that bore little resemblance to any at the York and Boroughbridge assemblies and what seemed to be hundreds of fashionably-dressed ladies and gentlemen. Half-dazzled and half-terrified, Elizabeth wondered whether she would ever get used to any of it.

The gavotte that had begun just as they had arrived was still in progress and during it Rockliffe had presented three gentlemen who had requested introductions and all of whom begged the honour of a dance. Even before that, her card had held the names of Mr Audley, Lord Sarre and the Marquis of Amberley. Elizabeth, who had little experience of even provincial balls, could only pray she would acquit herself adequately.

Nell Caversham, a vision in foaming rose-pink and white, rustled over to join them and said, 'Sherbourne is here and been dragged off to receive his orders. Personally, I don't consider that helpful – but Nick has a bee in his bonnet about the man.'

'In which he isn't alone,' observed Cassie. 'However, I've agreed to join the rest of you in giving Sherbourne a second chance – so I will. It's up to him not to make me regret it.'

'And here he comes,' murmured Adeline. 'Perhaps we could all *not* stare?'

Elizabeth watched from the corner of her eye as Sherbourne shook hands with Rockliffe and exchanged what looked like genial pleasantries. He wore a coat of dull gold brocade, over an embroidered vest and he was more attractive than she remembered. Seeing him again and knowing that, if it became necessary, he would offer her his name ... that, in doing so and had she been able to accept, he would make her a countess ... gave her a very odd feeling. And then he was bowing over her hand with that faint half-smile and the odd feeling abruptly became a sort of quivery warmth.

Hoping she wasn't blushing, she curtsied, smiled and said, 'It is a pleasure to see you again, my lord. I am quite sure that I didn't thank you adequately for your help.'

'It was my pleasure,' he replied suavely. 'But if you *wish* to thank me and your card is not already overflowing ... a dance would be more than enough reward for whatever small assistance I was able to provide.'

Unseen by anyone but Nell, Cassie rolled her eyes.

'I should be delighted, sir.' Elizabeth hesitated briefly. 'Perhaps ... the supper-dance?'

The hawk-like gaze widened a fraction, before briefly filling with something that might have been resignation as he said, 'The supper-dance, then. I shall be honoured.' With another slight bow and scarcely a pause, he turned his gaze on Nell. 'May I also solicit your ladyship's hand? You should know that I have been granted permission to ask.'

The caustic note was slight but Nell heard it and frowned. 'The only permission you need is mine, my lord. And you may have the first dance *after* supper.'

'I thank you.' He half-turned to go and then said softly, 'Mistress Audley, pray understand that, on the advice of Lord Nicholas, I am ... sparing us both a refusal.'

'When I need Nicholas to decide who I will or will not dance with, I'll let him know,' remarked Cassie. 'The gavotte is finishing and I am not engaged for the next set. It's yours, if you want it.'

'You mean it is mine if I am brave enough to accept it,' he retorted smoothly, offering his arm. 'And yes, ma'am. I believe my courage is adequate.'

As they moved away, Nell whispered, 'You're right, Arabella. He isn't stupid. But here is Lord Sarre to claim you. You'll like dancing with him. He's lovely.'

Elizabeth discovered that Lady Elinor had not exaggerated. Lord Sarre danced well, conversed easily and gradually banished her earlier nerves so that she was able to greet subsequent partners with less trepidation than she might otherwise have done. But for the next two hours, although she danced nearly every dance and enjoyed all of them, something inside her was waiting with illogical anticipation for the minuet before supper.

From time to time during the earlier part of the evening before he disappeared from the ballroom, she glimpsed Lord Sherbourne dancing with this one or that; Cassie, then Lady Sarre ... and later, a beautiful and extremely sophisticated-looking brunette who seemed to be enjoying his company very much indeed. It was at this point that Elizabeth edgily reminded herself that his lordship had only solicited *her* hand because he had been told to.

In fact, aside from the measure he had trodden with Caroline Sarre, Ralph was deriving little pleasure from the evening. He'd had to tolerate Cassandra Audley telling him it was time to mend his fences with his half-sister and her husband ... and then spent a

176

half hour deflecting Alicia Denning's attempts to lure him into bed. And when he'd escaped gratefully to the card room, a potentially enjoyable hand of piquet with Harry Caversham had been spoiled by the unsmiling presence of Nicholas Wynstanton. Had he not been promised to Lady Elinor for the quadrille immediately after supper, Ralph rather thought he would have left the instant his dance with Mistress Brandon was concluded.

It was this more than anything that, whilst waiting for the music to begin, was responsible for him asking Elizabeth why she had suggested the supper-dance.

'There wasn't any particular reason,' she replied, startled. 'Should I not have?'

'Perish the thought. I am looking forward to taking supper among Rockliffe's family and friends immensely. I am sure Nicholas Wynstanton has many more criticisms he would like to hurl at me. And I do *so* enjoy being told what I may and may not do.'

Before Elizabeth could reply, the music started – thus injecting a pause into the conversation. But as soon as they were close enough for her to be able to speak without being overheard, she said rapidly, 'I don't blame you for being annoyed, my lord – but I am not responsible for whatever Lord Nicholas may have said. And you needn't have pointed out that you are dancing with me for the sake of appearances. I'm already aware of it.'

Another pause, as the dance required them to move apart and circle another couple before coming together again. The instant they did, Ralph said, 'Who told you that?'

'You – a bare moment ago.'

'Pardon me – but I did no such thing.'

'No? Were you just not complaining about being told what to do?'

'I did not --' Once again, the dance sent them in opposite directions and he had to wait until he was facing her again. 'I was not referring to you.'

'Really? But if not me, then what?'

Elizabeth wasn't sure where the words were coming from and had a vague suspicion that she would regret them later. Ralph realised that he was on the verge of indulging in an argument in the middle of the ballroom and didn't know whether to be irritated or entertained. While he still had the chance, he murmured provokingly, 'Please stop scowling. It does not create the correct impression.'

'I am *not* --' began Elizabeth through gritted teeth, '- scowling.'

'No? You give a very good impression of it. Whose idea *was* this, by the way?'

'Whose idea was what?'

Having by now settled into the rhythm of when not to speak, Ralph waited for the opportune moment. 'Gathering me into the ducal fold.'

'Lady Elinor suggested it.'

'Ah. Of course.'

Neither of them spoke for a little while. Then Elizabeth said abruptly, 'At Stevenage ... why didn't you tell me who Lady Sutherland was?'

He remained silent so long, she didn't think he was going to reply. But finally he said, 'It would have served no more purpose then than it does now.'

The forbidding note was plain but she chose to ignore it and, as soon as she had the chance, said, 'Perhaps not. But I can't help wondering if --'

'I am sure you can't.' Ralph shot her brief hard glance. 'I am equally sure you have been fed numerous titbits to my discredit. Fortunately, my past is not your concern.'

They completed the dance in silence. Elizabeth managed to pin a smile on her face but wasn't sure how convincing it was. The single sideways glimpse that was all she permitted herself told her that Lord Sherbourne was also smiling – but in a way that made her wish she had left the matter of Philippa Sutherland alone. Supper, she thought with a sinking heart, was going to be fraught with pitfalls.

* * *

'Well,' said Adeline later that night when she and her husband were alone together, 'that seemed to go well enough.

And Lord Sherbourne was a surprise. I'd expected some species of practiced seducer not a coolly collected gentleman who can barely summon a smile. But despite that impenetrable reserve, I didn't dislike him.

'His willingness to marry Arabella if necessary is certainly a point in his favour,' agreed Rockliffe. Clad in a dressing-robe of black silk, patterned in gold, he poured wine for them both and sat down beside her. 'The problems surrounding Sherbourne are the same they have always been. He killed a man in a duel ... and his brothers are a disgrace. With regard to the former, I have a suspicion that it may not have been as straightforward as one might suppose. As for the younger Harcourts, I imagine they are the bane of his existence and that he does his best to restrain them. One also notices that Sherbourne's own behaviour has recently undergone a change.' He leaned back, contemplating the contents of his glass. 'At supper this evening, I had the impression that he and Arabella had argued. Has she said anything of that?'

Adeline shook her head.

'Nothing. And an argument suggests a closer relationship than I'd like to think exists. The earl may be willing to do the honourable thing but if he is as big a libertine as he's reputed to be – though I'm by no means convinced of that – it is unlikely to change. And after the debacle of her betrothal, Arabella doesn't need more heartbreak. Yes – I know reformed rakes supposedly make the best husbands but I'm not convinced of that *either*.'

Amusement lurked in Rockliffe's eyes.

'How fortunate, then, that our friends are gently spiking Lady Sutherland's guns.'

'Isn't it? Did you hear any hint of gossip this evening?'

'Naturally not. No one is going to speculate to my face. But Sebastian says that Lord Moreton expressed disapproval at Sherbourne's presence and followed it with a less than subtle enquiry about whether a happy announcement was imminent.'

'Yes. Lady Wendover asked Dolly the same thing – and went away disappointed.'

'Good. As ever, Charles Fox has his ear to the ground. Should the talk escalate, I shall have a gentle word with Phineas

Sutherland. He would not, I feel sure, wish his lady wife to make herself ... unpopular ... or worse still, a laughing-stock.'

Adeline eyed him admiringly. 'You are truly atrocious, you know.'

'I do my best. Now ... why does Mrs Fawcett think Arabella mistrusts the maids?'

She groaned. 'Symonds didn't trouble you with *that*, did he? It's nothing of the sort and so I told Mrs Fawcett this morning when she broached the subject with me. It's merely that Arabella's bed is always made and the room tidied before the maids go in each day. They thought her own girl, Annie, didn't know that it isn't a lady's maid's responsibility to perform these tasks. But when they told her so, she let slip that Arabella does them herself.' Adeline smiled at him. 'Now ... who does *that* remind you of?'

'Of you, my love, when we were first married.' Rockliffe's smile was replaced by a thoughtful expression. 'You, however, were unused to having servants attend you. Arabella is not ... or rather, she shouldn't be.'

'I thought that myself,' admitted Adeline. 'I suppose she may be trying to be as little trouble as possible – though that isn't a characteristic Louisa's letters led me to expect. But it's early days, so perhaps she is still a trifle overwhelmed by ducal pomp and magnificence.'

'Pomp and magnificence? Do we *have* some of that?'

'*You* have a great deal of it,' grinned his wife.

'Really? How gratifying.'

* * *

The following day brought Elizabeth numerous bouquets of flowers from the gentlemen with whom she had danced the night before ... all of them, that was, except the Earl of Sherbourne. For five days, she did not once lay eyes on him. She looked in vain for him at the Crewe assembly, the Delahaye soirée, the Linton rout and Drury Lane. And then, seemingly out of the blue, he sent a note inviting her to drive with him.

'Should I accept?' she asked Adeline.

'Do you want to?'

'I'm not sure. And after our last meeting, I'm surprised he has suggested it.' She coloured faintly. 'I asked something I shouldn't. He wasn't ... pleased.'

'I daresay – but does that matter?'

This wasn't something that Elizabeth had previously considered. She said slowly, 'I think so – though I don't know why it should.'

Adeline felt the first twinges of disquiet.

'Be careful, Arabella. Although I've a suspicion that Sherbourne isn't quite the villain many people think him, he is *not* a gentleman to take lightly or at face value. He is probably – indeed *must* be – capable of charm. And I can understand the temptation to find out what lies beneath that chilly exterior. But you should not allow your judgement be clouded by his willingness to do the honourable thing. That can only lead to disappointment.' She smiled suddenly. 'And now we should go. Caroline will be expecting us.'

Elizabeth's heart sank a little. It wasn't that she did not like Cousin Adeline's friends because she did – though understanding the various connections between them hadn't been easy. Some were related by blood, others by marriage and two couples by neither. But there had already been afternoons taking tea in the homes of Lady Elinor and the Marchioness of Amberley and, no matter who else was present, Elizabeth discovered that she could always be sure of finding Cassie Audley, Caroline Sarre and Madeleine Wynstanton there as well. All this was perfectly fine – even comforting. But because the last year had seemingly seen a procession of happy events, Elizabeth had begun to feel that she was straying into a meeting of the Young Mothers' Society. In short, however the conversation began, it inevitably ended with babies.

Rosalind Amberley's three year-old son now had a nine-month-old sister. Lady Nell was the proud mama of three-month-old Charlotte and Caroline Sarre of six-month-old Benedict while both Cassie and Madeleine were newly pregnant for the first time. And unfortunately it didn't stop there. The ladies *also* talked about other friends, currently absent from town. Thus

Elizabeth learned that Althea Ingram had given her husband twins ... and that, having previously adopted a little girl, Philip and Isabel Vernon had finally been blessed with a son of their own. In addition to their children, all these ladies had loving husbands and blissfully happy marriages. And though Elizabeth tried hard not to envy them, she was becoming depressingly aware that she herself would never have any of these things. When these weeks in London were over, she would go home and either dwindle into an old maid in the house where she had been born or do what she had intended to do before she'd let Belle persuade her otherwise and seek a position. Neither was an alluring prospect.

Today at Lady Sarre's small house in Cork Street, there was a new face. A beautiful dark-haired lady who was introduced to her as Madame Delacroix and who was apparently Madeleine Wynstanton's sister-in-law. Although something about the lady's eyes seemed familiar, Elizabeth did not immediately make the connection. She merely sighed inwardly when the other ladies asked the newcomer whether Etienne was still teething. Then, a little later, the lady crossed the room to sit at her side and murmured, 'I don't think you've quite realised who I am, have you?'

Baffled, Elizabeth said, 'I'm sorry?'

'They told you that Madeleine – Lady Nicholas – is my husband's sister.' Genevieve smiled a little. 'You'll meet Aristide later when he and some of the other gentlemen arrive. But everyone always feels awkward about mentioning my half-brother in my hearing ... so they don't, even though today they probably should have done so.' She paused, a tiny frown creasing her brow. 'He is Lord Sherbourne.'

'Lord Sherbourne?' echoed Elizabeth faintly. 'Oh.'

'Precisely. I understand that you recently spent some time in his company. I can't imagine you found that enjoyable or even comfortable. He is not always ... pleasant.'

'Perhaps not,' agreed Elizabeth carefully. 'But neither is he always *un*pleasant. And had it not been for his assistance, my maid and I would have been stranded miles from London without any means of completing our journey. So I'm in his lordship's debt.'

The frown vanished and Genevieve said, 'Of course. Please forgive my asking. It's just that Ralph and I have never got on well and his attitude towards my husband has fractured our relationship completely. Sometimes it's hard to remember that other people see a side of his character that he has never shown to me.'

'Lord Sherbourne dislikes Monsieur Delacroix?'

Unexpectedly, Genevieve laughed. 'You could say that – and the feeling is entirely mutual. But what Ralph *really* objects to is that Aristide owns a gaming-house. God forbid, you see, that a Harcourt should marry anyone who actually *works* for a living.'

What that told Elizabeth was that if Ralph Sherbourne knew she was lowly Mistress Marsden from the vicarage in Knaresborough, he wouldn't be taking her driving. The knowledge twisted something behind her ribs but she said merely, 'I see. But that is a fairly commonplace sort of attitude amongst the *ton*, isn't it? And perhaps his lordship will get used to the idea in time.'

'I suppose anything is possible,' agreed Genevieve, rising and shaking out the skirts of her gold-striped taffeta. 'But neither Aristide nor I are holding our breath.'

* * *

Lord Sherbourne was by no means convinced of the wisdom of that invitation. He suspected that Mistress Brandon would refuse it or be advised to do so … and told himself that that would probably be for the best. Rockliffe's stratagems to crush gossip might be working in his own circles but, in those Ralph frequented, Philippa's poison was beginning to leak out and was having the effect of dredging up the past along with the present. Ralph supposed Rockliffe must know this and be taking measures to combat it. But if, against all expectation, those measures failed … if Arabella Brandon's name appeared in one of the scandal-sheets next to his own … marriage might yet become the only solution. And Ralph was by no means blind to the advantages of a well-bred bride who, not being fresh from the schoolroom, was actually capable of holding an intelligent conversation.

He didn't think that living with Arabella would be a hardship; and bedding her *certainly* wouldn't be. But beyond his personal feelings was one inescapable fact. The earldom *had* to be secured – and the debacle with Cedric only increased the urgency.

The library door banged against the wall as Bertram erupted into the room clutching a note. 'Ceddie says you're making him marry the Belcher chit. You ain't, are you?'

'Yes.'

This stopped Bertram in his tracks, his mouth agape. Finally he said, 'I say, Ralph … you can't mean it. Not really. Ceddie wed to a farmer's daughter? After everything you said about Genevieve marrying that fellow who owns Sinclairs? This is worse, ain't it?'

'It is necessary,' replied Ralph. 'After the way he has behaved, Cedric is lucky the girl still wants him. For the rest, I am washing my hands of him.' He looked up into his brother's witless gaze. 'Take it as a warning, Bertram. The next time you run into trouble, I may wash them of you with equal rapidity. Your days of expecting me to prop you up are over. It is time you learned to take responsibility for your own actions … just as I have to do.' Ralph turned away and picked up his glass. 'As for Cedric, he will doubtless require you to stand up for him at his wedding so I suggest you return to Gardington and hold his hand until the happy day. Close the door quietly on your way out.'

* * *

At much the same time and having spent an evening watching Arabella holding no less than four potential admirers at arms' length with cool smiles and almost monosyllabic answers, Adeline said, 'Do you know, Tracy … I'm beginning to think that Arabella is almost *too* sedate – which is odd when her mother described her as being something of a hoyden.' She paused for a moment and then added, 'Actually, she isn't as Louisa described her in other ways – her looks, for example. Louisa said she was no more than passably pretty – which is not even *close* to the truth.'

'No,' he agreed thoughtfully. 'It isn't, is it?'

Adeline shifted in the curve of his arm to look into his face. 'What are you thinking?'

'I am thinking that, when added to the business of her tidying her own rooms, there seems to be one or two discrepancies too many. My suspicious nature, I suppose.'

'You have a theory?'

'Not exactly. What I have is a thought I really do not want.'

'Which is what?'

Rockliffe took his time about answering but finally, he said, 'Unless my imagination is running away with me, an unfortunate and extremely bizarre explanation is raising its head.' He sighed, leaning back against the pillows. 'Unlikely as it may seem, do you think it at all possible that our young guest is not Arabella at all? That she is, in fact, Cousin Elizabeth?'

Adeline stared at him incredulously.

'You think they changed places? Without anyone being aware of it? No. They can't have done so, surely? And why on earth *would* they?'

'I have no idea. I am only entertaining the notion at all because I can think of no other way to account for Louisa seeming not to know her own daughter. Can you?'

'No. If you put it that way ... no, I can't. But it's too preposterous!'

'Quite. So preposterous that they may have thought no one would ever suspect it.'

'Clearly, they didn't bargain for you, then.'

'Thank you ... I think.' Rockliffe paused, considering the matter. 'However, as you say the concept does rather over-stretch the bounds of credulity, does it not?'

'That is putting it mildly. No. There has to be some other --' She stopped abruptly. 'Oh. I've just remembered something else that has bothered me from time to time.'

'And that is?'

'Her clothes. They are lovely ... but not the colours which would suit her best. And once or twice I've felt that they don't fit as perfectly as they should.'

'As if, perhaps, they might have been made for someone else?'

'Yes.' Adeline looked at him forebodingly. 'I hope you're wrong about this.'

'Given the complications involved in correcting the situation should I be right, so do I.'

'And if you're not?' asked Adeline, 'How are we to find out? Based on such scant evidence – not to mention the sheer unlikelihood of it – we can't just *ask* her.'

'No. But assuming they *have* changed places, then Arabella is where Elizabeth should be … so learning something about the new Earl of Chalfont would appear to be the logical place to begin. In fact, I was considering doing so anyway, purely to assure myself that his household is … suitably respectable. I believe I will set the matter before Mr Osborne. He has been under-employed lately … and gathering information is a speciality of his.'

CHAPTER FOURTEEN

Arabella was prepared for awkwardness on Julian's part following their kiss and, knowing it would be up to her to diffuse it, steeled herself to do so only to be denied the opportunity. It was Saturday and so, with no lessons at the vicarage, she was breakfasting with the children in the kitchen. Ellie and Rob were surreptitiously slipping bits of toast and bacon under the table to Figgy; Tom had either chosen not to do the same or was merely better at hiding it. But when his lordship wandered in to lean against the door-jamb, all three children broke into spontaneous applause.

With his usual slightly embarrassed smile, Julian sketched a bow and, avoiding looking at anyone in particular, murmured, 'Thank you. I hope I didn't keep everyone awake?'

'It was lovely,' said Ellie. 'The loveliest thing ever.'

Before anyone else could speak, Rob blurted, 'Can *anyone* learn to do it?'

Tom snorted. 'Don't be daft, Rob. Playing like that takes years, doesn't it, sir?'

Julian's gaze rested thoughtfully on Rob. 'It does. But you can enjoy playing without taking it as seriously as I do. So yes, Rob ... anyone can learn.'

'Could *I*?'

'Do you want to?'

The boy nodded earnestly. 'Yes. Yes, please.'

There was a breathless hush while everyone waited for his lordship to speak. Finally, he said, 'Then I'll teach you. Come to the library when you have finished eating and --'

Rob was on his feet before Julian could complete his sentence.

'I've finished,' he said, his face aglow. 'Can I come now?'

'In just a moment.' A hint of laughter tugged at Julian's mouth. 'I came down to say that I am promised to the Misses Caldercott this afternoon. They have said that if anyone wished to come with me, there will be cake.'

'Us?' asked Tom, dubiously. 'All of us?'

'And Miss Lizzie?' demanded Ellie.

'Everyone.' Glancing at Arabella for the first time, he added innocently, 'Clean hands at two o'clock.' And restoring his attention to Rob, 'Clean hands for you *now*, if I'm to let you touch my keyboard.'

It came as no surprise to Arabella that the entire household managed to find a reason to linger in the hall while Rob had his first music lesson. The door had been left slightly ajar so they were able to hear his lordship's voice, low and encouraging and what could only be his lordship's hands demonstrating a simple scale before inviting Rob to attempt it.

At one point, Arabella heard Rob complaining that his hands were too small. And Julian's reply of, 'Mine were smaller than yours when I began. Now ... try again and remember to cross your thumb beneath your middle finger on the way up and middle over your thumb on the way down. Yes. Good. And again. Five more times until it feels natural.'

And later, when Rob sounding jubilant, had mastered the scale, Julian's voice again, explaining about black keys and white ones and the relationship between the two while he played a long, slow chromatic scale to illustrate the point. The child asking a barrage of questions; the man, quietly and patiently answering; and somewhere along the way, Arabella found it necessary to dash foolish tears from her eyes. Then, after nearly an hour, she heard Julian say, 'That's enough for today, Rob. Well done. When you've had a few more lessons and I'm satisfied you really *do* want to do this and will treat the instrument with respect, you can come in and practise. But for now, only when I'm here.'

'Yes, sir. Thank you.'

There was an odd sound, as if Rob had seized Julian in a hug, then his feet running to the door. Arabella whisked herself out of the way before she was caught eavesdropping.

* * *

Trailed by three unusually neat and tidy children, Arabella and Julian set off towards the village without speaking. Then, almost in unison, they said, 'About last night --' And stopped, looking directly at each other for a moment before Arabella laughed and Julian's gaze slid away.

'You first,' he mumbled.

'Last night we agreed apologies weren't needed,' she replied simply. 'They're still not. Given the magic you'd been making, what happened between us is hardly surprising. I'm not sorry and you shouldn't be, either.'

'I'm not.' He glanced at her, then away again. 'But I know I ought to be.'

'In that case, so should I. I'd no business intruding upon you in my night-clothes, with my hair hanging down my back.' She shook her head and added mischievously, 'My mama would have a fit if she knew.'

'It was beautiful,' said Julian. And in case she hadn't understood, 'Your hair.'

'Oh.' Arabella's colour rose a little. 'I've never liked it much … but thank you.'

He didn't reply and, after letting the silence linger for a minute or two, she said, 'Do you think Rob's enthusiasm for the harpsichord will last?'

'I don't know. Perhaps.' He thought about it and then, with a shrug, added, 'I was like him once. It lasted with me.'

'I doubt you had as good a teacher as the one Rob has.'

'That remains to be seen.'

'Can you stop being modest just for a moment? Rob's bursting with happiness and it's thanks to you.' She waited and when he merely walked on, looking straight ahead, 'Who *did* teach you? When you first started, I mean?'

'The church organist. I was eight but I could already use both hands and play tunes I knew by ear … so half-a-dozen lessons later, he told my parents to get me proper tuition.' He finally sent a brief glance in her direction. 'And after I threw a few tantrums, they did.'

Arabella laughed. 'Tantrums? *You*? I don't believe it!'

'It's true. Learning properly was a – a compulsion. So I persevered until I got Mr Bell. He came for three hours, four times a week and, as well as keyboard lessons, he taught me musical theory. That lasted until I was fifteen. Then, like the organist, Mr Bell said there was nothing more he could teach me and I was left to my own devices until Cambridge.' Julian's mouth curled wryly. 'Music isn't given much weight there. But Professor Ringwood was grateful to finally have at least *one* serious student so I got his undivided attention for two years. And then ... well, I'll leave you to guess.'

'He also said you were beyond his capabilities?'

'He told me not to waste a third year at Cambridge. He said I needed to go to a conservatoire – Paris or Vienna – where I could mix with other musicians and measure my skills against theirs.' He hunched one shoulder and added, 'My parents were dead by then and I'd inherited a little money. Not much ... but enough to get me to Vienna, afford lodgings and rent a harpsichord. I was twenty.'

'And then?' she asked softly.

He shoved his hands in his pockets, a sure sign that he was about to retreat.

'There's not much more. Do you really want to know?'

'Yes.' *Yes*, she thought. *I want to know everything about you. I want to understand how you've become the man you are. I want to learn how much gruelling work has gone into honing your talent. And I'm beginning to suspect that I want something I don't have the right to want and which I couldn't have even if you offered it. But I'll settle for whatever friendship we have ... and be grateful for that.* 'Yes. I really do.'

'Well, then. I spent seven years studying and practising ... playing in ensembles and taking composition seriously. I made ends meet by giving lessons and accompanying singers and violinists ... but I didn't mind because I knew that it would eventually be worth it. And one day Herr Krassnig heard me play and decided to take a chance ... and I gave a concert at the Schönbrunn.' He stopped again, seeming restless. 'That's it. You know the rest.'

She did and it made her so angry that she wasn't sure she could keep it out of her voice. Fortunately, Ellie chose that moment to pull one of Julian's hands from his pocket so she could hold it and said, 'Are the ladies nice? The ones we're going to see?'

'Yes. Before my harpsichord was mended, they let me play theirs. Theirs is much prettier. It has a painting inside it.'

'Will they let us see it?'

'Oh yes. I think you may count on that.'

* * *

It seemed to Arabella that there were a good many people out and about in the village. Women in little knots by their gates and men clustered outside the Dog and Duck ... almost as if they were waiting for something. But the Caldercott ladies didn't appear to notice anything unusual. They merely greeted Arabella warmly and welcomed the children inside with a commendable lack of fuss.

Miss Abigail said, 'Well ... this has certainly taken a while, Mistress Marsden. We were beginning to think Lord Chalfont was keeping you prisoner.'

Arabella shook her head laughingly and said, 'Nothing like that, I promise you. It just took time to settle in – and I've found plenty to do. But I'm delighted to make your acquaintance, ma'am.' She glanced to where Ellie and Rob were staring in awe at the lovely rosewood harpsichord while Julian, one hand resting casually on Tom's shoulder, talked quietly about the pastoral scene which graced the underside of the lid. 'Your kindness in letting his lordship practise here has meant a great deal to him.'

'It has meant a great deal to us as well,' said Miss Beatrice gently. 'Indeed, it has been a privilege. The last time he was here he said he was starting to tune his own instrument. Has he completed it?'

'Yes.' Arabella felt herself turning slightly pink. 'He was able to play it for the first time last night. He played for *hours* and it was ... well, there aren't words to describe it. He is remarkable, isn't he?'

Miss Beatrice patted her hand. 'Yes. He is. Truly gifted ... and such a dear, sweet boy. Ah – here is Millie with the tea.'

'Excellent,' said Miss Abigail. 'Come, children ... Tom, Rob, Ellie, isn't it? Yes. Don't look so surprised. Of course we know your names. Now, Cook hasn't had any young people to bake for in a very long time so there is a great deal of cake – much more than my sister and I can eat. I hope you're not going to tell them not to spoil their appetites, Mistress Marsden?'

'No.' Arabella gazed at the vast and tempting array of sweet things. 'How can I do that when I shan't worry about spoiling my own?'

'That's the spirit,' boomed Miss Abigail. And to the children, 'Come along, you three. Take a plate each and help yourselves … and you, my lord. This may be a special occasion but the rules still apply.'

'Rules?' asked Rob uncertainly.

'For me, not you,' replied Julian with a grin. 'The ladies think I don't eat enough so the rule is food before music. Ellie … choose something for me.'

The child stood before plates of little honey cakes and ones topped with soft icing; tarts of every variety – lemon, custard and strawberry; gingerbread, fruit scones and slices of apple pie. A frown creased her brow and turning to his lordship, she said, 'I can't. It all looks nice. I can't choose.'

Miss Beatrice leaned forward, holding out a plate and a napkin. She whispered, 'He likes the apple pie but he's always secretly wanted one of the cakes with pink icing. Why don't you take him one of each? And Tom … be so good as to pass his lordship a cup of tea.'

Arabella watched Ellie carry the plate carefully across the room and then met Julian's eye as he took a heroic bite of pink icing. She was just suppressing a giggle when her attention was drawn to what was happening beyond him, on the other side of the window.

'Miss Caldercott … there are people in your garden. Quite a lot of them, in fact.'

'Yes,' agreed Beatrice. And calmly turned her attention to settling the children with instructions to help themselves to anything they wanted.

Arabella looked at Abigail. 'What are they doing there?'

'Waiting for the music to start,' came the cheerful reply. 'Word always gets out when his lordship is expected – don't know how, but it does. And the dear boy never disappoints them.' She patted Arabella's hand. 'You'll see.'

Julian demolished what was on his plate, swallowed the tea and meticulously wiped his fingers clean. Then he opened the window wide, bowed in response to a scattering of applause and took his seat at the keyboard before immediately launching into a fast and furious polka. For an instant, Arabella's jaw dropped while, in the garden, some folk were clapping in time and others invaded the road in order to dance.

The polka became a reel, then a succession of popular songs that had everyone singing along. Near the conclusion of one of them, a male voice called out, 'Play *The Owl*, m'lord.'

Julian shook his head slightly and, whilst bringing the current tune to its end, called back, 'Don't know it. Sing it for me.'

Outside, a pleasant baritone obliged him.
Of all the brave birds that ever I see
The owl is the fairest in her degree.

By the third line, two other voices joined the first in pleasing harmony. Julian's head turned and he rose to lean against the window-frame, listening; and when the song ended, he said, 'You don't need me, gentlemen. You do well enough without.'

'Good of you to say so, m'lord – but play it anyway,' said one of them.

Julian shrugged and resumed his seat. Unerringly finding the pitch of the singers, he played the opening bars of the tune, before slowing it into an introduction and calling, 'Sing it now.'

They began … and Julian promptly exchanged simple accompaniment for a delicate and more complex blend of support and decoration. The three voices swelled; no one else said a word. Arabella gripped one hand hard over the other and shut her eyes.

A torrent of applause greeted the end of the song and one of the singers pushed his way to the window, holding out his hand and saying, 'Thank you, m'lord. I don't know how you do it – but that was a pleasure and no mistake. Thank you!'

Rising, Julian accepted the hand and, grinning back, said, 'Don't thank me – I enjoyed it.'

And returning to his bench, embarked on another reel.

He played for an hour and, during it, the crowd outside continued to grow until it seemed that the whole village was clustered outside the Misses Caldercott's villa. Inside it, Rob stood at Julian's shoulder, riveted by every movement of those clever hands. But finally Julian said, 'One more – and one only, ladies and gentlemen. What is it to be?'

'Something by Mr Mozart,' shouted one voice ... and was promptly drowned out by a chorus of others calling for 'That piece you played last week. The one we liked!' ... and then *The Owl* trio singing a snatch of melody.

'Ah,' murmured his lordship, an odd smile touching his mouth. '*That* one.'

And he began to play.

It was the piece of his own that Arabella had heard twice the night before; and, watching these ordinary folk rendered utterly silent and gripped by the shifting emotions in the music, she felt something hot and almost painful swelling inside her chest. She wasn't aware of the glances exchanged by the Caldercott ladies or that Miss Beatrice had laid a hand over her own. The only thing she *was* aware of was an overwhelming desire to put her arms about the man at the keyboard and hold him forever.

* * *

Julian thought that, after their conversation on the way to the Misses Caldercott's, he had put the kiss as far behind him as it seemed Elizabeth had done. But that evening when she followed him into the library after dinner, he discovered that he hadn't. No matter what he played, awareness of her presence sang through every nerve and vein in his body. It was odd really. Outside the library, he managed, by and large, not to think of the kiss; *inside* it, he could think of nothing else. The sweetness of her mouth, the way she'd felt in his arms and the expression in her eyes. He'd known he shouldn't touch her. What he hadn't anticipated was the seven hells of torture he would suffer afterwards. Even sitting ten feet away, he could feel her ... and it was destroying his reason. He could keep his hands off her because he had to; but he had no defence at all against the maelstrom of emotion she created by merely sitting quietly while he played. And so, by the second night and with desperation coming ever closer, he decided he had to do something about it.

He couldn't bring himself to banish her completely but he could and *must* change the usual routine. So for exactly an hour on the following evening, he played anything she requested, interposed with pieces she'd never heard before. Then, as the clock struck nine, he said, 'And that ends tonight's concert, I'm afraid. I've been neglecting parts of my repertoire for long enough and need to do some serious work.'

Startled, Arabella said, 'You want me to go?'

'Please. I'm going to be hammering away at the same phrases over and over again – so you won't be missing much.' He sent her a fleeting half-smile but didn't quite meet her eyes. 'Better close the door, as well. I don't want to drive everyone in the house demented.'

She watched him turn back to the keyboard and embark upon a series of scales. He was still playing them when she shut the door behind her and leaned against it, feeling childishly hurt. She would have sat quietly and not interrupted no matter what he played. He knew that ... though admittedly he *didn't* know that she'd happily listen to him playing scales all night, just for the pleasure of watching him do it. But something had changed and she didn't know why. It couldn't be the kiss because they'd cleared the air about that ... and Julian seemed more comfortable relegating it to the past than she was.

Closing the door did not completely shut out either sound or, as now, the lack of it. Arabella sat down on the stairs and waited. A moment later, she heard something new ... a slow yet restless melody in a minor key, picked out only by the right hand. He played it again and then again, this time adding the left; the same phrase, over and over ... searching, melancholy and beautiful. She hugged her knees, and wondered how to find out what it was without giving herself away by asking.

Inside the library and concentrating on the complexities of rearranging the middle movement of a concerto for solo performance, Julian recovered his balance. This would work. He could give her one hour a night. He could manage that. If he was careful, she need never know the mess of confusion that was going on inside him. And meanwhile, he would work systematically through his repertoire, one composer at a time. Tonight, one of Bach senior's sons ... tomorrow Rameau ... the next Scarlatti ... and so on. It was sensible and productive and it would prevent him doing anything stupid.

Still sitting on the stairs, Arabella didn't care that she was being stupid. She was, however, determined to keep her stupidity to herself by slipping away to her room before Julian stopped playing.

* * *

Three days later, Julian returned in triumph from the auction in Newark and went immediately in search of Arabella.

'The wine made nearly two hundred pounds! One hundred and eighty-six pounds, seventeen shillings and sixpence, to be precise.'

She beamed at him. 'That's wonderful. I'm so glad.'

'I can pay the outstanding bills and we can get new clothes and shoes for the children. And I can rent the corn-mill for another month and buy a new plough and --'

'And have new clothes yourself,' she interrupted. 'Don't argue. You *need* them! Whether you like it or not, you are the Earl of Chalfont and occasionally you should look the part. So ... coat, vest, breeches ... everything. Do you promise?'

'Yes. Yes – all right. I promise.' Grinning, he dug in his pockets and held out a couple of letters. 'These were waiting for you at the Dog and Duck.'

One was a long-awaited letter from Lizzie – the first since a hasty note telling of her safe arrival in St James Square and saying that the duchess was lovely but the duke could be rather frightening. Arabella started to smile ... then saw the superscription on the other letter and felt all her muscles go into spasm.

It was addressed to Mistress E. Marsden – which was all right; but the black slash of handwriting belonged to someone it shouldn't. Max.

For a moment, she held it at arm's length as if it was a live snake.

Julian eyed her obliquely. 'Is something wrong?'

'Wrong? I – no. No. It's just … from someone I didn't expect to write to me.' And thought wildly, *Max wouldn't write to Lizzie. Why would he? But the alternative is that he knows … and how can he?* Summoning a weak smile, she said, 'Excuse me, please. I – I'd like to read this now because it's likely to need a reply.'

Seated at her desk in the little housekeeper's office, it was several minutes before she could bring herself to break the seal. And when she finally did, all her worst fears were realised.

Belle, Max had written. *What in God's name do you think you're doing – and did you honestly expect to get away with it? You and Lizzie have changed places, haven't you? Don't trouble to deny it. I know you must have done. You made no secret of the fact that you never wanted to go to London but that you thought Lizzie deserved to – so somehow you've talked her into this madcap scheme. I can only assume it never occurred to you that Mama and Aunt Maria would share letters from the pair of you. As soon as I read all that chatter about taking the children to rummage through the attics, I knew right away who had written it. That idea wouldn't have occurred to Lizzie in a million years – neither would she have been remotely enthusiastic about it if it had. She's never been as comfortable with dirt as you. That entire paragraph had your personality stamped all over it so clearly I can't understand why neither Mama nor Aunt Maria saw it – yet somehow they didn't. And no, I haven't told them. Yet. But let me be plain. The only reason I'm writing rather than already being on my way to fetch you home is that you sounded happy; happier than you have been for a long time. I also suspect I understand what lies at the root of all this – though it isn't something to be discussed by letter. However, if you want to remain at Chalfont, here is the small amount of leeway I'm prepared to offer. I want an* immediate *reply giving chapter and verse on the earl – who*

*you seem oddly reluctant to write about and who, I am assuming,
is as much in the dark about your charade as the rest of us. And
make it the truth, Belle. If you lie, I'll know and you can expect me
to arrive within the week – having already shared my knowledge
with both Mama and Aunt Maria. None of this is negotiable. In
case you haven't yet realised it, I'm bloody furious with you.
Max*

Arabella let the letter fall to the desk and dropped her head
in her hands. Stupidly, she found herself remembering what
people said about being careful what you wished for. For Julian's
sake, she had been wishing for Max ... and look what had come of
it? But she didn't have time to panic about that. She had to
respond – and quickly.

Pulling a sheet of paper in front of her, she stared helplessly
at its blankness for a few minutes. Then, *Dearest Max,* she
scrawled. *I'm sorry, truly I am. And yes, I did this for Lizzie as well
as for myself – but I* am *happy here. So don't come. Please,
please don't – even though I've wished I could ask your advice for
his lordship who is struggling with a neglected estate, lacking
workers and money. But he thinks I'm Lizzie and I don't know how
to tell him I'm not, even though I'd like to. As for telling you about
him ... I don't know where to start. The obvious things – the ones
you might think important – aren't important at all. The things
that* are *seem impossible to put into words. And the most
important thing of all, which you won't understand, is that he
simply doesn't belong here. It's such a waste. He should be in
Vienna or Paris or London. But I'll come back to that later. First –
rather than just saying he is a good, kind man yet also
extraordinary – the quickest way to illustrate all that is by
explaining about the children. You see, it's like this.*

It seemed that, once she *had* started, there was no end to it.
She wrote about how the children came to be there and what
Julian had done for them; the months mending the damaged
harpsichord; the recital he had given in Vienna; the lying lawyers
who had persuaded him into forsaking his career; the impromptu
concerts for the villagers; and finally – and at great length – the
brilliance of his playing. She poured it all out, praying that Max

would understand but by no means convinced that he would. And at the end said, *So you see why I don't want to leave – not yet, at least. If there was a way to give Julian the life he should have and someone to look after the children in my place without caring that they are illegitimate … then it might be different. But as things stand, they need me here. In a different way, I think I need them, too. So please keep the secret. I am safe, I am happy and I'm glad I came. The only thing I regret is that Julian thinks I'm Lizzie and I don't know how to put that right yet. But I will. I must. Try not to be angry, Max, and don't worry about me. All my love,*
Belle

She sealed the letter – not having the remotest idea of how much else she had given away – and opened the one from Lizzie.

This described the gowns the duchess had bought for her at London's leading modiste and listed the people she had met thus far. The rest of it was wholly taken up with Lord Sherbourne. *The duke wasn't pleased that we had been seen travelling together. And there's something else. He killed a man in a duel, Belle. It was years ago but everyone remembers it. Only I can't believe he's so very bad – not after he helped Annie and me. But I remember him saying that sometimes being able to believe one's sins could be blamed on Fate would be very comforting. And though I didn't know it at the time, he must have meant the duel, mustn't he? It will be odd seeing him again. I am to attend my first ball tonight at Cavendish House and am told he will be there. Dearest Belle, I pray every night that you are happy at Chalfont and don't regret what we have done. Write and tell me everything!*
Much love,
Lizzie

Arabella frowned over this. Lizzie … thinking a man who had killed couldn't be all bad and wanting to give him the benefit of the doubt? It didn't sound like her at all. But she didn't have time to worry about that now. She had to warn her that Max *knew*; and that, though Arabella hoped he wouldn't give them away, Lizzie should be especially careful in every possible way.

Having sent her letters to the village and trying not to worry about Max's possible response, Arabella spent most of the afternoon with the children. She listened to them read, set each of them a small and quite different task and, when these had been accomplished, sent them outside to play. As soon as she was alone, however, she could think of nothing but that her feelings for Julian were causing her deception to carve a hole behind her ribs. Try as she might, there did not seem any way of telling the truth that would not make it unforgivable – possibly even hurtful; because whichever way one looked at it, it had been a breach of his trust. She couldn't understand why this aspect of the masquerade had never occurred to her before. But then, she supposed miserably, the chances of falling utterly and irrevocably in love during the course of it had never occurred to her either.

* * *

Julian, who was frequently oblivious to anything that did not relate to music, noticed immediately that Elizabeth wasn't herself. Her smile was tense, she talked less than usual and she didn't laugh, even when he told her that the spinach Mr Phelps had planted in the kitchen garden had turned out to be marigolds.

Eventually, suspecting he knew what might be wrong but hoping he was mistaken, he said baldly, 'Was it the letter?'

Her eyes flew wide. 'What?'

'You seem upset. I thought it might have something to do with that letter. The one you said you didn't expect?' He hadn't thought of it right away – he'd been too euphoric about the wine money. But later, wondering about her odd reaction, he'd realised that the bold handwriting was masculine ... and for the first time, it had occurred to him that somewhere – Yorkshire, probably – there might be a man patiently waiting to marry her. A weight had promptly settled on his chest, making it hard to breathe. He could still feel it now. So he waited, staring down at his plate, and when she remained uncharacteristically silent, muttered, 'I beg your pardon. I shouldn't have asked. It's none of my business.'

It is, thought Arabella despairingly. *But I can't blurt out the truth just like that.*

Refusing to add any more lies to her existing tally, she said haltingly, 'It's all right. It was from my brother. He – he had concerns about my coming here and doesn't consider my letters adequately reassuring.'

Her brother? The weight lifted and he drew a grateful breath. *Just her brother.*

Amidst the waves of relief, something stirred vaguely at the back of Julian's mind. She had mentioned brothers before, hadn't she? Yes. He was sure she had. But hadn't her letters to Paul spoken of sisters? And why was it her brother expressing concerns, rather than her father? It seemed … odd. But since nothing mattered except that she didn't go away, he shoved his doubts aside and said, 'Is he worried because of me – or is it the children?'

'Neither. He just … he feels that I'm not where I should be.'

Julian wasn't sure what that was supposed to mean. 'And are you?'

'No. I'm *exactly* where I should be and I've written telling him so, hopefully setting his mind at rest.' Then, summoning a bright smile, she said, 'Now … I wondered, since Rob is learning to play, whether it would help if I taught him to read music so that you can use your time with him for the practical side. But I thought you might advise me how best to go about it.'

He realised that she was deliberately changing the subject. He also realised that it was the first time he had felt her setting him at a distance. He told himself he shouldn't mind … which did nothing to change the fact that he did. Very much indeed.

CHAPTER FIFTEEN

Elizabeth's drive with Lord Sherbourne had to be postponed for two days due to sudden gusty showers. But when, on the third day, the sun finally deigned to put in an appearance, his lordship sent a note promising to call for her at four in the afternoon.

Elizabeth dressed carefully and tried to ignore the butterflies in her stomach. The deep blue carriage-dress trimmed with cream silk and the pale straw hat with its profusion of matching blue ribbons were becoming and elegant. In the last weeks, she had learned that looking one's best was the surest – and sometimes the only – antidote to nerves.

Arriving promptly, Sherbourne left the crossing-sweeper to hold his horses and entered Rockliffe's house unsure of his reception. Even an hour ago, he had still half-expected to receive a reply from Mistress Brandon making her excuses. He could only assume that Rockliffe knew that Philippa was writing to all and sundry and had decided to keep his and Arabella's options open for the time being; either that or the girl herself had refused to rescind her acceptance.

The duchess awaited him in the drawing-room, her lovely aquamarine eyes cool.

'Lord Sherbourne,' she said. 'You will be aware of the speculation surrounding yourself and Arabella – but as yet speculation is all it is, so there is no need for Arabella to be troubled by it. I'm sure you agree.'

'Completely, your Grace.' He smiled faintly. 'Did you think I intended to spend the afternoon regaling her with salacious gossip?'

'I have no idea *what* you might do,' she returned crisply, 'or what possessed you to issue this invitation or why Arabella felt it necessary to accept it. I do, however, have very definite views on what is best for her.'

'And your point is well-taken.' The door opened to admit Arabella and he turned swiftly, bowing. 'Good afternoon, Mistress Brandon. You look delightful.'

'Thank you, my lord.' She looked at Adeline. 'I didn't have a parasol to match this gown, so Jeanne loaned me one of yours. I hope that is all right?'

'Of course.' With a brief glance at the earl, Adeline added, 'One should never go driving without adequate protection.'

'How very true,' drawled Ralph, meeting the duchess's eyes with a look of complete comprehension. Then, offering his arm to Arabella, 'Shall we go?'

'Yes.' She laid her hand on his sleeve and smiled at him. 'Yes, please.'

Once settled beside her in the carriage and setting his pair in motion, Sherbourne said meditatively, 'I did not think you would come.'

'Why not? I said I would, didn't I?'

'I thought you would be persuaded to change your mind.'

'By Cousin Adeline?' asked Elizabeth. And when he nodded, 'I believe she might have liked me to do so. But she merely cautioned me to be careful.'

That was more honesty than he had expected. On a note of what might have been wry laughter, he said, 'Unnecessary advice. Did you not once tell me that you never do anything that you should not?'

She coloured a little and, toying with the handle of her parasol, said awkwardly, 'I think I – I attempted to do so the last time we met.'

'Ah.' They had got to *that* quicker than he expected as well. 'Is that an apology?'

'Should it be?'

'No. It is I who should apologise for speaking so sharply. But you were about to open a conversation I prefer to avoid ... particularly in the middle of a ballroom.'

Elizabeth tilted her head to look at him. 'You knew what I was going to say?'

'Oh yes. I have heard it countless times. You wanted to know if I really killed a man; if I intended to do so and why; and how I felt afterwards. Correct?'

'No.'

His eyes met hers with sudden, sharp intensity. 'No?'

'Not at all.' She looked away, watching the park unfold before them as the earl guided his phaeton through the gates. 'I was going to ask if it's true that, had events been otherwise, you would have married Lady Sutherland.'

Well, thought Ralph. *That makes a change.*

'And why would you wish to know that?'

Because I once heard you described as "heart-on-his-sleeve, stars-in-his-eyes besotted" ... *which, if it's true, means there is a part of yourself that you keep remarkably well hidden*, was the truthful answer. But she said, 'Because it might explain her hostility. If she loved you – as I imagine she must have done – she *can't* have believed that you meant to kill her brother. Grief and anger are natural but they fade. Virulent animosity so long after the event is *not* natural; and it makes me wonder how real it is.'

'Real enough not to care whose reputation she destroys so long as mine is one of them.'

'But that's all part of it.' Elizabeth looked earnestly into his face and, without realising it, laid her hand on his arm. 'The line between love and hate is a very fine one. She loved you once and she hates you now. But somewhere inside that hatred is, at the very least, a *memory* of love ... and perhaps also a shred or two of mistaken jealousy.'

What a wonderful, comforting notion, he thought. *How lovely to believe it even for a minute.* But he couldn't. He knew perfectly well what motivated Philippa.

Having tried to read his expression but found it inscrutable, Elizabeth said, 'I suppose you think I'm being fanciful?'

'No. I think you are crediting Lady Sutherland with what your own feelings might have been in similar circumstances. I do not, of course, imagine that *you* believe the death of Edgar Wilkes might not have been deliberate.'

'What I believe doesn't matter, does it?'

'Perhaps. Perhaps not.' He fell silent for a moment, trying not to ask a question to which he might not like the answer. Finally, however, he said, 'Just out of interest ... would you accept my word if I gave it?'

Elizabeth surveyed him gravely and said slowly, 'Yes. Since I've a feeling you don't give it lightly, I would.'

This time, the pause was a long one. Ralph tried to remember the last time anyone had been prepared to trust anything about him. Then he reflected on the fact that, if he was considering courting Arabella Brandon, he was going to have to tell her at least part of the truth and hope to be believed. He did not relish the idea. But since one had to start somewhere, he said slowly, 'Well, then. I fought Edgar at his own insistence and with no intention of killing him.'

'Thank you.' She hesitated and then said, 'I wouldn't have asked, you know.'

'No. I am beginning to realise that.' Needing to change the subject, he said, 'Are you enjoying your first taste of London society?'

'Yes. I was nervous at first but most people have been kind. Of course, I know there is some talk and I've caught a few speculative glances. But no-one has said anything within my hearing – which, in one way, is a pity.'

Ralph's brows rose. 'Is it?'

'Yes. One can't correct stupid, malicious gossip unless one hears it said.'

'Forgive my asking … but *would* you correct it?'

'Yes,' she said firmly, thinking, *I have to protect Belle's name as best I can.* 'Since I object to us both being unfairly slandered, I wouldn't mind the opportunity to say so.'

'Not that I don't appreciate the thought,' he remarked, hiding his inevitable surprise, 'but confrontation doesn't necessarily make the stupid, malicious gossipers back down.'

'I know that. Tongues wag just as much at home as they do here. The only difference is that it is more likely about whether the fishmonger is overcharging or Mr Smith has taken to drink.'

'Or whether Jack, having been caught kissing Jill, will do the honourable thing?'

'Probably. But that doesn't apply to you and me. No one saw us doing anything improper because there was nothing improper to see.'

Ralph sighed. 'That is beside the point. Surely Rockliffe has made it plain that, as far as the polite world is concerned, opportunity is sufficient?'

'Yes. But --'

'And I presume he has also told you of our conversation on the subject.'

Elizabeth nodded, colouring a little.

'That was ... good of you. And I appreciate it. But there will be no need for either of us to – to make such an irrevocable sacrifice.'

'I would suggest that you speak for yourself,' murmured Ralph, 'except that I suspect that is exactly what you *were* doing.' Forced to slow the carriage due to the dawdling progress of two horsemen ahead of them, he used the time to study her face. 'I will probably regret asking ... but is the idea of marriage with me completely repellent?'

'No!' said Elizabeth, aghast. 'That isn't it at all – truly it's not! It is merely that I can't ... I don't *wish* to marry anyone just at present.'

Able to drive on, he thought, *If that is not true, she has just made it impossible to accept another offer. But she started to say she* cannot *marry ... and why would that be?* He said, 'I am duly reassured. Is there some reason for your reluctance to wed?'

Elizabeth could feel the pit of deception opening beneath her. For a fleeting instant, she wondered if she dared tell him the truth ... but immediately knew she couldn't. The knowledge hurt more than she expected and made her realise that, although she didn't want Lord Sherbourne to marry her because he felt *compelled* to do so, she would have been far from reluctant to consider it if he was doing so freely. As things stood, however, it didn't matter a jot *why* he asked – since he thought she was someone she wasn't.

Falling back on Arabella's own excuse, she said baldly, 'I was betrothed for three years. But the gentleman in question married someone else.'

'Ah.' He frowned slightly. 'You must forgive me. I am sure you would have preferred not to tell me that.'

'Yes. But I couldn't have you thinking what you thought.' She summoned a smile. 'As for my former betrothed, at least he had the tact to jilt me from Massachusetts, rather than the neighbouring estate.'

'Did that make it easier?'

'Not really.' Elizabeth looked at him curiously. 'Am *I* allowed a question?'

'Ask it and we'll see.'

'Do you *wish* to marry? Not me specifically – but at all?'

'Aside from the choice of bride, my wishes have little to do with it,' he replied dryly. 'It is my duty to secure the earldom ... and that requires an heir. So, yes. I must marry – and relatively soon.' He slanted an odd smile at her and added, 'You may wish to consider that.'

* * *

The following morning, Arabella's brief letter containing the news that Max had somehow worked out their deception turned Elizabeth's insides to jelly. It was all very well for Belle to say she thought she had persuaded him to keep the secret ... but what if she hadn't? What if, right now, Max was sharing what he knew with Mama and Aunt Louisa? If he was, the axe could fall at any moment. And what price then this possibility of something between herself and Ralph Sherbourne? Even though she knew it could never amount to anything, she couldn't help wanting to let it develop ... wanting to know what, if anything, it was. If Papa found out what she had done, that wasn't going to happen. She'd be summoned home immediately.

Had she but known it, darker and more dangerous clouds were looming upon her horizon. Lady Sutherland had returned to town and, according to Nell Caversham, had immediately started talking "faster than anyone can listen."

'I had hoped,' sighed his Grace, 'that Phineas Sutherland might have prevented this. Since he hasn't, I had better have a word with him.'

'Before you do, let me go straight to the horse's mouth,' said Adeline. And with a smile, 'That way, we can save the really big guns until we're sure we need them.'

'Big guns?' enquired Rockliffe. 'How very flattering. Or is it?'

* * *

Adeline was admitted to the Sutherlands' house in Dover Street and shown up to the drawing-room where her ladyship waited with an expression of nervous defiance.

'Your Grace.' She curtsied. 'This is an unexpected pleasure.'

'Let us not pretend that this is a social call,' said Adeline crisply. 'You must be as aware as I am that it is not.'

Philippa Sutherland's colour rose. 'I'm sure I don't know what you mean.'

'Yes, you do. You are busy smearing the reputation of the duke's young cousin. It would be in your best interests to cease doing so.'

'If that is a threat --'

'It is a civil warning. If you continue with this, my husband will step in – and I am sure that is something you would rather avoid.'

Her ladyship looked back mutinously. 'I am only saying what I saw.'

'What you *think* you saw – and what you assumed was everything.'

'Mistress Brandon was travelling unchaperoned with Sherbourne and --'

'Due to an accident to her own carriage and lack of any alternative, Mistress Brandon completed one stage of her journey with Lord Sherbourne. And she was accompanied by both her maid and her aunt.'

Philippa managed a scornful laugh. 'I saw no aunt – nor heard any mention of one.'

'In a brief, chance meeting, why should you have done? Your mistake was in jumping to conclusions that suited your own purposes.' Adeline held the other woman's gaze with a very direct one of her own. 'I have no axe to grind on Sherbourne's behalf, Lady Sutherland. Whatever ill-will you bear him is entirely your own affair. But neither the duke nor I will permit you to continue involving Mistress Brandon in it.'

'She was seen driving with him only yesterday,' muttered Philippa.

'Yes. And do you really suppose that if the *slightest* impropriety had occurred she would have been permitted to do so?' Adeline paused to let this sink in. 'If you are wise, you will begin admitting to your friends that you may have been under a misconception ... that you were not in possession of all the facts ... and that Mistress Brandon has been in no sense compromised. If that is beyond you, try remaining silent. But if you persist in spreading malicious gossip, do not be surprised if your standing in society begins to ... diminish. As I am sure your husband will tell you, you will not enjoy the results of being openly cut by Rockliffe. Good day.'

* * *

Aware of Lady Sutherland's arrival in town but not that the Duchess of Rockliffe had taken matters into her own hands, Lord Sherbourne set off for Dorset and his brother's wedding. The brief missive he had received from the father of the bride had given the time, date and place of the ceremony – and also told him that the prospective groom had made two unsuccessful attempts to bolt. Ralph was not surprised by this. He did, however, wonder why closer acquaintance with Cedric had not caused either the bride or her father to call off the wedding – since, if Jenny Belcher was with child, no one had mentioned it.

Cedric, sporting a black eye and under the close escort of Jenny's burly brothers, whined to Bertram all the way down the aisle and then cast piteous looks in Ralph's direction. His mumbled vows and responses were only made at all due to the Belcher boys' ungentle reminders. And when he and Jenny were pronounced man and wife, his expression was that of a condemned man with the rope already about his neck. A couple of people sniggered. Had the butt of the joke been anyone but his idiot brother, Ralph might also have enjoyed the funny side. As it was, it merely made his jaw ache.

And the day wasn't over. Regardless of the circumstances, Mr Belcher and his wife were determined to celebrate the occasion with a gargantuan wedding breakfast, followed by dancing in the assembly rooms. Ralph endured it until he saw Bertram sitting down to a game of cards with a clutch of Belcher men, at which point his heart sank still further.

Bertram would start cheating. He always did. The men he was playing against would notice. They always did. Then there would be a fight. There always was. All this because Bertram never learned and nothing Ralph could do would change that.

He could control one thing, however. He didn't have to watch.

With a final glance towards the place where, hemmed in by his new brothers-in-law, Cedric sat glowering into an ale pot while his pretty bride danced with one of her cousins, Ralph left the room and ran down the stairs to the stables. Tired, depressed and, if he was honest with himself, more than a little lonely, he rode the short distance to Gardington, contemplating seeking solace in a bottle.

He didn't, of course. He sought it in the only things that never failed him.

Aristotle, Socrates and Heraclitus.

* * *

Although Elizabeth knew that Lord Sherbourne had left town, she was unaware of his reasons for doing so. She was equally unaware that, with his customary efficiency, Rockliffe's man-of-law had arrived to report his findings about the Earl of Chalfont.

'You have been uncommonly quick, Mr Osborne,' remarked Rockliffe. 'I am impressed.'

'As to that, your Grace, it was not so very difficult. I have prepared a fully-detailed account of everything I have learned ... possibly more than is pertinent.'

'You may leave it with me. But for now, perhaps you might précis it?'

'Certainly, your Grace.' Mr Osborne cleared his throat. 'Julian Langham, twenty-eight years old, only child and parents deceased. He spent two years at Cambridge but did not take his degree, departing instead for Vienna where he spent the next seven years studying music. Since that appears an inordinate length of time, I have sent an enquiry to a colleague in Vienna but will be waiting some weeks for a reply. At any rate, Vienna is where the late earl's lawyers, Bartle, Bartle & Fellowes, finally found the gentleman. I am told he was living a somewhat unconventional existence; that he was reluctant to assume the title; but that, though his relationship to the fourth earl was tenuous in the extreme, no other heir could be found – thus making Mr Langham a last resort.'

'You say 'told', Mr Osborne. By whom exactly?'

The lawyer smiled aridly. 'By Mr Fellowes, your Grace. He and his partners were eager to shed their responsibility for the Chalfont earldom – and did so immediately Mr Langham was in place. The fourth earl was a gentleman of expensive tastes and dissolute habits. By the time of his death, the estate was barely functioning and close to bankrupt.' He paused and, with more than a hint of disapproval, added, 'Young Mr Langham was told none of that and therefore had no idea what he would be facing. According to Mr Fellowes, he was similarly unaware that the late earl's three illegitimate children were running wild in the vicinity.'

'Did you say *three*?' asked Rockliffe faintly.

'Yes, your Grace. Three.'

'Dear me. The fourth earl was nothing if not … prolific … was he?'

'So it would seem. During the current earl's seven month tenure, he has been attempting to halt the downward slide with none of the necessary resources.' Another, rather different, smile. 'But this is where the gentleman becomes interesting, your Grace.'

'He does?'

'Indeed. I did not confine myself to the usual sort of enquiries. I also sent Hopkins, one of my young clerks, to the village closest to the Chalfont estate, to discover the reality of the situation. I had expected to learn that the new earl was … let us say, less than popular. In fact, the reverse is true. He has not attempted to solve his financial problems by raising rents and he has taken all three children into his own house. These two things alone were sufficient to create general approval. But during his sojourn in Beckingham, Hopkins witnessed something astonishing.'

The lawyer paused, as if for dramatic effect.

Rockliffe did not disappoint him. He said, 'Do go on, Mr Osborne. I am agog.'

'His lordship is apparently a harpsichordist of uncommon ability – an ability he regularly shares. He performs once a week from inside someone's parlour with the windows open. According to Hopkins, virtually the entire village gathers outside to hear him. He plays reels and jigs and songs they all know. But he also plays Bach and Mozart ... and complicated pieces by composers Hopkins did not recognise.' Mr Osborne looked at the duke over the rim of his spectacles. 'Your Grace ... young Lord Chalfont is a pleasing enigma.'

'He is certainly unusual,' agreed the duke. 'Did Mr Hopkins happen to catch sight of his lordship's new housekeeper?'

'He did. She and the children accompanied his lordship to the village on the day of his recital. Hopkins said that the lady was of dainty stature and her hair, a most striking silver-blonde colour. Unfortunately, he was unable to meet either her or the earl.'

'I doubt that doing so would have added to what we know.' Rockliffe rose. 'As always, you have been most commendably thorough, Mr Osborne. I am most grateful.'

* * *

A little later, having passed on the bulk of Mr Osborne's discoveries to Adeline, Rockliffe said pensively, 'The question now is whether or not to pay Lord Chalfont a visit. I find I am rather tempted by the idea. This is partly because I do not find the notion of Elizabeth ... let us continue for the moment to assume that it *is* Elizabeth ... living with a young man of unconventional habits and three illegitimate children entirely suitable. But I confess that I am also intrigued by the idea of his lordship giving impromptu recitals to the villagers.'

'And if you go there and find that it *isn't* Elizabeth? What then? You won't be able to leave her there. And how do we explain having *two* Arabella Brandons?'

'Yes,' he sighed. 'That will undeniably be a problem. I suppose you are going to suggest that we raise the issue with the one we already have?'

'It would be simpler, yes.'

'I am glad you think so.'

Adeline's brows rose. 'You don't?'

'No. I am imagining myself saying, *"This may seem an odd question, Arabella ... but are you by any chance really Cousin Elizabeth?"* And then I am imagining her reaction if it turns out that I am wrong.'

'Put like that, I suppose you may have a point. On the other hand, you are rarely wrong ... and wouldn't pose the question unless you were sure.'

'Being absolutely sure requires a journey to somewhere near Newark – for which this may not be the best time.' The dark eyes rested on her invitingly. 'I have been exceedingly patient, my love. But if you felt able to confirm my suspicions, I would be ... grateful.'

Laughter tugged at Adeline's mouth but she said, 'There are times when I find your famed omniscience rather trying.'

'I'm sure. But in this particular instance – given the fact that, other than those few days each month when you prefer to sleep alone, we habitually and most unfashionably share a bed – I hardly think omniscience comes into it.'

'Unfashionably? Perhaps that *may* be true. Though I'd be surprised if both Nicholas and Madeleine and also Nell and Harry did not do as we do – thus setting a fashion.'

'Do you know,' said Rockliffe looking mildly pained, 'I really would prefer *not* to contemplate the mating habits of my siblings.'

'Mating habits? Is *that* what we are discussing?'

'You were. I was attempting not to. *I* was attempting to establish whether I might begin planning an elaborate and wildly expensive gift in the anticipation of a happy event ... some time during March, perhaps?'

Adeline rose and crossed to settle comfortably on his knee, arms around his neck and mouth against his throat. 'Yes. You may. And don't be thinking it will be like Vanessa. I have never felt so well in my life – not a whiff of sickness.'

'I rejoice to hear it.' He settled her closer against him. 'So this time I will not be required to hold the basin at some ungodly hour of the morning?'

'I sincerely hope not.' And trailing smiling kisses along his jaw, 'But if it should become necessary, you will be the first to know. Meanwhile, go to Newark and solve the mystery. I'll await your return with bated breath.'

CHAPTER SIXTEEN

Having spent the previous night at the Woolpack in Newark, Rockliffe arrived at Chalfont just before noon. It was Saturday and it was raining. His Grace, having sent his coachman to the back of the property in search of shelter for himself and the horses, was about to become aware of the significance of these facts.

The first clue was when he was left standing in the meagre shelter of the porch while the door went unanswered. Rockliffe rang the bell again ... waited again ... then lifted the latch and let himself in. It was immediately clear that the reason no one had responded to the bell was because it was unlikely anyone had heard it over the din. Someone, somewhere was playing slow, painstaking scales on a harpsichord, while from the landing overhead came a series of thuds, yells and shrieks of laughter, mingled with shrill yapping. The duke hesitated and had just decided to track down the would-be musician when a maid shot into the hall to stare at him out of startled eyes and say breathlessly, 'Beg pardon for nobody answering the door, milord. But if you was looking for the earl, he's not at home just now.'

'Is he not?' Rockliffe stripped off his gloves. 'Then I will wait. Meanwhile, I would appreciate a word with the ... er ... housekeeper.'

'Housekeeper? Oh. Miss Lizzie. Yes, milord. She's upstairs --
'

A particularly loud thump from above caused her to stop speaking. The harpsichord also fell silent and a young voice yelled, 'Will you all *shut up*? I'm *practising*!'

'Upstairs playing skittles with the children,' finished the maid helplessly. 'If you'll just follow me to the parlour, milord, I'll get her.'

'Thank you,' nodded Rockliffe. 'Perhaps someone could ensure that my coachman has found the stables? And both he and my groom will need the opportunity to get dry – if it isn't too much trouble.'

'Mr Phelps went to see to it. It was the coach as told us we'd got a visitor.' Rose dropped a curtsy. 'Please sit down and I'll fetch Miss Lizzie directly.'

Leaving the duke to absorb the shabbiness of his surroundings, Rose pelted up the stairs to say, 'Miss Lizzie – a gentleman's come and he's ever so elegant and there's a crest on his carriage, only his lordship isn't here and he's asking for you instead so I've put him in the parlour.'

'Breathe, Rose,' grinned Arabella. 'I'll come down.'

'In your old gown and with your hair all adrift?'

'It's either that or keep him waiting,' she shrugged. And over her shoulder to Tom and Ellie as she descended the stairs, 'Carry on with the game if you wish but please keep the noise down a little. We don't want our visitor to think he's come to the mad-house. Rose ... you'd better see about some tea. His lordship is tuning the Caldercott ladies' harpsichord this morning so he may be some time.'

Entering the parlour with a smile and a curtsy, Arabella had greeted their visitor before she actually *looked* at him properly; so when she did, it took a moment for her to behave as if she received striking, aristocratic gentlemen every day of the week. She said, 'I'm sorry Lord Chalfont isn't here to receive you, my lord and I'm not entirely sure when he'll be back. But in the meantime, perhaps you'll take some tea and tell me if *I* may help you in any way.'

Even without the confident manner, the duke knew instantly who she was. He had met her late father only once ... but he remembered those storm-grey Brandon eyes quite clearly. He said gently, 'Allow me to introduce myself. I am Rockliffe.'

The ground shifted under Arabella's feet and she took an uncertain step back. All the colour ebbing from her face, she whispered, '*Rockliffe?* Oh.'

'Quite. You look shocked. May I suggest that you sit down?'

She folded bonelessly into a chair. 'You ... you *know*. Don't you?'

'Yes – though until this moment I was not entirely sure.'

'Wh-What gave us away?'

'A number of small things made me wonder. As yet, however, neither the duchess nor I have said anything to Elizabeth. Who else is aware of your … masquerade?'

'To begin with, nobody. But Max – my brother - has also guessed. He wrote to me.'

'And Lord Chalfont?'

'No.' Her eyes widened and she shot to her feet. 'And please – *please* don't tell him! I have to do it myself. I *must*! I wanted to do so anyway and … and I have to make him understand. He isn't … he won't … I d-don't want him to think I deliberately set out to deceive him.'

'Forgive my saying so, but you appear to have set out to deceive quite a number of people – of whom Lord Chalfont is only one.'

'Yes. But we – Lizzie and I never meant to harm anyone. And I didn't know Julian – his lordship, then. I didn't know he would be … well, the way he *is*.' She stopped, then added helplessly, 'Everything is different now.'

'In what way?' Rockliffe asked, already sensing that there was more going on here than guilt at being caught out.

'It – it just *is*,' she said miserably. 'You wouldn't understand. I --'

'Miss Lizzie?' Tom stamped in to stand beside her. 'Is that man upsetting you?'

'No.' She managed a tense smile. 'No, Tom. I'm fine – really. Go back to Ellie.'

'You don't *look* fine.' He turned a baleful scowl on the duke and then, reaching a decision, turned back to the door and yelled, 'Rob! Come here and stay with Miss Lizzie. I'm going to get Sir Julian.'

'Don't!' said Arabella rapidly. 'His lordship won't be able to leave what he's doing half-finished and --'

Appearing with Ellie hard on his heels, Rob said, 'What the matter?'

'This man's upsetting Miss Lizzie and I'm fetching Sir Julian.'

Instantly, the two younger children flanked Arabella and took her hands. Before either of them could speak, however, Violet also stalked in to deposit the tea-tray on the table, saying, 'You don't need to go, Tom. Mr Phelps already went off in the farm-cart.'

At this point and having to suppress a smile, Rockliffe decided he might as well sit down. He said mildly, 'You may observe that I am not attempting to threaten anyone.'

Violet sniffed. 'Do you want me to stay with you, Miss Lizzie?'

'No.' Pulling herself together as best she could, Arabella said, 'None of you need to stay – though I thank all of you for offering. This gentleman doesn't mean me any harm. He is the Duke of Rockliffe ... and he is a – a relative.'

'Of yours?' demanded Tom; and when she nodded, he spun to face Rockliffe, turning from protective to belligerent in the space of a heartbeat. 'Well, duke or not, you ain't taking her away – if that's what you've come for. We won't let you. Sir *Julian* won't let you.'

Ellie's fingers tightened convulsively on Arabella's and Rob said, 'You wouldn't go, would you? You wouldn't really leave us?'

'You c-can't,' quavered Ellie, her eyes filling with tears. 'We're a – a *family*.'

The lump in Arabella's throat made it impossible to say anything.

'Do you think everyone might cease jumping to conclusions?' murmured Rockliffe. And looking at Arabella, 'At present, all I require is some private conversation – preferably before Lord Chalfont returns. And a cup of tea would also not be unwelcome.'

She swallowed hard and nodded. 'Violet ... perhaps you and Rose could see to the best of the spare bedchambers in case --'

'Please do not go to any trouble on my account,' murmured Rockliffe smoothly. 'I have taken rooms in Newark and will return there presently.'

'Oh. Then you may go, Violet.' Trying not to look too relieved, Arabella turned to the children. 'Tom ... take Rob and Ellie upstairs, please. I – I'll join you in a little while.'

On a sound of undisguised disapproval, Violet stalked from the room. Tom, on the other hand, stood his ground, saying, 'I'm not going nowhere till Sir Julian gets here.'

'Tom, *please*! I know you only want to help but this is upsetting Ellie.'

'She'll be more upset if he makes off with you while we're not looking. We *all* will.'

'Perhaps,' sighed the duke, 'I might suggest a compromise?'

'What's that?' asked Rob suspiciously.

'It is a means whereby we all get a part of what we want. If, for example, you were to stand guard on the other side of the door, *I* could speak to … this lady … and *you* will be on hand to stop me if I attempt to abduct her. Does that sound reasonable?'

Rob and Ellie looked at Tom. After a moment he said grudgingly, 'I suppose.'

'Excellent. Then perhaps we can progress.' He waited with raised brows until the children had trooped reluctantly from the room, then directed a faint smile at Arabella and said, 'Might I now have some tea? Very little milk and no sugar, if you please.'

Arabella reached for the teapot and without looking up, said, 'I'm sorry. They don't usually behave like that.'

'You need not apologise. They love you.'

'It – it would seem so.' She placed the tea beside him. 'They love his lordship, too.' And added abruptly, 'They aren't his, by the way.'

'I know they are not.' Rockliffe took a sip of tepid tea and managed not to grimace. 'Did you think I came here without learning a little about Lord Chalfont?'

Arabella eyed him with sudden suspicion. 'What else do you know?'

'I know that he inherited an impoverished and mismanaged estate; that he is housing three children who have no claim upon him; and that he plays the harpsichord. What I do *not* know and am hoping that you will tell me is if the … attachment … between you is mutual.'

'*What?*' The word came out as a strangled gasp and Arabella could feel herself turning scarlet. 'Attachment? Th-there isn't one.'

'Forgive me … but your whole attitude towards his lordship tells a very different story.' The enigmatic dark gaze remained fixed on her face. 'My question is whether he returns your regard and, if so, whether he has already declared himself.'

She stared at him for a long moment and then looked down at her hands.

'You are mistaken. There is nothing of that nature between us. But if you're thinking that he – that *we* have behaved improperly --'

'I do not think it and it is not what I asked.' Rockliffe paused, his mind busy with how this muddle could be straightened out. 'Arabella ... for numerous reasons, I ought to remove you from here but the children will clearly not release you without a fight. And if --'

'The children aren't the only ones who will fight,' she burst out. 'I will, too.'

'I gathered that. And if, as I was about to say, his lordship is of the same mind --' He stopped, listening to the sound of voices in the hall. 'Ah. Well, it seems we shall soon know.'

The door opened and Julian strode in, extremely damp and dishevelled, but his looks not in the least diminished by either. Barely glancing at the duke, his eyes settled on Arabella and he said rapidly, 'What's happening? Ellie is crying, Tom is in a temper and all three of them seem to think you're going away. It isn't true, is it?'

'Not if I can help it.'

'*What?*'

Trying to ignore the plummeting sensation in his chest, Julian looked at Rockliffe.

His Grace had no difficulty in interpreting the expression in the earl's eyes because there had been a time when he had been all too familiar with the feeling that caused it. He thought, *Well ... that answers one question*. And rising slowly, he held out his hand, saying, 'Lord Chalfont ... I am Rockliffe.'

'He means,' muttered Arabella, 'that he is the *Duke* of Rockliffe.'

'Oh.' Accepting the outstretched hand, Julian nodded. 'Your Grace?'

'I must apologise for arriving on your doorstep uninvited and unannounced,' continued the duke, 'but I am afraid we find ourselves in an unfortunate situation.'

'Do we? That is ... I've no idea what you mean or why you're here.' And, to Arabella, 'Or how you and the duke know each other, come to that.'

'Until an hour ago, I'd never laid eyes on him,' she replied bitterly. 'I wish I still hadn't. But I know *who* he is because he – he's a sort-of relative. The same sort, if you like, as the fourth earl was to you.'

'You ... you're related to a duke?' He stared at her, becoming increasingly alarmed. 'How? No. You can't be.'

'I think,' said Rockliffe smoothly to Arabella, 'that you should explain. If you wish to be private, I will brave the infantry in the hall.'

She shook her head. 'Finish your tea, your Grace. We'll talk in the library. Julian?'

'Yes. Now.' Sick with anxiety, he led her from the room and when the children showed signs of asking questions, said tersely, 'Later. Don't worry.'

Once inside the library, he locked the door, leaned against it and said, 'You needn't explain anything. I don't care who he is or why he's here. I don't care about *any* of it. Just tell me you aren't leaving.'

'I don't *want* to,' she said, her voice low and raw. 'But he – the duke --'

'Can he *make* you?'

'I don't know. I hope not.' Arabella lifted her head and looked into his eyes. 'I'm sorry, Julian. I'm so, so sorry I didn't tell you the truth before this. I wanted to. And if it had just been about me, I would have. But --'

'Elizabeth ... will you please, for the love of *God*, just tell me whatever it is you and he think I need to know?'

'Well, that's it, you see. I - I'm not Elizabeth.'

'What?' For a handful of seconds, Julian thought he'd misheard, followed by the peculiar feeling that the floor was slowly dissolving under his feet. He said carefully, '*Not* Elizabeth?'

'No.' She dragged in a painful breath and forced out the words. 'Elizabeth is my cousin. I – my name is Arabella Brandon. We ... we changed places.'

He shook his head, as if to clear it. 'I'd ask if you were joking. But you're not, are you?'

'No. We were both invited to stay with the duke and duchess and Lizzie's been in London all the time I've been here. But somehow, Rockliffe has guessed what we did and he came here to make sure.'

'And now he *is* sure?'

'Yes. So he probably thinks it's his duty to either take me to London or send me home.'

'*Christ.*' Julian shoved a hand through his already windblown hair and tried to quell a rising tide of panic. 'But why did you *do* it? It – it doesn't make sense.'

'I ... I didn't want to go to London. Lizzie did but her father wouldn't let her. She would never get another chance and it seemed stupid and unfair that she was denied this one. So when you offered her the position here, changing places seemed the perfect solution.' She stopped, absorbing the expression of hurt bewilderment in his eyes. 'I'm sorry. Not that we did it – I'll never be sorry for that. But I'm desperately sorry I didn't tell you the truth sooner. You have no idea how much I wanted to.' She waited for him to speak and eventually when he still did not do so, said, 'Please say something. I don't blame you for being angry and --'

'I'm not angry.' In a futile attempt to hold back the words boiling inside his head, he folded his arms tight across his chest. 'How can I be angry? It doesn't matter what your name is. It doesn't change who you *are*. I don't know your cousin. But I'm *glad* you came instead of her.' He hesitated and then, staring down at his feet, added unevenly, 'It's not just the children who don't want to lose you. I don't either – and not only because of them. I can't ... the thought of you not being here ... of how it was before you came ... I can't go back to that. So no matter what this duke says or threatens ... please don't leave. Promise that you won't?'

'I'm not sure I can promise,' she said unhappily, 'but I'll do my very best not to let it happen.' Everything he'd said made Arabella hope and wish and hurt. Mostly it made her want to cross the floor and hug him; the only thing that stopped her doing so was those defensively folded arms. 'Taking me to London will be awkward because Lizzie's already there using my name. And I can definitely refuse to let him send me home.' She risked going a few steps closer. 'I don't want to leave, Julian. I'm *happy* here. I love – I love the children.' *And you*, she thought, *I love you more than anything*. 'And if you can forgive me for deceiving you --'

'I'll forgive you anything as long as you'll stay,' he cut in doggedly, finally letting his arms fall loose at his sides and peeling himself away from the door in order to unlock it. Then, with a crooked smile and reaching out to lace the fingers of one hand with hers, he said, 'It may take me a while to get used to thinking of you as Arabella, though. But for now, let's just go and tell the duke that you're staying.'

* * *

Having reassured the children as best they could on their way back to the drawing-room, promising to explain properly later, they stood side by side and told Rockliffe that Arabella would absolutely *not* be leaving Chalfont.

Having expected it, Rockliffe merely sighed. 'If only it were that simple.'

'It is,' said Julian. 'It's what I and she and the children all want. How much simpler can it be? And you've already got an Arabella Brandon of your own, haven't you?'

'What I *have*,' corrected his Grace, a hard note entering his voice, 'is a problem, the complications arising from which are legion. To begin with, the duchess and I have unwittingly introduced an imposter to London society. No, please don't interrupt, my lord. I feel sure you were about to say that I am exaggerating the case or that it is of scant importance – but you are wrong on both counts. You should also understand that I am more than a little annoyed. But let us move on to Elizabeth ... who, since she is known to all as Mistress Brandon of Brandon Lacey, obviously cannot accept a proposal of marriage even if she wished to do so. And finally *you,* Arabella, are now in the frankly ludicrous position of never being able to appear in London under your own name at all.' He paused briefly, then added, 'Under the circumstances, what either you or his lordship *wants* is of no consequence whatsoever. The longer this charade goes on, the worse the situation will become … which means that I have no choice but to put an end to it.'

His words were greeted by a tense silence. Then, 'How?' demanded Julian, becoming unpleasantly aware that the situation was more complicated than he had supposed.

'Ah. A sensible question at last.'

'And what is the sensible answer?'

Rockliffe subjected the younger man to a long, cool gaze and finally said, 'Lord Chalfont … being fully aware that you are currently labouring under strong emotions I am prepared to be tolerant. You would be wise, however, to retrieve a few of your manners from wherever you left them before you exceed my patience.'

Julian flushed slightly. 'I beg your pardon, sir. I didn't intend to be rude. Sometimes I don't … things just come out the wrong way.'

'So I have noticed,' murmured Rockliffe with a hint of dry amusement. 'But returning to the issue at hand --'

'Wait a moment,' interposed Arabella quickly. 'I realise you can't ignore what you know – but must you act immediately? If you could wait just a few more weeks, Lizzie will be going home again and no one will be any the wiser.'

'I am not sure if that is wishful thinking or rank naiveté. It needs only one person who knows either of you to catch sight of Elizabeth in town and both her name and yours are likely to be plastered across the gossip pages. The fact that your cousin was seen travelling unchaperoned with the Earl of Sherbourne has already made this a possibility. I hope that particular danger has been averted. But if I am mistaken and marriage becomes the only solution, we will be left with the difficulty of explaining to his lordship that his prospective bride's name and background are not what he currently believes them to be.' He paused, waiting for this to sink in. 'It is all very well for you to hide your head in the sand and pretend that nothing is wrong, Arabella ... but, in addition to what I have said so far, the hornet's nest you and Elizabeth have created puts my wife in an awkward position – and *that* I will not tolerate.'

'I'm sorry,' she whispered. 'I really am. We thought it would be all right and --'

'It is beginning to strike me,' said Rockliffe, a shade grimly, 'that neither of you considered the eventual ramifications at all. However ... a little earlier, you told me that Lord Brandon knows the truth. What --?'

'*Lord* Brandon?' demanded Julian suddenly. 'Who is he?'

There was a brief silence while Arabella wished that she could make the duke vanish in a puff of smoke. Seeing this clearly written on her face, he said blandly, 'Ah. I gather you neglected to tell Lord Chalfont that your eldest brother is a baron. Probably one of several things that slipped your mind, I suspect.'

'The subject didn't come up,' she muttered uncomfortably. And to Julian, 'Max knows I'm happy and don't want to go home. He won't tell Mama. At least, I don't *think* he will.'

'In which case, his lordship has been placed in the same unenviable position as myself,' observed Rockliffe, rising to his not inconsiderable height. 'I can think of only one way out of this tangle. It is not one either of you will like but perhaps it need only be of relatively short duration ... so I ask you to hold that thought and not to interrupt. Arabella, you will return with me to London where you and Elizabeth will confess the fine joke you have played upon us all. My entire --'

'It wasn't a joke!' protested Arabella.

'It was most certainly a joke,' repeated the duke firmly. 'And I believe I desired you not to interrupt.' He waited until she pressed her lips together and then resumed. 'My friends will enjoy this enormously and have a great deal of fun at my expense ... but they will also ensure that the story filters out to society at large in the least damaging way, carefully omitting all mention of your recent whereabouts. The two of you will probably become a nine-day-wonder but if you are charmingly contrite, you will be forgiven. In a few weeks, when the dust has settled, you will be free to either go home to Yorkshire or return here – depending on the wishes of your family. As for Elizabeth, if her father can be persuaded to agree, she may remain in St James Square with the duchess and myself for a while longer.' He stopped speaking and eyed Julian and Arabella with an air of sardonic detachment. 'You will wish to discuss it. Do so, by all means. I shall return to Newark for the night. But you may expect me by ten o'clock tomorrow morning in the happy anticipation, Arabella, of finding you ready to travel south with me.'

'And if she isn't?' asked Julian.

'If she is not,' returned Rockliffe blandly, 'we shall probably all regret it.'

* * *

Left looking helplessly at each other, Arabella was the first to speak. She said, 'We have to talk about all this – but first, we should stop the children worrying.'

'By telling them what?' Julian refrained from admitting that *he* hadn't stopped worrying; that the unlikelihood of her coming back if she once left was lying like a stone in his chest.

'The truth. And if I make it sound like an adventure, they may not mind very much.'

The second Arabella walked into the nursery, Ellie hurtled across to hug her, saying fiercely, 'You can't go. You can't leave us. Sir Julian – *tell* her!'

'I have told her,' he replied quietly. 'And now she has something to tell *you* ... so perhaps we could all sit?'

Rob joined Ellie in towing Arabella down between them on the sofa. Tom stayed where he was, staring into Julian's eyes. He said, 'Has the duke gone?' And when Julian nodded, 'Good. I knew you'd get rid of him. You won't let anybody upset Miss Lizzie, will you?'

'I'll certainly do my best to stop them ... and if I'm not here, I know I can rely on you. Now come and sit by me and listen.'

All three children fell silent, staring expectantly at Arabella. She cast a slightly wild glance at Julian and then said simply, 'It's a story about two girl cousins who were more like sisters – though one of their families was much richer than the other. They were invited to stay in London with a duke and duchess – yes, Tom, *that* duke. The first girl – the one from the poorer family – wanted to go but her papa wouldn't let her. The second girl *didn't* want to go and she thought that, if only one of them could go to London, it ought to be her cousin. So she had a clever idea.' Arabella paused and shut her eyes for a moment. 'She suggested that she and her cousin should change places without telling anyone.'

Ellie's eyes grew wide. 'Ooh! Do they look like twins?'

'No. But that didn't matter because no one where they were going knew what they looked like.' Glancing across at Tom, Arabella could see that he already knew where her story was going. So far as she could tell, neither Rob nor Ellie had any idea as yet. 'They travelled from their homes together and changed places when they got to Newark. One cousin – Elizabeth – went on to the duke's house in London; the other one – me – came here to look after you.' She paused and clasped her hands tightly together. 'I'm sorry ... but my name isn't Lizzie. It is Arabella. At home, everyone calls me Belle.'

The silence when she finished speaking was a long one but inevitably it was Tom who broke it. He said bitterly, 'Was you ever going to tell us? If that duke hadn't come, would you even be telling us now?'

'I wanted to tell you – *all* of you. But the secret belonged to Lizzie as well, so it didn't seem right to share it. Are you angry with me, Tom?'

'I don't know. A bit, maybe.'

'Why?' asked Ellie. 'It's like a story in a book. I don't mind. Do you, Rob?'

Rob shook his head. 'I suppose we call you Miss Belle now?'

'Yes – though it may take you a while to get used to it.'

'That's not important,' said Tom impatiently. 'What matters is that duke. He knows, doesn't he? It's why he came here. So what's he going to do?'

'He says that what Lizzie and I have done is causing all sorts of problems,' confessed Arabella. 'So he wants me to go to London for a little while to help put it right.'

All three children absorbed this. Then Ellie said, 'Then you'd come back?'

She nodded, not quite daring to promise but adding persuasively, 'It need only be for a few weeks. Would that be all right?'

'I suppose,' mumbled Tom. 'What do *you* think, sir? Is this duke being fair?'

'This isn't about what is fair,' replied Julian evasively, coming to his feet. 'And nothing is decided yet. Meanwhile, I want a bath and dry clothes.'

And time, he thought as he walked out, *to make sense of it all*.

CHAPTER SEVENTEEN

While Julian sat in the usual shallow depth of water that was also less hot than he would have liked, it started to dawn on him that there were a number of holes in what he'd been told so far.

Why hadn't Arabella wanted to go to London? Wasn't that what all girls wanted? Parties and balls, pretty clothes and sophisticated admirers ... perhaps even a husband? He could understand the other girl agreeing to the exchange because she was getting the better end of it. But what had Arabella got out of it? A dilapidated, understaffed house, three illegitimate children and a man who was only ever complete when he sat at a harpsichord. If there was sense in that, he couldn't see it. What he *could* see, only too clearly, was that when she had first come to Chalfont, she had planned to stay only as long as her cousin remained in London. There had never been any intention of permanence ... so why should that change now?

He wondered about her family. He thought about some of the suggestions she had made regarding the home farm and tenants ... and what knowledge like that said about her background. She was related to a duke, for God's sake; she had also spoken of brothers – though he couldn't remember how many – and one of them was a baron. He found himself dwelling on that fact along with the possibility of wealth. It did not occur to him that, leaving money aside, the Earl of Chalfont substantially out-ranked Baron Brandon. He merely saw his personal limitations and liabilities ... and total lack of assets.

And yet, regardless of any of that, Arabella insisted that she didn't want to leave. If she truly meant that – and he couldn't begin to imagine why she would – then she must also mean what she said about coming back. But if she thought that would be possible, she hadn't considered the matter properly because, whatever her feelings were, Julian couldn't imagine her family allowing it. They would probably be horrified that she had been living under his roof at all.

Climbing out of the bathtub before the water was completely cold and reaching for a towel, he tried convincing himself that losing her wouldn't be the end of the world. He had music again; the children were less of a mystery; and the wine money had temporarily eased his financial burdens. Life without her would go on as it had before and he'd manage because he had to. The trouble was, the prospect left his insides frozen with misery.

Two rooms away, Arabella was telling herself that everything might have been much worse. Rockliffe hadn't dragged her away with him; he hadn't threatened to write to Mama; and, if he really *was* angry, it didn't show. The children – even Tom – had taken her revelations better than she had expected. And Julian had brushed the whole thing aside ... seeming to care for nothing at all so long as she stayed.

He had said it wasn't purely because of the children. He had said ... things that made her hope for something she had tried very hard *not* to hope for. But if he *truly* couldn't bear the thought of her leaving, didn't that mean that – even if he didn't know it himself yet – he had perhaps grown fond of her?

But that wasn't a possibility she dared contemplate, so she set it aside and forced herself to go back over everything the duke had said ... particularly the parts that affected Elizabeth. Then she was suddenly struck by a breath-taking possibility; a possibility which would give Julian at least one of the advantages she wanted for him. She turned it over and over in her mind ... wondering how best to make it happen. And finally, wanting to look her best for the evening ahead, she put on the prettiest of her cousin's gowns and sent for Violet to tidy her hair.

The latter took some time because the maid wanted a proper account of the garbled tale Ellie had taken downstairs to the kitchen. Typically, at the end of it all, Violet said, 'So everything you told me about your cousin – all of that was really *you*, was it?'

'Yes.'

'Well, God knows why you'd want to be here when you could be going to balls and suchlike in London. You must have windmills in your head.' And then, with a sly smile, 'Not that his young lordship is hard to swallow, is he?'

'No. Is my hair finished?'

Violet nodded, then said casually, 'A girl could do worse.'

'I'm late.' Arabella rose and headed for the door. 'And only ladies' maids of very long-standing are allowed this sort of conversation.'

Julian was already in the parlour, tidier but looking no less tense than he had done an hour ago. Almost before she had got through the door, he said, 'What have you decided?'

'I haven't decided anything – and I won't until we have discussed it.'

'Why? You already know what I think – what I want. But that's beside the point, isn't it?' Hands in his pockets, he kept his eyes on the carpet at his feet. 'You'll do what you have to. The duke hasn't left you with much choice.'

'It isn't his decision,' she began.

'It's not mine, either.' He turned away to stare out of the window. He couldn't look at her. Since the night he'd kissed her, the temptation to do it again had become a constant ache. Right now, he wanted to snatch her up in his arms and never let go. His control was hanging by a thread. If he looked at her, it would snap. He said, 'Just don't make any promises you can't keep.'

'I wasn't planning to. Julian, can we please sit down and --'

The jangling of the doorbell caused her to stop speaking. Without a word, Julian stalked away to throw the door open ... and found himself face to face with Dr Featherstone.

'Paul?' he said blankly. 'What brings you here?'

'A pleasure to see you, too,' retorted the doctor. 'Am I allowed inside?'

'Of course.' Julian stepped back. 'Sorry.'

Dropping his hat and gloves on a table, Paul said, 'But for Davy Padgett breaking his leg, I'd have been here sooner. Abigail Caldercott sent a note saying you'd been summoned home because of an alarming visitor.' With a grin and a bow for Arabella, he said, 'Good evening, Mistress Marsden. I apologise if I intrude but Miss Abby was worried enough to think someone ought to check that all is well.'

Groaning inwardly and wondering how many times she'd have to do this, Arabella said briskly, 'We had a visit from the Duke of Rockliffe, to whom I am distantly related. He came because he has guessed that my cousin and I exchanged places and that it is Elizabeth, not I, who is currently a guest in his London house.' Holding her head high, she dropped a curtsy and added, 'I am Arabella Brandon, by the way. And I apologise for the deception.'

He stared at her in awed fascination while he absorbed this remarkable revelation and then said, 'Well that certainly explains a few things Janet and I had wondered about.' And to Julian, 'Did you know about this?'

'Not until today. It doesn't matter.'

'*Not matter?*'

'No,' said Julian stubbornly.

'So the duke travelled from London just to pay a social call, did he?'

'Not exactly,' admitted Arabella. 'He wants the situation corrected.'

'Yes. I imagine he would – and quickly, too. Is he still here?'

'No. But we can look forward to a return visit tomorrow.' Julian poured a glass of wine and handed it to his friend. 'Are you staying for dinner?'

'If that was an invitation and you're not wishing me at the devil – yes.'

'Don't be an idiot,' mumbled Julian. 'Just sit down, will you?'

Paul grinned at Arabella. 'Graciousness personified, isn't he?'

'It's been a difficult day,' she replied repressively. 'But since you're here to keep Julian company, it might be a good idea if I ate with the children this evening.'

'Please don't run away on my account,' he said quickly.

'I'm not running away at *all*. I'm making sure the children aren't still anxious and I'm giving the two of you a chance to talk – which I presume is what you both want.' She smiled at Julian. 'You'll be in the library as usual?'

He hunched one shoulder. 'Yes.'

'Then we'll speak later.'

When she had left the room, Paul said quietly, 'I'm guessing that the duke – Rockliffe, is it? – has some idea of how this bizarre business can be straightened out?'

'He says the only way is for the girls to make a clean breast of everything and pretend it was a joke. Not that *he's* laughing.'

'Well, you can't really blame him, can you? He's been put in a very awkward position. So I suppose he wants to take Liz – *Arabella* to London?'

'Yes.'

'Will she go?'

'I don't know.' Julian stared into his untouched glass. 'Probably.'

Paul said slowly, 'You don't have to answer if you'd rather not ... but I'm gathering you don't want to lose her.'

'No. But it's not up to me, is it?'

'Does she know you want her to stay?'

'Yes.' Inwardly cringing at his earlier behaviour, Julian thought, *How much more pathetic could I be? Christ – I might as well have begged on my knees.* He said, 'But I doubt if it's going to be up to her either. From what I've seen of him so far, whatever happens next will be dictated by bloody Rockliffe.'

'Not necessarily,' demurred Paul. 'She certainly stood up to *me.*'

Julian shook his head. 'You didn't meet him. He's not the sort of man people say no to. And he made a damned good case – all about the other girl being left to face the music on her own and not being able to accept some fellow who might ask her to marry him. Arabella won't leave her cousin in the lurch. She'll go to help put things right there, just as she's been doing here.' He paused, dragging in a long breath. 'She says she'll come back. I think ... I think she actually wants to. But they're not going to let her, are they? Rockliffe, her mother and her brother – who is a baron, by the way. They're not going to let her come back here to this. Why the hell would they?'

For the first time, Paul saw what was in the other man's face. It was an expression he hadn't seen since before Julian had first sat down at the Caldercott ladies' harpsichord ... and one he'd hoped never to see again. Utter bleakness coupled with desperate longing. Keeping his tone casual, he said, 'No. Arabella can't come back as your housekeeper-governess. But perhaps she could come back as something else.'

For a second, Julian stared at him blankly. Then, on a bitter laugh, he said, 'Now why didn't *I* think of that? I'm sure her family would be *delighted* to see her married to a poverty-stricken joke of an earl with three baseborn children. As for Arabella – she'd have to be demented to even consider it.'

Paul didn't think so. Once or twice he had seen the look in those expressive grey eyes as they rested on his lordship ... as, apparently, had Abigail and Beatrice Caldercott. All three of them shared the same suspicions. The real problem, he thought, wasn't going to lie with Arabella or even her family. The root of it was going to be Julian himself.

He said, 'That's merely your opinion. Too cowardly to find out for sure, are you?'

'*What?*'

'Leaving the question of marriage aside, it's simple enough. If you love her, you should tell her. True, there's a risk she might not feel the same. But at least you'd know.'

Julian let his head fall back against the chair and shut his eyes. He said wearily, 'Yes. I'd know. But what good would that do? She'll still have to leave and with scant chance of being allowed within a mile of me again. If things were different ... but they're not. So somehow I have to get through this without making it worse than it need be.'

* * *

Once the children were settled for the night, Arabella sat in her room thinking. It seemed Julian was leaving the decision on whether or not to go with Rockliffe up to her and because she now had a dazzling ulterior motive to do so, she found it easy to make. There was no point taking Elizabeth's clothes to London when her own were already there, so she packed only what she would need for the journey ... then, leaving her door slightly ajar, she sat by the hearth and waited.

It was over an hour before the first notes of the harpsichord drifted up from the library ... a soulful, lingering melody in a minor key. Arabella ran lightly down the stairs. The library door stood open but the room was lit by only one branch of candles. In the shadowy gloom, Julian had begun toying moodily with a piece by Couperin. Continuing to play and without turning his head, he said, 'Well? Are you leaving?'

Closing the door behind her, she walked slowly to his side.

'For Lizzie's sake, I think I must.'

The melody froze briefly and then resumed. 'Yes. Of course.'

'But it need only be for two or three --'

'Don't.' The Couperin went on unabated. 'Please don't say it.'

'Say what?'

'That you'll come back. We both know that somebody will stop you.' For the space of half a dozen bars, he said nothing because he was terrified of what might come out if he opened his mouth at all. Then, 'And you never intended to stay here permanently, did you?'

Uncertain, ashamed and guilty, Arabella wished he would stop playing and look at her. 'Not when I first came. But nothing that seemed true *then* is true *now*.'

'Isn't it?'

'No.'

'So you'd have told me who you were even if Rockliffe hadn't turned up?'

'I – I wanted to. But there was Lizzie, you see. And --'

'And there still is.' Couperin became a menacing Bach fugue, as he fought the choking sensation in his chest. 'So there's really no more to be said, is there?'

'What? Of course there is. We need to discuss this properly and --'

'*Stop!*' He played a single, crashing discord, rose and spun round to face her. 'What is there to discuss? You are leaving and there's an end of it. So will you please do us both a kindness and just *go away.*'

Arabella's jaw dropped. In the five weeks since she had first met him, she had never once heard him raise his voice. Now he stood there looking rumpled and aggrieved and beautiful and so inexpressibly *dear* that she wanted to cry. But since that wouldn't solve anything … and since her emotions were as raw as his … she lifted her chin and said, 'Why are you being so difficult?'

'I'm not being difficult. I--'

'Yes you are – and totally unreasonable, too. You think I'm any happier about this than you are? I'm not. But this stupid tangle was my idea, so it's up to me to put it right.'

'I've gathered that. So go and do it.' He turned away again and sat down before he lost the battle to keep his distance. He lifted his hands to the keyboard and because, in that first moment, music wouldn't come, played a series of dark, descending chords. 'But don't promise the children anything. I understand the situation. They won't. Now please go away and leave me alone.'

And finally, his fingers found their way into something which, if asked, he couldn't have put a name to.

Arabella stood mute and irresolute for a moment before realising there was nothing she could say that he would listen to whilst in this particular mood. Just loud enough to be heard over the music, she said, 'We'll speak in the morning, then. Goodnight.'

As soon as he heard the library door close behind her, Julian strode across and locked it. Then he slid down to the floor and dropped his head in his hands.

She was leaving. That was the last he would ever see of her. And it was tearing him apart.

* * *

Having spent a large part of the night writing a long letter to Max, Arabella donned Elizabeth's grey wool travelling gown, laid out her cloak and asked Violet to put her valise in the hall. Downstairs, she found the library door locked – but without music pouring from the other side of it. This was unusual. Julian had stopped locking it over a week ago which, but for the silence, suggested that he was inside. Arabella tapped on the door, called his name … and waited. Nothing. Sighing, she went to take breakfast with the children.

Tom took one look at her gown and said, 'You're going, then?'

'Yes. I have to. And though I can't promise when I'll be back, I *can* promise to try my very best to make it soon.' She smiled round at the three of them. 'I'll write to you and you can write back. That will make the time go quicker. And meanwhile, I want all of you to look after his lordship. Will you do that?'

Rob nodded, looking gloomy.

Ellie said stoutly, 'I always look after him.'

'I know. I know you do.'

Arabella rose, unable to swallow anything past the lump in her throat. Following her to the door out of earshot of the others, Tom said accusingly, 'You're not promising to come back at all, are you?'

She shook her head. 'His lordship asked me not to. He – he thinks I may be prevented.'

'By the duke.'

'Or my family. And when the duke arrives this morning, please be polite to him. This is my fault, not his.' Arabella paused and, trying to think past her sense of incipient doom, pushed the letter to Max into the boy's hand. 'Take that to be collected please, Tom. And now I need to speak to his lordship. Do you know where he is?'

'Where do you think?'

Arabella stopped dead and swung to face him. 'But he's not playing.'

'No. He isn't, is he?'

Suddenly alarmed, she ran to the library and rattled the door handle.

'Julian? *Julian!* Open the door.' And banging on the panels with her fists when there was no response, 'This won't help. Rockliffe will be here any minute and you and I have to talk. Julian – *please!'*

The door remained stubbornly locked but the silence was abruptly fractured by a thunderous series of rhythmic and harmonically-shifting chords. Relief caused Arabella's hands to relax and she pressed her palms against the wood. After a moment, the music stopped as suddenly as it had started; there were a few seconds of seemingly acute silence, followed by the gentle opening bars of something by Rameau.

'Julian?' she called. 'Please open --'

Rameau dissolved into the same deafening sequence as before, drowning out her words and this time continuing into complex snatches of phrase, punctuated by brief, unexpected pauses. Arabella leaned her brow against the door, knowing exactly what the music was telling her and feeling as if her heart was being sliced open. She was aware that, behind her on the far side of the hall, Rose, Violet and the children stood in a bewildered huddle. Ignoring them, she waited until the musical fury slid back into Rameau and called Julian's name again.

Staring sightlessly down the length of the harpsichord, Julian heard her voice and immediately plunged back into the explosion of sound that would drown it out. He hadn't played *Vertigo* since Vienna ... had almost forgotten he'd ever played it. But right now, those passages of dark, violent chords were exactly what he needed. If she'd stop calling to him, he could seek safety and balance in Couperin or Bach. He needed both before he dared leave this room if he didn't want to risk disgracing himself.

In the hall, the wild music drowned out the doorbell, Rose's voice and Rockliffe's arrival, so that the first Arabella knew of the duke's presence was when, over an impossibly rapid run of notes, he said, 'What *is* that he's playing?'

'I don't know.' She moved away from the door, drawing the duke with her so she need not shout to make herself heard. 'He's never played it before. It sounds so ... so turbulent.' *And hurt*, she thought. *So very hurt.*

Rockliffe nodded, a slight frown creasing his brow. Whatever that piece of music was and however great the emotional turmoil revealed by it, its execution required a player of exceptional skill ... so he leaned against the newel post at the foot of the stairs and waited. A minute or two later there was a brief lull, followed by the first crisp notes of Bach.

Arabella heaved a sigh of relief. 'The *Fantasia*. It's one of his favourites. Can we give him a few minutes, please?'

'I can resign myself to a short recital. I gather he isn't taking your departure well?'

'He's trying to. He knows I have to go. But he doesn't believe I'll come back.'

In which he is almost certainly right, thought Rockliffe, falling silent to listen.

After the *Fantasia* came a fragment of Mozart and then something astonishingly lovely. Seeing Arabella brushing tears aside, Rockliffe murmured, 'His own work?'

'Yes.'

His brows rose but he said nothing, waiting until the harpsichord finally fell silent.

Then, strolling back to the library door and scarcely raising his voice, he said, 'Thank you, Lord Chalfont. That was a privilege – as, indeed, was the earlier piece which I would enjoy hearing in its entirety on some future occasion. However, I am having Mistress Brandon's valise loaded on to my chaise as we speak ... so if you wish to bid her goodbye, now would be the time to come out and do so.'

On the other side of the door, Julian pressed the heels of his hands over his eyes and tried to pull himself together – at least temporarily. Quite aside from Arabella and Rockliffe, the children must be wondering what was wrong with him. He drew a long, ragged breath, stood up and reached for his coat. His cravat was a crumpled mess, he needed a shave and his hair – still far too long – had, as usual, escaped its ribbon. Sighing, he realised that he must look every bit as deranged as his behaviour had suggested. Putting himself to rights as best he could, he summoned what resolve he could find and went to unlock the door.

The second he appeared, Ellie shot across the hall to grab his hand.

'Why are you angry? Is it us? D-did we do something?'

'No. Of course you didn't. And I'm not angry.'

'The *music* was angry,' she insisted, still looking worried.

Too tired and heartsick to explain, he merely shook his head and turned to the duke, managing a bow and wondering what the hell he could say. Sparing him the need to say anything at all, Rockliffe murmured, 'Who wrote that first piece? The … er … angry one?'

Surprised but glad of the neutral topic, Julian said, 'Pancrace Royer; French and not very prolific.' He thought for a moment and then, feeling more information was required, added, 'He's dead.'

'Ah.' Forced to suppress a smile, Rockliffe said, 'Your repertoire is extensive.'

Julian coloured faintly and shrugged.

'But now … Arabella, I shall wait in the carriage. Join me when you are ready.' Upon which note, he sauntered to the door.

The children were hugging Arabella while she told them to practise their reading and be good for Rose and Violet and to write to her and not to let his lordship be lonely. Then she disengaged herself, looked across at Julian and tried to smile.

Feeling like an automaton, he closed the distance between them and, bowing over her hand, said woodenly, 'Have a safe journey. I hope you and your cousin are able to – to resolve matters to the duke's satisfaction. We … the children and I … we'll miss you.'

'And I'll miss all of you.' Arabella's voice was noticeably unsteady and tears weren't far away. Julian looked every bit as miserable as she felt, yet he was behaving as if they scarcely knew each other. *Is this it?* she thought. *Is this all he's going to say?*

Drowning in misty, dark grey eyes, Julian felt his self-control begin to slip. Every muscle in his body was aching with the need to hold her. If she didn't turn away soon, he wasn't sure he'd be able to stop himself. Then, drawing a shuddering breath, she did turn away … and he could have wept.

With one last farewell for the children, she walked to the door and then through it and, without looking back, let Rockliffe's groom hand her into the carriage and close the door.

Julian felt as if all the air had been sucked from his lungs. He couldn't breathe and there was an odd roaring in his ears. The carriage rolled forward and …

'Well, you made a right mess of that, didn't you?' said Tom.

'I – what?'

'Made a mess of it. Oh – it was all very proper and polite but it didn't look as if you cared tuppence she was going. But perhaps you *don't*.'

'Of course I do,' said Julian. 'But --'

'So why didn't you kiss her – or at least give her a hug like me and Rob and Ellie did? You wanted to, didn't you?'

Mere wanting in no way described it. 'Yes.'

'Right. And anybody could see *she* wanted you to.'

Julian stared at him. 'She did?'

'Bloody hell,' breathed Tom. 'You're the grown-up. Couldn't you tell?'

Julian stepped into the open doorway and watched the ducal carriage making its ponderous way down his badly-rutted drive. Then he started to run.

Sitting beside the duke, Arabella told herself she would *not* look back. Looking back would make everything worse. Not that she was sure *how* everything could be worse; she only knew that if Julian wasn't on the steps watching her go or even if he was, the last shreds of her composure would fly out of the window and she'd probably start to howl.

Then, despite her misery, she heard Tom yelling, '*Wait! Stop!*'

She tried to let down the window, her fingers made clumsy by haste. Rockliffe reached across to do it for her before knocking on the roof to signal his coachman to pull up.

'Don't tell me,' he sighed. 'His lordship has recovered the use of his legs – if not his brain.'

With her head out of the window and her eyes fixed on Julian pounding after them, Arabella didn't hear him. Even before the carriage had come to a halt, she had the door unlatched so that when Julian arrived beside it, she was able to tumble out into his arms. She thought she said something ... or that he did. And then they were holding each other so tightly it was a wonder either of them could breathe.

Her hair beneath his cheek and his heart thundering against his ribs, Julian managed to murmur, 'I'm sorry. I know you have to go. I'm sorry about before. I just ... I couldn't --'

'It doesn't matter,' she whispered. 'You're here now.'

'Yes.' He lifted his head so he could look into her eyes. 'Yes, I am.'

Rockliffe gave a gentle cough, just enough to remind them of his presence.

'It is a pity you had to leave this until now, Chalfont,' he remarked lazily. 'But since you did ... and since there is a limit to what I can pretend not to have seen, not to mention the many miles between here and London ... I would appreciate you deferring the rest of this touching scene until another time. And yes,' he said, when both of them looked at him, 'you may hope that there *will* be another time. So please get back in the carriage, Arabella.'

Slowly, she disengaged herself from Julian to lay one palm briefly against his cheek.

'You'll be all right?'

'Yes.' He helped her back into her seat but didn't let go of her hand. 'May I write to you?'

'You had better. If you don't, I'll tell Ellie.'

'Tell Tom instead. I'm already in trouble with him.' He raised her fingers to his lips and then, looking at the duke, said, 'I apologise for my behaviour earlier, your Grace. I was somewhat ... agitated.'

'Agitated? Clearly, you have a talent for understatement.' Amusement lurked in Rockliffe's eyes. 'Expect to hear from me, Chalfont. And now, finally ... goodbye.'

* * *

A little while later, Rockliffe swayed easily with the motion of the carriage watching Arabella re-living those last moments with the earl and trying to evaluate what they meant. Finally, deciding that it was time to divert her attention, he said idly, 'Tell me about his lordship. His musical history, for example. Has he ever graced a concert platform?'

'Oh!' Arabella's eyes flew wide and, instead of answering, she clapped her hand over her mouth. Then, sounding thoroughly annoyed with herself, she said, 'I had a plan. And I forgot all about it. I wanted you to hear Julian play – properly, not through the library door. Then I was going to persuade you to sponsor him and provide him with a chance to perform – and I *forgot*. How could I have been so *stupid*?'

'I imagine knowing that his lordship was in the grip of a nerve-storm may have had something to do with it,' murmured Rockliffe. 'As for performing in public ... one can't help wondering if he has the mental resilience for it.'

'He's a different person when he plays. He's been performing for the village --'

'Recitals for the villagers can scarcely be compared with professional concerts.'

'I know that!' said Arabella crossly, wishing she could read the duke's enigmatic expression. 'But even from the little you heard, you *must* have realised how good he is.'

'Must I?'

'Yes. He's extraordinary. He --'

Sighing, Rockliffe held up one staying hand and when she fell silent, said, 'You are biased, Arabella. Set your opinions aside and give me facts – beginning, as I asked a few moments ago, with whether or not he has ever occupied a concert platform.'

'Yes. He has,' replied Arabella. And promptly launched into everything Julian had ever told her about Vienna.

Dear me, thought Rockliffe some three hours later and having learned more about obscure composers and the internal workings of a harpsichord than he ever wanted to know. *One forgets how exhausting young love can be. I must be getting old.*

CHAPTER EIGHTEEN

The Duchess of Rockliffe read her husband's letter for the second time and groaned.

Arabella is here, he had written. *I believe there is a way to resolve this – but I shall not know whether she will agree to it until tomorrow. An additional complication is that, although no declarations have yet been made, she and Chalfont are in love with each other. Whatever the outcome and barring unforeseen circumstances, you may expect me home on Tuesday. It might be best to leave Elizabeth in ignorance until then.*

'A way to resolve it?' muttered Adeline to herself. 'How? And as for Elizabeth … isn't it already bad enough that the only man who interests her is Ralph Sherbourne? Though any interest on *his* part may wither fast enough when he finds out she's the daughter of a lowly vicar with a dowry that probably wouldn't buy a decent horse.'

Had Adeline known it, the feelings that had assailed Ralph after Cedric's wedding had made him look inside himself and dislike everything he found. A man who had locked his feelings away because he no longer trusted them; who had convinced himself that he didn't give a damn what anyone said or thought; and whose nearest thing to a friend these days was his valet. What sadder fellow could there be than one who had to turn to Greek philosophers for comfort? That night had taught him that, unless he wanted to die a lonely and embittered old man, he couldn't marry a woman who would only tolerate him for the sake of the title … particularly when there was a lady who, for reasons that eluded him, actually seemed to *like* him.

At the Martindale ball, he danced with a three pretty young things whose parents were shopping for a title and trod a gavotte with a little widow whose gift for double-entendre might, had he been looking for one, have made her an amusing mistress. By the time the Rockliffe party arrived – minus the duke – Ralph was struggling to resist the lure of the card-room. Then Arabella Brandon's blue eyes met his with a smile that seemed to say '*Oh – there you are!*' … and the evening no longer seemed a desert.

He claimed her hand for the quadrille and, while waiting for the music to begin, said, 'Do you know, Mistress Brandon ... I find you pleasantly alarming.'

'Pleasantly alarming?' she echoed. '*Is* there such a thing?'

'I think so.' His mouth curled in a smile. 'You give the impression of being pleased to see me ... which is pleasant – but also alarming because I am unaccustomed to it.'

Elizabeth looked at him cautiously. She *was* pleased to see him but hadn't been aware of making it obvious. She said, 'No one else is ever pleased to see you?'

'Rarely.'

'Not even your family? Your brothers?'

'Them least of all. But since I would happily never lay eyes on either of them again, the feeling is entirely mutual.' He paused, his expression sardonic. 'My family is a perfect example of the truism which regrets that one can't choose one's relatives. And that is probably the *only* thing on which my siblings and I can wholeheartedly agree.'

Further meaningful conversation being impossible for the duration of the dance, Ralph spent the time watching her without appearing to do so. She was beautiful, graceful and not in the least flirtatious. Of those three qualities, it was the fact that she didn't flutter or simper or try to prise compliments out of him that appealed most. There was also honesty, oddly coupled with reserve ... and glimpses, from time to time, of warmth. She had told him she did not want to marry but had given reasons which, in Ralph's opinion, didn't seem adequate. Indeed, he could only think of one possibility that might account for it. But if he wanted her to confess that, she had to be given reason to trust him.

It occurred to him that he had recently thought quite a lot about trust and the reciprocal nature of it. Perhaps it was time to put that theory into practice. Perhaps, more pertinently, it was time to find out if whatever he felt for Arabella Brandon was equal to the amount of iron-clad nerve he would need to lay bare some part of his past.

As the quadrille came to an end and he escorted her from the floor, he said, 'Will you drive with me tomorrow? To the physic garden at Chelsea, perhaps, if the day is fine.'

A voice at the back of Elizabeth's mind told her that she ought to refuse. She was getting too close to him – and he to her. It was neither safe nor wise and would doubtless force her to tell more lies. She should smile and plead a previous engagement.

The smile came easily ... but the right words were beyond her.

She said, 'Thank you, my lord. I shall look forward to it.'

* * *

The following afternoon was one of those mid-October days of bright but only marginally warm sunshine. Having settled Mistress Brandon in his carriage, Ralph chatted on impersonal topics whilst navigating his way through the traffic. He talked of the opera, which he enjoyed and the theatre, of which he was less fond; when asked about books, he admitted that he had read none of the novels currently in vogue because his taste ran to ancient literature and philosophy in their original languages. Then, since Arabella seemed to find this interesting, he was tempted to continue talking about Aristophanes or Plato – or anything at all rather than the painful thing he had brought her here to confess.

Once at the physic garden, he tossed the reins to his groom and helped her down from the carriage, saying, 'Shall we begin with the rock garden? I'm told it is the oldest in England ... so I suppose one should see it.'

Taking the arm he offered her, she said, 'You haven't been here before?'

'No. I chose it today because it is less popular and therefore quieter than the various alternatives. And I have a story to tell you ... if you wish to hear it.'

Elizabeth glanced sharply at him. 'Yes. But only if you want to share it.'

He didn't. He actually felt faintly nauseous. But he nodded and said, 'Very well, then. The scene is Hyde Park at a little after dawn on a January morning some seven years ago. Two gentlemen stand back to back. Both are holding pistols pointing skywards. A short distance away are their seconds and the doctor everyone always hopes will not be necessary. One of the seconds begins the count and the principals pace away from each other in time to it.'

As always when he let himself think of that day, Ralph recalled the sulky gleam of the pistol barrels ... the crispness of the frosty grass beneath his feet ... the way his breath had smoked on the air. He remembered wondering why Edgar had removed his wig to reveal close-cropped hair of butter-yellow. He remembered it all in excruciating detail.

The count ended; they pivoted to face each other and the handkerchief fluttered down. Then, in the split-second before he fired, Edgar shifted a half-step to his left ... and in nightmarish slow-motion, crumpled to the ground.

An instant of horrified disbelief; his pistol falling from nerveless fingers; himself, racing across the turf, thinking, No! No, no, no!

Then he was on his knees, seeing that there was nothing to be done; aware of the doctor and the seconds closing in on him and saying helplessly, 'Why? Why, Edgar?'

Blood pumping from his chest and pooling bright against the frosty ground, Edgar Wilkes peered up at him. Then, his mouth contorting into something half-smile, half-grimace, he used his dying breath to say, 'See you in hell, Kilburn.'

He was on his feet without knowing how he'd got there. Augustus Wilkes was clutching his brother's hand. The doctor's expression was telling him something he knew but didn't want to hear.

'He's dead, my lord.'

Somehow he managed a coherent reply. 'I am aware.'

'I shall have to report it.'

'You may also wish to report that it wasn't my intention.'

Tears streaming down his face, Augustus said, 'You're a bloody murderer, Kilburn!' ... in counterpoint with Richard Lazenby, his own second, saying, 'Ralph? What the hell just happened?'

'Richard,' murmured Ralph, emerging from the play inside his head, 'could not believe the evidence of his own eyes; could not believe he had just seen Edgar move deliberately into my line of fire.'

'Why?' Elizabeth stared at him, shocked. 'I'm not doubting your word – but why would he *do* that? Why would *anyone* do such a thing?'

Richard and Augustus had both asked the same question. Even though he now knew it wasn't the whole story, Ralph gave Elizabeth the same answer he'd given them.

'Edgar Wilkes had a discreditable secret which he knew I shared and which he imagined I meant to make public. In fact, my reasons for confronting him with what I knew were quite different. I had hoped to make him stop what he was doing before someone else … someone with less reason than I to be helpful … ruined him – and the rest of his family as well. But Edgar could not accept that. He challenged me to fight in terms that made a refusal impossible.' Ralph's mouth curled wryly. 'His brother, Augustus, said that if such was the case surely Edgar would have done his best to kill me. Since I thought the same, I could only theorise that he had believed my death would result in exposure.'

That answer had not appeased Augustus.

'You've just killed a man and you're standing there like a block of ice talking about theories? *And what* damned secret?*'*

'You don't know?'

'If I did, I wouldn't be asking. Well?'

'Since it died with Edgar, there is nothing to be gained by revealing it now.'

And Richard, homing in on the crux of the matter, *'Forget the secret. Unless I'm missing something, we just watched Edgar commit suicide.'*

'That is how it would seem.'

His composure astounded him. Inside he was a seething mass of nausea.

'It's a bloody lie!' shouted Augustus. 'If you think to avoid a trial by branding my brother a suicide, you can think again, Kilburn. I'll see you swing for this.'

'No. I have fought three duels, all of them identical. Edgar knew that I would aim for a flesh wound to the left arm … so when, as you all saw, he shifted to his left in that last second, he did not do so accidentally.'

He had not believed it could get any worse … but it had.

'I don't watch you bloodthirsty idiots blowing holes in each other,' snapped the doctor, busy with his bag. 'I merely deal with the consequences. So I saw nothing.'

'Nor I.' How quickly Augustus had pounced on that. 'There was nothing to see.'

'You'll lie under oath?' And how naïve of Richard to imagine that he might not.

'Who says it would be a lie? You?' Wilkes' laughter was hard and mirthless. 'It'll be your word against mine, Kilburn – and nobody'll be surprised you finally killed your man. But don't blacken Edgar's name with this farrago about suicide. No one will believe it. When a gentleman wants to kill himself, he puts a pistol to his head. He doesn't need someone to do the deed for him.'

The silence stretched out to infinity while he considered his reply.

'He does if he wants to take that someone with him.'

Coming slowly back from the past, Ralph realised that they had completed a circuit of the rock garden while he had been speaking and that he had seen none of it. Striving for his usual tone, he said, 'My apologies. That might have been done with less … detail.'

Frowning a little, Elizabeth suspected that it might have been done with much more. She said slowly, 'You did not come to trial.'

'I did not come to trial because I left the country.' He hesitated and then added, 'Augustus was right in saying it would be my word against his. Richard suggested that labelling Edgar a suicide would do me no credit and that the truth would work better if it came from him. So I left and he did his best. It proved insufficient.'

'And Philippa?' she asked gently. 'I am guessing that she also knew this secret and would have spoken out in the event of your death?'

'That is what I believed at the time.' It had taken him months to work out that most of what he had believed before the duel was wrong; that it was not Philippa who had been the pawn in Edgar's misdoings but the other way about; and that by some muddled, convoluted logic, Edgar's sacrifice had been made to protect her … which was cripplingly ironic since Ralph had been trying to do the same thing. 'I knew, of course, that any hope of marriage died with Edgar.'

'But she must have known you didn't intend to kill him?'

'I hoped so,' he admitted. And thought, *I continued to hope until it finally dawned on me that it suited her better* not *to do so.* He drew a careful breath and forced himself to ask the all-important question. 'Do *you* believe that I did not?'

'Yes.' She replied without hesitation, seemingly unaware that she had laid her hand over his. 'I do. But I'm not sure why you told me.'

Relief and the warmth it brought with it made him feel vaguely light-headed and forced him to think carefully before he said anything at all. Finally, with a smile he hoped was convincing, he said, 'It has been a long time since I cared for anyone's good opinion. I find that I care a great deal for yours. I am also aware that if I am to tempt you into allowing me to court you, I need to earn your trust. Have I succeeded?'

Yes, thought Elizabeth instantly. But she couldn't say it. He was inviting her to tell him her own secret … and that if there was ever going to be a perfect moment to confess, this was it. But her heart which had opened to him through the last half hour turned into a lead weight as she remembered Arabella.

She said awkwardly, 'I – I appreciate the honour you do me, my lord. And your confidences are safe with me. But marriage is out of the question. I'm sorry.'

It wasn't the answer he had hoped for ... but knowing that the worst was behind him and she had not turned away, encouraged him to press the point. He said mildly, 'So you said when I raised the subject before. My difficulty is that you began to say that you *could* not marry – which is very different from not *wanting* to do so or, more specifically, not wanting to marry *me*. And though I may be wrong, I can only think of one reason which might account for that.'

She eyed him warily. She should not ask ... but since the chances of him guessing right were non-existent, she decided to risk it. 'And that is?'

Ralph doubted there was a tactful way of putting this, so he said, 'You were betrothed to a gentleman about to go to war. In such circumstances, anticipating your wedding vows would have been understandable. But if you did so and believe that now renders you ineligible, you are mistaken. It would only do so in the eyes of a saint or a hypocrite.'

Turning rapidly scarlet, Elizabeth stared at him in shocked disbelief.

'No! Of course I haven't – how could you think --?' she began. And then stopped abruptly as a previously unsuspected truth hit her like a blow. She thought, *Oh. That's it, isn't it? That's why Belle didn't want to come to London and wouldn't consider marriage. Why didn't I guess? And why on earth didn't she* tell *me?*

'Clearly, I am wrong,' Ralph was saying. 'I sincerely beg your pardon.'

'You n-need not. What you told me was – was kindly meant.'

'It was.' His smile was full of rueful amusement. 'But most ladies would have slapped my face before recognising that.'

That smile did what his words had not. Elizabeth looked at him and, for the first time, let loose the feelings that had been building since the day she had met him ... all of them adding up to one thing. She didn't merely *like* Ralph Sherbourne; she was physically attracted to him in a way she hadn't known existed. When he smiled, her pulse tripped and when he touched her, heat flared in unexpected places. She tried to imagine what it might be like to be kissed by him … regretting that she would never know. Now, looking at him, she realised something vital. She would *certainly* never know if she didn't harness her courage while he was offering her the chance. So she looked him in the eye and, before she could think better of it, said rapidly, 'You spoke of trust earlier … and having given me yours, you deserve no less from me. I can't marry anyone because I – I'm not who everyone thinks I am. Who *you* think I am.'

Ralph took a second to wonder if she meant this literally. On a faint note of incredulity, he said, 'You are an imposter?'

'*No!*' cried Elizabeth, aghast. And then miserably, as the truth of it struck her, 'I've never thought of it in that way … but yes. I suppose that is *exactly* what I am.'

'How intriguing.' With unimpaired calm yet also a certain amusement, he replaced her hand on his sleeve and said, 'Why don't you tell me about it?'

She stole a quick glance at his face, wondering if he really was as unmoved as he sounded. Since he did not *look* shocked or even disapproving, she drew a bracing breath and said, 'I am not Arabella Brandon. My name is Elizabeth Marsden. Arabella is my cousin and we – we agreed to change places for a time. It is she who should be here, not me.'

Out of the half dozen questions that immediately suggested themselves, Ralph eventually said, 'Well, *that* is not something I would ever have guessed. Does Rockliffe know?' And when she shook her head, 'Really? My congratulations. He is not an easy man to deceive. Indeed, many would say it cannot be done.'

'I don't know about that,' sighed Elizabeth. 'But the only person who seems to have guessed is Belle's eldest brother.' She hesitated. 'You will be wondering why we did it.'

'Somewhat. Why did you?'

She drew a long, bracing breath and, in as few words as possible, told him. At the end and without giving him chance to speak, she said, 'So there you have it. I'm Lizzie Marsden of St Mary's vicarage – and you can't imagine how often I've wished I'd never let Belle talk me into this. *She* may be comfortable with it but *I* just feel guiltier by the day.'

Distantly, Ralph wondered why what he had just learned mattered less than might have been expected. 'You haven't confided in anyone else? Mistress Audley or Lady Sarre, for example?'

Elizabeth shuddered. 'No. Heaven only knows what they would think – or what *you* do, for that matter. Why aren't you shocked?'

'My dear, I am too busy being stunned by your audacity,' he replied truthfully. 'And I would *dearly* love to see Rockliffe's face when you bring the curtain down on your little comedy. However, you need not fear that I shall tell him … though I would advise *you* to do so. He will take it much better than if he hears it some other way.'

'I know. And if it was just about me, I'd probably have told him already. But it isn't – so I can't.' She stopped walking and looked up at him, seeing the hint of laughter lurking behind his eyes. 'You ought to be angry. I don't understand why you're not. But it's a relief to have told you. And at least now you understand why – why I can't think of marriage.'

'Yes,' agreed Ralph enigmatically. 'Yes. At least I understand that.'

* * *

Two days later and just in time for dinner, Rockliffe and Arabella arrived in St James Square. While Arabella took in the magnificence of her surroundings, the duke handed his hat and cloak to the butler and ascertained that the duchess was in the drawing-room but had invited no additional company.

Rockliffe nodded and then glanced quizzically at Arabella. 'Shall we?'

'Are you sure you ought not to warn Lizzie?' Three days spent travelling with Rockliffe had largely banished Arabella's initial awe. 'What if she faints?'

'Let us hope that she doesn't.'

As soon as the door opened, Adeline was at Elizabeth's side. For the merest instant, Elizabeth glanced questioningly up at her … then her gaze drifted, first to the duke and finally to the figure beside him. Eyes widening and hands creeping to her mouth, she rose whispering, 'Belle?'

Arabella flew across the room to seize her cousin in a hard hug.

'It's all right, Lizzie. The duke says it can be straightened out without too much harm if we do it together. And – oh, I'm so happy to see you!' With an apologetic glance for Adeline, she said, 'Forgive me… but you see …?'

'I do – and there is no need to apologise, Arabella. It was bound to be a shock.' Adeline directed a mildly astringent look at her husband and added, 'Your habit of producing rabbits out of hats is not always the best policy.'

'I am duly rebuked,' he murmured, not looking in the least chastened and crossing to kiss first her hand and then her cheek.

Meanwhile, the colour draining slowly from her face, Elizabeth stood passively in her cousin's embrace and stared blankly across at the duke.

'How long have you known?' she asked. '*How* did you know? And why – why didn't you say anything to me? I feel so *stupid*.'

'You need not,' said Rockliffe. 'Before I met Arabella, I had only a handful of suspicions which might have been wholly incorrect.'

'Lizzie?' Arabella gave her a little shake. 'How do you think *I* felt when he arrived and introduced himself?'

Elizabeth shook her head. 'It's not the same. I must have done something wrong. I --'

'You weren't as stupid as me – writing all that stuff about crawling around the attics with the children, without having the sense to realise that *of course* our mothers would share the letters, which meant Max was bound to read them too. So stop crying over spilled milk. Aren't you at *all* pleased to see me?'

Managing a weak smile, Elizabeth said, 'Yes – yes, of course I am.'

Arabella nodded, released her and turned to curtsy to the duchess, saying, 'I'm truly sorry for any trouble and you mustn't blame Lizzie. It was all my idea. But the duke says that if we pretend it was just a foolish prank, people may not blame us too much.'

'Does he indeed? Then we must hope that he is right.' Adeline took Arabella's hands in hers and smiled. 'Meanwhile, welcome to London, my dear. The room next to Elizabeth's has been prepared for you and I daresay you will want to reclaim one of your own gowns. I will have dinner set back a half hour. Any longer than that and I fear Cook may give notice.'

Upstairs, with Annie in nearly as big a state of shock as Elizabeth, Arabella said, 'Half an hour, the duchess said – so we must make haste. Which gown can I wear?'

'Whichever you like – they're yours, after all. Belle, there's too much to take in. Aside from coming to find you, what else has the duke done? Has he written to our families? Because if he has, Papa will demand that I go home immediately.'

'You can't.' Arabella stepped out of the blue wool gown and headed for the wash-stand. 'Rockliffe wants us both here until everybody's got used to the idea that I'm you and you're me and that our masquerade was just a silly hoax.'

Annie looked around from where she was laying out a blue-grey taffeta gown.

'He reckons that's going to work, does he? That folk will say *Oh, just a bit of girlish fun, was it? Well, that's all right then.*' She shook her head. 'I doubt it.'

'Have you got a better idea?' asked Arabella, patting her face dry.

'No. But --'

'Then we'll assume Rockliffe knows best.' She stepped into the gown and stood still while the maid laced her into it. 'Speaking for myself, I'll be glad to be done with the pretence. Won't you, Lizzie?'

'Yes.' With Annie still in the room, Elizabeth deferred admitting that she had already confided in Ralph Sherbourne. 'But what did Lord Chalfont say? Was he furious?'

'No. He said it didn't matter because I was still me.'

'Really?' Elizabeth looked mildly sceptical. 'Did he mean it?'

'Yes. Julian doesn't know how to lie ... and he's not much good at saying the right thing, either.' Sitting down so that Annie could deal with her hair, she said, 'The only part he couldn't cope with was the possibility that, if I left, I'd never go back. But --'

'Go back?' exclaimed Annie, shocked. 'Of *course* you're not going back, Miss Belle! The very idea! How could you think it?'

Correctly interpreting the glance Arabella sent her in the mirror, Elizabeth took the brush from the maid's hand, saying, 'Thank you, Annie. I'll finish this while you explain the situation to Jeanne and ask what she suggests telling the rest of the staff.'

'Ha!' snorted Annie. '*That's* going to be fun, isn't it?'

When she had gone, Elizabeth said, 'Well?'

'I love him, Lizzie. He's kind and sweet and shy and so beautiful he takes my breath away.' Arabella briefly described the events of the morning of her departure from Chalfont, finishing with, 'When he ran after the carriage and held me as if he was never going to let go, I understood what people mean when they say they felt as if their heart might burst.' She stopped, holding the other girl's eyes in the mirror. 'He *needs* me, Lizzie. I *know* he does. And when he plays ... I can't begin to describe it except to say that he makes magic.'

Continuing to pin up her cousin's hair, Elizabeth said, 'Are you hoping to marry him?'

A shadow crept into the dark eyes. 'I haven't thought of it.'

'Why not – if you love him?'

Arabella shrugged, said nothing and stared down at her hands.

Suddenly certain that her suspicions were correct, Elizabeth said quietly, 'I think I know why. What I *don't* know is why you never told me.'

'Told you what?'

'About you and David ... and the real reason you didn't want to come to London.'

Arabella drew a long breath and discarded any notion of pretending not to understand.

'I didn't tell anyone. I was too ashamed. And I thought you would think as badly of me as I did of myself. I – I regretted it so bitterly, you see. I still do. And that's why I can't – daren't – let myself hope. Also, it isn't as if Julian has ever said anything to suggest that he might want to marry me.'

Frowning a little, Elizabeth said slowly, 'If it helps, Lord Sherbourne says that anticipating one's wedding vows with a gentleman one expects to marry but doesn't, only makes a lady ineligible to a man who is either a saint or a hypocrite.'

The grey eyes grew wide. 'Well, Julian isn't either of those. But what on earth made his lordship tell you that?'

'He thought he was being helpful. He thought he was talking about *me*. But it made me realise the truth about *you* – though I didn't tell him that. I merely said he was mistaken. We were only having the conversation at all because I'd told him I couldn't marry.'

Ignoring her own circumstances for a moment, Arabella gazed thoughtfully at her cousin's image in the looking-glass. 'Has he asked you?'

'Not in so many words. He just intimated that he was … considering it.'

'Well, that's good, isn't it? Your letters suggested that you liked him.'

'I do like him. Very much, as it happens. He isn't sweet or shy … and though he *can* be kind, that isn't the first quality anyone would apply to him. He's elegant and impeccably mannered and – and handsome in a dark, stern sort of way.'

'So why aren't you happy?'

'Because he was *considering* it before I told him I'm not you,' replied Elizabeth, as lightly as she was able. 'That was two days ago – and I haven't laid eyes on him since then.'

CHAPTER NINETEEN

On the following evening, some of the Duke and Duchess of Rockliffe's family and friends – together, at Elizabeth's request, with the Earl of Sherbourne – gathered in St James Square for an informal supper. Surprised to have been invited, Ralph folded his arms and waited to learn why he had been. Thus far, his only clue had been the brief and slightly wild glance thrown at him by Elizabeth.

All suddenly became clear, however, when a second young lady entered the room to stand hand in hand with her. Flags of colour flying in her cheeks, Arabella introduced both herself and her cousin ... and then proceeded to confess what they had done and, to a limited degree, what had prompted them to do it.

Only at the very end, did she depart from the truth by saying, 'It was just intended as a joke. I thought it would be fun to find out if we could get away with it for a little while. It didn't ... it never occurred to either of us that we were involving the duke and duchess in our deceit; that by presenting Lizzie as me they were introducing an imposter to all of you and to the rest of society. It was stupid not to realise that – and I'm sincerely sorry. Indeed, Lizzie and I want to apologise to all of you and hope you will be able to forgive us.'

There was a brief, stunned silence into which Lord Nicholas eventually said, 'Speaking for myself, I'll forgive you right now. Anyone who can fool my brother for ... *how* long did it take you to figure it out, Rock?'

'Long enough,' sighed his Grace. 'Thank you for pointing that out, Nicholas.'

'My pleasure.'

This provoked some laughter and various teasing remarks, all of them at the duke's expense. Having expected it, Rockliffe merely shrugged and responded with lazy resignation. And Arabella was just beginning to think that she and Elizabeth were going to get away with it much more easily than either of them had dared hope, when Cassandra Audley said, 'Forgive me if I missed something, Arabella. But *where* did you say you were while Elizabeth has been here?'

On the journey from Chalfont, Rockliffe had made it plain to Arabella that it was going to be impossible to keep her recent whereabouts out of the story. *'You may play it down and try to disguise it,'* he had said, *'but people will ask. Be careful how you answer, do not give away more information than you must – and do* not *mention the children.*

So Arabella smiled brightly and said, 'In Nottinghamshire. Lizzie had accepted a position as a housekeeper. I went in her place.'

'A *housekeeper*?' echoed Lady Elinor, incredulously. 'I don't know whether you're brave or mad. Why on earth would you want to do that?'

'It was the only way we could change places. I had to go *somewhere*, after all. And it was rather nice not being myself for a while.' Arabella knew there was a way to reduce the flow of questions; a way which, two months ago, she would have been incapable of using but which now, because of Julian, was ridiculously easy. She said, 'It was *especially* nice being among people who didn't know that, after a three-year betrothal, my future husband left it to his brother to tell me that he'd married someone else.'

As she had hoped, everyone looked either sympathetic or shocked. Sebastian Audley broke the silence by saying bracingly, 'If he was *that* big a coward, you were well rid of him.'

'Hear, hear,' murmured Cassie.

Arabella thanked them with a grateful smile and left the floor to the duke.

'I am sure,' he sighed, humour lurking behind his eyes, 'that I will never be allowed to live this down. However ... a foolish but harmless practical joke is the story we will be telling. Neither Arabella nor Elizabeth will be seen in public until the Queensberry ball on Friday, where they will appear together and be presented as themselves. The general idea is to create a delightful novelty rather than a scandal.'

'That shouldn't be difficult,' grinned Nicholas. 'Most folk will be too busy enjoying the idea of these two minxes hoaxing you, of all people.'

'Which should facilitate matters a great deal,' agreed Rockliffe. 'But an unexpected development has arisen from Arabella's sojourn in Nottinghamshire. Her employer there was the new Earl of Chalfont. As some of you may recall, the title was left vacant for over a year while the lawyers hunted for an heir.' He paused, smiling faintly. 'I am seldom surprised and almost never impressed but Chalfont has achieved both. He is a musician of rare and extraordinary ability. Consequently, it is my intention to arrange for him to make his London debut under my patronage.'

Amidst a few raised brows and some curious glances, Arabella felt all her nerves go into spasm. Staring incredulously at the duke, she said weakly, 'Do you mean it? Do you really *mean* it?'

'Yes – though not due to your lengthy persuasions. I had decided before I stepped into the carriage.'

She did not need to ask why. 'Because you'd heard him play.'

'Because I'd heard him play under less than ideal circum--'

Rockliffe's words were cut off when Arabella hurled herself on his chest, sobbing, 'Thank you! Oh – *thank* you! You don't – you can't know what it will mean to him.'

'I believe I have some inkling,' he replied, returning her embrace with tolerant amusement before gently taking her shoulders to set her away from him. 'And though I am naturally delighted you are pleased, I really must ask you to respect my coat.'

Several people laughed.

Lady Amberley said, 'What is his lordship's instrument?'

'The harpsichord.' Arabella swung round to face the room, glowing with excitement and pride. 'He is *brilliant*! He plays for hours on end without a scrap of music in front of him and he composes and he's already given a concert in Vienna. Just wait till you hear him!'

'I can tell,' smiled the marchioness, 'that you are not at *all* biased.'

'No. I'm not.' And to Rockliffe, 'Am I, your Grace?'

'You are not,' he agreed. 'But let me make one thing very clear. You will not inform his lordship of my intentions until I have done so myself. And that is quite final.'

Arabella opened her mouth to argue, then sensibly closed it again and nodded.

'Excellent.' Toying absently with a silver snuff-box, the duke turned back to the rest of his guests. 'If Chalfont was not something completely outside the common way, you may believe that I would not be exerting myself on his behalf. As it is, he is exceptionally gifted and, if matters are handled correctly, will take London by storm. Consequently, Adeline and I have agreed that his debut will be made in this house, before a specially invited audience.'

'My agreement had little to do with it,' remarked Adeline dryly, 'though I'll confess to a large degree of curiosity.'

'And curiosity is what I wish to create,' nodded Rockliffe. 'A few whispers about my having discovered that the lost earl is, in fact, a hitherto unknown virtuoso and rumours that his lordship's first performance will be by invitation only. That should be sufficient to stimulate speculation whilst also deflecting attention from Arabella and Elizabeth.' He sent a gentle smile around the room. 'I leave the matter in your capable hands.'

Throughout all of this, Ralph wondered whether Elizabeth had told Rockliffe that he already knew the secret or had asked that he be invited so that she wouldn't have to. He waited until conversation became general before approaching her to say quietly, 'When did Rockliffe produce your cousin?'

'Yesterday. The first I knew of it was when she walked in with him.'

'Quite a shock, I imagine.'

'Yes.' She took a breath and met Ralph's eyes. 'I haven't told the duke and duchess that I confided in you. I didn't want to have to explain *why* I had.'

'Thank you.' He smiled at her. 'Your cousin did an excellent job of delivering the prepared speech. Had I not known better, I would have thought it spontaneous. And it was noble of her to shoulder all the blame.'

'She insisted on it.'

'Ah. Most commendable,' murmured Ralph. 'Are you feeling duly relieved?'

'I will be after Friday evening.' She hesitated and then said, 'Will you be attending the Queensberry Ball?'

His smile became caustic. 'Her Grace has neglected to send me a card. But Rockliffe has chosen well. The Queensberry Ball is one of the great events of the season and will be the perfect occasion for you and your cousin to resume your own identities.' He paused, gauging her expression. 'You need not be nervous. You are under Rockliffe's protection. And since he is prepared to accept a small chip in the veneer of his legendary reputation, it will go without a hitch.'

'Yes. I suppose so. And it is good of him – because I'm sure he can't like it.'

Ralph's tone grew mildly sardonic.

'Don't be too grateful, my dear. It is a very *small* chip – no more than a scratch, really. In no time at all, society will recall that Rockliffe had never seen either of you before ... from where it will be a short step to marvelling that he should work it out at all. And in the meantime, he intends to have everyone talking about his harpsichord virtuoso. His Grace,' concluded Ralph, 'invariably has at least *one* ace up his sleeve.' He paused, glancing away from her. 'Ah. Here comes your cousin.'

Arabella swept down upon them saying, 'Are you ever going to introduce me to Lord Sherbourne, Lizzie?'

'An introduction would seem to be redundant,' remarked Ralph, bowing. 'How do you do, Mistress Brandon? That was a masterful performance you gave earlier.'

'Thank you. ' Arabella grinned, curtsied and turned to her cousin. 'Lady Sarre and Mistress Audley want to assure you that tonight's revelation doesn't change anything as far as they are concerned. They're both very kind, aren't they? On the other hand, Lady Elinor is bursting with curiosity – so you'd better be careful.'

'Dear me,' said Ralph mildly, as Elizabeth nodded and moved away to join the other ladies. 'Never say that there are yet *more* secrets.'

'None that need concern anyone here,' shrugged Arabella. 'But if we are to talk about secrets ... I am wondering why, despite clearly having other friends, Lizzie chose to confide our deception to *you*?'

Ralph eyed her meditatively. 'You think Nell Caversham a better choice?'

'I don't know her – or any of the other ladies – well enough to judge. What I *do* know is that Lizzie trusts you more than any of them.'

'I am honoured.' He bowed slightly. 'I am also discreet ... if that was your question ... and hope, since Rockliffe is unaware of my prior knowledge, that the same is true of you.'

'Of course it is.'

'I am duly reassured.' He paused before adding delicately, 'May one ask at what point you confided in the mysterious and talented Lord Chalfont?'

'No. One may not.' Aside from being irritated by the way he had referred to Julian, Arabella thought she had caught a fleeting glimpse of mocking amusement in those unusual tawny eyes. But since what she *really* wanted was to find out if Elizabeth's inexplicable affection for this man was returned, she said pensively, 'Lizzie's parents will know the truth by now – as does my own family. Since her father was adamant that she wasn't to come to London, he will almost certainly demand that she goes home immediately.'

'Ah. You are asking if I will mind.'

A hint of colour rose to her cheeks. He wasn't just irritating. He was also quicker than she had thought. Standing her ground, she said pleasantly, 'And will you?'

Unwilling to admit, even to himself, that he would probably mind a great deal ... that recently he only accepted invitations in the hope of meeting Elizabeth ... he smiled coolly and said, 'Oddly enough, I am no more willing to answer that question than you were to discuss Lord Chalfont.' And putting an end to the conversation, 'May I fetch you some refreshment?'

* * *

Later, sitting on the end of Elizabeth's bed and after bubbling with excitement about Julian's forthcoming concert, Arabella said cautiously, 'Lord Sherbourne is older than I expected.'

'He is thirty-five,' replied Elizabeth, busy braiding her hair for the night. 'That isn't old.'

'No. Of course it isn't. And he *is* very elegant.' She gave a tiny laugh. 'Compared to Julian, *any* reasonably tidy gentleman looks elegant ... but I've a feeling that Lord Sherbourne is never less than immaculate.'

There was a long, thoughtful silence. And then, 'You didn't like him, did you?'

Arabella sighed. 'I didn't *dis*like him, Lizzie. To be honest, I didn't know what to make of him. He's rather sphinx-like, isn't he? And cynical ... and cold.'

Elizabeth came to curl up beside her.

'He's good at hiding his thoughts. But cold? No. I think he shut his emotions away a long time ago and no longer knows how to reach them. And I think he's lonely.' She smiled faintly. 'You think I'm choosing what to believe, don't you? I'm not.'

Arabella considered this for a moment. She said slowly, 'I asked him why you confided in him rather than one of the ladies I met tonight. He wouldn't tell me. Will you?'

'I told him because he had earned the truth. He trusted me with something personal and painful, even though he had no expectation of being believed. He didn't have to do that. I hadn't asked and he knew that I wouldn't but he told me anyway.'

'Did you believe him?'

'Completely.' Elizabeth stretched out a hand to clasp one of Arabella's. 'He may offer me marriage or he may not. I don't know. But you won't persuade me I'm mistaken in him, Belle. And I'd ask you to suspend judgement until you know him better.'

'That's fair, I suppose. Will we see him at the ball on Friday?'

'Unfortunately not.' Elizabeth's mouth twisted wryly. 'He hasn't been invited.'

* * *

Queensberry House was ablaze with the light of hundreds of candles and the air, at least at the beginning of the evening, was redolent with the scent of hot-house flowers. Arabella had told herself she would not be nervous because there was really nothing for her to be nervous about. But when she stood in the receiving line ... when she and Elizabeth were presented to the Duchess of Queensberry under their own names ... and when her Grace's narrow, arched brows nearly met her hairline ... she felt her knees start to tremble.

'You changed *places*?' said the duchess incredulously. 'I never heard of such a thing! Surely you did not *condone* this masquerade, Rockliffe?'

'Until very recently, I was unaware of it,' he replied urbanely. 'And I will admit that I did not immediately perceive the humour in it. Age probably has something to do with that. Do you not agree, Margaret?'

The duchess gave a sharp laugh and prodded him with her fan.

'No, you atrocious man – I do not. And the only reason I forgive you for choosing my ball to tell the *ton* it's been hoodwinked is because you've been hoodwinked yourself.' She grinned at Adeline and said, 'Take him away, my dear. And good luck.'

Arabella released a sigh of relief and, seeing it, Adeline murmured, 'Don't relax too soon. That was only the first hurdle.'

'Their Graces, the Duke and Duchess of Rockliffe.' The major-domo's powerful baritone rang out over the strains of the orchestra. 'Mistress Arabella Brandon and Mistress Elizabeth Marsden.'

At first there was little reaction. Then heads began to turn and a sort of silent whisper seemed to spread through the room ... which was when Mr Audley and Lord Sarre strolled over to claim both Arabella and Elizabeth for the quadrille that was currently forming.

Waiting for the music to begin and recognising that the real Mistress Brandon was virtually vibrating with tension, Lord Sarre said, 'So ... tell me about the virtuoso earl. Where did he study?' And watched with interest as the girl he had thought no more than passably attractive gathered a glow that suddenly made her beautiful.

At the end of the dance when he was escorting her from the floor, Sarre said quietly, 'I'm sure Rock has told you that, aside from his musical ability, it will be best to say as little as possible about Lord Chalfont, which means you'll have to find some way of dodging the questions. When in difficulty, my advice is to raise your brows and say nothing at all until he or she begins to wish they had not asked.'

Arabella laughed up into silver-grey eyes. 'I can imagine that working for *you*, my lord. However, I'm not sure that I have the necessary stature.'

In fact, mostly thanks to what Adeline called her husband's 'looming presence' and the fact that the girls were never left completely alone to fend for themselves, the evening progressed more smoothly than either Arabella or Elizabeth had expected. There was a great deal of surprise but little evident shock; and though some ladies shook a reproving head, many others were inclined to consider the charade audaciously amusing. The gentlemen, of course, enjoyed a good many jokes at Rockliffe's expense but soon discovered that he was impervious to provocation and consistently able to turn the tables.

Everything, in fact, went beautifully until Elizabeth entered the ladies' retiring room ... and found herself face to face with Philippa Sutherland.

'Dear me,' said her ladyship. 'If it isn't the imposter.'

Elizabeth's nerves tightened and, realising that they were alone, she was briefly tempted to say, *And good evening to you, Lady Spite.* But because she refused to sink to this woman's level, she said merely, 'Not any more, I'm happy to say. Goodbye, Lady Sutherland.'

Seeing her about to walk out, Philippa said tauntingly, 'Don't go. Only think what a lovely chat we could have! Or are you too scared to face me?'

Turning slowly, Elizabeth surveyed her from plumed headdress to jewelled slippers.

'Hardly. As for your invitation to chat ... well, let us just agree that it would be a mistake.' And for the second time, she turned to leave.

'Ralph won't marry you now, you know. Not Miss Nobody from nowhere.' Philippa waited until Elizabeth once again pivoted slowly to face her. 'He *might* have, I suppose ... while he thought your family wealthy and if I had kept the gossip-mill turning ... though even then it was unlikely. But the remote possibility of it was why I stopped telling what I knew. You may have enjoyed sharing his bed for a time but I can guarantee that you wouldn't have enjoyed being married to him if he felt he'd been forced into it.'

'I am confused,' remarked Elizabeth. 'You are commiserating with me because Lord Sherbourne will no longer consider me a fit bride and simultaneously congratulating me on escaping an enforced marriage. Which is it? As to the reason you stopped smearing my reputation – I suspect it was less to do with my future welfare than anxiety about what Rockliffe might do if you didn't.'

'Believe that if you wish.' Philippa's laugh was a little off-key. 'I daresay you know that Ralph wanted to marry me – was quite desperately in love with me, in fact. And yet, despite swearing eternal devotion, he murdered one of my brothers in cold blood. Doesn't that tell you what sort of man he is?'

'No.' Elizabeth decided to meet fire with fire. 'You can stop pretending. I know how your brother died – and so do you. Your other brother was a witness to it and though he may have chosen to lie to the world, I can't believe he lied to you.' She paused, holding the other woman's gaze. 'Your brother wasn't murdered. He committed an act of desperation bordering on insanity. Precisely what he thought to escape by that act is the only piece of the puzzle that I don't have. But those pieces I *do* have lead me to suppose that, whatever your brother's sins may have been, you were not completely innocent yourself.'

Just for a second, Philippa froze and some of her colour leaked away. Then, hearing voices in the corridor outside, she snapped, 'You are delusional and I am leaving.'

Aware that they would soon have an audience, Elizabeth stepped into her path and said, 'You wanted to chat – so let us chat. You don't hate Lord Sherbourne because he killed your brother. You're terrified of him because he knows something about you. And you imagine that if you continue blackening his name at every opportunity --'

She was forced to stop speaking as Lady Sutherland attempted to shove past her. Instinctively, Elizabeth stood her ground and shoved back. Behind her, someone giggled.

'You blacken Lord Sherbourne's name,' Elizabeth repeated grimly, 'so that, if he *should* speak out, everyone will dismiss it as a case of tit-for-tat.' Folding her arms and still blocking the doorway, she added, 'Personally, I think you'd do better to stop provoking him. If he hasn't said anything in seven years, he won't start now. You ought to be more worried about what you will do if I confide my suspicions to a few friends – because the gossip-mill you are so fond of works both ways, doesn't it?'

And stepping abruptly aside, she let Philippa storm by both herself and the two unknown and very young ladies hovering at the door with their eyes on stalks.

CHAPTER TWENTY

Three days after Arabella's departure, Julian received the first of several letters. It was from Arabella and it told him that she missed him and then, after inexplicable urgings for him to visit a tailor, apologised for forgetting to warn him that she had written to her brother.

I wanted to tell Max that Rockliffe knew so he could prepare Mama, she had written, *but I was worried about leaving you and the children, so I got a bit distracted and said more than I should have. At any rate, I wanted to warn you that Max may write to you or even send one of his own people who can advise you better than old Mr Ridley. Rockliffe will also be writing to you – but I'm forbidden to say any more about that.*

Although he was not entirely sure what most of this meant, it still made Julian smile. By contrast, the duke's letter which arrived the next day, left him light-headed with shock, disbelief and an urgent need to sit down.

Rockliffe came directly to the point.

From the little I heard, I have concluded that a gift as rare as yours should not be wasted. I can offer you both a platform and an audience – and Arabella has left me in little doubt that you want them. I imagine that your repertoire is equal to the task of preparing a recital programme in a relatively short space of time and this I leave in your hands. But rather than attempting to make all the necessary arrangements by letter, I am sending my secretary, Matthew Bennett, to discuss them with you in person. I trust that this will meet with your approval.

Yours etc.

It took Julian the best part of the afternoon to convince himself that this was real ... that the duke's letter was not some macabre practical joke and that Rockliffe meant what he said. And even then, he kept it to himself in case there was some mistake. But the following day brought a deliriously ecstatic letter from Arabella; and two days after that a cheerful, pleasant-faced young gentleman arrived on the doorstep.

Holding out his hand, he said, 'How do you do, my lord? I'm Matthew Bennett, Rockliffe's secretary. I believe you've been expecting me.'

And that was when it finally started to sink in that this was really happening.

'With regard to the practicalities,' Mr Bennett began, 'the duke feels that your debut should be made under his own roof, before an exclusive, specially-invited audience. He says this will set up a clamour among those who aren't invited but, more importantly, the first to hear you play will be people with either the influence or the power to promote you further.' He glanced up, grinning, from his notes. 'All right so far, sir? You're looking a bit stunned.'

'More than a bit. This is ... beyond my wildest dreams.'

'Ah. Seems too good to be true, does it? But I can assure you that the duke is serious. He's already started a buzz of speculation but given the gossips virtually nothing to go on. I sometimes wonder how he does it. However ... where were we? Yes. His Grace suggests a two-part recital, separated by an interval. Does that sound reasonable?' And when Julian agreed that it did, 'Excellent. I've been told that you will compile the programme and supply it in time for it to be printed. Will that be possible?'

'Yes.' Managing to engage his brain and unlock his jaws, Julian said, 'I could do it in the next hour or so. But has the duke any specific pieces he would like included?'

'The *duke* has only one. Mistress Brandon, on the other hand, has several.' Mr Bennett laughed and consulted his notes. 'His Grace asks for – and I quote – Miss Ellie's 'angry' music.'

For the first time, Julian grinned. '*Le Vertigo* by Royer. Yes. I can do that. What else?'

'The lady insists on the Bach *Fantasia* and one of your own compositions – she says you'll know which. She also asks for the new Mozart concerto.'

Julian could feel himself being overtaken by a sense of unreality.

'The Bach and my Sarabande, yes,' he managed. 'But not the concerto.'

'You don't know it?'

'I know it. But it requires an ensemble and I can't put his Grace to that expense.'

'His Grace likes the idea of giving something of Herr Mozart's which London has probably not yet heard. He is already taking steps to acquire the full score and --'

'I doubt he'll get it,' interrupted Julian, trying not to contemplate the enormity of what he was turning down. 'Mozart rarely hurries to get his compositions printed.'

The secretary looked up. 'If that is so, how come you know it?'

Silently damning himself for an idiot, Julian muttered, 'I have some hand-written pages. But they're barely legible and --'

'If they are all that is available, they will have to do,' said Mr Bennett serenely. 'Perhaps you can furnish me with them before I leave?' He continued thumbing through his notes, apparently oblivious to the fact that Lord Chalfont's expression suggested that he had just been hit on the head with a mallet. 'His Grace suggests that the first part of the concert should be the Mozart concerto, with your solo recital after the interval – if that is agreeable to you, sir?' Looking up again when no answer was forthcoming, he said gently, 'My lord?'

An orchestra, thought Julian. *He's offering me the chance to play the E flat major with an* orchestra, *for God's sake! This can't be happening. I must be dreaming it.*

'My lord?' prompted Mr Bennett again, this time more forcefully. 'May I tell his Grace that you will play the Mozart? I need an immediate decision on that because --'

'Yes.' The word emerged in a sort of strangled croak. 'Yes. I'll play it. *God!* Does Rockliffe realise what he's doing for me? I never expected – never dared hope I'd perform again at *all*. And to be offered an *orchestra* ... I'm sorry. It – it's just too huge to take in.'

'Yes. I can understand that.'

Julian doubted it. But as his brain started to function again, he said suddenly, 'Tell his Grace to cut the brass and woodwind by half – and the same with all the strings except the violins.' Then, seeing the secretary's raised brows, added, 'I'm not saying it to reduce costs. Mozart writes for the pianoforte – probably one of those iron-framed things they're making these days that can cope with heavy orchestration. The harpsichord can't. It will be drowned.' He hesitated, pressing his fingers against his temples and added, 'You can take the orchestral parts but ask his Grace to get them copied.'

'Of course. If, as you say, they are almost illegible --'

'It's not that. Some of them are in Mozart's own hand. They'll be worth something one day – if they aren't already.'

It was the secretary's turn to stare. 'Good God.'

'Exactly.'

'Yes. I promise I will take very good care of them, my lord,' said Mr Bennett, still scribbling furiously, 'and I will explain all your requirements to the duke. Now, just a few more details and I'll leave you in peace. Mistress Brandon believes you would prefer to be billed as Julian Langham, rather than the Earl of Chalfont. Is that correct?'

'Yes.'

Mr Bennett ticked something else off on his sheet.

'The date of the concert will need to be fixed in order for invitations to go out. Does three weeks on Friday sound reasonable?'

This time Julian merely nodded. His mind was spinning.

'And how long will you need in order to rehearse with the orchestra, sir?'

'I don't know. A – a few days, I suppose, if they've already learned the music.'

'In that case, his Grace instructs me to tell you that he will send a carriage to convey you to Wynstanton House eight days before the event. Allowing for the length of the journey, this should give you ample rehearsal time.' Mr Bennett shuffled his papers into a neat pile and restored them to his case. 'I think that is everything, my lord – unless you have any questions?'

'Dozens, probably – but my brain isn't working well enough to think of them.' Julian shoved a hand through his hair and said vaguely, 'Give me an hour – or better yet, stay here tonight – and I'll complete the concert programme for you.'

'Thank you, my lord. I'd be glad to – if it is no inconvenience.'

'It isn't. Just don't tell anybody – especially the children, if you come across them – why you're here. And for God's sake, please call me Julian.'

* * *

Mr Bennett departed for London, leaving Julian floating two feet above the ground on the twin prospects of performing and seeing Arabella again sooner than he'd dared hope. And finally, since he was beginning to believe that the concert was really going to happen, he decided it was safe to tell people about it.

Miss Beatrice enclosed him in a warm, gentle embrace and said, 'Dear boy … that is such wonderful news and no more than you deserve. You will be a huge success, I am sure.'

Miss Abigail said, 'Excellent. But you must let us know what we can do to help – with the children, for example. If you are to be away for several weeks, you will not be comfortable leaving them in the care of servants.'

'No. I hadn't really thought that far ahead,' he admitted slowly.

'Of course you hadn't. So if no other solution presents itself, consider letting them have a little holiday here with Bea and me.'

'That is … that's extraordinarily generous of you,' said Julian, startled. 'Are you sure? They can be quite … boisterous.'

'Well, they're children, aren't they? It's to be expected. What do you think, Bea?'

'They would be very welcome,' agreed Miss Beatrice, 'and it would relieve you of any anxiety, Julian. You must be free to concentrate on your music.'

'Then, thank you. I won't impose on you if there is any other way – but I thank you.'

Next, Julian shared his news with Paul and Janet Featherstone. Janet kissed his cheek and said, 'How marvellous! You must be very excited.'

'Yes. Yes, I am.'

'Try sounding it, then,' grinned Paul, grasping his hand and slapping him on the back at the same time. 'You've got the patronage of a duke, for God's sake! When do you leave?'

'In a couple of weeks.' Something flared in the dark green eyes. 'He ... he's engaging an orchestra and wants me to play the Mozart E flat concerto. I can't begin to explain what that means. In Vienna, I often played in ensembles ... just groups of friends, you know. But a real orchestra? I'm having trouble believing Rockliffe would go to so much expense.'

'I daresay he can afford it,' remarked Janet. 'But with you and Liz – *Arabella* – both away, what will you do about the children?'

'The Misses Caldercott have offered to have them.'

'Mm. That *might* work, I suppose.'

'It won't,' said Paul. 'They'll want to come with you. You know that, don't you? They'll want to come because they'll worry you might not come back. And they'll want to attend the concert so they can cheer and clap and stamp and generally behave the way sophisticated audiences never do. So you'd better think of something.'

* * *

Another letter from Arabella again stressed the importance of new clothes. Julian, immersed in music, forgot about it until Paul turned up one morning and dragged him off to visit a tailor in Newark. Then a further missive from Rockliffe informed him that invitations for the concert had already been despatched and his fellow musicians were busy rehearsing the Mozart. Towards the end, his Grace said, *Since you will be staying with the duchess and myself, I should warn you that, at Arabella's request, I have also invited Lady Brandon and her eldest son to join the party.* And in a brief postscript, *Should you have concerns about leaving the children for an extended period, I am sure we have an empty attic.*

The attic reference made Julian grin. The prospect of meeting Arabella's family didn't ... but he told himself he need not think about that yet and, in order not to do so, he went upstairs to ask the children if they'd like to go to London with him.

For almost a minute, all three of them stared at him open-mouthed. Predictably, Ellie was the first to recover. She said, 'Where's London?'

'A long way from here. But it's where Miss Belle is and where *I* have to go ... because the Duke of Rockliffe wants me to give a concert.'

Rob's face lit up. 'For lots and lots of people?'

'I think so.'

'A concert like the ones at Miss Bea's house?' asked Ellie dubiously.

Tom snorted and Julian had to hide a smile.

'No. Not quite like that. This one will be in the duke's house, in front of his friends. And for part of the time, I'll be playing with other musicians.' He waited for a moment. 'What do you think? Tom?'

'Do you mean it?'

'Which bit exactly?'

'All of it. Do we want to come to London and go to the duke's house and – and be there with you when you play for his friends? *Us*. Rob and Ellie and me.' Tom stopped and shook his head. 'Of course we *want* to – but we can't, can we?'

'Why not?'

'Because we'd embarrass you. Folk will ask who we are and why we're there and *then* what will you say?' Tom turned away and shoved his hands in his pockets, exactly the way Julian often did. 'You can't tell the *truth*.'

'Yes. I can. I'll tell them that my wards have every right to hear me perform. And I'll tell them that we are a family ... and that I am proud of you,' said Julian gravely. 'And if any of these people don't like it, we shall ignore them. So will you come? Or are you going to make me travel all that way on my own?'

Ellie climbed on to his lap and nestled against his shoulder. 'I'll come.'

'And me,' said Rob, still beaming. 'A *real* concert. With an *orchestra*. It'll be *splendid*!'

'I certainly hope so,' agreed Julian. 'Tom?'

The boy turned around and said gruffly, 'Of course I'll bloody come. You just said it yourself. We're a family.'

* * *

For the next five days, happily submerged in hours of rehearsal, Julian lived in a bubble of near-perfect bliss that needed only Arabella's presence to make it complete. It might have continued a while longer had not the outside world intruded in the shape of the last thing he had expected.

* * *

'I wish you'd stayed at the inn and let me do this on my own,' Max grumbled as the carriage turned on to the rutted drive of Chalfont Hall. 'You'll meet him in London, after all. And I'm only going because of Belle's letter. Two sentences saying Rockliffe was taking her away – and then a page of anxiety, as if Chalfont wasn't safe to be left. I mean, Mother – *really*? God alone knows what we're likely to find.'

'We're going to find the young man Arabella has been deceiving for weeks and with whom – though Rockliffe's letter said nothing of it – you believe she has fallen in love,' replied Lady Brandon calmly. 'And I have not entirely forgiven you for withholding your prior knowledge of her whereabouts, Max – so please don't argue. I know *why* you did and it doesn't appear to have done any harm ... but I shall judge Lord Chalfont for myself, thank you. And you will *not* pin him to a wall on the assumption that he has behaved improperly.'

'I wasn't going to!'

Louisa lifted one satiric brow. 'No?'

'No.' And with a reluctant grin, 'Well ... probably not.'

'My point, exactly. And I suggest that you bear a few things in mind. Rockliffe apparently approves of him. So *if* Belle loves him and *if* her feelings are reciprocated --'

'They'll be reciprocated fast enough if she's mentioned her dowry.'

'Don't be such a cynic. And stop pre-judging a gentleman who, for all we know, may end up becoming your brother-in-law. As for the question of impropriety, if any *did* occur it was as likely to be Belle's doing as his.' She stopped speaking as the house came into view. 'Oh dear. Parts of that roof look decidedly dubious, do they not?'

'Belle said the previous earl had run the place into the ground. I was hoping she'd exaggerated. If the house is in this state, goodness only knows what the land is like.'

The front door swung open before they reached it and a boy stared out at them. Max muttered something under his breath. Ignoring him, her ladyship smiled and said, 'Hello. Unless I have it wrong, you must be Tom.'

'Yes,' said Tom, plainly taken aback. 'Who are you?'

'I am Miss Arabella's mama – and this is her brother. We've travelled a very long way to meet you and your brother and sister … and Lord Chalfont. Is he at home?'

'Yes. He's practising for the --'

He stopped, as Violet half-ran across the hall behind him saying, 'Tom? You know you're supposed to leave answering the door to Rose or --' Then she also stopped for a moment, looking confused. Dipping a curtsy, she said, 'Sir – ma'am – I'm so sorry. Please come inside. Tom – go and tell his lordship he has visitors. Oh. Beg your pardon, sir but who shall he say --?'

'It's Miss Belle's mother and brother,' interrupted Tom, already heading for the library from which the silence was suddenly broken by a crisp, complex cascade of notes.

'Wait!' Louisa Brandon stopped dead, her hand gripping her son's arm. 'Tom, wait a moment, please.' And when the music continued through bar upon flawless bar, 'Oh Max. Do you hear that? I know both Belle and Rockliffe said he could play but …'

'Good, is he?' asked Max, unimpressed and impatient. 'But let's stick to the point, shall we?' And shooting a grin at Tom, 'Off you go, there's a good fellow.'

In the library, Julian had been working on *Vertigo* and finding it recalcitrant. He played the same phrase in three different ways and felt frustration building. Then Tom was beside him, saying something that he couldn't hear through the notes inside his head.

Used to this problem, Tom solved it by grasping his wrist and saying forcibly, 'You've got to leave this, sir. Miss Belle's mother is here – and her brother as well. You need to come and meet them. *Now.*'

Julian stared at him, his expression gradually gathering focus. 'What? Her mother, did you say?'

'And her brother. Violet will have put 'em in the parlour.' The boy scanned the room until he saw Julian's coat lying across a chair. Grabbing it, he said, 'Put this on – and straighten your cravat. Your hair could do with a comb as well but it'll have to do. I don't reckon her brother's used to being kept waiting.'

Julian could feel knots forming in his gut. This wasn't meant to happen. He was supposed to meet Arabella's family in London, not here. Arabella had said her brother might *write* to him – not turn up on the doorstep. So he'd counted on them not seeing the dilapidated state of his house. He had also counted on meeting them for the first time in a coat that wasn't creased and with neatly-tied hair.

Trying to appear more confident than he felt, he entered the drawing-room and managed a creditable bow before flushing at the realisation that the lady was staring at him – probably on account of his dishevelment.

In fact, Lady Brandon was thinking, *Heavens! Even shabby, rumpled and in need of a shave, he's perfectly beautiful. No wonder Belle is head over heels. All that and music, too? How could she resist?*

Looking shyly back, Julian could see nothing of Arabella in her blonde, blue-eyed mother ... and thought the same was true of her raven-haired brother until he encountered a pair of familiar dark grey eyes. Then awareness that Max Brandon's expression was far from friendly drove all the proper courtesies from his mind and he said haltingly, 'Forgive me. I hadn't expected ... that is, welcome to Chalfont. I apologise for – for my appearance. I was ... well, that doesn't matter. It is a – a pleasure to meet --'

He stopped as the door behind him opened an inch or two and appeared to become the victim of a tug of war.

'No!' hissed Tom. 'You can't go in – neither of you. And what's Figgy doing down here, Ellie? You know he's not allowed.'

Then Rob's voice, saying, 'I only wanted to ask if --'

And Ellie interrupting with, 'Miss Belle said to look after Sir Julian – so I shall! And Figgy is going to help.'

'Not now!' snapped Tom, sounding at the end of his tether.

Julian wondered if this moment could get any worse. He muttered, 'I'm so sorry. If you would excuse me for a moment …?' And he stepped out of the room to a chorus of voices.

Eyes brimming with laughter, Louisa warned Max to be silent with a quick shake of her head and shamelessly proceeded to eavesdrop.

'One at a time,' Julian was saying, desperation threading his tone. 'Rob?'

'Have they come to take you away?'

'No. They just want to meet me because Miss Belle has been staying with us.'

'Oh. That's all right, then. So can *I* practise now?'

'Yes – but shut the door. You're not at performance level yet.' He looked down at the owner of the two small hands wrapped around one of his. 'Ellie?'

'I'm staying with you. I promised Miss Belle I'd take care of you.'

'And you do. But I must speak to our guests now and it would be better if Figgy was … somewhere else. Tom, can you --?'

'Yes. Come on, Figs. You too, Ellie.'

'No.' She clung stubbornly to Julian's hand. 'I'm not leaving you.'

Shoving his free hand through his already disordered hair, he said rapidly, 'Ellie … nobody is going to hurt me or carry me off so --'

The door opened fully and Lady Brandon smiled at them. Her smile was so like Arabella's that for a moment Julian felt slightly dizzy. Then she said, 'It's all right, my lord. If she will feel better keeping you under her eye, let her.' And to the child, 'It's Ellie, isn't it? Arabella wrote all about you in her letters. I am her mama … and this is one of her brothers.' And over her shoulder, 'Do stop looming, Max. It's no wonder Ellie doesn't want to leave his lordship alone with you. I wouldn't either, if I were in her place.'

The uncompromising line of Lord Brandon's mouth relaxed a little. He said, 'I am not looming, Mama. I am merely waiting – very politely – to be offered a seat.'

'Of course – please!' said Julian, with a vague wave of his hand. He looked down at Ellie and said hopefully, 'Perhaps you might ask Violet to bring tea?'

'And some of the biscuits Miss Beatrice sent yesterday?'

'Yes. Some of those, too.'

Seemingly reassured, Ellie nodded and ran off.

Left looking at his unexpected guests, Julian said again, 'I'm sorry. The last visitor we had was Rockliffe and he took Arabella away with him. It's left them a bit ... un-unsettled.' He'd very nearly said 'unhinged', since that was what the last ten days had felt like. A sudden thought struck him and he said edgily, 'You *do* know they aren't mine?'

'Oh yes,' agreed Max, silkily. 'We do at least know *that*.'

'Don't be tiresome, Max,' said Louisa. And to Julian, 'It is we who should apologise to you, Lord Chalfont. It wasn't fair of us to arrive without warning ... but we couldn't resist the opportunity to meet you on our way south.'

'To meet you and hear *exactly* what's been going on here,' added Max. 'I can imagine only too easily Belle coming up with this mad escapade and talking Lizzie into it. But doesn't it bother you that she came here pretending to be her cousin?'

'No. I'm just glad she did,' replied Julian truthfully. And, colouring slightly, 'I realise you must be wondering whether I – whether I've taken unseemly advantage ... but I can assure you that I w-wouldn't dream of doing so.'

'Of course you wouldn't,' said Louisa kindly. 'Neither Max nor I have thought such a thing for a moment.'

'Speak for yourself, Mother,' said Max. '*I'd* thought it ... but can see now how very unlikely it was.'

The unspoken sub-text of *"I doubt you could take advantage of a girl even if she asked you to"*, sailed over Julian's head – but Louisa heard it well enough. Sending her exasperating son another look of reproof, she said, 'I understand that Rockliffe is arranging for you to give a recital, my lord. You must be finding the prospect rather daunting.'

Julian stared at her, faintly nonplussed. 'Daunting? No. Why?'

'The prospect of playing in front of so many people?'

'No. I enjoy performing.'

'You've done it before?' asked Max, faintly surprised and half-disbelieving.

'Yes. And I'm hoping this concert will lead to other professional engagements.'

Max still looked sceptical. 'When you say professional engagements ... do you mean ones for which you will be paid?'

'Well, of course.' A glance into the hard grey eyes told Julian that Lord Brandon was still unconvinced and made him say impatiently, 'I *am* good enough, you know. Do you want me to prove it?'

'Though I'd love to hear you play, there's no question of proving *anything*, Lord Chalfont,' said Louisa firmly. And as the door opened on Violet with the tea-tray followed by Ellie carefully carrying a plate of biscuits and assorted pastries, 'Ah tea ... excellent. Find out if your brothers want to join us, Ellie – and then come and tell me about your dog. Figgy is a very unusual name.'

Leaving them to it, Max looked sideways at Julian and said, 'I didn't mean to imply you couldn't play. Obviously, you *must* be able to if --'

Feeling suddenly thoroughly annoyed, Julian snapped, 'I don't just *play*. I'm not some dilettante trotting out pretty tunes for the ladies. I'm a damned *virtuoso*. And if I could bring a Viennese audience to its feet, I can certainly make London sit up.'

If Max's jaw didn't quite drop, his expression was as stunned as if the dog had trotted in and recited Shakespeare. It occurred to him that perhaps he'd been premature in his judgement of Lord Chalfont. It further occurred to him that – little though he looked or behaved like one – the fellow was, in fact, an earl.

Eventually – and suppressing an unhelpful desire to laugh, he said, 'My apologies. The truth is that I know next to nothing about music.'

'I'd guessed that,' muttered Julian.

Max grinned and held out his hand. 'Perhaps we could start again?'

'Or not.' But Julian accepted the offered hand and was about to say something further when Tom appeared in the doorway, took one look at his face, then stared Lord Brandon in the eye to say belligerently, 'Just so as you know, Sir Julian's the best man in the world. So if you've been bullying him, you can leave right now. And if Miss Belle was here, she'd tell you the same.'

This speech stole Julian's breath. Fortunately, Max spared him the need to speak by saying pleasantly, 'Yes, Tom. I know she would. I also know that I was less than fair to his lordship and have apologised.'

'Gentlemen often like to hurl insults at each other before they decide to be friends, Tom,' offered Louisa. 'You will be exactly the same yourself one day. Now ... have a cake.'

'Do *you* want cake, Chalfont?' asked Max in a wicked undertone. 'Or – since Belle said I was to help – would you prefer to walk me about your land?'

'I'd prefer it to cake,' replied Julian, making it sound like the lesser of two evils. Then, looking from the contents of the plate to Arabella's mother, he added, 'My cook made them – so your ladyship would be wiser sticking to the biscuits.'

* * *

Strolling towards the Home Farm, Max asked a half-dozen questions regarding acreages, tenants and livestock and then, at the end of it all, said, 'How bad *are* things?'

'Not as bad as when I first got here. The children are more settled and happier, thanks to Arabella.'

'Oh? Well, I'm sure Belle's presence has helped. But Tom thinks you're ten feet tall, Ellie adores you and ... and if you're giving the other boy music lessons, it's presumably because he asked you to – which speaks of a different kind of hero-worship.' Glancing sideways, he grinned at Julian's heightened colour and added, 'Then again, none of it would have happened if you hadn't brought them under your roof in the first place.'

Julian stared down at his feet. 'What else could I do?'

'What most other men would have done. Shut your eyes to a problem that wasn't of your making,' replied Max bluntly. And with a sideways glance, 'Why didn't you?'

'I intended to. I even thought I could. Naively, I imagined that – having taken the children in – I could walk away and everything would go on as I'd left it. But finally it began to dawn on me that it wouldn't; that with neither money nor the presence of the so-called earl, the children would be homeless again as soon as I turned my back.'

'And you couldn't let that happen.'

'No. It would have been ... cruel. Worse than if I'd never taken them in at all.'

Max was beginning to understand what Arabella saw in this man. He said, 'So you stayed and continued to support them – even though you scarcely had two shillings to rub together. When, for example, was the last time you had a new coat?'

Refusing to ask why everyone was so concerned with the state of his wardrobe, Julian said, 'I'm having one made now. Arabella wrote to my friend, Paul and he dragged me to a tailor in Newark.' His expression darkened. 'That wasted half a day and the idiot wanted the damned coat to fit so close on the shoulders I could scarcely lift my arms. And as if *that* wasn't bad enough, he wanted to put lace ruffles on my shirt-sleeves. How the hell am I supposed to play trussed up like a chicken, with bits of lace flapping about all over the place?'

'With difficulty, I imagine,' agreed Max, managing not to laugh. 'The trouble is, people will expect you to look the part.' And quickly changing the subject, 'However, aside from the children, what else have you been doing here?'

'Rebuilding the harpsichord. It took months and I – I don't function well when I can't play.' Julian thought for a moment. 'For the rest, we've re-roofed the main barn and planted two of the fields that had been left idle for the last three years. Then the wine money paid some bills and made it possible to lease the corn mill.'

'Wine money? And why did you need to lease a mill? Don't you have your own?'

So Julian told him about Arabella's discovery in the cellar and the even bigger surprise that what his neighbours paid for use of the mill almost covered the cost of renting it. At the end, Max said, 'You should buy it before somebody else does. In a few years, it will have paid for itself.' And then, as they toured the Home Farm, 'Leaving money out of it, what would you say is the worst of your difficulties?'

'Ignorance. There's no one but Ridley to advise me and he's an old man who only stayed because he had nowhere else to go. Arabella suggested that I try to get the Home Farm and the tenants to work in unison – planting, shearing, reaping and so on at the same time as each other. But when I talked to Ridley about it, he wasn't ... enthusiastic.'

'Well, that needs to change. The system Belle suggested is similar to the one our great-great-grandfather set up at Brandon Lacey after the Civil War. Actually, his situation was almost identical to your own. He unexpectedly inherited a failing estate but no money to plough into it. Land had been left untended and a good many of his tenants were widows whose menfolk hadn't come back from the battlefield. So Gabriel turned the estate into a sort of cooperative where the tenants sold their wool to him, after which he paid them to do the spinning and weaving on the estate. We still do it that way because it benefits everyone ... and I believe some parts of it could be made to work for you here. But you're going to need a good land-steward and three or four fellows to work with him. Men who know what they're doing and can start the process of bringing the land back into full production while you're giving concerts in London.' He paused and then added casually, 'If you like, I can send you those on loan from Brandon Lacey.'

Julian stopped walking and stared at him.

'I – that's extremely generous of you,' he said awkwardly. 'But I can't possibly --'

'Yes, you can.' He grinned. 'Close your mouth and stop looking so shocked. Belle knows I can help you and will have a lot to say to me if I don't.'

'Yes. But --'

'Also, the information Rockliffe shared with us from his lawyer's extremely detailed dossier made it clear that your need is acute.' He glanced into Julian's face. 'Ah. You didn't know about that?'

'No.' On an uncharacteristically arid note, he said, 'I'm surprised you put yourself to the trouble of meeting me.'

'Well, as to that I was hoping we'd arrive on a day when you were giving the village a concert through somebody's parlour window. Yes. I told you it was thorough, didn't I?' This as Julian simply stopped walking to gape at him. Setting him in motion again with a hefty buffet to the shoulder, Max said, 'Now ... did Belle make you sell *all* of the wine or might you be able to offer me a glass?'

Lady Brandon and the children were playing a card game which seemed to largely consist of Ellie swooping triumphantly on everyone else's discards. The second she clapped eyes on Julian she said, 'Look – Aunt Louisa has taught us a new game and I'm winning!'

Max looked at his mother. '*Aunt* Louisa? That was fast work.'

'Wasn't it? Although I didn't mind Ellie calling me grand-mama, I was less happy hearing it from two strapping young men ... so we decided I could be an honorary aunt instead.' She rose from the table, leaving the children to finish the game. Then, reading her son's expression while Julian poured wine, she said, 'It seems the two of you have come to terms with each other. Good.'

'We have discussed a few things,' agreed Max, 'principally that I'll be asking Adam to send Garrett and a handful of other fellows here to start knocking the estate into shape. It's the quiet time at home, so they can be spared easily enough.'

'Dear me,' said his mother, a shade dryly. 'I know Belle asked you to help, but --'

'She didn't *ask* so much as *order*.' He accepted the glass Julian offered him and nodded his thanks. 'So I'm helping. What's wrong with that?'

'Nothing. I'm merely wondering if Lord Chalfont has been given any say in it.' She raised enquiring brows at Julian. 'Have you?'

'Not much. But I'm neither too proud nor too stupid to refuse help when it's offered. I'm just grateful.'

'Make sure you tell Belle that,' muttered Max. And glancing at the clock, 'We should be starting back to Newark soon, Mother ... so if you want to hear his lordship play, I suggest you ask him now.'

Louisa looked at Julian. 'Will you?'

He surprised her with a shy, sweet and completely beguiling smile.

'It will be a pleasure.'

Following his mother and the earl to the library, Max listened to a muted conversation going on behind him.

'I hope he doesn't play the angry music,' muttered Ellie.

'It's not angry,' objected Rob.

'Some of it is. He played it when Miss Belle was leaving and I don't like it.'

'He won't play that one.' Tom's voice this time. 'He's still working on it. You know what he's like. Perfect's never good enough.'

Interesting, thought Max. *But perfectionism and skill isn't all it takes.*

Personally, he wondered how this retiring, uncertain, socially awkward fellow would manage to play before an audience without dissolving into a puddle of nerves. The ruined casing of the harpsichord didn't inspire confidence either.

Pulling off his coat, Julian sat down on the bench and, after a moment's thought, raised his hands to the keyboard. At which point, the retiring, uncertain, socially awkward fellow was replaced by a wholly different person; a confident, commanding and dazzlingly brilliant man with magic in his hands.

CHAPTER TWENTY-ONE

Rumours of a confrontation between Philippa Sutherland and the lady who was *not* Arabella Brandon took less than twenty-four hours to reach the ears of both Rockliffe and Ralph Sherbourne. There were various versions – ranging from a heated exchange of words, to a jealous quarrel about Lord Sherbourne, to actual physical assault. The one that interested both the earl and the duke most was the one that said Sherbourne knew something scandalous about Lady Sutherland which she feared he might make public.

Rockliffe took Elizabeth to one side and said, 'I will not ask what Sherbourne has told you or what really took place between you and Lady Sutherland. But I will be eternally grateful if – in the wake of all our other complications – you could attempt not to draw any further attention to yourself. Do you think you might manage that?'

Flushing hotly, Elizabeth nodded and apologised.

'Thank you. A few days respite will be a relief.'

Lord Sherbourne caught up with her on the following evening at Lady Wroxton's ball and with practised expertise drew her into the semi-privacy of an alcove to say, 'You will forgive my bluntness, I am sure ... but precisely *what* did you say to Philippa Sutherland?'

Elizabeth swallowed and toyed with her fan so she wouldn't have to look at him.

'I wouldn't have said *anything* if she had let me leave instead of spilling poison. But by the time she said you murdered her brother, I was too annoyed to let it pass. So I told her what I thought.'

'Which was?'

'That it wasn't murder and she knew it perfectly well. And that the reason she's intent on discrediting you is because you know something damaging about her which she's afraid you'll reveal.' The ensuing silence lasted so long that Elizabeth was forced to look up. The hawk's eyes held an odd expression that, as usual, she couldn't interpret. 'It's true, isn't it?'

He took his time about replying but finally he said, 'Yes.'

Elizabeth realised that she hadn't expected him to answer. The fact that he had done so left her unsure how to respond. Fortunately, Ralph saved her the trouble of deciding.

'What led you to that conclusion? And why did you choose to defend me?'

'I thought about the things you'd told me ... and wondered about those you'd left out ... and after that, I started reading between the lines. Also, I wasn't about to let that woman get away with calling you a murderer. Perhaps she'll think twice about it in future.'

Ralph doubted it. Philippa was nothing if not tenacious.

He said slowly, 'You still haven't told me why.'

'Does it matter?'

'Yes. I think so. But since we've been closeted here long enough, I suppose I must let it go. However ... if you have not already promised it, may I claim the supper-dance?'

'Yes,' said Elizabeth. And in the hope that it disguised her surge of pleasure, 'But only if we can talk of something else. I'm quite *tired* of Lady Sutherland.'

An hour later, she was dragged into a corner by Arabella who said, 'Is it true?'

'Is what true?'

'That you and the sister of the man Lord Sherbourne killed came to blows over him at Queensberry House.'

Elizabeth stared at her. 'Did you really need to ask that?'

'No,' grinned Arabella. 'I just wanted to see your face.'

'I hope you're satisfied.'

'Not particularly. But it's what half the people here are saying and I rather hoped it might be true. As it is, Cassie is asking anyone who raises the subject how a slight disagreement becomes a cat-fight and Lady Nell is sighing over how unbelievably credulous some people are. What really happened? And why didn't you tell me?'

'I didn't expect it to become common knowledge,' replied Elizabeth tautly. 'It wasn't nearly as dramatic as people would like to think. I merely admitted to knowing something her ladyship would prefer that I didn't. And no – I'm not going to tell you what.'

'Oh. Lord Sherbourne again.'

'Yes – though probably not in the way you're thinking. Now, unless you can talk of something else --'

'All right – I give up.' Arabella laughed and then said thoughtfully, 'He asked me to dance the quadrille with him, by the way. Will he interrogate me?'

'More to the point,' retorted Elizabeth, moving away, 'will *you* interrogate *him*?'

As it turned out, Arabella and Lord Sherbourne managed the quadrille without treading on the other's toes either literally or metaphorically and ended the dance with a better opinion of each other than they'd had at the start of it. Arabella discovered that his lordship had a dry wit coupled with acute observation. And Ralph found Arabella's cheerful, unselfconscious manner a pleasant change to the usual, fashionable *ennui*. As he escorted her from the floor, he said, 'I have received an invitation to Lord Chalfont's concert and look forward to attending. Is he due to arrive in London soon?'

'No,' said Arabella, only half-joking. 'Not for another eight whole days.'

'As long as that?' A faint smile touched Ralph's mouth. 'Will time be hanging equally heavy on his lordship's hands?'

'Not at all.' Her laughter was full of rueful affection. 'He will be spending every available hour at the harpsichord and enjoying it immensely.'

Sitting at supper beside Elizabeth and having to lower his voice so his words were not overheard by those around them, Lord Sherbourne said, 'If I am not permitted to ask why you took up the cudgels on my behalf ... may I at least thank you?'

'There's no need for that.' Warmth stole into Elizabeth's heart and touched her cheeks. 'Surely anyone who knew the truth would do the same?'

'No. They wouldn't.' He thought about it and then said dispassionately, 'The last and, to the best of my recollection, the *only* person who ever tried was my second on that fateful day. It wasn't his fault that he failed.'

'You are saying it won't be mine either, if her ladyship continues spitting venom?'

'No. I am saying you shouldn't be surprised if she does and that you would be wise to steer clear of her in the future. But I am also saying that I ... value and appreciate the fact that you tried. And that I am grateful.'

* * *

Although she was counting the days until Julian arrived, Arabella settled more easily into fashionable society than Elizabeth had done. It helped that she had always been less conscious of her dignity than her cousin and that the occasional spiteful remark or disparaging glance did not worry her in the least because they came from people whose opinions simply did not matter. Also, unlike Elizabeth, she did not find contemplating Cassie or Caroline's marital bliss painful and was frequently to be found visiting someone's nursery. In short, she enjoyed her visit to the full ... but was aware that, when the time came, she would walk away without a backward glance.

No one saw what happened when letters arrived from Chalfont because she took them to her room and locked the door. Letters from Julian made her cry because missing him was like a hole in her chest. Letters from the children made her cry because they were so dear and sweet and unintentionally funny. All of them had to be read and re-read and treasured. None of them made up for the emptiness of waiting. And nothing Julian wrote told her what that long, desperate embrace had meant at the time ... or might mean in the future.

It helped to focus on the forthcoming concert and so, when a pleasing idea occurred to her, she wasted no time putting it into action. She asked favours of Cassie Audley and Caroline Sarre; she coaxed two concert invitations from Rockliffe; and then, having filled in the names, she despatched them to people she thought Julian would like to be present at his London debut.

Elizabeth, meanwhile, received the dreaded letter from her father. The Reverend expressed his disappointment in her behaviour, had a great deal to say about deceit and demanded that she return to Yorkshire immediately. With lagging steps and depression clogging her throat, Elizabeth sought out the duke.

'Yes,' said Rockliffe calmly. 'I have received a similar communication – though mercifully lacking the sermon. I intend to inform Reverend Marsden that returning you to the fold is not convenient just now ... the organisation surrounding Lord Chalfont's concert, complex as it is, being my primary concern.' Amusement lurked in the dark eyes. 'I am sure you can tell your father how exceptionally occupied I am at present.'

Perfectly aware that, since initially planning the event, his Grace's role was merely that of overseer, Elizabeth swallowed and said, 'Oh yes. *Exceptionally* occupied.'

'Quite. You may also tell him – as will I – that your return journey will be made in one of my own carriages and will be arranged as soon as is practically possible. In the meantime, he should not worry unduly. He might also contemplate the notion that my household is a good deal less ... haphazard ... than that of Lord Chalfont.' He smiled a little and said, 'On another matter entirely, Sir Alastair Vennor has asked my permission to pay his addresses to you. I took the liberty of suggesting that he should spare himself the disappointment. If, however, I have misread the situation --'

'You haven't,' said Elizabeth, startled and faintly aghast. 'I am sure Sir Alastair is a very worthy gentleman but I hadn't realised – that is, I can barely --' She stopped, aware that it would not do to admit that it had taken her a moment to recall Sir Alastair's face. 'Thank you for dealing with the matter, your Grace.'

'Not at all.' He paused, toying idly with his snuffbox whilst watching her without seeming to do so. 'Is there any other gentleman from whom I may expect a similar approach in the near future?' And when Elizabeth shook her head, 'I ask only because the prospect of your forthcoming departure may spur some hitherto dilatory gentleman into action.'

Elizabeth eyed him with fascination, thinking, *Is he telling me what to do if I want to spur some gentleman into action?* But keeping both face and voice demure, she said, 'Thank you ... but I am no more in expectation of other offers than I was in the one from Sir Alastair.'

And escaped to her room to come to terms with the entire conversation.

Twenty minutes later when Elizabeth had begun the task of writing to her parents, Arabella bounced in brimming with delight and brandishing a letter.

'Julian is bringing the children! Although Rockliffe hasn't said a word to me about it, he's told Julian that he may bring them with him and he's sending a coach for them all. Isn't that wonderful? I never dreamed he could be so kind. And Julian is still reeling at the idea of being able to play with an orchestra. He sounds so happy, Lizzie. And he deserves to. He really, really does.'

'Yes. I'm sure he does,' agreed Elizabeth, abandoning her letter. 'But how will he explain the children? People are bound to ask who they are – and he can scarcely tell the truth, can he? Also, will they know how to behave? If they're going to be running wild all --'

'They will not be *running wild*, as you put it,' snapped Arabella, a storm brewing in her eyes. 'Given the chance, Rob will barely stir from Julian's side while he's rehearsing; Ellie is a delight ... and Tom will take care of her when I cannot. As for explaining who they are, Julian will do what he always does and tell the truth. He won't care what people think unless anyone is *stupid* enough to say something unkind in the children's hearing.'

Elizabeth coloured faintly. She said, 'I'm sorry. I didn't mean to sound as if --'

'As if they should be hidden away?'

'No! I never meant that!'

'I certainly *hope* you didn't.' Arabella drew a steadying breath and, somewhat more calmly, added, 'I'm sorry, Lizzie. But I love them – and so does Julian, though he probably hasn't realised it yet. So neither of us will be tolerant of – of *in*tolerance. They are *children* – though I don't believe Tom has ever had a childhood. If you knew how long it took him to believe there might be some kindness in the world and how hard it was for him to trust that Julian wouldn't abandon them --'

'Stop!' said Elizabeth, pressing the heel of one hand against her brow. 'I'm *sorry* – truly I am! I wasn't thinking clearly. Papa has written, ordering me home but the duke is going to hold him off until after the concert and Sir Alastair Vennor apparently wants to marry me, though I can scarcely recall which one he is. And I've absolutely no idea what Lord Sherbourne may be thinking – or whether he's thinking anything at all as far as I'm concerned. But if you're glad the children are coming, then good – so am I.'

'Thank you.' The spurt of temper evaporating as fast as it had come, Arabella sat down and said, 'If you ask me, Lord Sherbourne doesn't know what he's thinking himself. I've seen the way he sometimes looks at you and it's obvious there's *something* there. But for what it's worth, I think you were right when you said he's shut his emotions away where he can't find them because it's almost as if he's observing the world from behind a glass wall.' She paused, thinking it over. 'He'll be there tomorrow evening, won't he – at the Audleys' dinner-party?'

'Yes,' agreed Elizabeth. And with a groan, 'And so will his half-sister and the husband Cassie swears Lord Sherbourne will refuse to speak to. So if you think it's going to fun – think again.'

* * *

In Wynstanton House, preparations were already taking place for the concert. The chandeliers in the ballroom had been taken down for polishing and the room itself given a thorough cleaning; the harpsichord – a particularly beautiful instrument with inlay, gilding and a lovely Classical scene on the underside of the lid – had been carefully carried there from the music room. Flowers had been ordered, the silver polished and the kitchen was busy with menus for the after-concert supper. Members of the orchestra arrived every afternoon for two hours of rehearsal ... and gilt-edged invitations had been despatched to over a hundred guests. Lord Brandon and his mother were due to arrive the day after the Audley party ... which meant that the only thing missing would then be the virtuoso himself.

Rockliffe had found Julian's programme surprising. The first half, of course, was to be the Mozart concerto. The second was comprised of five sections, each by a different composer and each containing two or three short pieces; Bach and one of his sons, Rameau, Scarlatti and Royer. Of all the music listed, Rockliffe was familiar with less than half. Next to the Royer piece he himself had requested, Julian had scrawled, *A good choice – though it may surprise you.* And at the bottom of the page, *The timings are for your own information. If an encore is requested, I'll play something of my own.*

Smiling with gentle anticipation, his Grace handed the programme back to Matthew Bennet and said, 'Excellent. Take it to the printer – and let no one else see it.'

* * *

In Bruton Place, Cassie Audley's nerves were in knots about Lord Sherbourne coming face to face with Monsieur Delacroix. She had lived in constant expectation that one or other of them would send their excuses … but neither had. And though it was easy enough for two gentlemen to ignore each other at a large gathering, it wasn't even remotely possible in a party of sixteen.

She had invited Genevieve and Aristide because she and Sebastian liked them; she had invited Ralph Sherbourne because she suspected that Lizzie Marsden *more* than liked him; and she'd hoped that getting Aristide and the earl into the same room on neutral territory might make them come to terms with each other.

'It won't work,' Sebastian had said. 'I agree it's ridiculous for two adult men to be incapable of giving each other a polite nod. But one of them has to be the first to do it and both of them will happily leave it to the other – which is why it won't work.'

Consequently, Cassie was looking forward to her cosy dinner about as much as she would to a tooth extraction.

By a half after eight, the only guest missing was the Earl of Sherbourne.

Inevitably, Nicholas started taking bets on whether or not he'd show up.

'Perhaps he's not coming,' said Elizabeth to Cassie. And then, just as she was about to remark that it might be for the best, the butler appeared in the doorway and, in the voice of doom, announced, 'The Earl of Sherbourne.'

The room might have fallen silent but for the determination of Caroline, Lord Amberley and Adeline. For just one critical instant, nearly everyone else froze before resuming their conversations with renewed vigour.

A small, sardonic smile curling his mouth, Ralph bowed over Cassie's hand and said, 'My profound apologies, Mistress Audley. It appears that I am late.'

'Not at all, my lord – merely the last to arrive. *Someone* has to be, don't they?'

'That is indisputably true,' he agreed. And with no more than a nod and a smile in Elizabeth's direction, he turned to accept Sebastian's outstretched hand, saying, 'Mr Audley … a brief word, if I may?'

Sebastian's brows rose. 'Of course. In private?'

'That might be best.'

Having led his guest through to the library, he said, 'What can I do for you?'

'You can accept my apologies for my behaviour the last time I was in this room. I was angry, of course … but that is no excuse for bad manners.'

For a second, Sebastian was too stunned to speak. But finally he said, 'It is forgotten, my lord. But I appreciate the sentiment and will pass it on to Cassandra.'

'Thank you.' Ralph had been late because it had taken a long time to find the frame of mind necessary to do what, with extreme reluctance, he knew had to be done. Even now, he had to force the words past his lips. 'Everyone in the next room is waiting to watch Monsieur Delacroix and I cut each other. I am a guest in your home, as is he … and *I*, at least, have no wish to be a cause of embarrassment to you or your lady. Therefore I thought you might ascertain whether …' *God*, he thought grimly, *this is going to choke me.* '… whether, if I offer Delacroix my hand, he will accept it. I do not ask him to meet me half-way. I do, however, refuse to put myself in the position of being insulted in public.'

First an apology – and now this, thought Sebastian. And then, *Why? What's changed? Or are you just making Aristide the villain of the piece if he won't kiss and make up?*

He said, 'Understandable. And I respect you for making the offer – as, hopefully, will Aristide. I take it you don't want me to bring him in here?'

'Hardly. That would raise speculation to new heights, would it not?'

'Oh almost certainly, I should think. Very well. Give me a few moments, will you?' And he left the room, wisely suppressing an impulse to laugh.

With Genevieve on his arm, Aristide was talking to Adrian and Caroline – which meant that Sebastian did not need to bother drawing the Frenchman to one side. He said, 'Excuse the interruption – but I am charged with a mission.'

'A mission?' echoed Caroline. 'How intriguing!'

'You have no idea,' murmured Sebastian. Then, looking at Aristide and coming directly to the point, 'Lord Sherbourne is prepared to offer you his hand. And since he is naturally reluctant to be made a fool of in front of everyone, he wants to know if you'll accept it.'

If Monsieur Delacroix's jaw didn't quite drop, it certainly slackened in shock.

In the seconds it took her husband to find his voice, Genevieve said, '*Ralph* said that?' And when Sebastian nodded, 'Why?'

'He says he doesn't want to be the cause of awkwardness under my roof. I see no reason to disbelieve him. I also think he deserves credit for bending his pride.'

'I daresay,' returned Aristide tightly. 'But the current situation is of his making.'

'And he's prepared to mend it – at least, in part.' Seeing that Aristide's expression remained unforgiving, Sebastian said, 'If you refuse now, he won't offer again – and I, for one, wouldn't blame him. But if it helps, do it because it's plainly killing him.'

Adrian laughed. 'Not exactly the right spirit for a rapprochement, is it?'

Ignoring this, Sebastian turned to Genevieve. 'What do you think? He's your brother, after all.'

She said slowly, 'It is up to Aristide, of course. But on the rare occasions we meet Ralph in company, the three of us cutting each other is ... awkward.'

Aristide looked at her and then sighed. 'You are right, of course. And if I refuse, that awkwardness will be my fault, will it not? Very well, Sebastian. Tell him I'll do it.'

A few minutes later when Sebastian returned, chatting amicably with Lord Sherbourne as they crossed to where Aristide and his wife still stood, conversations all around the room faltered and then resumed at seemingly increased volume. Face and voice both carefully neutral, Ralph looked his brother-in-law in the eye and extended his hand, saying, 'A pleasure to see you, Monsieur. I trust you are well?'

'Perfectly, I thank you,' responded Aristide, matching the earl's manner precisely as he accepted his hand. 'And you, my lord?'

'Never better.' And turning, 'Genevieve – you are quite in your best looks, I see. Motherhood obviously suits you. Ah ... you have a son, I believe.'

'Yes. His name is Etienne.' Smiling and perfectly aware that it would be a cold day in hell before Ralph came to Duke Street, she added sweetly, 'If you wish to make his acquaintance, you know where to find us.'

'Indeed,' he agreed, his answering smile not quite reaching his eyes. 'Perhaps when he is a little older? I am forced to admit that babies are not my *forte*.' He made a slight bow which encompassed both his sister and Aristide and then, with a glance across the room, said, 'Forgive me – but I have yet to greet Mistress Marsden.'

He had gone no more than six steps when his path was blocked by Cassie Audley.

'That was uncommonly well-done of you, my lord – and not easy,' she said with a warm smile. And, beckoning a footman bearing a tray, added, 'Have some wine … and perhaps you might take a glass to Elizabeth. You will be leading her in to dinner, you know.'

By the time he finally reached Elizabeth's side, the bile was beginning to drain from Ralph's throat. Handing her the glass, he said, 'Not the ideal way to begin an evening, perhaps … but unfortunately necessary.'

Not pretending to misunderstand, she said, 'How long is it since last you spoke?'

'Over a year. The occasion was not … pleasant.'

'It will be easier next time. And it has done you no harm at all to have been seen to make the first move.'

His mouth curled faintly. 'You think I wasn't aware of that?'

'No. I'm sure you were. But it doesn't detract from the fact that you did it.' She smiled and changed the subject. 'Acceptances for the concert invitations are flooding in and Arabella's mother and eldest brother are due to arrive tomorrow or the day after. Belle asked the duke to invite them so we can apologise for deceiving everyone.'

'Ah. Not, then, because an announcement is imminent?'

This time she *did* pretend not to follow him. 'An announcement?'

'Between your cousin and Chalfont. One can't help noticing that every time his lordship's name is mentioned, Mistress Brandon glows like a beacon – and not, I imagine, purely on account of his skill at the keyboard.' He paused briefly, setting down his glass and relieving her of hers, then offering his arm. 'You need not answer … and we are being summoned to table. Mistress Audley informs me that I am to have the pleasure of your company at dinner – for which I am suitably grateful.'

Despite the fact the company included a duke, a marquis and two earls, dinner was a cheerful affair during which no one adhered very strictly to the usual etiquette. At one point during the second course, Sebastian silenced everyone else by addressing Arabella, three places down on the other side of the table.

'Mistress Brandon, why has it taken the concert invitation for me to find out that the Earl of Chalfont is actually Julian Langham?'

'Well, Julian *is* the Earl of Chalfont,' said Arabella, baffled. 'But he prefers to use his name rather than the title. Why do you ask?'

'Because I'd never heard of Chalfont until Rock mentioned him ... but I know Julian Langham.'

'You do?'

'Yes. We were at Cambridge together – and he played like a demon even then. The music professor was in awe of him. But he disappeared after the second year.' Sebastian grinned invitingly. 'So where's he been all this time?'

'In Vienna.'

'Doing what?'

'Studying.' Abandoning any attempt to look indifferent, Arabella beamed at him. 'Composing ... learning to play like *ten* demons ... meeting Mozart.'

If she hadn't had everyone's full attention before, she had it now. Several people spoke at once, some impressed, others incredulous.

From his place across the table, Ralph watched her meditatively. Her cheeks were pink, the big grey eyes brilliant and a sweet, tender smile hovered about her lips ... all of it purely from speaking of Chalfont. Ralph found himself wondering how it must feel to be the object of a love like that. Extraordinary, he supposed. Extraordinary ... and something he found himself envying.

Transferring his gaze Elizabeth, he murmured, 'What I said earlier about your cousin? I rest my case.'

Cassie, meanwhile, was saying, 'Does his lordship *really* know Herr Mozart?'

'He does,' confirmed Rockliffe, thinking of the hand-written pages locked safely in his own desk and which he was still amazed Chalfont had allowed out of his possession.

'I'm not sure how *well* they're acquainted,' remarked Arabella truthfully. And on a gurgle of amusement, 'All I *do* know is that he and Mozart got drunk together.'

Into the inevitable laughter, Rockliffe said gently, 'I don't believe we needed to know that – about either gentleman.'

'Speak for yourself,' objected Sebastian. 'Aside from his music, all any of us know about Mozart is that he's a genius. It's comforting to know he's human, too. However ... when is Chalfont due to arrive?'

'Next week,' sighed Rockliffe. 'I must admit, I shall be delighted to see him. Perhaps he will be able to stop the concerto ensemble squabbling among itself. I am quite tired of being summoned to arbitrate on matters entirely beyond my comprehension.'

* * *

On the following afternoon, Max and Louisa arrived. Inevitably, since Max had never previously met Rockliffe and neither he nor his mother knew the duchess, their welcome took rather longer than it might otherwise have done and it was nearly an hour before Arabella was finally alone with them. Hugging both of them again and shedding a few tears, she said, 'I'm sorry. Truly, I am. But I didn't care about London and Lizzie *did* ... so changing places gave both of us what we wanted. And no real harm seems to have come of it. There's been a bit of gossip since the truth came out but most people have accepted it for what we said it was – just a foolish joke.'

'At the risk of stating the obvious,' said Louisa, 'a great *deal* of harm might have come of it. It's only thanks to Rockliffe that it hasn't. So promise me that you won't even *think* of doing something so idiotic again. Otherwise I'll be forced to lock you in the attic.'

'The cellar,' corrected Max. 'She'd enjoy the attic too much.' And, holding his sister's gaze, 'On our way here, we took a slight detour and called on Lord Chalfont.'

'You did *what*?' asked Arabella, aghast. 'Why?'

'Why do you think? We wanted to see for ourselves the kind of man you've been living with these last weeks.'

Her eyes narrowed and she stood up. 'Did you bully him?'

'No. For God's sake, Belle! I could forgive young Tom – but you should know better.'

'Well ... perhaps. But if Tom *thought* you were, he must have had a reason.'

'He didn't. He just jumped to conclusions. What he *actually* walked in on was Chalfont biting my head off because I hadn't properly appreciated his virtuoso status.'

She stared at him. '*Julian* did that? No. He can't have.'

'He did,' confirmed Louisa, 'though I wouldn't say he exactly bit your head off, Max.'

'He snarled,' muttered Max. Then, 'Why is nobody defending *me*?'

'Because you don't need it,' retorted his mother. 'However, the two of you were friendly enough when you came back to the house. So why don't you tell Belle what you and his lordship agreed?'

'Yes,' said Arabella suspiciously. 'Why don't you?'

Max sighed. 'You asked me to help him, didn't you? Well, I'm helping. I've written to Adam telling him to send Garrett and a handful of others to Chalfont to see what can be done and to start doing it. That *is* what you wanted, isn't it?'

Her eyes suddenly luminous, she opened her mouth, closed it again and then, throwing herself into her brother's arms, said, 'Yes. Oh *yes*. He needs help so badly, Max – so thank you. *Thank you*.'

Behind her daughter's back and knowing that, if Arabella would talk to anyone about her feelings for Lord Chalfont, it would be Max, Louisa gave her son a meaningful smile and, receiving a nod of acknowledgement in return, slipped from the room. When the door closed behind her, Max said, 'I'm glad you're pleased, minx ... but do you think you could stop strangling me?'

'Sorry.' With a watery giggle, she relaxed her hold on him. 'D-Did you like him?'

'I think I can probably get used to him,' he replied with a touch of mordant humour. 'Mama, on the other hand, took to him right away.'

'Oh?' Arabella stepped back and realised they were alone. 'Where did she go?'

'She made a tactical retreat.' He pulled her down beside him on a sofa and put his arm around her. 'I'm not going to demand every detail of the weeks you spent with Chalfont – but one thing is clear enough. You love him, don't you?'

'Yes.' It was a mere whisper against his cravat. 'So much.'

'That's what I thought. Since he said nothing of it, I am assuming there is no understanding between you. But I imagine you are hoping there will be one?'

This time the tears were not happy ones. Lifting an impatient hand to brush them aside, she said, 'Yes. But … it's complicated. And I – I can't explain.'

'You don't need to explain. I guessed a long time ago that you and David lay together,' replied Max, his tone decidedly grim. 'I'm right, aren't I?'

'Y-Yes.' There was a long silence and then, 'Does Mama know?'

'I don't believe so. If she did … if she even suspected … she would have raised the matter with you.' He paused and then said, 'You changed at around the time David left. Mama put it down to you growing up. I didn't. I realised something must have caused it – and from there it wasn't hard to work out what that something was.'

'I'm sorry.' She burrowed into him. 'I'm so sorry. I wish I hadn't done it, Max. I've wished it every day since. I don't even know why I did. Aren't … aren't you angry with me?'

'I can't pretend to be pleased, love. But I don't doubt that it was David's idea, not yours. Spent a lot of time talking you into it, did he?'

'Yes. But I needn't have given way. I knew better than --'

'As he should have done. There was no predicting how long he'd be away – he might have died over there, for God's sake! Consequently, seducing you wasn't just bloody stupid; it was downright dishonourable. You were foolish, Belle – but at eighteen, so are we all. And what's done, is done. It's not the end of the world nor even a hanging offence, so it can't be allowed to ruin the rest of your life.' He dropped a kiss on her brow and added, 'We won't speak of this again … but I'll give you just one piece of advice. If Chalfont asks you to marry him, you'll say yes … and you'll tell him about David. And then you'll find out if he loves you enough not to mind.

CHAPTER TWENTY-TWO

In the last week before departing for London, Julian set himself a gruelling routine. He played for three hours in the early morning and a further four in the evening. Between these, he did the tasks demanded of him by the estate and spent the time he had left with the children. Violet and Rose, ably assisted by Tom, prepared for the journey without subjecting his lordship to questions and, as far as was possible, saw that he was spared the inevitable household chaos. There was a tacit agreement that even Ellie understood. The music must come first. And soon all of them knew the concert programme by heart.

Julian gave up part of the last afternoon to play the solo part of his recital for the Misses Caldercott, Paul and Janet Featherstone and, it being a pleasant day, half the village. The penultimate Royer piece left his audience in a state of stunned silence for almost a full minute before applause, whistles and cheers broke out. The ladies hugged him, Paul thumped him on the back ... and Julian went home completely unaware that, behind him, his friends were making plans.

He arrived at the house to find the hall occupied by four strangers. His mind still elsewhere, it took him several moments to understand what one of them was saying to him.

'I'm Ben Garrett, my lord – and these are three of my best men. Mr Adam sent us from Brandon Lacey to see what improvements need making and maybe get a start on them.'

Gradually the sense of it filtered through. Julian said helplessly, 'But I'm leaving for London tomorrow.'

'We know that, my lord – it's why we was anxious to get here beforehand. Now, there's nothing you need to worry about. We'll introduce ourselves round and about till we know what's what ... so all we need from you is your authority to get to work.'

'Right. Yes. Whatever you think best. Thank you.'

From beside him, Rose said, 'They're putting up at the Dog and Duck, milord. But there's a couple of the spare bedchambers that haven't got damp in them so Vi and me can put 'em to rights.

If it's all right with you and the gentlemen don't mind sharing, they can stay here instead after you and the children have gone.'

'Yes. Good.' And to the foreman, 'Will that suit you, Mr ...?'

'Garrett, my lord. And yes, that'll suit a treat. Much obliged to you.'

The men set off back to the village, leaving Julian vaguely wondering what he'd just agreed to but disinclined to delve too deeply. He was just heading back to the library, when Ellie skidded to his side, hotly pursued by Tom and a wildly yapping Figgy.

Ellie said, 'Tom says Figgy can't come to London. But he *can*, can't he?'

'What?' asked Julian. Then, 'No. He can't. Absolutely not.'

'I've explained why four times,' growled Tom. 'She won't listen.'

The little girl fixed big, beseeching eyes on Julian. 'Please! He'll be good.'

He drew a long breath and struggled to find his usual tone.

'I'm sorry, Ellie – but no. We can't take Figgy to the duke's house – never mind having him in the carriage with us for hours on end. It won't do. He'll stay here with Rose and --'

'But he'll miss me!' She clutched Julian's hand. '*Please* let him come.'

'I can't. It's impossible.' And when she opened her mouth to argue, he added firmly, 'Enough, Ellie. The answer is no.'

And for the first time ever, he walked away.

'Told you,' muttered Tom. 'Now stop pestering him. This isn't the time.'

* * *

The duke's coach – an elegant, well-sprung vehicle – pulled up outside the front door promptly at nine on the following morning. Inside the hall were neat piles of luggage which Tom, Rob and Rockliffe's groom carried outside for loading. Ellie, meanwhile, helped Mistress Phelps stow wicker baskets of food under the seats. When everything was ready, both Rose and Violet seized the opportunity to hug his lordship, kiss his cheek and wish him luck. Then Julian and the children climbed aboard ... and they were off.

They hadn't reached the end of the drive before it became clear that one of the wicker baskets contained something other than food. Tom sent Julian a long-suffering look; Rob dissolved into giggles; and Julian rapped on the roof, signalling the coachman to pull up. Then, in an unusually crisp tone, he said, 'Get Figgy out, Ellie. Now.'

Reluctantly and without looking at him, she did as he'd asked. Rob stopped laughing and Tom pressed his lips together so he wouldn't start.

'I forbade you to bring him. Did I not make that clear?'

She nodded. 'Yes. But I thought --'

'You thought you would disobey me and do it anyway.' He regarded her sternly, knowing a sign of weakness would be fatal right now. 'Tom ... take Figgy back to the house. Ellie ... you can either stay at home with Figgy or you can come with me. Which is it to be?'

Ellie's chin quivered. She buried her face in the dog's neck and finally mumbled, 'I'm sorry. I'll come with you.'

'Good choice,' said Tom briskly, taking Figgy from her and hopping down from the carriage. Then, flashing a grin at Julian, 'It could have been worse, sir. We might've been half-way to Newark. As it is, the journey'll fly by now.'

* * *

It didn't. Rob, it turned out, was carriage-sick – forcing them to halt five times in three hours. After the second occasion and praying that it would help, Julian transferred the boy to the front-facing seat. This, because Ellie refused to sit anywhere but by Julian, resulted in him giving up his own seat to Tom and occupying the rear-facing seat instead. After three further stops, Rob was green-tinged and miserable and, by Julian's reckoning, couldn't have anything left inside him to bring up. Part-way through the afternoon, Ellie grew tired and climbed on Julian's lap to sleep; then Tom, the only one of them enjoying the journey, pulled a chicken-leg from the picnic basket – the scent of which set Rob off again; and by the time they stopped for the night,

Julian was wondering how he was going to endure two more days of this.

Thanks to some sensible advice from a sympathetic chambermaid, Rob (and therefore Julian) survived the next day's journey rather better. Ellie slept through most of it, leaving his lordship with cramp in one arm. And Tom passed the miles with an almost continuous commentary on whatever caught his attention through the window.

One more day, thought Julian grimly as he settled the children down for the second night. *Just one more day. I can manage that ... as long as I don't let myself think about doing all this again in reverse.*

* * *

When the carriage entered the outskirts of London and the press of traffic therein, Ellie forgot to be tired, Rob forgot to feel sick and all three children grew increasingly excited. The only thing keeping Julian mildly sane was the prospect of seeing Arabella. In every other respect – and for the first time ever – he was acutely aware that he was going to arrive at Rockliffe's door grubby, crumpled and looking even more disreputable than he usually did. The butler, he reflected gloomily, would probably send them all round to the tradesmen's entrance – which might actually be for the best.

Their first sight of Wynstanton House rendered the children mute for the first time in an hour and Ellie crawled on to Julian's knee. She whispered, 'It – it's too big.'

'Yes. It is rather large, isn't it?' He somehow managed to hide the fact that his insides were in knots. 'But Miss Belle is in there and – and her mama, I think. So there's nothing to be scared of. Come on. We have to get out.'

But Ellie refused to budge, leaving Julian with no alternative but to step down with her clinging limpet-like to his neck. Then the door to the house swung open, a pair of liveried footmen trotted down the steps to begin unloading the carriage and the butler said sonorously, 'Good afternoon, Lord Chalfont. Their Graces have been greatly looking forward to your arrival. I hope your journey was pleasant?'

'Not particularly.' Hemmed in by Tom and Rob, Julian allowed the butler to usher them all inside and made another unsuccessful attempt to dislodge Ellie. Finally, in desperation, he said, 'I'm sorry. But could someone find --' And then, hearing running footsteps, looked towards the stairs in time to see Arabella come to a halt on the half-landing.

For a handful of seconds, their eyes met and Julian lost the ability to breathe. She looked beautiful; but the flowered green silk gown over its cream, lace-trimmed underskirt made her a stranger. Then, with a small inarticulate sound, she was skimming down to the hall, with the boys running over to meet her and Ellie was suddenly fighting to be free. He set the child down, then stood like a stone as Arabella, careless of her billowing petticoats, tried to hug all three children at once while all of them talked at the same time. Julian's chest hurt. He hauled in a lungful of air and found it didn't help very much.

When the children finally released her, Arabella smiled radiantly at Julian, gathered up her skirts so she could run to him … and then abruptly realised that she shouldn't. Not because Symonds was watching but because she couldn't hurl herself into Julian's arms without being sure he would welcome her doing so and not feel embarrassed. So she settled for walking as quickly as dignity allowed, while he took two hesitant steps towards her. Then they were face to face and his fingers were curling warm and close around hers, making her dizzy and speechless with pleasure.

Her eyes told Julian everything her lips could not say … and all the things he had been worried about ceased to matter. She had not changed. Aside from the lovely, expensive clothes, she was still the same girl she had been at Chalfont. More than anything, he wanted to wrap his arms about her, to breathe in the scent of her hair, to kiss her until the world went away. But he retained just enough sense to know that he'd better not. So he bowed over her hand, brushed the lightest of caresses on her knuckles and, on a mere breath, said, 'I missed you.'

Still gazing into his eyes, she whispered, 'And I, you. I thought you'd never get here – and now I can't believe you have.'

Very reluctantly, he released her fingers but was unable to stop smiling at her.

'Neither can I.'

Having waited for a few moments, Symonds gave a discreet cough and said, 'Perhaps your lordship would care to follow me up to the drawing-room?'

This swept the smile from Julian's face.

'Right now? Do I have to? I'm not fit to be seen.'

'Yes, you are.' Arabella was unable to stop herself brushing back the lock of rich brown hair that habitually escaped its ribbon. 'To *me*, you are.'

'That's because you're used to my clothes looking as if I've slept in them.'

She shook her head and, laughter trembling in her voice, said, 'Julian, everyone knows you've been travelling for days. I promise you that they'll understand. Now come with me and stop worrying.'

Seeing that he still looked unconvinced, she slid her hand back into his and squeezed it gently. He shot her a brief, startled glance and looked swiftly away ... but not before she glimpsed the beginnings of a smile and was filled with such a powerful surge of tenderness that it threatened to overwhelm her. To hide it, she offered her free hand to Ellie – currently hopping from foot to foot behind her – and grinned at the boys. 'Let's go.'

Rob and Tom sent Julian imploring glances. He shrugged helplessly and let Arabella tow him upstairs. A footman threw open a pair of doors ... and he found himself facing Rockliffe, Lady Brandon, Max ... and an elegant lady in turquoise.

Rockliffe strolled over to offer his hand.

'Welcome to Wynstanton House, Chalfont. I gather you are already acquainted with Lady Brandon and her son ... but allow me to present you to my duchess. Adeline, my dear ... rescue is finally at hand. Our virtuoso is here.'

'And a good thing, too,' said Adeline, with a warm smile that embraced both Julian and the children. 'I am happy to meet you, my lord. Have you had a perfectly awful journey?'

'It wasn't good,' he agreed, bowing over her hand. 'Your Grace, I apologise for my appearance but --'

'Don't.' It was Louisa, already heading towards Ellie and the boys, who spoke. 'Three days in a carriage with three children? I doubt there are many gentlemen who could survive the experience with their sanity and temper intact.' Startling each child with a quick hug, she said, 'Did *you* enjoy riding in the carriage, Ellie?'

'Sometimes. But Rob kept being sick.'

Rob's ears turned red. Tom groaned and stared at his feet.

'Oh dear,' murmured Louisa unsteadily. 'How ... unfortunate.'

'That must have been fun,' remarked Max, slanting a grin at Julian but holding out his hand to the boy standing ramrod straight beside him. 'How do you do, Tom?'

It was Tom's turn to flush. 'I'm well, my lord. Thank you.'

'And you?' Max ruffled Rob's hair. 'Still practising your music?'

'Y-Yes,' stammered Rob. 'But Sir Julian's needed the harpsichord more than usual.'

'I'm delighted to hear it,' said Rockliffe. And then, 'Louisa ... may I ask if you would be good enough to take the children up to the nursery floor and have Symonds send suitable refreshments? I imagine Lord Chalfont needs a brief respite.'

'I was about to suggest that very thing,' agreed Louisa cheerfully. 'Come along all of you. Belle and his lordship will join you later. But for now, you'll have to make do with me.' And she shepherded them firmly from the room.

When the door closed behind them, Adeline said, 'Please sit down. Arabella, I think you may now safely let go of his lordship's hand and pour him a cup of tea.'

Arabella looked down, as if unaware that her fingers were still firmly locked with Julian's. Releasing him with a tiny embarrassed laugh she said, 'I'm sorry. I'm so happy to see him that I'm scared he'll vanish again.'

'You cannot possibly be as happy as I,' drawled Rockliffe, waving Julian into a chair and seating himself in an adjacent one. 'The concerto ensemble will be here as usual tomorrow afternoon. I rejoice to say that they are now solely your responsibility.'

Frowning a little and absently accepting the cup Arabella put in his hand, Julian said, 'Is something wrong with them?'

'They are ... fractious.'

'You mean they argue?' Julian's brow cleared. 'Yes. Of course they do.'

Looking mildly entertained, Max said, 'Perfectly normal, is it?'

'Yes. They've been rehearsing a harpsichord concerto without the harpsichord and reducing the orchestration will have raised questions. But everything will settle down now I'm here.' He hesitated before adding, 'I can't tell your Grace what this opportunity means to me. The concert alone would have been more than enough. But the chance to play with an orchestra --'

Rockliffe silenced him with a wave of one indolent hand.

'You thanked me quite adequately by letter, Chalfont. And I am eagerly anticipating your performance. The programme you have put together is ... intriguing.'

'It's also gained the proportions of a State Secret,' remarked Max. 'Even *Belle* hasn't been allowed to see it – never mind the rest of us.'

Arabella laughed again but said smugly, 'Julian will tell me, though.'

'No, he will not,' said Rockliffe flatly. 'You hear me, Chalfont?'

'Yes,' agreed Julian. Then, looking at Max and dragging his mind to more mundane matters, he said, 'Your men arrived the day before we left, Lord Brandon. I – well, I'm extremely grateful.'

Shrugging this aside, Max said, 'Adam worked fast. How many did he send?'

'Four. They'll live in the house and I gave them authority to do whatever they think necessary.' Setting his cup aside, he stood up and said diffidently, 'If it's all right, I should make sure the children aren't --'

'*I'll* see to them,' interposed Arabella in a tone that brooked no argument. '*You* will take an hour to yourself and catch your breath. I imagine you'd like a bath?'

'I would *kill* for a bath. What with Ellie spending half the journey in my lap and Rob throwing up every five miles or so --' He stopped abruptly, colouring a little. 'My apologies. I shouldn't have said that.'

'I don't see why not.' Adeline smiled at him. 'Speaking for myself and knowing just a little of the horrors of travelling with only one small baby, I admire your stamina. Arabella ... pull the bell for a footman to show Lord Chalfont to his rooms. And -- '

'Forgive me,' blurted Julian. 'But please ... could everyone stop calling me Chalfont? If no one minds, I prefer my given name.'

'Julian, then. And don't feel obliged to re-appear until dinner.'

He nodded but said, 'When I've made myself presentable, may I see the harpsichord?'

'By all means,' sighed Rockliffe. 'I'm amazed you are willing to wait that long.'

* * *

Bathed, shaved and clad in what had recently become his second-best suit of clothes, Julian and the children followed Arabella to the ballroom ... he fending off her attempts to prise the concert programme out of him and the children gazing about them in awe whilst chattering about their rooms, Lily the nursemaid and Lady Vanessa Jane – who had immediately, if temporarily, occupied a Figgy-sized space in Ellie's affections.

In truth, Julian was glad of the distraction. It made it possible to *almost* ignore the warmth of Arabella's hand on his arm and the emotions and desires it aroused in him.

'I don't see why you won't tell me,' she grumbled. 'I suggested some of the pieces myself, after all.'

'You heard the duke.'

She turned her head. '*You'll* tell me, won't you, Tom?'

'Not if Sir Julian says not.'

'Which I do. And *please* don't ask Rob, Arabella. He'll sing.'

'Rob's singing never sounds like *anything*,' observed Ellie. 'And when he tries to do the angry bit, it's *worse*.'

'Angry bit?' prompted Arabella, feeling a slight quiver run through Julian.

'It's *not* angry,' said Rob crossly. 'And I'm sick of saying it.'

'I think it is,' argued Ellie. 'And anyway, I like the bouncy music best.'

Arabella looked up into Julian's face and laughed. '*Bouncy*?'

'Apparently.' He'd missed her laughter and was rediscovering what it did to him. 'Your brother says he's helping me because you asked him to. Why did you?'

'Because he can and you need it,' came the simple reply. And then, throwing open tall double-doors, 'Here we are.'

Julian stepped inside the ballroom and froze – as did the children. Gleaming floorboards, crystal chandeliers and windows along one side hung with moss-green velvet and separated by gold-painted, ceiling-height caryatids.

Christ, he thought. *It's massive. Beautiful – but massive. And I won't know about the acoustics until the audience is in and I start playing.*

'What do you think?' asked Arabella.

He shook his head. 'How many people has Rockliffe invited?'

'Over a hundred, I believe. Why? You're not nervous, are you?'

'No. I'm praying to God this won't turn out to be an echo-chamber.'

A low platform the width of the room had been erected at the far end and on it stood the harpsichord. Shadowed by Rob, Julian advanced on it as if magnetised while Tom continued to stare about him, dumbstruck. Then Ellie said, 'The gold ladies are pretty. But why aren't they wearing more clothes?' And the tension shattered.

The harpsichord was exquisite and in pristine condition. After a moment, Julian stretched out a hand and played a few notes. Then he uttered a muffled curse.

'What?' asked Arabella, wrenched from the pleasure of simply looking at him.

He didn't answer. Instead, he played a couple of arpeggios, followed by a series of chords. Finally he said, 'It's flat.'

'It can't be! His Grace had someone tune it only two days ago.'

'And it's tuned perfectly note-to-note. But the whole thing is almost a quarter-tone flat. If I wasn't giving a recital, it would be acceptable. Since I *am*, I'll have to re-tune it.'

Seeing his hand sliding towards his pocket, Arabella grabbed it before it could get there.

'Stop. You can't do it now.'

'It won't take very long,' he protested, his attention instantly riveted on the sensation of her fingers about his wrist. 'I'll just need to --'

'*No*. Dinner is in an hour. If you set to work now, you'll tune it and then you'll start playing – and no one will see you before tomorrow. You can do it in the morning.'

'All right.' His gaze travelled slowly from her hand, to her eyes and finally to her mouth. His voice, lower in pitch and a little husky, he said, 'Tomorrow. If you say so.'

Arabella's breath caught and a ripple of heat flickered along her veins. Without realising it, she swayed towards him and ...

'Can I watch?' demanded Rob.

Taking a guilty step back, Julian said, 'What?'

'Can I watch while you tune it? I promise I'll be quiet. So can I? Please?'

'Yes. If you wish.'

He wondered if Arabella was relieved or disappointed that they had brought three chaperones with them. *He* didn't feel nearly as grateful as he knew he ought to. If he had kissed her, he would have had to say all the things he'd vowed *not* to say until the concert was behind him. Pushing the thought aside, he said, 'I haven't thanked you, have I?'

'For what?' she asked.

'For persuading Rockliffe to do this.'

'I didn't persuade him. Oh – I'd planned to. Aside from Lizzie, it was my main reason for agreeing to come to London with him.'

'Was it?'

She nodded. 'You once told me that a concert required money and patronage and I knew Rockliffe could supply both so I decided to badger him until he did. Only, as it turned out, after hearing you play – even from the wrong side of the library door – he'd already decided to do it. Truthfully, I can't imagine how I ever thought he might not.'

'I hope I'll justify your faith. I still can't explain how it feels to be given something I thought I'd never have again.'

'You don't have to explain. I know.' For several minutes neither of them spoke. But finally Arabella said reluctantly, 'We should re-join the others.'

'If you're not going to let me tune the harpsichord, I suppose we might as well.' He grinned suddenly. 'I hope you're going to guide us back. Left to ourselves, we could all be wandering this house for days. What do you think, Tom?'

Tom grinned back. 'I think that if *you* were left to yourself, you'd tune the harpsichord and spend the night in here with it. Right, Miss Belle?'

'Absolutely right,' she laughed, dropping an arm about the boy's shoulders for a quick, impulsive hug. 'He must think we don't know him at all.'

* * *

On the following morning, Arabella announced that she and her cousin would begin the children's visit by taking them to shake out the fidgets in Hyde Park.

'And tomorrow, when the harpsichord is re-tuned and Rob is free to join us, we'll go to the Tower of London. What do you think?'

Tom and Rob voted this a capital idea.

Ellie said gleefully, 'The bloody tower that Norman built?'

Julian watched Arabella struggling not to laugh and Cousin Elizabeth trying to hide a quiver of shock ... at which point he silently thanked God for a narrow escape. He had a feeling that the *real* Miss Lizzie would have had all the children marching in step – or died trying.

In this, he did Elizabeth an injustice. The second after she recoiled from what she had initially thought was the child's profanity, she realised her mistake. She also, with a good deal of dismay, realised something else. She didn't want to be jealous of her cousin's unconcealed joy in Lord Chalfont's company – she wanted to be glad for her. But seeing Arabella glowing with happiness and witnessing the expression in his lordship's eyes when he looked at her was suddenly excruciatingly painful.

Since the day in the physic garden when she had told Ralph Sherbourne the truth, she had seen him on only three occasions and, though he had sought her out on all of them, he had not said anything to suggest that he was still considering making her an offer. Elizabeth told herself that she ought to have expected this. He was an earl, after all. And there was a vast difference between the well-dowered sister of a baron and the scarcely-dowered-at-all daughter of a vicar. She also told herself that she had no right to feel either disappointed or hurt. He had promised nothing … and she had taken Arabella's place expecting nothing. She had certainly not expected to meet a man who made her blood run faster merely by looking at her; and one whose deep and impenetrable loneliness made her heart ache.

The concert was less than a week away and, after it, she must face music of a different kind at home. She did not delude herself with the notion that she would forget Ralph Sherbourne. She simply told herself that dwelling on her memories would bring nothing but misery … and life had to go on.

* * *

It took the best part of three hours to re-tune the harpsichord and Rob insisted on staying throughout. When it was done, Julian rolled his shoulders to ease the stiffness in them and then sat down on the bench.

'Are you going to play something?' Rob asked.

'Yes. All instruments have their funny little ways so I need to get to know this one.'

Rob nodded and made himself comfortable on the first violinist's chair.

Julian was part-way through a piece he'd originally considered for his debut concert but decided to hold in reserve for a future occasion when he realised Rockliffe had wandered in and was standing some distance away, listening. Julian stopped playing and said, 'Were you looking for me, your Grace?'

'No. I was merely curious. I take it that the harpsichord is now at … do we call it concert-pitch?'

'We do and it is.' He sent a smile at the boy, 'Rob's been helping me.'

'Excellent. And the piece you were playing just now?'

'A good test for both the instrument and myself.' Julian added a few more bars. '*Fandango* by Antonio Soler … a Spaniard.'

'Ah.' The duke strolled closer and asked curiously, 'You don't require sheet music?'

'No. I have some, of course – like the Mozart concerto. Newer pieces I was still working on when I left Vienna. But once I've learned the music, the pages are just a distraction.' He stopped playing again and turned around. 'May I ask how we are going to keep the concert programme secret? Given half a chance, Arabella will be listening at the keyhole or in here hiding behind a curtain.'

'Ah. Then I shall have the room regularly scoured for spies and a footman on guard at the door.' Rockliffe smiled back. 'That should do the trick, don't you think?'

* * *

Choosing to do a little eavesdropping of his own, Julian lurked in a small room near the ballroom until the attendant footman informed him that all the members of the ensemble had arrived.

Nodding his thanks, Julian folded his arms and leaned against the wall by the partly-open door. From inside the ballroom came the sounds of instruments being tuned and snatches of desultory conversation. Then, after a few minutes, someone said clearly, 'I thought the soloist was supposed to be here today. Has anybody been told different?'

'No – which means he could walk in at any minute. And since sitting about waiting won't create a good impression, I suggest we get busy. Take it from the top, shall we?'

Julian smiled to himself. Musicians didn't vary much the world over, it seemed. He remained where he was, listening to the opening bars of the *Allegro* minus his own part and then sauntered quietly into the room. The first person to notice him was the cellist, swiftly followed by the second violin. Gradually, everyone stopped playing ... came to their feet ... and stared at him as if he had two heads.

'Good afternoon, gentlemen,' he said. 'You look surprised. Weren't you expecting me?'

'Yes.' The first violinist laid down his instrument. 'Yes, we were. But for some reason, we all thought you would be ... older. However, I am Henry Bassett, first desk, sir.'

'I'm pleased to meet you, Mr Bassett.' Having shaken the fellow's hand, Julian said, 'And your colleagues?'

Having been introduced to the other six musicians, Julian said bluntly, 'I daresay you're all wondering if I'm any good. In your place, *I* certainly would be. So let's get that out of the way, shall we?'

And taking his seat, he launched into a furiously dramatic piece he'd be playing towards the end of the recital. After some three minutes of it, he broke off to look at them. All seven were staring at him open-mouthed.

'Well?' he asked. 'Will I do?'

'Yes,' agreed Mr Bassett weakly. 'I reckon you will, sir.' And then, 'What *was* that?'

'Pancrace Royer. Something of an acquired taste, isn't it?' Julian stood to shed his coat and roll up his sleeves. 'Your turn now, gentlemen. Let's attack the first movement and see what comes of it.' He grinned suddenly. 'Don't worry. I know my absence has caused you some difficulties but I'm here now and we'll work through them as they arise. So, if everyone is ready ...?' He lifted one hand and with a seemingly careless gesture, brought them in.

For the first few minutes, Julian gave way to the sheer elation of playing with an ensemble. Gradually, however, he forced himself to play closer attention to his fellow musicians. And when they arrived at the end of the *Allegro*, he was able to say, 'Well, that could have been worse, couldn't it?' Before adding, 'But I hope we can all agree that it could also have been better. The horn is a fraction too loud throughout, Mr Grey ... and something peculiar happened between yourself and the oboe at the recapitulation of the main theme. Can we try oboe one and horn two at that point?' He waited while everyone shuffled their pages and scribbled notes. 'Good. Now again, from the top.'

CHAPTER TWENTY-THREE

After the Audley supper-party, Lord Sherbourne did not see Elizabeth again for four days – despite attending two balls and a soirée purely in the hope of finding her there. He had been teetering on the brink of a marriage proposal for two weeks but still hadn't taken the ultimate step and wasn't sure *why* he hadn't. It wasn't because he thought she might refuse him. He had sufficient experience to know when a woman wanted him; and beneath Elizabeth Marsden's cool and extremely proper demeanour he had occasionally glimpsed a look he knew very well indeed. Neither, oddly enough, was it because he had believed she came with a substantial dowry and now knew she didn't. In truth, he was surprised how little her changed identity mattered to him. And he was sure, wasn't he? Sure that Elizabeth was the only woman since Philippa Wilkes with whom he could contemplate sharing his life; sure also that, unlike Philippa, Elizabeth did not possess feet of clay. True, he did not entirely understand his feelings for her and was oddly afraid to probe too deeply. And equally true that, if he didn't do something soon, he might find himself chasing her to Yorkshire.

* * *

Julian's third day in London began with the information that Rockliffe's own tailor was to attend him immediately after breakfast.

He said, 'I don't need a tailor. I had a new suit made in Newark and --'

'In *Newark*,' agreed Rockliffe with a faint shudder. 'Yes. I can imagine.'

'But I don't have time to waste on --'

'Please do not argue, Julian. You will see Mr Lassiter this morning and that is the end of the matter. Good tailoring may not be the most important thing in life but there are times when one must treat it as such. This is one of them.'

So Julian gritted his teeth through two seemingly interminable hours with the damned tailor and then, learning that Arabella and her mother had taken the children shopping, fled to the ballroom and locked himself in. He went through his solo pieces three times and then worked solidly on his arrangement of Mozart's cadenza. He was still doing it when the ensemble arrived and had to hammer at the door to be let in.

The afternoon's rehearsal went relatively smoothly. Having solved the last of the problems with the first movement, they were able to progress into the *Andantino* and, at the end of the session, he went in search of the children feeling moderately cheerful. He eventually found them in the billiard room where Max Brandon and a red-haired fellow Julian thought looked vaguely familiar were attempting to teach Tom and Rob the rudiments of the game while Ellie circumnavigated the table, towing a large fluffy dog on wheels. As he entered the room and in her haste to reach him, Ellie's new pet collided with Tom's shins, causing him to take his next shot with more force than accuracy. The ball flew off the table and would have hit the red-haired gentleman squarely on the nose had he not caught it in time.

Tom apologised, adding, 'Nice catch though, sir.' Rob dissolved into gales of laughter. And Ellie cried, 'Look, Sir Julian! See what Aunt Louisa bought for me so I won't miss Figgy. Isn't she pretty? Her name is Amelia.'

'Whoever heard of a dog called *Amelia*?' snorted Tom. 'It's worse than Figgy.'

'I can call her what I like! I can, can't I, Sir Julian?'

'Absolutely.' One glance at the children's new clothes told Julian that Amelia wasn't the only thing Lady Brandon or Arabella had bought. 'But perhaps you could take her for a walk in the hall while the boys finish their game?'

'I *suppose* I could,' she sighed grudgingly. And heading for the door, said, '*Heel*, Amelia. Good dog.'

Throughout all this, Max had been resting on his cue, silently laughing. He said, 'Try some practise shots, boys – but remember the rule about keeping the cue tip off the baize or the duke will have all our heads on spikes.'

Meanwhile, the man Julian felt he ought to know strolled forward with his hand outstretched saying, 'A pleasure to see you again, Langham. Or should I call you Chalfont?'

'Langham will do.' Julian accepted the proffered hand, wished Max would help him out by supplying a name and then, realising he wasn't going to, said, 'I'm sorry. I know we've met but I can't recall where.'

'Cambridge,' came the cheerful reply. And taking pity on him, 'Sebastian Audley?'

Light dawned. 'Oh. Yes – of course. You used to play by ear.'

'I still do,' grinned Sebastian. '*You*, on the other hand, are the fellow who got drunk with Mozart – which is a thing I wouldn't mind hearing about.'

Julian flushed. 'There's not much to tell. I remember the first part of the evening and the crashing headache when I woke up on the floor next morning but not very much in between.' He caught the look on Tom's face and added, 'You didn't hear that.'

'Didn't hear what?' asked the boy – before spoiling it with, 'Does Miss Belle know?'

'Who do you think told Mr Audley?' muttered Julian. 'Where is she, by the way?'

'Drinking tea with Lizzie, my mother and Audley's wife,' replied Max. 'They're all going to some ball or other this evening so Audley suggests dining at his favourite club. Join us.'

'No. I mean – thank you for the invitation but I lost half the morning with the blasted tailor and I need to work.'

'Rubbish. You can't spend every waking hour locked in the ballroom, only emerging to eat. You need to relax and have a little fun.'

'But I don't play cards or --'

'Or drink very much, by the sound of it,' laughed Sebastian. And to Max, 'Only think ... if we get him drunk enough, he'll tell us all his secrets.'

'I don't have any -- '

'Excellent,' said Max, clapping him on the shoulder. 'You can just tell us about your concert programme instead. And now take

Ellie and Amelia up to the ladies while we and your boys finish the game.'

* * *

Upon learning, with some amusement, that the gentlemen were intent on dragging Julian to Sinclairs, Arabella elected to miss the Bedford House assembly in favour of a quiet evening with the children. Elizabeth wasn't sorry to be spared her cousin's company. In the last couple of days, Arabella had had far too much to say about what appeared to be Lord Sherbourne's withdrawal and, aside from being heartily sick of the subject, Elizabeth didn't trust Belle not to say something embarrassing directly to Ralph's face if she got a chance.

At Bedford House and although Elizabeth had ordered herself to stop hoping, the habit of searching the room for one particular face seemed impossible to break. Then, when she did not find it, she danced the opening set with Lord March, promised the supper-dance to Richard Penhaligon and let her dance card gradually fill up with the names of any gentleman who asked her.

Ralph walked in mid-way through the evening and saw Elizabeth immediately. The corn-gold hair gleamed in the candlelight, her skin glowed with pearl-like lustre against the rich blue of her gown, she was smiling brightly at Lord Rayne ... and she looked tired. Something shifted inside Ralph's chest. He told himself it was relief. Then he conversed desultorily with one or two acquaintances whilst waiting for the dance to end.

The first Elizabeth knew of his presence was when he emerged at her side, frightened poor Lord Pelham away with a single look and calmly placed her hand on his sleeve. Her nerves vibrating like violin strings, she said unevenly, 'That was naughty of you. This was his lordship's dance.'

'*Was* being the operative word. Do you have any objection?'

'Would it make any difference if I did?'

'Usually, yes. But not tonight.'

Elizabeth became aware that he was leading her away from the floor. Surprised, she said, 'Are we not to dance?'

'Later, perhaps.' He sent an obliquely amused smile in her direction. 'Your card may be full ... but you have seen how slight an impediment that can be. First, however, I would like to hold an entire conversation in consecutive sentences ... and for that, a degree or two of privacy would be helpful.'

'Privacy?' She managed to ignore the sudden thud of her heart and gestured to the crowd around them. 'Here?'

'There is generally a way. And I am an expert at finding it.'

If there was an answer to that, Elizabeth decided it was better left unspoken. She merely let him lead her from the ballroom, along a slightly less congested corridor and eventually into a small parlour, lit only by the light from the flambeaux outside the windows.

'This will do,' remarked Ralph, gently closing the door behind them and turning to face her. 'We should not linger here longer than necessary, so I will come directly to the point. Since you reclaimed your own name, your reason for being unable to contemplate matrimony no longer exists. If you are inclined to contemplate it now, I ask your leave to approach Rockliffe with a formal offer.'

She stared at him, half-inclined to wonder if she had misheard. He looked as coolly composed as ever and if one listened to the tone of his voice rather than the words, he might have been asking whether or not she thought it would rain tomorrow. She said faintly, 'Are you ... are you asking me to marry you?'

'Yes. Was I not clear?'

'N-Not ... entirely.' She found herself struggling with a slightly hysterical bubble of laughter. 'You might have wanted to m-marry Rockliffe.'

Ralph frowned. 'That's nonsense.'

'I know.'

There was a long enigmatic silence. Then, with a hint of strained patience, he said, 'Perhaps I should begin again. Would it clarify things if I went down on one knee?'

She shook her head. The bubble was expanding into something different; something that was slowly filling her with wonder and joy; something that, even now, she could scarcely believe. She said truthfully, 'I didn't expect you to speak of marriage at all. I thought ... I thought that, having learned I am not who you thought I was, you wouldn't --'

'You are *exactly* who I thought you were.' And before she could ask what he meant, 'If you disliked me ... would you marry me purely to become a countess?'

'No. I wouldn't.'

'Precisely.'

'But fortunately I *don't* dislike you. You must know that.'

'I have thought it – but I thank you for saying so.' He hesitated, opened his mouth to speak – and was suddenly conscious of a feeling of paralysis. The internal barrier he'd set around himself seven years ago might as well have been a granite wall ... and the words he needed were trapped on the other side of it. But she was waiting and he had to say something so he unlocked his tongue and, with a lack of expression that made him despair, said, 'I would be deeply honoured if you would consent to be my wife, Elizabeth. I hold you in great esteem and – and affection. I believe we would deal comfortably together and, along with my respect, you have my word that I would do my best to make you happy.' An unkind little voice at the back of his mind said, *Esteem? Affection? What woman could resist?* So, in desperation, he added, 'I can also promise physical pleasure ... if that helps. But if none of this is enough, please tell me now.'

His tone throughout had been as calmly dispassionate as ever but, for the first time, Elizabeth saw a flicker of anxiety in his eyes and guessed that, on some level, he had disappointed himself. She drew a long steadying breath and, repressing the temptation to say that she would love him if he would let her, contented herself with reaching out to touch his hand.

'It is enough. It is more than enough.'

He shook his head ruefully. 'I had hoped to do better. But perhaps I will, in time.'

She smiled at him and shook her head.

'You should learn to like yourself more, Ralph.'

His fingers curled around hers. 'You think so?'

'Yes. There's quite a lot to like, you know.'

The shock of her words slammed through him like a blow. With something less than his usual suavity, he said, 'Does that mean I may speak to Rockliffe?'

'Yes. It also means that I will marry you no matter what he or anyone else says.'

He was tempted to ask why but decided not to risk her saying something he wouldn't know how to answer. 'You're sure?'

'Perfectly sure.' Elizabeth summoned her nerve, hoped she wouldn't blush and added, 'There is just one condition though. I'd like ... I'd very much like you to kiss me.'

Another shock which this time brought laughter in its wake. He said, 'It would be my very great pleasure – though it shames me that you had to ask.'

And gathering her into his arms, he proceeded to demonstrate that what the ladies whispered about him behind their fans was not an exaggeration.

* * *

Having agreed to say nothing to anyone until Ralph had spoken to the duke the following afternoon, Elizabeth was glad that Arabella and Aunt Louisa had final fittings at Phanie's for their 'concert gowns' and had taken Ellie with them. This left her free to pace up and down in her bedchamber or hover at the window until the earl's carriage pulled up outside.

Shown without delay into Rockliffe's study, Ralph came directly to the point.

'I imagine you can guess why I am here.'

'I believe so. You wish to pay your addresses to Elizabeth – and she has presumably already signified her willingness to receive them.'

'She has done me that honour, yes. But since you are currently acting in *loco parentis*, I considered it proper to seek your consent.'

'You do not need to stress that this is a mere courtesy call,' remarked Rockliffe dryly. 'I am perfectly well aware that Elizabeth is of age and presumably knows her own mind. As for my role as her temporary guardian ... both her maternal aunt and the eldest of her male cousins are currently under my roof. You might more properly apply to them.'

'I shall speak with them, of course, and also write to her father. But since any objections are more likely to come from you than from Elizabeth's relatives, I am here so that we may clear the air. In short, ask what you wish and let us be done with it.'

'Very well.' The night-dark eyes regarded him meditatively. 'I take it you *do* know that Elizabeth is not well-dowered?'

'Yes. It is of no consequence.'

'Is it not?' Rockliffe's brows rose. 'Forgive me for being surprised.'

'Unnecessary. I am surprised myself.' Ralph paused and then, in somewhat clipped accents, added, 'I shall treat her with both courtesy and respect.'

'And conduct your other liaisons with the utmost discretion?'

It was impossible to tell whether the hint of colour staining the earl's cheekbones was caused by embarrassment or anger. He said coldly, 'Since I have never previously found it necessary to sleep with more than one woman at a time, I don't envisage that changing after marriage. Doubtless something else you find surprising.'

'No. Clearly I made a mistaken assumption.'

Silence fell and lingered. Finally, when Rockliffe showed no sign of asking further questions, Ralph said, 'Is that it? You are not going to ask how Edgar Wilkes died?'

'If I did, would you tell me?'

'If I did, would you believe me?'

'Since there would seem to be no point in lying, yes.' His Grace frowned a little. 'Have you told Elizabeth?'

'I have told her what happened but not *why* it did. I have never told anyone that and aside from myself, the only person who knows the truth is Philippa Sutherland.' Ralph shut his eyes for a moment and then, opening them again, said, 'I will break my silence if I am assured that nothing I say will ever leave this room.'

'Consider yourself duly assured.' The frown deepened. 'How bad is it?'

'It is an abomination.'

'Ah. Then you had better start at the beginning.'

'I will start with what you already know. Edgar Wilkes forced a duel on me with a false accusation of sleeping with his wife. We will come to his real reason later. Suffice it to say that I accepted his challenge and we met. You will doubtless recall, as he did, that I had fought three previous duels. All of them resulted in my opponent taking a bullet in the left arm. In the second that I fired, Edgar ... moved. My shot took him in the heart – or as close to it as made no difference. He was dead within minutes.'

'Suicide by duel? Yes. That is the story Richard Lazenby told after the event.'

'The story which no one believed because I was not there ... because Augustus Wilkes was singing a different tune ... and because there seemed no explanation for it.' Ralph paused, staring bitterly down at his hands. 'It is hard to credit how naïve and incredibly stupid I was. It took me months to work out why Edgar did it – and yet the answer had been staring me in the face all the time if only I had not been too besotted with Philippa to see it.' Still avoiding Rockliffe's gaze, he drew a long breath and said, 'It began when Edgar's wife, Sarah, turned up on my doorstep – not for amorous purposes, but because she had discovered something about Edgar that both terrified and sickened her. With no male relatives to turn to and knowing I wanted to marry Philippa, she thought I could make it stop.' He gave a tiny hard laugh. 'Of course, I didn't believe what she told me. How could I? But with perseverance, she eventually convinced me. Then she laid all the blame on Philippa which, once again, I decided could not possibly be true. The fault had to lie with Edgar. It *had* to. Philippa was not at fault. She *couldn't* be. She was as much a victim in all this as Sarah was ... or as I would be.'

'I begin to understand why you have refused to speak of this,' said Rockliffe distastefully. 'So let us have it out in the open. You are talking about incest.'

'Yes.'

'And I am guessing that you confronted Edgar Wilkes about it.'

'Yes. I told him it had to stop immediately before anyone else found out. He denied it, we argued ... I assured him that I had no intention of exposing him and left, hoping sense would prevail. Instead, on the following evening he threw a glass of wine in my face.' As it had throughout, Ralph's tone remained almost but not quite impersonal. 'When we met, I expected him to try to kill me. I did *not* expect him to make me his scapegoat. But then, as I said earlier, it took a long time for me to realise that I had been refusing to see the whole picture ... that it wasn't Philippa who was the victim of Edgar's obsession but he who was the victim of hers. I had painted her in the colours that would enable me to continue loving her – but they were false. And beneath them, she was someone I could not recognise.'

Rockliffe sensed the pain behind the words. He said quietly, 'And Edgar?'

'As far as one can hope to understand what drove him, I eventually came to the conclusion that suicide put him out of his misery. It also made me the villain of the piece – and left Philippa safe from exposure.' His mouth twisted in something not quite a smile. 'They say the road to hell is paved with good intentions. Everything I did was well-meant ... but all of it was wrong. If I had walked away from the entire mess --'

'That is hindsight talking. And it is rarely helpful.'

'Oh – quite.' Ralph came abruptly to his feet. 'One last thing. Even after all this time, Philippa still fears that I may reveal what I know. Having deduced something of this – though obviously not the precise nature of it – Elizabeth said as much to her face. I doubt this will become a problem ... but, should it do so, I shall deal with it. And now, if you have nothing further to ask, perhaps I might speak to Elizabeth?'

Rockliffe also rose and pulled the bell to summon a servant.

'May I offer a glass of brandy first? You look as if you need it.'

'I do ... but I will not go to her smelling of spirits. She might take it for Dutch courage.'

'Later, then.' And when the butler appeared, 'Have someone ask Mistress Marsden to join Lord Sherbourne here, Symonds.

And perhaps you might ascertain whether or not Lord Brandon is in the house.'

'I believe he is in the mews with Lord Chalfont's boys, your Grace. They expressed an interest in seeing the horses.'

'In that case, ask him to join me at his convenience.' As the door closed behind Symonds, Rockliffe gave Ralph a faintly resigned smile and said, 'We have been attempting to keep the presence of the children relatively quiet. But since you are about to join the family, you may as well know that they are not Chalfont's progeny. He has, rather remarkably, taken responsibility for no less than three examples of the fourth earl's sexual carelessness. And now I shall leave you. No one will disturb you, so you may bring Elizabeth to the drawing-room when you are ready.'

Ralph nodded his thanks and, when the duke had gone, wheeled away to the window where, bracing himself against the embrasure, he attempted to clear his mind of the last hour. He was still there when Elizabeth entered the room ... and if he had thought he had his expression under control, he discovered his mistake when she walked towards him saying, 'What is wrong? What has Rockliffe said to you?'

'Nothing at all unpleasant,' he began – then stopped in surprise when she reached out and took his hands in hers. 'You think I need comfort?'

'Don't you?' She smiled at him. 'Doesn't everyone from time to time? It isn't a crime, you know – or even a weakness.'

'I shall bear that in mind.' He lifted one brow. 'Do you intend to cosset me?'

'I intend to make you happy, if I can.'

'Ah. Then in that case – Rockliffe having no objections – perhaps it is time I proposed to you in time-honoured fashion.'

Taken by surprise, Elizabeth said hastily, 'You don't have to.'

'I think I do. You made it easy for me last night – but I would advise you not to make a habit of that. I am likely to take advantage.' And before she could reply, he dropped smoothly to one knee, her fingers still locked in his. 'Elizabeth ... will you give me the very great pleasure of accepting my hand in marriage?'

'I – yes.' She swallowed hard. 'Yes, my lord. I will.'

'My lord? I was Ralph last evening, was I not?'

'You were. You still are.'

'Well, then?'

She shook her head at him, a smile quivering on her lips.

'Yes, Ralph. I'll marry you.'

'Excellent.' He rose to drop a light kiss on each of her wrists followed by a more lingering one on her lips. 'And now, before we go and share the glad tidings with Lord Brandon, let us discuss when and where you wish to be married.'

* * *

In fact, Max was not the only one who had joined his Grace in the drawing-room. He was, however, the only person aside from Adeline to whom Rockliffe revealed that the Earl of Sherbourne was currently offering Elizabeth marriage.

Adeline had not been surprised. Max was. He said, 'Lizzie is to be a countess? Well ... that's good. At least, I suppose it is. What is Sherbourne like?'

'I am inclined to believe him a better man than I had previously supposed,' replied Rockliffe. 'But they will join us shortly and you may judge for yourself.' And, as the door opened on Louisa, Arabella and Ellie, with Tom and Rob bringing up the rear, 'As, it appears, will everyone except Julian. But I am sure Lord Sherbourne's habitual composure will be equal to the occasion.'

By the time Julian sauntered in radiating his usual air of post-rehearsal distraction, everyone was on their second cup of tea and Adeline, seeing the depredations made by Tom and Rob, had rung for more cakes. Before Arabella could take more than a step in Julian's direction, Ellie had pulled him down beside her and was chattering about the new dress she was to wear at his concert.

'It's pink and it has *frills*,' she told him in awed accents. 'And ribbons and – and special *petticoats*!'

'Petticoats? Really? That sounds very grand,' he replied seriously. Then, aware that Arabella was within earshot, 'And does Miss Belle have them, too?'

Arabella made a small choking sound, her eyes full of laughter.

'Yes – only hers are blue with lace and little flowers sewn on,' replied Ellie. 'You just wait, Sir Julian. She looks more beautiful than *anybody*.'

'Yes. She always does.'

'Flatterer,' grinned Arabella, handing him a cup of tea and telling Ellie to fetch him something to eat. 'How was rehearsal today?'

'The *Allegro* and *Andantino* are both going well and we'll attack the *Rondo* tomorrow.' He paused and, not looking at her, added, 'It wasn't flattery. I meant it.'

'Oh. Thank you.' Her colour rose a little. 'And your evening at Sinclairs?'

'Better than I expected. Everyone was very kind.' This time he did look at her. 'I don't understand why you're surprised. It isn't just gowns. You *are* beautiful.' Then had to turn away to accept the heaped plate that Ellie had brought him.

Across the room and still standing beside Rockliffe, Max said meditatively, 'What *is* it about Julian?'

'What is what?'

'Well, he ought to be thoroughly exasperating, yet somehow he isn't. Within an hour of meeting him, I found myself actually *wanting* to dig him out of the hole he's in at Chalfont. Then last night, he wouldn't play cards and scarcely drank ... with the peculiar result that nobody else did much drinking or gambling, either.' He began ticking off things on his fingers. 'The children idolise him; his servants and the villagers think the sun shines out of him; Belle's totally besotted and Mother wants to adopt him. How does he *do* it?'

'I have no idea – and suspect that Julian himself is equally ignorant. Perhaps that is the secret.' The duke toyed absently with an emerald-studded snuffbox. 'Have he and Arabella arrived at an understanding yet?'

'Not that I know of,' replied Max grimly. 'But if he walks away, it will break her heart.'

He stopped speaking – as did everyone else – when the door opened on Ralph and Elizabeth. Strolling across to them, Rockliffe murmured, 'Yes, I know. Rather more people than you were expecting. But there is something to be said for getting everything over at once.' And, in his normal tone, 'I have a happy announcement, ladies and gentlemen. Lord Sherbourne and Elizabeth are to be married.'

Arabella was the first to react. Flying over to her cousin, she threw her arms about her and said, 'Oh Lizzie – this is the *best* news! I'm so happy for you – and for you, too, my lord. No gentleman could have made a better choice.'

'I entirely agree,' replied Ralph suavely, 'and consider myself undeservedly fortunate.'

'Very nicely put,' said Louisa with a warm smile. 'I am Lizzie's aunt and I wish you both every happiness. Lizzie, dearest – I couldn't be more pleased for you and am sure your parents will be equally delighted.'

'I certainly hope so, Aunt Louisa.'

'Aunt Maria will be ecstatic,' said Max, reaching out to shake Ralph's hand. 'A pleasure to meet you, my lord – and many congratulations. When is the wedding to be?'

'Soon, we hope – though the subject is still under discussion. I shall be showing Elizabeth our London home tomorrow and would hope to reach a decision then.'

* * *

Escorting Elizabeth into his house on Curzon Street, Ralph said, 'As you will see, Kilburn House is fairly modest. Also, it hasn't been touched since my mother's time – so if you wish to change anything, you must tell me.'

'You call this modest?' asked Elizabeth, absorbing the wide, elegant hall while following him up the stairs. Then, entering a drawing-room decorated in shades of gold and green, 'And why would I wish to change anything? This is lovely!'

Ralph smiled a little. 'You may feel differently when you're living here some months of the year and wish to entertain.'

She smiled back. 'Perhaps. We'll see.'

He drew her hand through his arm and laid his free one over it.

'Come and inspect the rest, then. After which, we should attempt to reach a conclusion about our wedding.'

She nodded, enjoying the sensation of his body, warm against her side.

The breakfast and dining rooms were light and of good proportions. The shabbily comfortable library was very clearly Ralph's own domain, its shelves crammed with well-used books. She said, 'I imagine you spend a great deal of time in here.'

'I do. While my brothers shared the house, this was the only room where I could usually be sure of avoiding them.' His tone grew dry as dust. 'When you meet them — as, unfortunately, you are eventually bound to do — you will understand.'

'Aside from saying there is no love lost between you, you've scarcely mentioned them.'

'Deliberately. Cedric and Bertram get on well enough with each other - both of them being equally asinine.' He began leading her up to the next floor. 'If you want an example, Cedric recently seduced the daughter of a respectable neighbour by promising her marriage. It was left for the girl's father and me to ensure he kept his word.'

'Oh,' said Elizabeth.

'Oh,' agreed Ralph. 'I will not sully your ears with what Bertram gets up to.' He paused, ushering her into a pink and cream bedchamber. 'This will be yours.'

'Mine?' she asked, colouring a little.

'Yes. There is a dressing-closet and a small parlour. My own rooms are through there.'

Elizabeth advanced a few steps into a masculine room hung in dark blue silk and dominated by a large bed. Suddenly feeling as if she was intruding, she turned hurriedly ... and promptly bumped into Ralph's chest.

'I'm sorry,' she began. Then stopped as his arms came around her.

'Don't be,' he said. And kissed her.

He had intended it to be the same as when he had kissed her at Bedford House. Within seconds, he knew it wasn't going to be. It was as if a fast-burning fuse had been lit between them. She sighed into his mouth, her hands rising to cup his face; he pulled her flush against the length of him and was suffused with an instant and wholly unexpected surge of acute desire. His brain shut down and just for a few, critical moments control completely deserted him. Later he would wonder about that. Now he was aware of nothing but the woman in his arms and what every cell in his body was demanding. He dug his fingers into the gold silk of her hair, sending hairpins flying; he ravished her mouth, then moved on to the smooth column of her throat and the hollow below her ear; he let his hands go where they would and felt her tremble with response whilst pressing herself even closer.

Inside his head, a primitive voice shouted *Yes!* ... while an even more primitive growl vibrated through his chest. Inexplicably, it was the latter which awoke some small degree of reason. He froze and thought hazily, *What am I doing?* Then, with greater clarity, *This isn't me. I don't ... holy hell, I never lose control. Not ever. What is wrong with me?*

Stepping back from her, his hands as unsteady as his breathing, he said, 'I beg your pardon. That was ... inexcusable.'

'Was it?' Flushed and confused, yet seemingly less shocked than he was, Elizabeth pushed her hair from her face. 'Is that not for me to decide?'

'No. I am the arbiter of my own behaviour ... and I do *not* behave like *that*.'

'I know.' Stooping, she began gathering up hairpins. 'You always behave perfectly.'

He opened his mouth to thank her and then, recognising that something in her tone wasn't complimentary, said cautiously, 'And that is a bad thing?'

'By no means. But impeccable manners are your shield and armour, aren't they?'

'*What*?'

'And very effective they are, too.' She rose to face him, hoping she looked calmer than she felt. 'But you don't need them with me. I could quite easily love the man they are hiding if only you would let me know him.'

The floor shifted beneath his feet and his mind went blank. He said, 'Elizabeth … I can't … I have lost the ability to – to --'

'It isn't lost, Ralph. It is merely … misplaced. And I understand why. I also think that, in time, we might find it again.'

His brain still seemed to be moving very slowly. 'You don't understand.'

'Actually, I do.' Turning back into the pink room, she located a mirror and began tidying her hair. 'You believe yourself incapable of love. *I* think you capable of a great deal of it … but am aware that you need to find out for yourself. Fortunately, I don't mind waiting.'

Ralph struggled to find his usual manner.

'You sound very sure. That … concerns me more than a little.'

'It need not. You could have chosen any number of ladies but you didn't. You chose me. I am assuming that counts for something. Does it?'

'Yes.' He swallowed and, exerting the full force of his will against the self-made impediment inside him, managed to add 'Yes. It … counts for a very great deal.'

'Good. Then nothing else matters.' She smiled at him over her shoulder. 'As to what took place between us a few moments ago … I didn't find it inexcusable in the least. I believe I was flattered.'

'And that is even more worrying.' Since the right words were clearly beyond him, he closed the space between them to turn her into his arms and kiss her with slow thoroughness. Then he simply stood holding her, his cheek against her hair for a long, somehow significant moment before murmuring, 'Upon which note – and before I forget myself again – perhaps we should go downstairs and discuss our wedding?'

Elizabeth nodded and let him lead her from the bedchamber. Neither of them spoke until they were seated in the drawing-room and then it was she who said, 'Why don't we begin with what *you* want?'

'It is less a matter of what I want than of the practicalities. I know you would like to be married by your father in his own church ... but it presents various problems. The distance involved and the time it would take to cover it; a three week stay in your father's parish while the banns are called; and a return journey in December through winter weather. None of these things are insurmountable, of course ... but they cannot be discounted.'

'No,' she agreed reasonably. 'So what do you suggest instead?'

'I suggest having the banns called in St George's, Hanover Square and setting the wedding for the first available date. Meanwhile, I will arrange for your parents and sisters to come to London for the ceremony. It may not be possible for your father to actually marry us but it should be possible for him to perform a blessing.' Ralph paused, uncharacteristically uncertain. 'I know this is not what you would prefer and I'm sorry for it. But might you find it an acceptable compromise?'

'Yes.' She reached out and took his hand. 'Yes. More than acceptable, actually.'

'And your father?'

Elizabeth laughed suddenly. 'My father isn't going to find anything I have done in the last two months *remotely* acceptable. Fortunately, Mama's reaction and that of the rest of my family will make up for it. As for the wedding, we'll tell everyone that St George's was *my* choice and you allowed yourself to be persuaded.'

His fingers tightened on hers. 'You would do that?'

'Why not? It's no sacrifice. I want to marry you, Ralph. The when matters to me; the where is less important. And it's *our* wedding – no one else's.'

Seconds ticked by in silence until, finally, he kissed the hand he held and said, 'I cannot promise that you will never regret it, Elizabeth. I *do* promise to try never to give you cause.'

CHAPTER TWENTY-FOUR

On the day before the concert, Arabella and her mother paid calls on the Earl and Countess of Sarre and Mr and Mistress Audley. In Cork Street, Lady Brandon made the acquaintance of the Misses Caldercott and, in Bruton Place, that of Paul and Janet Featherstone. No one, it was agreed, would breathe a word of their arrival in London to Julian.

'It must be a surprise,' Arabella had told them. 'I know that he would want all of you to be present at his first concert – but he won't expect it. And I want the occasion to be as special for him as we can possibly make it. Having all of you visit him just before he walks out to perform, will mean a great deal.'

'You don't think he'll find playing for a hundred fashionable folk in a duke's house quite exciting enough?' Paul had asked.

'Exciting, yes – and of course success tomorrow is vital. But an audience of strangers isn't the same as knowing that his friends cared enough to travel here to wish him well.'

'Such a dear, sweet boy,' said Miss Caldercott, brushing away a tear.

And, 'It was a very kind thought, Arabella – both for Julian and for us – so we thank you for arranging it,' said Miss Abigail. 'Now ... go back and hold our boy's hand until it's time for him to show the world what he can do.'

Julian didn't need his hand held. He tolerated a final fitting with Rockliffe's tailor and spent what was left of the morning checking the tuning on the harpsichord and running through certain passages. Then, the afternoon being his final rehearsal with the concerto ensemble, he concluded the session by performing the solo part of the recital to an enthusiastic reception.

'Excellent,' said Mr Bassett simply. 'Very well-balanced, if I may say so.'

'And my arrangement of the Johann Christian *Andante*?'

'Ah. *There* I must admit to feeling somewhat aggrieved, sir. My colleagues and I would have greatly enjoyed playing that lovely thing with you in its original form.'

'I daresay. But is the arrangement all *right*?' demanded Julian. 'Does it *work*?'

'It is most interesting, sir. It--'

'Cut line, Henry,' said the cellist. 'The arrangement is bloody genius, Mr Langham. So I hope you've got an encore or two up your sleeve – because you're going to need them.'

* * *

Since it had never happened before, Arabella was astonished to find Julian in the drawing-room before dinner. She said, 'Is something wrong?'

'Wrong? No. Why would you think that?'

Shaking her head, she laid a hand on his brow.

'You don't *feel* feverish but --'

'That's because I'm not.' He stepped back and finally saw the laughter dancing in her eyes. 'Oh. Right. Very funny.'

'Well, we usually have to send a footman to fetch you. And even then --'

'Oh! Forgive me, Belle – I didn't realise you had company,' said Max from the doorway. And with only slightly exaggerated incredulity, '*Julian?* Is that you? Freshly-shaved, hair that's seen a brush sometime in the last day or so and a coat – a very nice coat, by the way – without a single crease? No wonder I didn't recognise you!'

Arabella tried to turn a giggle into a cough.

'If you *really* want to know, I took a bath as well,' retorted Julian, 'Now – can the two of you please *leave* it?'

'Leave what?' asked Louisa, entering in time to hear this. Then, 'My goodness, Julian – how very elegant you look this evening.'

Max gave a choke of laughter and Arabella hid behind her fan.

'Thank you, my lady,' said Julian, grittily. 'Since everyone takes such an interest in my appearance, I thought I'd better rehearse that as well.'

Her ladyship slid a hand through his arm. 'Have they been teasing you?'

'You might put it that way, yes.'

'Learn to ignore it, my dear. It's the only way. Max … stop tormenting Julian and bring me a glass of sherry, if you please. It is only we four tonight. Rockliffe and Adeline are taking Elizabeth to a ball where she and Lord Sherbourne can accept the usual felicitations.' She huffed a small breath. 'Unless I'm imagining it, something fundamental has changed between those two since he took her to view his house. But I must say that I am *not* looking forward to Josiah's views on their wedding plans.'

'He'll get over it – and sooner rather than later, if he has any sense.' Handing his mother her sherry, Max said, 'Not working tonight, Julian? With the concert imminent, I'd have expected you to be burning the midnight oil.'

'There's no need. Everything that can be done already has been.'

'You sound very relaxed.'

'Yes. Why wouldn't I be?'

'Oh – I don't know. The weight of expectation resting on you, perhaps?'

'Stop it, Max,' said Arabella. 'If Julian isn't nervous, don't try to make him so.'

'It's all right,' shrugged Julian. 'He's not saying anything I don't know. And nothing he can say is going to turn me into a bundle of nerves – if that is what's worrying you. The ensemble is ready, *I* am ready and the harpsichord is perfectly in tune. There's nothing left to do now except give the actual concert.'

* * *

The day of the concert dawned pale with wintry sunshine. The fact that Julian did not appear at breakfast did not particularly surprise anyone. But just as Adeline was rising from the table, Symonds entered the room and said, 'Pardon me, your Grace … but Mrs Fawcett wonders if we can begin setting up the ballroom for later – his lordship not seeming to require it this morning?'

'By all means,' began Adeline, a second before Rockliffe said, 'Where *is* his lordship?'

'I am not sure, your Grace. But if you will give me a moment, I will ascertain.'

Rockliffe nodded and, when the butler had gone, Arabella said, 'He's probably with the children. I'll go up and find out.'

Five minutes later, Symonds re-appeared.

'I can only assume that Lord Chalfont has left the house, your Grace.'

'Left the house?' echoed Max. 'After being a recluse for the last week? Why?'

Arabella skidded back into the room, almost colliding with Symonds.

'He's taken the children and gone out. Lily says he came for them an hour ago but she doesn't know where they went.' She shrugged. 'It's not so surprising. He said last night that there was nothing left to do. Why *wouldn't* he want some time away from it all?'

'But why take the children?' asked Elizabeth dubiously.

'That was sensible of him,' said Louisa firmly. 'It will stop them becoming over-excited about this evening. And I daresay they will be back by noon.'

* * *

They weren't.

After exploring the gardens, marvelling at the cascade and finding some ducks to feed, noon found them sitting in the rotunda at Ranelagh, eating bread-and-butter and listening to the regular breakfast concert. When it ended and without any warning at all, Julian said, 'How would you feel about being adopted?'

'What's that?' asked Rob and Ellie, more or less in unison. And, 'By you?' blurted Tom, too stunned to think about it.

'Yes.'

Bread-and-butter dropped from suddenly nerveless fingers. 'You – you'd really *do* that?'

'Yes. But only if it's what all three of you want.' Leaving Tom to get over his shock, Julian turned to the younger children and said, 'If I adopted you, you would take my name – just as if I were really your father. You'd be Tom and Rob and Ellie Langham. But it would mean that you'd be stuck with me and there'd be no getting away.'

'Ever?' asked Rob.

'Ever.'

'Yes!' Nearly upsetting the tea-cups, Ellie threw herself on him. 'Oh yes – *please*!'

Julian gathered her on to his knee but held out his hands to her brothers and, when they had taken them, said, 'What do you think? Shall we do it?'

Seeming beyond words and his face one big, happy smile, Rob nodded.

Tom said gruffly, 'You've always been more than good to us. But this ... this isn't a small thing and I can't ...' He stopped. 'Thank you isn't nearly enough.'

'It'll do. And I'll take that as a yes.' Julian grinned, restored Ellie to her chair and leaned back in his own. 'All I have to do now is find out how to go about it.'

'Don't you know?' asked Rob.

'I haven't a clue. Fortunately, however, I think I know a gentleman who will.'

* * *

When, at nearly two o'clock with the whole house in a frenzy of preparation and the truants still absent, Rockliffe was conscious of a mild quiver of disquiet. The concert was due to begin in four hours and though he didn't doubt that Julian would return ... he *did* wonder how late he might leave it. But some twenty minutes later, in the wake of Rob and Ellie who raced across the hall shouting for Miss Belle, Julian sauntered in with Tom at his side.

Rockliffe said softly, 'Julian ... I would admire your nerves better if you had shown some consideration for my own. Where have you been?'

'Ranelagh.'

'Ranelagh.' A faintly pained expression touched the duke's gaze. 'Really.'

'Yes. You weren't worried, were you? You must have known I'd be back.'

Before Rockliffe could reply, Ellie and Rob – having failed to find Arabella in the drawing-room – hurtled back through the procession of footmen engaged in carrying chairs to the ballroom in time to find their quarry descending the stairs.

'What is all this noise about?' asked Arabella. 'His Grace must be deafened.'

They tripped over themselves in their haste to tell her their news.

'We went to a garden with a waterfall --'

'There was a concert--'

'And ducks--'

'And bread-and-butter--'

'And the best bit,' shouted Ellie, determined to be heard above Rob, 'is--'

'Shut up, the pair of you!' bellowed Tom. 'Sir Julian should tell her.'

Julian dropped a hand on the boy's shoulder. 'It's all right Tom. Let them.'

'We're going to be *adopted*!' announced Rob, triumphantly beating Ellie to it.

'And I'm going to be Ellie Langham,' added his sister, unwilling to be defeated.

Suddenly, for the first time since they had entered the house, there was silence. Arabella stared into hesitantly smiling green eyes, her hands creeping to her mouth. Finally, she whispered, 'You're going to adopt them? Truly?' And when he nodded, 'Oh … Julian. That is the *best* thing … the very best thing you could do for them. It's quite - quite splendid. *You* are splendid.' And, as she had wanted to do all week, she flew across the hall to throw her arms about him. 'I am so – so very *proud* of you!'

He held her close and muttered, 'Well, since I'm keeping them, it's the only thing to do.'

'You will *not* make it sound like nothing,' said Arabella fiercely while tears soaked into his cravat. 'It's not nothing. Not to them – and not to me either. You're giving them your *name*! And look how h-happy you've made them. It's m-magnificent.'

'I'm going to tell Aunt Louisa,' said Ellie single-mindedly. '*Me*, Rob – not *you*!'

Without haste, as Arabella reluctantly stepped back and wiped her face with her hands, Rockliffe strolled across, saying, 'You will need a lawyer, Julian.'

'I know. I was hoping you might be able to help with that.'

'And I will. But only on condition you go to your rooms, take a bath and rest.'

'I don't need to --'

'It is an order – not a topic for discussion,' sighed the duke. 'My valet will attend you at half-past four. And yes, I realise you don't need him either but you will humour me on this occasion. Now, please go.'

* * *

Those favoured with an invitation to the most talked-of event of the season began arriving shortly after five o'clock, some going directly to the ballroom and others lingering with the duke and duchess in the drawing-room.

Julian, splendidly attired in darkest green silk over a gold embroidered vest, was led through the servants' passageways to a small room from which he could access the platform and left there with an order from Rockliffe's valet to neither remove his coat nor sit down and risk creasing it. Smiling and looking the picture of docility, Julian took this as permission to do what he intended to do anyway. He was leaning against the window embrasure wishing he'd brought a book when the door opened and Arabella said, 'I thought you might like company – so I've brought you some visitors.'

'Does Rockliffe know?' began Julian. And stopped when, beyond Arabella, he saw who his visitors were. For an instant, he looked stunned. Then a dazzling smile dawned and he walked into Miss Bea's warm embrace, followed by a brisk one from Miss Abigail and a laughing one from Janet.

'My goodness, Julian!' she said. 'You actually look like an *earl.*'

'You didn't think we'd miss this, did you?' grinned Paul, shaking his hand. 'We know you don't need moral support or good luck wishes – but we wanted to bring them anyway.'

'I – I don't know what to say,' stammered Julian. 'I never expected or thought it might be possible ... but *God!* It's so good to see you all. Thank you. Thank you for coming.'

'Thank Arabella,' said Miss Abigail. 'She arranged everything.'

'You did?' He turned to Arabella. 'Do the children know?'

'I told them half an hour ago. Before that, I couldn't trust them to keep the secret. But we mustn't stay – it's nearly time and we ought to take our seats. I just wanted you to know your friends were here.'

With a final round of well-wishing, the Beckingham party withdrew leaving Arabella and Julian alone. Impulsively, she placed her hands on his shoulders, reached up to brush his mouth with hers ... and instantly found herself being thoroughly, if briefly, kissed. Then Julian said, 'Thank you for that.'

She smiled at him and turned to go. 'It wasn't any trouble. They are staying with --'

'Thank you for that, too. But I meant the kiss.'

By the time Arabella took her seat, having found a cushion for Ellie to sit on and sandwiched all three very smartly-dressed children between herself and Janet Featherstone, it was five minutes to six. She looked at the platform, ablaze with tall candelabra and set with chairs and music-stands for the ensemble, strategically placed around Rockliffe's superb harpsichord. A small shiver of mingled excitement and apprehension slithered down her back and she wondered how Julian was feeling.

Decorated with enormous pots of flowers on pedestals, the body of the ballroom was illuminated only by wall sconces which gave it a shadowy air of mystery. Every seat was occupied and the room was buzzing with laughter and conversation as Rockliffe's guests speculated upon the contents of the scrolls tied with blood-red ribbon, one of which lay waiting on each chair. Arabella, her heart still filling her chest from Julian's unexpected kiss, looked at hers for a long moment before slowly untying it.

The concert was to begin with the Mozart concerto, with Julian's solo programme following after the interval. This was laid out by composer – the first being Johann Sebastian Bach.

Arabella smiled, happy to see that Julian had chosen to begin his recital with the *Fantasia in C minor*, followed by an *Allemande* she didn't think she knew and finally the *Allegro* from the Italian Concerto – which she did. Next came three pieces by Rameau, one she recalled being a pretty thing with a series of complex variations. And then came the *Andante* from a concerto by Johann Christian Bach ... intriguingly labelled *Arranged for solo harpsichord, J. Langham.*

Oh, thought Arabella, with a frisson of excitement. *I didn't know that was possible – and imagine most other people don't either. It sounds clever ... and it will pave the way for one of his own compositions later.*

But neither of the remaining items on the programme were Julian's own. They comprised a pair of Scarlatti sonatas and two pieces by Joseph-Nicholas-Pancrace Royer who Arabella didn't think she had ever heard of. Or had she? Not that it mattered. What *did* matter – at least to her – was that Julian hadn't included any of his own music, most specifically, the *Sarabande* she had asked for. Just for a moment, she felt disappointed. Then she reminded herself that Julian knew what he was doing. If he had left his own compositions out, he'd done it for a reason.

Somewhere, a clock chimed the hour. The ensemble players filed out to take their places and, once they were seated, Rockliffe strolled into the centre of the platform. Silence fell throughout the room.

'The duchess and I welcome you to Wynstanton House and to what we believe will be a memorable occasion. I shall not sing Mr Langham's praises because you are about to witness his gifts for yourselves. I shall merely say that I am as eager for this evening's performance to begin as you are – since I have not, you will be amazed to learn, been permitted to hear so much as a note of it.' He was rewarded by a ripple of amusement and when it died away, added simply, 'Ladies and gentlemen ... please welcome Julian Langham.'

Applause filled the air; some of it polite and some, from obvious quarters, wildly enthusiastic. And into it, Julian walked unhurriedly on to the platform. He bowed to Rockliffe, shook hands with the first violinist and finally, with a faint smile, bowed to the audience – at which point, the polite applause became noticeably warmer. From behind her, Arabella heard a gentleman murmur, 'There's not a sheet of music on the harpsichord and he's brought none with him. How on earth--?' And a lady promptly shushed him, adding, 'With looks like that, who cares?'

Julian took his seat and played an A so that his fellow musicians could check their tuning. Then, this done and all of them appearing ready, he placed his own hands above the keyboard, gave one decisive nod ... and they began.

The music was, quite unmistakably, Mozart's. Elegant, tuneful and charming, it couldn't have been composed by anyone else. Arabella had always loved Mozart. Listening to it now, she supposed she still did. But as the *Allegro* progressed, she began to realise that it wasn't taxing Julian at all. True, it was beautiful ... but it was also comfortable and, compared to other pieces she now knew, just a little bit *safe*. A glance at the faces around her, most of which were smiling, told her they didn't share her opinion. She wondered if that would change later when they learned the full scope of Julian's ability.

In fact, Julian didn't make them wait that long. He demonstrated it in the *Rondo* by performing his own sizzling arrangement of Mozart's cadenza. Since the concerto was new to them, the audience could not know that. But the new heights of technical complexity were impossible to miss ... and when the piece drew to its close, the surprised and enthusiastic reception told Arabella that people were beginning to realise they could look forward to something truly extraordinary.

Julian bowed and turned immediately to acknowledge the ensemble who also bowed. He and the first violinist shook hands again and, since the applause was still continuing, everyone took another bow. Then, with a nod and a smile, Julian led the way from the platform, leaving Rockliffe to invite the audience to withdraw for a restorative glass of wine while the stage was re-set for the second part of the concert.

Rob said eagerly, 'Can we go and see Sir Julian now?'

'Yes – but we mustn't stay long. He still has a lot of work ahead of him,' replied Arabella, half her attention tuned to snatches of conversation going on around her.

They found Julian still surrounded by the ensemble, all of whom wore huge smiles. The cellist said, 'Sir – working with you has been a privilege. I'm sure I speak for us all when I ask that, if you ever have need of a chamber consort again, you will bear us in mind.'

'I will indeed, Mr Roland,' agreed Julian promptly. 'And I thank all of you for your support and patience – as well as a first-class performance.' Catching sight of Arabella and the children hovering in the doorway, he added, 'Now go and take up the duke's offer of a drink. You've earned it.'

They filed past Arabella, looking bashful when she added her own compliments. Meanwhile, Ellie winnowed her way through to demand that Julian admire her new dress.

'It's lovely,' he said gravely. 'I particularly like the frills. And the hair-ribbon.' He looked at Arabella. 'What are they saying out there?'

'They loved it. They're marvelling that you played the whole concerto without a note of music in front of you and I heard a couple of gentlemen arguing about the cadenza. One assumed it must be Mozart's own – the other said it wasn't.' She smiled at him. 'It was yours, wasn't it?'

'It was mine ... with Mozart's wrapped up inside it.'

'Is that allowed?' asked Rob dubiously. 'Changing it, I mean?'

'Yes. Cadenzas are the soloist's chance to show off.' Julian grinned. 'So I did.'

'Spectacularly.' Arabella eyed him thoughtfully. 'Did you enjoy yourself?'

'Yes. But I'll enjoy the second half more.'

'I think I will, too ... though I wish you had included something of your own.'

He laughed and shook his head. 'Wait and see what happens.'

* * *

By the time everyone returned to their seats, the platform had been cleared of everything except the harpsichord, its music-rest still empty and folded flat. This time, Rockliffe made no announcement but merely sat chatting to Lord Amberley until Julian emerged to immediate and welcoming applause. He bowed, smiled and took his place on the bench to sit perfectly still, his hands lying loose and relaxed on his thighs and his head slightly bent while the audience settled into an expectant hush. Then, lifting both head and hands, he sent the opening bars of the *Fantasia* singing bright and clear through the air … and Arabella promptly stopped breathing. Gradually, it occurred to her that she wasn't the only one who had done so. The entire audience seemed suddenly frozen; fans stopped fluttering and no one moved or spoke or coughed. For four-and –a-quarter minutes, every single person's attention remained utterly focussed on the man at the harpsichord. And then, as one, they broke into a storm of applause.

They should not have done … so Julian hadn't expected it. This was an educated audience, perfectly aware that the correct form was not to applaud until the end of the section – in this case, after the *Allegro*. Clearly no one cared about that. His mind still largely in the place it went when he played, he turned a gaze of baffled amusement on his audience and lifted one staying hand. Then, not waiting for silence but simply commanding it, he embarked on the *Allemande*.

Arabella watched him, captivated as she always was by the changing expressions on his face, by the tilt of his head and the times he played, eyes closed, plainly engulfed by the magic he was creating. He didn't just play with his hands. He seemed to play with his whole body … as if he felt each note and chord and phrase in every part of him. And this time, when he brought the *Allemande* to its end, his audience remained quiet and still, waiting for whatever jewel might come next. But at the conclusion of the *Allegro*, there was more deafening applause … and this time Julian rose from the bench, walked to the edge of the platform and bowed, hand on heart. There was a sort of touching humility to that bow which wasn't lost on his audience and which caused the applause to go on for longer than it might otherwise have done. But when it finally dwindled, Julian did what not even Arabella had expected – though she quickly realised that she should have done. Asking for silence with the same small gesture he'd used before, he said simply, 'I ask your forgiveness, ladies and gentlemen – but I shall play better without this.' And he took off his coat.

There were a few gasps. Then, from somewhere away to her left, Arabella heard a crack of laughter and Sebastian Audley's voice calling, '*Just* the coat, Julian. Otherwise the ladies may faint.' Which, naturally enough, provoked still more laughter – making it clear that the audience was ready to forgive anything.

Julian merely smiled, handed his coat to a footman and resumed his seat to begin the sequence of delicate Rameau pieces. During them and for the first time since the concert had begun, Arabella let her eyes stray to the children. Ellie was wide-eyed, Rob looked dazzled and Tom wore an expression of such fierce pride that she had to blink back tears. Not one of them had fidgeted or said a word since Julian had played his first note.

The pause before the Johann Christian Bach *Andante* was a long one. Julian sat perfectly still, his gaze resting on the keyboard, apparently unconcerned that his audience was silent and waiting with eager anticipation to hear what he had done with the music of Johann Sebastian's youngest son. But finally, he drew a long steady breath … and began.

From its very first notes, the main theme emerged haunting and beautiful … tugging mercilessly at the heartstrings as it promised fulfilment before once again falling away into loneliness and searching. Every emotion the harpsichord expressed was written on Julian's face and in his posture. By the middle of it, half the ladies in the audience – Arabella included – had recourse to their handkerchiefs while the gentlemen sat tight-jawed. If anyone had doubted that they were listening to a true virtuoso, the masterly dynamics and perfectly controlled emotion in Julian's performance of the *Andante* banished them.

When his hands left the keys and the last, gentle notes died away there was utter silence. Julian didn't appear to notice it. Even from where she sat, Arabella could see the disruption in his breathing.

'Why aren't they clapping?' whispered Ellie, confused. 'It was good, wasn't it?'

Unable to trust her voice, Arabella merely hugged the child and nodded.

Then, from the back of the room, a gentleman stood up and began to applaud, calling out, 'Bravo! Bravo, indeed!' Astoundingly, it was Ralph Sherbourne. And as if waking from a trance, more and more people followed his example until the entire audience was on its feet, wildly applauding. Rob and Ellie jumped up and down. Tom shouted himself hoarse. Arabella turned to Max, sitting on her other side and said helplessly, 'What has he done? He can't possibly eclipse that. No one could!'

Max merely shrugged, grinned and continued clapping.

On the platform, wearing a faintly dazed expression, Julian bowed and bowed again. Then, as if he didn't know what else to do, he resumed his seat on the bench and waited.

Eventually the tumult died down, people settled back into their places and Julian launched into the Scarlatti sonatas. The first was an unashamed display of technical brilliance; the second, softer and more lyrical. The audience appreciated both ... but Arabella detected an air of increased anticipation. As if everyone believed that something remarkable lay in wait. Around her, she could hear people asking each other if they'd heard of Langham's final choice of composer. And in the end, unable to bear it any longer, Rob turned around and informed the row behind him that Royer was French – and dead.

'Really?' asked one gentleman lazily. 'You're a very well-informed young man.'

'*Vertigo* is my *favourite*,' replied Rob. 'I'm going to learn it one day.'

'And is that why Mr Langham has saved it for the end?' the same gentlemen enquired.

'No.' Tom turned his head. 'He did it because it's the only piece the duke asked him for especially.'

Arabella's eyes widened a little. She hadn't known that Rockliffe had requested anything. Max murmured, 'This should be interesting.'

On the platform, Julian took his time adjusting the settings within the harpsichord. Once again, he was content to let the silence linger because the effect of what he was about to do would be the greater for it. *La Marche des Scythes* was going to shock them. He doubted any of them had ever heard anything like it … and he knew it was a risk. If they recognised that the reason they had never heard it before was because few harpsichordists had either the skill or the courage to play it, the risk would pay off. If not … well, he refused to think of that. Instead, he brought his hands down on the keyboard with sudden ferocity and plunged into the piece's darkly furious opening.

Jaws dropped, some people physically flinched and the numerous gasps went unheard against the thunder of the music – which suddenly sounded like four instruments, rather than one. Head down and eyes on his flying hands, Julian hovered between exultation and incipient laughter. Wild, dramatic and fiendishly difficult, *La Marche* yet had its unexpectedly playful moments. But none of it left room in his head or the world around him for anything but the explosive torrent of notes, spilling over like a surging tide.

La Marche stopped as abruptly as it had begun, leaving a deafening silence behind. Julian turned slowly and surveyed the audience, undismayed by the expression he glimpsed on most faces. He'd thrown down a musical gauntlet and they didn't know what to make of it. Then Rockliffe came to his feet and said, 'Congratulations, Julian. You promised me a surprise and have certainly delivered one. That was … extraordinary.' And he led a round of applause which grew less and less ragged as the shock started to wear off.

Julian bowed but didn't return to his seat. When the room fell quiet again, he said, 'Most of you are probably unfamiliar with Monsieur Royer's work. Allow me to reassure you that *Le Vertigo* is easier on the ears.'

A few people clapped and there was a scattering of laughter over which someone said, 'Thank God for that. Mine are still ringing from the last one.'

Julian shoved back the usual recalcitrant lock of hair and, over his shoulder as he sat down, said, 'Mine, too.'

Leaning closer to Arabella, Max said, 'Is he *supposed* to chat to the audience?'

'Why shouldn't he? Rockliffe doesn't mind. And they like him, don't they?'

'Oh yes. They like him. He has them in the palm of his hand – even after that unholy racket he just played. God only knows how he had the nerve.'

'Shh,' hissed his mother. 'Julian's ready to begin.'

A melodic, almost lazy sequence of notes drifted through the room, followed by rippling runs and trills which resolved themselves into dreamy arpeggios. All the emotion of the Johann Christian Bach *Andante* seemed to be waiting in the wings and the audience settled into a state of comfortable expectation ... only to be jerked awake by a pounding series of harmonically shifting chords.

Julian had a particular fondness for *Le Vertigo* because it twisted and turned, never doing quite what one expected. Half a dozen contrasting themes, from lyrical to fierce, chased each other apparently at random. If there was a pattern, Julian had never found it. He had also never decided whether Royer was a genius or merely possessed of a wicked sense of humour – because *Vertigo* contained pauses which tempted premature applause. After being caught out by the first of these and glimpsing Julian's glance of amused reproof, the audience grew more cautious – with the result that, when the piece *was* over, he signified it by immediately rising from the bench.

This time the applause was deafening and it went on and on, punctuated by demands for an encore. Julian merely smiled, bowed, waited ... and sought Rockliffe's gaze.

'Oh – by all means,' replied the duke with a lazy gesture. 'I doubt that I will be the only person disappointed if you leave the platform without playing something of your own.'

'In that case ... *Sarabande* in D minor and *Rondo* in G major,' said Julian. And added awkwardly, 'Both of them dedicated to the lady who unknowingly inspired them.'

Several romantically-inclined ladies sighed.

And too excited to keep his voice down, Rob said, 'That's you, Miss Belle!'

Over the ensuing gust of laughter as virtually every head in the audience turned to find the source of this remark, Mr Audley called out, 'She knows now, Julian!'

Despite the bud of awed pleasure blossoming inside her, Arabella slid down in her seat wishing she dared sit on the floor. Max murmured, 'It's no good hiding. The secret's out. You may as well get up and take a bow.'

'Be quiet!' she hissed back. 'Does Julian look embarrassed?'

'It's hard to tell. He's sitting down and will probably start to play when he's decided how to kill Rob.'

The first notes of the *Sarabande* drifted softly from beneath Julian's fingers. Arabella folded her arms about her middle, trying to contain the enormity of knowing he had written this bitter-sweet piece – the one she and the villagers had always liked best – for her. If there was a greater gift than this one, she couldn't imagine it. She didn't know whether to laugh or cry. And when the *Sarabande* became a *Rondo* ... light as a feather and full of teasing ripples and trills ... she lost the ability to breathe.

When it was over, Julian rose and accepted the applause hand on heart with a bow, a smile and his usual air of faint abstraction. Then he left the platform.

The audience summoned him back with a standing ovation during which Rockliffe strolled over to shake his hand and offer his congratulations. Julian shrugged, bowed once more to the auditorium, left the stage again ... and didn't return.

Leaning across Max to grasp Arabella's hand, Louisa said softly, 'Oh my darling ... to think he wrote those pieces for you! *Such* a lovely thing to do.'

Gradually, the room quieted sufficiently for the duke to announce that supper awaited and people began to leave. Telling the children to stay with Max and her mother, Arabella started making her way in Julian's wake. She passed one lady voicing her shock at Mr Langham's state of undress and being pooh-poohed by the Duchess of Queensberry on the score that genius was allowed its little foibles.

'But truly – I didn't know where to *look*!' the first lady exclaimed.

'You must have been the only one, then,' retorted the duchess.

Arabella was just about to leave the ballroom when Rockliffe detained her, saying, 'I suspect he needs a few moments of quiet, Arabella. Share them with him, by all means ... then bring him to join the other guests. There are at least three gentlemen who are eager to speak with him.' He smiled a little. 'You may tell him that one of them is from the Queen's House.'

CHAPTER TWENTY-FIVE

Arabella found Julian sitting on the window-seat, eyes closed, one wrist resting loosely on his raised knee ... and grinning with post-performance elation. She wanted to walk across and put her arms around him but to do that now after what had happened at the end of the concert would look like an assumption. If a first move was to be made, it would be up to Julian to make it.

And so, without waiting for him to either open his eyes or speak, she said softly, 'Thank you. You know I've always loved the *Sarabande* but I never dreamed --'

'That I wrote it for you?' He turned his head and looked at her, his expression somehow both relaxed and exhilarated. 'No. You wouldn't, I suppose. Did you like the *Rondo*?'

'Very much. It ... you'll think I'm foolish, but it sounded like laughter.'

'Yes. Yours.'

Arabella stared at him. '*Mine*?'

'From the first time I heard it and every time thereafter. I knew it needed to be a *Rondo* – but it took a long time to come right.' He swung his feet to the floor and stood up in one smooth, collected movement. 'I'm glad you liked it.'

'I ... Julian, it's the most beautiful gift any woman ever received. I just – I can't find the words.' She paused, then added, 'I'm sorry about Rob. You must want to throttle him.'

'It's a bit late for that, isn't it?'

'Somewhat. Were you embarrassed?'

'Not especially – though I'll admit I'd have preferred not to have the entire audience expecting me to go down on one knee there and then.'

Arabella's heart gave a single odd lurch. Striving to sound amused, she said, 'Not *quite* the entire audience, surely? And most people won't know which lady you meant anyway.'

'I don't care about them.' He prowled towards her, his eyes holding hers with unusual intensity. '*You* knew, didn't you? Even without Rob, you must have known it was for you. And why.'

'Perhaps ... but it isn't the kind of thing one can take for granted.' Seeing his expression change but unable to interpret it, she said quickly, 'Are you ready to face your public yet? There are people waiting to speak with you and --'

'In a minute.' With the sort of predatory grace Arabella would never have suspected he possessed, Julian closed the space between them. 'We'll go in a minute. First --'

'No.'

She stared into dark pools of forest green and held him back with the flat of one hand as she realised what she should have seen instantly. He was still the man he became in performance; the confident, invincible virtuoso without a nerve in his body. Arabella stared at him, wondering how long this might last ... but aware that it was the incarnation which would serve him best while he met the men Rockliffe had spoken of.

She said firmly, 'No, Julian. We will go *now*. This evening was all about one thing – and you will *not* waste it by keeping people waiting. One of the gentlemen wishing to speak with you is from the Queen's House, for heaven's sake!'

He frowned slightly. 'Does that mean what it sounds like?'

'Yes. A lot of people still call it Buckingham House – which is what it was before the King bought it. Now, the Queen and all the royal children live there – and the King as well, most of the time. So come and make use of your success now you've earned it.'

Julian removed her palm from his chest, dropped a warm kiss in the centre of it and kept a firm hold on her hand. 'But you and I will speak later. Yes?'

'Y-Yes.'

'Good.' He turned away and shrugged back into his coat. 'Let's go, then.'

* * *

Julian entered the drawing-room to a fresh burst of applause and was immediately surrounded by gentlemen wishing to shake his hand and ladies wanting to engage the beautiful young virtuoso's interest. Arabella slid away to join the Audleys near the buffet-table and began loading food on to a plate.

Grinning, Sebastian said, 'Hungry, are you?'

'It's for Julian. He won't have eaten before the concert and he won't get the chance now if something isn't done about it.' She handed the plate to him. 'Take it, please. You've got more chance of elbowing your way through than I have.'

Collecting a glass of wine *en route* from a passing footman, Sebastian reached Julian's side by simply telling everyone to make way before Mr Langham expired from starvation. Then, dropping his voice, he murmured, 'Bloody well done, Julian. The piece that put everybody into a state of catalepsy wasn't just a brave choice – it was inspired. Now ... drink your wine and eat something before Rockliffe starts introducing you to the men he invited purely to meet you.'

During the next hour and beginning to feel light-headed with euphoria, Julian accepted an engagement to play at the Pantheon the following week and another for a concert at Queensberry House. Then Max walked up and, in a rapid undertone, said, 'A few minutes ago I heard the Misses Caldercott telling Lady Amberley and some others about your impromptu concerts for the villagers. And Mother and Mistress Featherstone lost track of Rob and Ellie for a short while – with the result that half the people here know *exactly* who they are and that you plan to adopt them. So now, in addition to your official status as a genius, you are well on the way to recommendation for sainthood.' And seeing Julian wince, 'Yes. That's what I thought, too.'

Eventually, some of the guests started to leave and Rockliffe asked Julian to join him in the library. There, he presented him to Sir Alec Kinross who shook his hand and said, 'Allow me to congratulate you on your performance, my lord. It was truly extraordinary.'

'Thank you.'

'I am here at Her Majesty's behest, of course – but I have seldom enjoyed an evening more. Indeed, the Queen might have attended in person but that she is, once again, *enceinte*. She has a great fondness for music, you understand, and is keen to nurture it in her children – particularly the young princesses.'

'Come to the point, Alec,' sighed Rockliffe. 'I'm sure Julian would like to enjoy his triumph for what is left of the evening.'

With an easy smile and a shrug, Julian said, 'By no means, sir. I'm at your disposal.'

Kinross laughed. 'Of course you are. But Rock is right. I am instructed to invite you to give a private recital for the royal family. They won't pay you, of course. They never do. But the *cachet* ought to go some way to making up for that. What do you say?'

He bowed slightly. 'Naturally, I would be honoured.'

'Excellent. Expect to hear from me in the next few days with possible dates.' He shook Julian's hand again and added, 'You'll go far, young man – and you deserve to. But when you play for the Queen, you had best keep your coat on.'

When he had gone, the duke said, 'Allow me to add my own congratulations, Julian. I had very high expectations ... and you exceeded them.'

'I'm glad I didn't disappoint you. I owe this evening wholly to you and --'

'That isn't entirely true,' interposed Rockliffe with a hint of laughter. 'But for Arabella and Elizabeth's idiotic masquerade, your path and mine might never have crossed. So I think we must give them some of the credit.'

At the end of a further hour, the company had shrunk to the duke's particular friends, Arabella's family, the Beckingham delegation and the children. Although elation was still fizzing through his veins, Julian was slowly coming down to earth ... and there remained one thing necessary to make the evening complete. Unfortunately, he didn't know how he was going to get it without everyone jumping to conclusions; and the fact that they would be the *right* conclusions didn't make it any better. Finally, seeing that Rob was yawning and Ellie about to fall asleep, he stood up saying, 'Time for bed, you three. I'll see you on your way and then, if no one minds, I'd like to go back to the ballroom for a little while.'

'You've just given a concert and you want to play some *more*?' asked Max incredulously. 'Are you *completely* insane?'

Julian shrugged and avoided his lordship's eyes. 'Probably. But it's habit, mostly. And after a performance ... well, I just need time to recover my balance.'

'Go,' said Arabella. 'I'll see to the children. Ellie will need help with her new dress and the nurse-maid has enough to do.' She waved a dismissive hand at Julian. 'Go and take a half hour for yourself. You've earned it.'

Upstairs in the nursery suite, she made short work of Ellie's ribbons and laces and smiled ruefully when the child fell asleep even before her goodnight kiss. Then Tom was at her elbow saying quietly, 'Now *you* go, Miss Belle. Nobody needs to know you weren't here with us all the time – and I reckon he's waiting for you.'

'Thank you,' whispered Arabella, surprised and touched by the boy's perceptiveness. '*Thank* you, Tom.' Then she was gone.

Having re-lit a branch of candles, Julian threw off his coat and sat down on the bench. Without conscious thought, his hands drifted lightly through a bit of Couperin he'd considered for the concert and then discarded. He wondered if she would come. He *thought* she would. She always had at Chalfont. And tonight ... he'd told her that he wanted to talk to her, hadn't he?

He heard the door open and spun round to watch her tripping quickly down the length of the room towards him. Rising, he said, 'I wasn't sure you'd come.'

'I wasn't sure you wanted me to.'

'Why? We agreed, didn't we?'

'Yes. But you always play late at night and, after this evening, it wasn't surprising that you'd want some peace. However, Tom said you would be waiting ... so here I am.'

'Tom understands too damned much for a twelve-year-old – though there are times I'm glad of it.' Julian reached out a hand for one of hers. 'Will you sit? I want ... there are things I want to say to you but it may take me a while to find the right words.'

Arabella sank down upon the bench and looked up at him.

'The right words don't matter. Just tell me.'

He nodded, shoved his hands in his pockets and said, 'I wrote the music for you. I did it because I couldn't help it and because, at the time, it was the only thing I *could* do. But tonight has changed everything. I have three further engagements.' He grinned faintly. 'I'll even be paid for two of them.'

'You'll have a dozen more when word gets out that you played for the Queen.'

'I hope so. But until tonight, I couldn't be sure. If it hadn't been a success --'

'There was never any chance of that.'

'I couldn't take the risk. With things as they are at Chalfont, even given Max's help ... and me not exactly being much of a catch ...' He hesitated and hauled in an unsteady breath. 'I didn't think there was the remotest chance that – that you'd marry me.'

The candlelight flickered oddly and there was a faint roaring in her ears. She said weakly, 'Are you asking me to?'

'Yes. *God*, yes. Will you?' And without giving her the chance to answer, 'I'm aware that you could do a hundred times better – but you must know how I feel about you. You saw how the prospect of you going away and not coming back turned me into a gibbering idiot. I didn't know how I would bear it. The mere thought made me feel ill. And that wasn't because of the children. It was me, panicking.' He stopped again, looking vaguely helpless. 'I love you. At least, I suppose that's what it is. I've never felt this way about anyone ... as if losing you would be as bad as never being able to play another note.' He shut his eyes and added despairingly, 'I'm making a mess of this, aren't I? I probably should have said that I love you and *then* asked you to consider marrying me. I probably also ought to be on my knees. Would it help if I did that?'

Throughout what he was already realising was possibly the worst marriage proposal in history, Arabella had been staring at him, wide-eyed. Now, with a tiny uncertain shake of her head, she said, 'No.'

'Oh.' Something cold and hard slammed through his chest. 'No. Of course.'

'No – I meant, don't kneel. There's no need.'

'Oh.' It took him a second to allow hope back in. 'Then you'll consider it? Please? I'll be content with that until you decide. Just don't say no right now.'

'I don't want to say no at *all*.' Unable to help herself, Arabella stood up to put her arms around his waist and lean her brow against his shoulder. He immediately wrapped her so close that she could feel the fast thundering of his heart. 'I want to say that I love you and I'll marry you and that, out of all the men in the world, there is no one better for me than you; that I'd choose you over a hundred or even a *thousand* other men because not one of them would be a fraction as remarkable as you are. You're unfailingly kind, you never complain or put yourself first and what you're doing for the children is ... well. There aren't words for it.' She stopped and then added miserably, 'But I can't, Julian. I can't say any of those things without telling you something else first.'

The silence was so long that she wondered if he'd understood. Finally, he asked unsteadily, 'Do you mean it?'

'Every word.'

'Even the bit about loving me?'

'Especially that bit.'

Relief and gratitude shuddered through him.

'Then nothing else matters.'

'This does. It – it might make you change your mind.'

'It won't. It couldn't.'

'We'll see.' She freed herself from his embrace and stepped back to look him in the eye. 'I was betrothed once. We were both very young and his regiment was being sent to the Colonies so it was agreed that we wouldn't marry until he came back. But he didn't come back. He married a girl in Massachusetts instead.'

'Oh.' Julian shifted uncomfortably. 'I'm sorry.'

'Don't be. I'm not sure I ever loved him, so I wouldn't have minded him jilting me. I might even have been *glad* of it if only I hadn't let him persuade me to – to lie with him before he left.' Arabella forced herself not to look away. 'I've regretted it every day since then but that doesn't make it any better. So you see ...?'

'See what? See that he'd no business seducing you, then marrying someone else? Yes. I see that. But I'm hardly likely to wish he'd come back and married you, am I?'

For an instant, she was completely nonplussed. Then, in case he had missed the point, she said quietly, 'Julian ... I'm telling you I'm not a – a virgin.'

'Yes. I gathered that. But what of it?' He shrugged. 'Neither am I.'

Shocked into a choke of laughter, Arabella said, 'That's different. Gentlemen are expected to be ... experienced. Girls are supposed to be untouched.'

'Convenient nonsense made up by men,' he retorted impatiently. 'I don't give a fig for it. So you're not untouched. So what?' He bathed her in a sudden dazzling smile. 'Since we're telling the truth, *I'm* not especially experienced ... but I'll be happy to work on that side of things if you'll give me the chance by marrying me.'

Unable to believe that, after all her fears, it could possibly be this easy, she said, 'Are you sure? Are you *sure* it doesn't matter?'

'Positive.' He closed the space between them, his eyes brilliant. 'Say yes.'

'Yes,' whispered Arabella shakily. 'Oh yes. Please.'

'Thank God,' breathed Julian. And sweeping her back into his arms, he kissed her as if he had been starving.

And perhaps, without knowing it, he had been. In the second his mouth touched hers, the entire world was full of music ... rare, elusive and utterly compelling. A melody more beautiful that any he had ever either heard or even imagined. She was the purity of flutes, the poignancy of oboes and the warm promise of violas. He slid his fingers into that incredible mass of silvery-fair hair while he kissed her brows, her eyelids, her jaw; then, groaning with pleasure at the exquisite sweetness of it, he found her mouth again so he could drink in the taste of her.

Arabella merely let go, allowing him to carry her away on a tide of sensual promise. His lips asked and hers answered. Her hands traced the line of his shoulders, found the nape of his neck, wound their way through the silky, dark brown hair she had always yearned to touch. She pressed close and then closer, until his fingers skimmed the neckline of her gown, making her blood run quicker and sending sparks exploding through her veins. She kissed a path up his throat, breathed fire against his skin and felt the answering tremor that rippled through him.

Long moments later and keeping her close within the circle of his arm, he drew her down beside him on the bench and, breathing rather hard, said, 'How long do we have to wait?'

'What?' Coherent thought was beyond her.

'To be married. How long must we wait?'

'Not very long.'

'Good.' He stroked her hair again and then, on a groan, added, 'I suppose I have to ask Max's permission, don't I? Will he give it?'

Arabella laughed. 'Yes. He knows I love you. He knew it before I did.'

'Did he? How?'

'Reading between the lines of a letter I wrote. He'd asked about you ... and I told him more than I realised.' She reached up to touch his cheek. 'He likes you. If he didn't, he wouldn't be helping with Chalfont.'

'He said he was doing that because you told him to.'

'That's only partly true. He visited you to see things for himself because I asked him. But if he hadn't liked what he found ... if he had considered you negligent or uncaring ... he'd have walked away.' She thought for a moment and then said, 'Did he ask what your worst problem was?'

'I – yes. I think so.'

'What answer did you give him?'

'I don't remember exactly. Probably that it was my own ignorance.'

'Ah.' Arabella smiled and kissed his jaw. 'And *that* was when Max decided to help. You earned it yourself, you see.'

They fell silent for a time, savouring this new closeness and all it meant for the future they now knew they had. But eventually Julian said, 'Are we going to tell everyone?'

'Tonight? While they are all together?' She stood up and pulled him to his feet. 'Yes. I think so – though it's a pity the children are in bed.'

'We'll tell them in the morning. They'll be ecstatic. Aside from knowing you'll never leave them, it means you and I can adopt them together.' A hint of anxiety touched his eyes and he said, 'Are you really sure about that? It can't be how you'd imagined --'

'No. It isn't. It's *better*. So play my *Rondo* again – and then we'll join the others and you can make our grand announcement.'

'God help me!' muttered Julian, obediently sitting down at the harpsichord.

'Don't be silly.' Arabella leaned against his back and put her hands on his shoulders. 'You've just played the most incredibly difficult music I've ever heard to a packed audience. And you *talked* to them – as casually and confidently as you'd talk to Tom. Compared to that, standing in front of our friends is *nothing*. Now … play for me.'

* * *

They re-entered the drawing-room hand in hand and smiling. Consequently, before Julian had a chance to say anything at all, several other people all spoke at once – over which Max's remark of, 'And about time!' emerged triumphant.

Trying to frown but on the verge of laughter, Arabella said, 'You might have let Julian break the news, Max. He had a speech all prepared.'

'No,' confessed Julian. 'I really didn't.'

And then the room erupted into congratulatory hugs, kisses and hand-shaking.

Slapping Julian on the back, Paul said, 'Finally found the courage, did you? Well done!'

Louisa folded Arabella in her arms and said, 'Oh my dear … he is an exceptional man and he will make you so very happy. I just *know* it.'

Miss Beatrice kissed Julian's cheek, saying, 'Dear boy – *such* a lovely girl. Abby and I are so happy for you.'

Cassie, Caroline and Elizabeth, all talking at once, tried to embrace Arabella at the same time. And Max grinned at his future brother-in-law and said, '*Aren't* you glad I spared you the need to ask my permission?'

During the course of all this, Rockliffe rang for champagne and toasts were drunk. But eventually Adeline said, 'When is the wedding to be? And more to the point – where?'

Sitting beside Arabella, her fingers wrapped in his, Julian said, 'We hadn't got that far. We'd just like it to be soon.'

'There's a surprise,' grinned Sebastian. 'But since you have professional engagements, *soon* means London, doesn't it? And --'

'If I might make a suggestion?' interposed Rockliffe gently. And when everyone fell silent, 'As you know, Elizabeth and Sherbourne have agreed on banns and will be married next month. I assume neither bride wants a double wedding?'

Arabella and Elizabeth exchanged glances and said simultaneously, 'No.'

'Then perhaps Arabella and Julian would like to consider being married from this house by special licence – on a date to be decided after Julian has heard from Kinross. Aside from leaving him free to fulfil his obligations, it has the added advantage that – with the exception of your other brothers, Arabella – everyone you would wish to attend the happy occasion is already here. Or am I missing something?'

'I doubt it,' remarked Adeline dryly. 'You're just assuming that everyone can remain in London for an unspecified period. Dr Featherstone might find that difficult.'

'A retired colleague from Newark is covering for me,' said Paul. 'But Sebastian and Cassie can't possibly want --'

'Of course you must continue to stay with us,' said Cassie firmly.

'As must Miss Bea and Miss Abby with Adrian and me,' added Caroline.

Adrian grinned at Sebastian. 'That would appear to be settled, then.'

'Perhaps,' suggested Louisa, 'Belle and Julian might be allowed a word?'

Arabella stared hopefully into her love's eyes. They smiled at her. Then Julian turned to Rockliffe and said, 'Thank you, your Grace. We accept – and are grateful. As for everyone else ... if you will all be present to wish us happy, our day will be perfect.'

* * *

On the following morning, they told the children. For a handful of heartbeats, all three stared at them open-mouthed. Then Rob and Ellie hurled themselves on Arabella with mingled expressions of glee.

'That's brilliant!' exclaimed Rob. 'The best news ever!'

'Almost as good as being adopted,' cried Ellie. 'We'll be just like a real family. For ever and ever.'

Despite grinning from ear to ear, Tom tried to hang on to his new-found dignity. He shook Julian's hand and said, 'Congratulations, sir. I know you'll both be happy.'

Smiling back, Julian pulled the boy into a hug.

'No, Tom. We'll *all* be happy,' he said. 'And we won't be *like* a real family. We'll *be* one.'

CHAPTER TWENTY-SIX

Reasoning that his audience at the Queen's House would be completely different from that at the Pantheon, Julian decided to play the Wynstanton programme at both. The only change he made was to substitute *La Marche des Scythes* for a less disturbing Royer piece. Then a note arrived from Sir Alec Kinross, setting a date a fortnight hence and adding, *'Her Majesty asks that you repeat your solo performance – of which she has heard so much – in its entirety.'* Julian's brows rose a little at that. Then he merely shrugged and agreed. One didn't, after all, argue with royalty.

One also did not argue with Rockliffe who, having obtained a special marriage licence and placed the complexities of adopting Tom, Rob and Ellie in the hands of Mr Osborne, coolly suggested that, with ten days between the Pantheon and the Queen's House, the wedding should take place the day after the first of them.

Julian began to experience the odd yet somehow not alarming feeling that his life was spiralling out of his control. Then Max Brandon made him sit down and talk about financial matters … and petrified him by bringing up the subject of Arabella's dowry.

'Wh-What?' stammered Julian, thinking he must have misheard. 'F-Fifteen *thousand*? No. You can't mean it.'

'She's never mentioned it?'

'Not a word.'

'Well, I suppose she has her reasons. But why are you looking so horrified? You can put some of it to good use – first and foremost by installing a reliable roof over her head.'

'No! I mean, yes – I know the roof needs repairing. But I can't use Arabella's money for that. It – it wouldn't be right.' He could feel a chill invading his veins. 'I don't understand why you agreed to me marrying her. You can't have wanted to.'

Max sighed. 'Julian … try not to be a bigger ass than you can help. I know you love Belle and I know you're not after her money. I also know what she'd do to me if I tried to come between you – and it wouldn't be pleasant. We're only discussing this because marriage settlements and the like are a necessary formality. So will you please stop panicking and pay attention?'

'I'm not panicking. I'm attempting to come to terms with a sum of money beyond my comprehension. And if *you'd* never had more than fifty pounds to your name, you might understand what I mean.'

'I understand it now. How much is the Pantheon paying you, by the way?'

'A hundred.'

'A hundred for an hour's work? And you're complaining?'

Julian looked him in the eye and said something pithy and extremely rude.

Max laughed. 'Good. It's nice to know you're human after all.'

* * *

Adam and Leo Brandon arrived two days before the wedding, made the acquaintance of their future brother-in-law and, after an hour or so, agreed that the fellow seemed to be sound. 'Odd,' said Adam, 'but sound. I can't imagine him performing in public, though – wouldn't have thought he had the stomach for it. Still … we'll know tomorrow.'

The Pantheon was packed. Word that the virtuoso earl was to make his first public appearance had caused a scramble for tickets. Every seat was taken, people were standing wherever they could find room and others were still trying to get in.

The Duke of Rockliffe's party which – as well as the Amberleys, the Sarres, the Audleys, the Brandons and Ralph Sherbourne, now also included the Featherstones and the Caldercott ladies – occupied two of the boxes overlooking the main floor. Only the children were missing. Since all three had roles to play in tomorrow's wedding, Louisa and Arabella had decreed an early night with no additional excitement.

Sitting more or less directly above the platform on which the harpsichord stood, Arabella looked down at it and wondered why her nerves were twitching when she knew perfectly well that Julian's wouldn't be. She also wondered if she would ever get used to the change that came over him when he walked out before an audience ... and concluded that she wouldn't.

There was to be no Mozart concerto tonight – only Julian's solo recital. As unruffled as he had been in Wynstanton House, he strolled out to welcoming applause. Hand on heart, he bowed first to the audience and then, looking up, directly to Arabella. She laughed down on him and blew a kiss. The audience laughed with her and the applause doubled in volume. Julian took a moment to glance about him ... and, in what those who knew him suspected was probably to become as much an expected idiosyncrasy as that charmingly modest bow, he shrugged out of his coat and sat down at the harpsichord. The audience fell gradually silent ... and the *Fantasia* in C minor filled the vast space.

Even before he played the Christian Bach *Andante*, they loved him. After it, he got a standing ovation. The first Scarlatti sonata dazzled them and Le Vertigo brought calls for an encore pouring in from every corner. With another, even deeper bow for Arabella, Julian played her *Sarabande* and *Rondo*. But the audience refused to be satisfied. They demanded more. And that was when Sebastian Audley leaned over the parapet of the box and shouted down, 'You can't leave it there, Julian. Play the piece you thought would be too much for them. I'll wager it isn't. And if I can take it, I dare anybody to admit they can't.'

No one knew what he was talking about – but they cheered him on anyway.

Julian held up a hand for silence and, speaking for the first time, said, 'Very well. I would have spared you this, ladies and gentlemen ... but *La Marche des Scythes* it is. And if you don't like it, please remember to blame Mr Audley.'

Seeing only smiles and expressions of anticipation, Arabella suspected that Julian had brought them to a place where they were prepared to enjoy anything – even the piece Max insisted on calling *Langham's Nightmare*. And so it was. Despite flinching at the violently turbulent opening ... despite staring in frankly open-mouthed confusion ... despite even possibly not actually liking the music ... they appreciated and responded to the skill required to perform it. Or perhaps, thought Arabella when the Pantheon was ringing with another ovation, they just couldn't help responding to Julian himself.

'You might as well listen to somebody banging on cooking-pots,' grumbled Max. 'Lord only knows how he gets away with it.'

'It's the sort of thing that grows on you,' grinned Sebastian. 'So are warts.'

* * *

Janet and the Caldercott sisters having undertaken to ready the children, Arabella dressed for her wedding amidst a great deal of laughter, attended only by her mother, Elizabeth and the duchess's personal maid. While Jeanne turned her normally ungovernable hair into an elaborate arrangement, cunningly twined through with ribbons, Louisa and Elizabeth laid out the gown of violet silk and silver tissue, debated the question of jewellery and eventually concluded that none was necessary.

'The gown is adventurous enough,' remarked Louisa. 'Not your usual style at all, Belle.'

'I know. But I saw the silk and remembered the portrait of Great-Great-Grandmother Venetia wearing that colour. Since I've inherited her hair, I hoped it might look as good on me as it did on her.' She smiled at the maid and said, 'That is so pretty, Jeanne. Thank you. And please thank her Grace for letting me borrow you.'

As Jeanne curtsied and left the room, Elizabeth reached for the gown ready to help her cousin into it and said, 'This is perfect, Belle. Julian won't be able to take his eyes off you.'

Arabella laughed. 'You must have realised by now that Julian never notices what anyone is wearing – including himself.'

'I still can't equate the two sides to him,' mused Louisa. 'Off the platform, he's diffident and endearingly shy. *On* it, he's relaxed, confident and totally in command.' She shook her head. 'And when he *plays* ... well. The ladies are going to flock around him, Belle. You do know that, don't you?'

'Yes. If they do it when he's standing in front of a harpsichord, he'll smile and reply in as few words as possible. If they do it elsewhere, he'll find somewhere to hide.'

'I'd worry about your confidence if I didn't suspect that you're probably right. Now ... stand still while I lace you up.'

Despite her initial doubts, Louisa had to admit that the violet silk beneath the silvery overlay looped up polonaise-style, was a triumph. She contemplated Arabella from head to toe and, eyes a little bright, said, 'You look beautiful, my darling ... and you're marrying a man who actually deserves you. And now I shall go before I ruin my face by crying.'

Arabella watched her leave and then turned in time to see Elizabeth reaching for a handkerchief. She said, 'Don't, Lizzie. If you cry, I will, too. And aside from the fact that – unlike yours – my eyes would end up pink and puffy, we've had scarcely a minute to talk about your wedding. Are you regretting not being married at home?'

'No. Papa will bring Mama and the girls to London for it – partly because he will see it is best for everyone and partly because Ralph's letter gave him no excuse to refuse.' She gave a small sardonic smile. 'There's a lot to be said for having an earl in the family. And if Papa doesn't immediately understand that, Tilly and Flora will doubtless explain it in detail.'

'But you're not marrying him because he's an earl,' remarked Arabella. And after a tiny hesitation, 'Tell me to mind my own business, if you wish ... but I can't help wondering if he abandons that chilly reserve of his when you're alone together.'

There was a long silence. Then, 'He – yes. I think you might say that he – he does.'

Watching the tell-tale colour blooming in her cousin's face, Arabella said accusingly, 'Lizzie Marsden! What have you done?'

'Nothing!'

'All right. What has *he* done? And don't say nothing. It's written all over you.'

Elizabeth, recalling those minutes of unchecked passion in Ralph's arms, pressed her hands to her hot cheeks and said, 'Let's just say that, though the words are beyond him as yet, the feelings are – are not.'

'That sounds very half-and-half,' observed Arabella.

'It isn't. If you *must* know, when Ralph lets go of his usual restraint, the results are ... astonishing. Now – can we please leave it at that?'

'Yes.' And quickly, as the door opened, 'If it means what I *think* it means, we'd better!'

'I'm ready,' announced Ellie, 'and the boys have gone to find Sir Julian. So I'm going to stay here with you and keep my dress clean. That's all right, isn't it?'

* * *

Julian, meanwhile, was having a less enjoyable time. He had managed to take a bath in peace ... but had barely pulled on his ancient chamber-robe when he found himself once again at the mercy of Rockliffe's valet.

'If your lordship will kindly sit,' said Perkins in a tone that defied his lordship to do otherwise, 'I will begin by shaving you.'

'I've already shaved. And I don't need --'

He was subjected to an unnervingly intense scrutiny.

'I believe that we can improve upon that, my lord. It will take but a few minutes.'

Before Julian knew what was happening, he was in a chair and swathed in a towel. He attempted a mild objection ... and got a mouthful of shaving-soap. Spitting it out, he prepared to let the annoying fellow do his worst.

'Which coat will your lordship wear?' asked the valet, plying the razor.

Wisely, Julian said nothing.

'My lord? Which coat?'

Perkins winced as his wrist was suddenly trapped in a grip strengthened by two decades of harpsichord playing. Julian said, 'Do you mind if we chat later? Preferably when you haven't got a cut-throat near my face?'

Looking offended but having the sense to wait until his wrist was his own again, Perkins turned this set-back to his advantage. 'Your lordship removed his coat during the concert. I sincerely hope you will not feel obliged to do so during your wedding ceremony?'

His lordship gritted his teeth and willed the man to shut up and go away.

He didn't. He finished Julian's second shave of the morning, wiped away the excess soap and smothered him in a hot towel. Julian promptly wrenched the thing off and got to his feet. The valet tutted reprovingly and, sighing faintly, said again, 'Which coat?'

'The brown one.'

More tutting. 'It is not *brown*, my lord. It is bronze brocade and, if I may say so, the epitome of Mr Lassiter's craft.'

Julian could feel himself beginning to unravel.

'Fine. It's a bronze work of art which I can put on myself. Moreover --'

But Perkins was having none of that. With steely and unshakeable resolve, he persisted until Julian was clad in shirt, breeches, gold-embroidered vest and cravat. Then he said, 'And we will now attend to your lordship's hair. I noticed that one lock has a distressing tendency to shake itself free. But --'

'I know. I'm used to it.'

'But we may correct this deficiency with the aid of a small hairpin.'

This, in Julian's opinion, was an atrocity too far. Ducking out of the valet's reach, he said, 'No. You will leave my deficiencies alone. In fact, you will leave *me* alone.'

'But my lord --'

'No!' snapped Julian, unaware that Tom and Rob stood in the doorway. 'Just *go*!'

Tom walked forward, took the valet's arm and began propelling him from the room.

'I think you ought to do as he says, sir. Agitating him is never a good thing.'

'That,' returned Perkins grittily, 'is very evident.' And he stalked out.

Julian dropped into a chair. 'Thank you. He was driving me demented.'

'I noticed.' Tom grinned. 'You won't be getting a valet yourself, then?'

'Not if I can help it. And *certainly* not one who wants to put pins in my hair.'

'He didn't!' said Rob, revolted.

'He did.'

'Like a *girl*?'

'Yes.' Feeling suddenly better, Julian grinned. 'Do you think he does that to Rockliffe?'

* * *

Since the wedding was to be a small one, Adeline decided that the main drawing-room would be a pleasantly intimate setting and had decorated it accordingly. Baulked of grander designs, Rockliffe limited himself to engaging the concerto ensemble to play from the adjoining room and was touched but unsurprised when they refused payment, saying earnestly, 'Anything for Mr Langham, your Grace. Anything at all.'

Descending the stairs to the strains of Mozart, Julian was about to visit its source when Max Brandon dropped a firm hand on his shoulder and said, 'No. You can speak to them later.'

'But it's my concerto ensemble. I'd know the sound of that cello anywhere.'

'I daresay. But this isn't the time to get distracted. The guests are already arriving and you should be in your seat. Where's Tom?'

'Here.' Tom ran down to join them. 'Sorry. I was taking Rob to Miss Belle.'

'Well, you're in charge of the bridegroom now.' Max grinned at him. 'Don't let him out of your sight. Do you remember what you have to do?'

'Yes, sir.'

'And you've got the ring?'

Tom patted his pocket. 'Right here.'

'Good man.' He turned to Julian and lifted one brow. 'Nervous?'

'No.'

'Sure?'

'Yes,' said Julian impatiently. 'Arabella won't run away or say 'I don't' instead of 'I do'. So what is there to be nervous about?'

'Concert mood,' Tom told Max laconically. 'Just as well, really.'

Julian walked to his seat amongst smiles and good wishes. Both Paul and Sebastian had offered to stand up with him today but he had refused them in favour of giving the task to Tom ... who, almost bursting with love and pride, walked beside him now, head held high.

When he was sure that everyone had arrived, Max sent a footman upstairs to summon Arabella. Flanked by Ellie and Rob clad in their best new clothes, he watched his little sister float down the stairs in a silvery-violet cloud, her face radiant with happiness. Feeling his throat tighten, he said, 'A hand-maiden and a page-boy, Belle? *Very* smart!' Then, unable to help himself, he pulled her into his arms and added, 'You look beautiful, love. Julian's a lucky man.'

She clung to him briefly. 'He's a good man, Max.'

'I know that. If I didn't, I wouldn't be letting him have you.' Releasing her to tuck her hand through his arm, he smiled at the children. 'Ready?'

Rob grinned back and nodded vigorously. Ellie said, 'We've been ready for ages!'

'Excellent. Then let's take Julian his bride – before he starts to worry.'

The music changed from Mozart to a Bach *Pavane* as Arabella let her brother lead her slowly between the beaming faces of their friends and relatives. Ahead of them, near the waiting cleric, Julian turned to look at her, his initially solemn expression dissolving into a bone-melting smile ... and then she was beside him, drowning in his eyes. The music stopped; there was a moment of pure silence; and then, 'Dearly beloved,' began the Reverend Sir Henry Brockhurst, sonorously ... and the time of waiting was over.

Although he made his responses clearly and without hesitation, Julian was to remember little of the marriage service because everything in him was focussed on Arabella. At some point, he found himself entertaining the hazy notion that this moment had been pre-ordained; that she and Elizabeth had changed places because Fate knew that Julian Langham and Arabella Brandon belonged together. He liked that idea. But all he wanted now was to drink in the sight of her and the knowledge that, despite everything, she was now his ... as he, body and soul, was hers.

He heard Sir Henry informing him that he could kiss his bride.

'*Finally*,' he muttered. And wrapping Arabella in his arms, captured her mouth with his – hungrily and for far longer than was proper.

Punctuated by a few teasing remarks, a ripple of indulgent laughter ran around the room and eventually caused Julian to remember where he was – if not to care very much that they had an audience. Touching Arabella's cheek with light, slightly unsteady fingers, he whispered, 'Are we really married – or did I dream it?'

She laughed up at him and brushed back the recalcitrant lock of hair that her enthusiastic response to his embrace had dislodged. 'Well, if you dreamed it, so did I.'

'It must be real, then.' He let his arms fall away and took her hands in his to kiss each of them in turn. 'In which case, I don't mind waking up ... because you're here and I love you.'

From the next room, music began afresh and, over it, Rockliffe said mildly, 'Perhaps, Lord and Lady Chalfont, you might finish your conversation later? Your guests are waiting to felicitate you ... and the champagne is growing warm.'

'We beg your pardon,' grinned Julian, not sounding at all sorry. And Arabella said suddenly, 'Listen! They're playing my *Rondo*!'

'They're playing an *approximation* of your *Rondo*,' agreed Julian, finally leading her back down the aisle, 'which, considering they've only heard it twice, is no mean feat.'

The champagne was ice-cold and crisp. Rockliffe proposed a toast to the happiness of the newly-wedded pair; Max proposed one to Tom and Rob and Ellie – all of whom, he said, had performed their various roles to perfection; and the ensemble stopped playing long enough to congratulate Julian and raise a toast of their own to the bride. Then, after the usual round of congratulatory kisses and hand-shakes, everyone adjourned to the dining-room for the wedding-breakfast.

On one of the rare occasions when her attention strayed from Julian, Arabella noticed the new light in Ralph Sherbourne's eyes when they rested on Elizabeth and the way his fingers seemed to gravitate to hers. *Perhaps Lizzie's right*, she thought. *Perhaps he does love her but hasn't found a way of saying it yet. I hope so. I want her to be happy.*

After the food, Max rose to thank the duke and duchess for hosting his sister's wedding before formally welcoming his new brother-in-law to the family. Then he added wickedly, 'Your turn, Julian. If it's any help, you're supposed to begin with the words *My wife and I ...*'

There was some laughter, during which Julian found himself on his feet. He said, 'My kind, clever and incredibly beautiful wife and I ...' And stopped, seemingly at a loss. Then, since everyone was smiling and waiting for him to continue, he added simply, 'We just want to thank all of you for your good wishes and for sharing today with us. It – it has meant a great deal. I'd also like to thank his Grace for everything he's done for me. And most of all, I want to thank Arabella for knowing all my failings but marrying me anyway.' And he sank, with even greater gratitude, back into his seat.

More laughter and some applause, over which Rockliffe said, 'And upon that happy note, ladies and gentlemen, I suggest we retire to the drawing-room where there will be tea for those who want it and something stronger for those who do not.'

Holding fast to Arabella's hand, Julian whispered, 'How long before we can slip away?'

'Not long. As soon as we've spoken to the children?'

While most of the guests drifted towards the drawing-room, Rockliffe drew the bridal pair to one side and handed Julian three letters, saying, 'These arrived this morning but I thought they could wait until now. Open them. I suspect they bring good news.'

The first was from the Duchess of Queensberry saying that she suggested deferring Julian's concert until he had put together a new programme – at which point they would set a convenient date. The second was from Mr Spalding at the Pantheon, respectfully asking if Mr Langham would accept two further engagements. And the third was from the Controller of Vauxhall Gardens, begging Mr Langham to honour them by performing at the opening concert of the spring season.

Rockliffe murmured, 'And so it begins. Do not be surprised if, in due course, you get invitations to perform in Paris. Word is already spreading.'

'Paris,' breathed Arabella, awed. 'Oh Julian – just *imagine* it!'

'I am,' he agreed, for the first time uneasily aware of how his professional life might impact on his family. 'But let's not count on it happening.'

They sat down with the children in a quiet corner. Arabella said, 'Max was right. You were all splendid today. I was very, very proud of you.'

'So was I,' agreed Julian. 'Tom – I couldn't have managed without you.'

Tom coloured. 'You would have, sir. I reckon you can manage just about anything.'

'Then you've got more faith in me than I have.'

'Now you're married to Miss Belle,' said Ellie, snuggling up at Julian's side, 'does that mean she is our – our guardianess?'

Tom gave a crack of laugher and Julian had to bite his lip in order not to do the same.

'Why is that funny?' demanded Ellie. 'If you were a prince and Miss Belle married you, she'd be a princess, wouldn't she? So she *must* be a guardianess, mustn't she?'

'I suppose she must,' said Julian a little unsteadily. 'Though it might be better to find a different name for her, don't you think?' And turning to the younger boy before Ellie could speculate further, 'You've been very patient, Rob – but once the excitement has died down, we'd better resume your music lessons. If you want to, that is?'

'Yes, please. I want to learn more than *anything*.'

'Then you shall. I'll be playing the same music for the Queen that I played here, so I don't need to work every hour God sends –

which means that you and I can make up for lost time. And now,' he concluded, rising and holding out his hand to Arabella, 'if none of you mind, Miss Belle and I will say goodnight. We'll see you tomorrow – but, in the meantime, be good for your Aunt Louisa and Max.' He glanced at Tom and added dryly, 'And you, young man, can take that look off your face.'

'What look?' asked Tom, sounding innocent but still smirking.

'*That* one. You're not old enough for it. Yet.'

* * *

Having escaped from their well-wishers and obtained directions, they strolled with their arms about each other to the suite of rooms the duchess had ordered to be made ready for them. Their first glimpse of the bedroom caused them to stop dead and stare for a moment ... then Arabella dissolved into laughter.

'Goodness! They've put us in the royal apartment. Just look at the coat of arms over the fireplace – and there's another above the bed. This is *absurd*!'

'That's one word for it.'

She danced across the room, opening doors which led to a grand withdrawing-room and a dressing-room so large that their own clothes looked somewhat lonely. Then, skipping back to throw her arms about Julian's neck, 'But it has advantages. Only think ... it's on the far side of the house from the other guest rooms.'

'I am thinking of it.' He cuddled her close, finally giving free rein to the anticipation which had been humming inside him for several hours; anticipation of the night to come ... when they would each give themselves to the other and become one. He said, 'I'm thinking of a lot of other things as well. But there is no hurry. All day, I've been looking forward to being here with you ...' He paused, glancing dubiously at the quantities of gold leaf. 'Well, perhaps not here, precisely, but somewhere ... just you and me, alone together with no interruptions. So now I'd like to take a little while to savour it. What do you think?'

'The same. *Exactly* the same, if you really want to know.'

'Ah. Good. Not just me, then.'

Smiling, he bent his head and kissed her ... a slow and tender gift that asked nothing but offered everything and which filled the world with unimagined sweetness. It was a kiss that spoke of mystery and delights to come. And responding to it, Arabella let him know that what he wanted ... *anything* that he wanted ... he could have.

After a time, he said, 'Can I remove my coat now?'

'Can I stop you?' she retorted. 'Can *anybody*?' And then, sighing, 'If only corsets were as easy to be rid of.'

'Oh?' Heat flared but he chose to ignore it. 'I could ... help, if you like.'

Arabella's pulse tripped. 'Since I can't reach anything myself, you'll have to ... beginning with the gown.'

'The gown? Yes. I think I knew that.'

Stepping back, he shed his coat and then set about untying her laces. Naturally, it was impossible to resist the soft skin of her nape or the place where her neck joined her shoulder ... so he kissed both of those, then had to remind himself what he was supposed to be doing. His fingers wanted to hurry. His brain ordered them not to. But eventually the gown slid away, revealing uncharted inches of pearly-pink skin. His mouth went dry. Moistening it, he said huskily, 'You are so beautiful. Do I ... is it the corset now?'

She nodded, reaching up to start pulling pins and ribbons from her hair. The first heavy locks fell loose. One coiled itself around Julian's wrist and he hauled in an unsteady breath.

'Unfair,' he muttered.

'Is it?' Arabella removed more pins and felt the deft, musician's hands go more swiftly to work. 'Why?'

He didn't answer but concentrated on getting rid of the corset before the cascade of silver-gilt destroyed what was left of his brain. When it was done, he closed his arms about warm, slender curves and drew her back against his chest, murmuring, 'Anything else?'

'Yes.' She turned in the cage of his arms and set about removing his cravat. 'Since we're to talk about fairness ...' And, tossing the cravat aside, she began unbuttoning his vest.

His heart threatening to explode, Julian tried to think of something else. The vast, crimson-hung bed looked intimidating and was saying things he didn't want to hear yet. But there was an armchair near the hearth and so, as soon as he was able to shrug off the vest, he picked Arabella up and sat down with her on his lap.

She laid one palm against his cheek and rained kisses along his jaw. He threaded his fingers through her hair, enjoying the cool weight of it. For a long moment neither of them spoke. Then Arabella said, 'I love you so much. And I'm madly, *ridiculously* proud of you.'

The possibility he'd thought of earlier stirred again.

'Even though performing may sometimes take me away from you?'

'Yes.' She looked up at him. 'If that happens – and I understand that it may – I'll miss you and so will the children. But it's a small price to pay for seeing you become what you were born to be.'

'Not so small.' The fingertips that had been drifting over her shoulders, moved on to the temptation of her clavicle. 'Spare a thought for me missing you.'

'You'll have your music for company.' She kissed him again, heat and new sensations blooming all through her body at the scent and closeness of his. 'Do you ever think of what would have happened if Lizzie and I hadn't changed places?'

'No.' With an apparent laziness made possible by iron restraint, he traced the line of her chemise and then, almost but not quite by accident, let his fingers seek the loveliness beneath it. 'If you hadn't, we'd never have met – and that doesn't bear thinking of.'

He felt the tremor that ran through her and heard a small, involuntary sound. Since this indicated that she liked what he was doing as much as he did, he slid the chemise from her shoulder. This did nothing to lessen his hunger but, with something new to investigate, he found it possible to continue distancing himself from it for just a little while longer.

382

So pretty, he thought. *All delicate bones and shadowy hollows and inches of delectable petal-soft skin.* He began exploring with feather-light fingertips, learning texture and contours as he would a new and fascinating piece of music. He traced her jaw and her throat; he marvelled at the slenderness of her arms and the fragility of her wrists; everything he found brought a lingering wonder as he absorbed and committed each of them to memory before finally allowing himself to find one small, perfect breast.

Arabella rewarded him with a shuddering sigh. Her mouth grazed his throat and she slid a hand inside his shirt to the hard warmth of his chest. Suddenly the crimson monstrosity started to look less intimidating than it did inviting. His breathing uneven and his voice raw, Julian said, 'We can continue ignoring that enormous bed for a while longer... or we could find out if it's more comfortable than it looks. What do you think?'

She buried her face in the curve of his shoulder.

'I think we should definitely give it a try.'

'You do?' He rose, still holding her in his arms and then hesitated. 'Good. Right. Yes.'

Feeling his hesitation, Arabella said, 'You can put me down, you know.'

'I'm going to.'

He crossed to the vast bed and tossed her on to it amidst a tangle of petticoats. Laughing, she watched him kneel on the edge of the mattress and somehow throw off his shoes whilst also kicking the steps away.

'Julian ... what are you doing?'

'Narrowing the boundaries.' He crawled towards her, smiling. 'The damn bed is big enough to lose you in – never mind the rest of the room. Now I have you trapped.'

'I hadn't planned on escap--'

He stopped the words with his mouth, kissing her until she was clinging to him and they were both breathless. For a long, sweet moment, they gazed silently into each other's eyes and then, tugging at his shirt, Arabella said, 'Too many clothes.'

He nodded, pulled it over his head and cast it aside. She stared at him, reaching out to touch lean but well-defined musculature beneath smooth, lightly-golden skin. With the usual lock of hair brushing one cheek and a vagrant smile lurking in his eyes, he looked tempting as sin even before he raised one brow and, as he had earlier, said, 'Anything else?'

'Everything.'

Another nod and a look of intense concentration. 'Yours first, then.'

Without haste and pausing to discover hitherto hidden delights along the way, ribbons and laces melted away until the only garments separating his body from hers were his breeches and stockings. These he disposed of swiftly, to draw her close against the length of him. On a gasp of surprise at the exquisite meeting of flesh, Arabella pressed her mouth against his throat. Sensation and anticipation were building inside her and everywhere he touched, her skin caught fire.

To the skill in his hands, Julian added the adoration of his mouth ... gradually learning the melody of her body, as she, in her turn, released the music in his. It was a flawless duet of shared pleasure, played in both harmony and counterpoint. He worshipped her slowly and with dedication ... from the hollow at the base of her throat to the arch of her instep and everything in between. And for the first time words, which had never come easily to him, flowed, albeit a little disjointedly.

'So beautiful. Always so beautiful ... and with a heart even lovelier than your face. I love you. How could anyone *not* love you? I'm yours. All the days of my life. Only yours.'

Lying entangled with her, he continued soliciting her senses until he could not tell her heartbeat from his own. And when she moulded the line of his back whilst trailing hot kisses across his chest, desire thundered through him like timpani.

For Arabella, the world outside Julian's arms ceased to exist. There was nothing but the singing of her blood and the sizzling heat of his caresses. Every nerve and fibre of her being was ablaze with sensations she could hardly contain. Her breath came in sobbing gasps and she could no longer remain still. She dissolved under the delicious assault of clever, confident hands ... melted against his mouth and was overwhelmed by responses she had never imagined existed. Feeling herself soaring up and up towards some indefinable place, she uttered a few involuntary and incoherent words, one of which was his name.

Ablaze with fires of his own making, Julian managed to say, 'Yes. My love ... my heart ... my *wife*. Yes.'

Adagio grazioso ... legato ostinato. Long, exquisite moments of resonance; breathing as one, feeling as one ... being one. The stars, perfectly aligned and in tune.

Accelerando ma non troppo ... cantabile. Then, all too soon and impossible to resist, *appassionata con fuoco*. And finally, tumbling effortlessly over the cliff ... *volante*.

After which came peace, wrapped close in each other's arms.

Much later, Arabella said, 'I thought you said you weren't very experienced.'

'I did.'

'It doesn't show.'

'Thank you.' There was a smile in his voice.

She drew one foot invitingly up his calf. 'Is it even true?'

'Do you think a man would lie about a thing like that? But perhaps,' he added hopefully, 'it's like the harpsichord; a matter of natural talent.'

'That would seem to be the only explanation,' agreed Arabella gravely.

'And experience is just another word for practice, isn't it?' He accepted her invitation by sliding his thigh between hers. 'Are you familiar with the musical term *Da Capo*?'

Although the drift of his hands was providing a clue, she shook her head.

'No?' He smiled enticingly into her eyes. 'Then I'll show you.'

Author's Note

Thank you for reading *Cadenza*.

If you are interested in the precise programme of Julian's debut concert, visit the Extras page at http://stellarileybooks.co.uk where you will also be able to hear some of the pieces played by French virtuoso, Jean Rondeau.

The story of Arabella's great-great-grandparents, Gabriel and Venetia, can be found in *Garland of Straw* – a tale told against the backdrop of the months leading to the execution of King Charles I.

Printed in Great Britain
by Amazon

14978284R00224